Operation Music Man

Jennifer Haynie

Copyright © 2021 Jennifer M. Haynie

Published under the On-the-Edge Publications Imprint

All rights reserved. No part of this book may be reproduced, stored in a retrieval system, or transmitted in any form or by any means—electronic, mechanical, photocopy, recording, or otherwise, without written permission from the author, except for brief quotations in printed reviews.

The persons and events portrayed in this work are the creations of the author, and any resemblance to persons living or dead is purely coincidental.

Scriptures taken from the Holy Bible, New International Version®, NIV®. Copyright © 1973, 1978, 1984, 2011 by Biblica, Inc.™ Used by permission of Zondervan. All rights reserved worldwide. www.zondervan.com. The "NIV" and "New International Version" are trademarks registered in the United States Patent and Trademark Office by Biblica, Inc.™

Cover design by Indie Designz, http://www.indiedesignz.com

All rights reserved.

ISBN:
978-1-943398-18-8

Other Books by Jennifer Haynie

Last Chance Series

Operation Shadow Box
Operation Peacemaker

Unit 28 Series

Panama Deception
Loose Ends
Orb Web (short story)

The Athena Trilogy

The Athena File
No Options

Other Books

Exiled Heart
Hunter Hunted

Other Books by Jennifer Haynie

Last Chance Series

Operation Shadow Box
Operation Peacemaker

Unit 28 Series

Panama Deception
Loose Ends
Orb Web (short story)

The Athena Trilogy

The Athena File
No Options

Other Books

Exiled Heart
Hunter Hunted

To Wilson Huntley, friend, brother in Christ, husband to Tracy, father to Allan, Reid, Mary, Natalie, and Judy.
We miss you.

To all of those who have come out of human trafficking and have learned to thrive.
You are brave.

Blessed are the poor in spirit, for theirs is the kingdom of heaven.

—Matthew 5:3

The Team

Victor Chavez (call sign One) — Team leader, former Special Forces captain and Secret Service agent, owner of Sentry Securities, Flagstaff, AZ

Suleiman al-Ibrahim (call sign Two) — Sniper/observer, former Hezbollah sniper, university student, Flagstaff, AZ

Sana Jain (call sign Three) — Breaking-and-entering specialist, former Olympic gymnast and cat burglar, owner of Pause Café, Flagstaff, AZ

Shelly Wise (call sign Four) — Computer and security system specialist, independent computer contractor, Flagstaff, AZ

Butch Addison (call sign Five) — Mechanic / escape-and-evasion expert, former Special Forces soldier, currently owner of an auto mechanic shop, Flagstaff, AZ

Diana Kasem (call sign Six) — Doctor, former Army cardiothoracic surgeon, currently practicing cardiothoracic surgery, Flagstaff, AZ

Fiona Mercedes (call sign Seven) — Pilot, former Army helicopter pilot and CIA contract pilot, owner of Kitchen Sink Air Cargo, Flagstaff, AZ

Skylar James (call sign Eight) — Procurement officer / disguise specialist, former CIA agent, currently owner of Regions Café, Flagstaff, AZ

The Supporting Team

Deborah Chavez — Wife of Victor Chavez

Anna Fields (15) — Oldest daughter of Deborah

DJ Fields (14) — Only son of Deborah

Gracie Fields (8) — Second daughter of Deborah

Marie Fields (7) — Youngest daughter of Deborah

Sugar (a.k.a. Marvin LaMott) — Owner of La Femme Nue Jazz Clubs, New Orleans, LA, and Nashville, TN

Loquacious — Sugar's bodyguard

1

Friday, March 18, 2016, 0600 hours CDT, Nashville, TN

"Hon, someone's come to bail you out."

Morgan Walton cracked her eyes open. Bright light seared her retinas. Her neck hurt from huddling upright all night on a bed in a corner of the holding cell.

A female sheriff's deputy approached. Keys clinked on a ring dangling from her fingers.

Mom had changed her mind. Hope unfurled in Morgan. "Where is she? Where's my mom?"

"Your mama?" The deputy shrugged. "I don't know about her, but there's a gentleman here who's certainly worried about you. At least enough to pay your bail." She opened the door. "This way, young lady."

Morgan followed her. When she reached the lobby, Wes Sampson straightened as he stuffed his wallet into his jeans pocket. His warm brown eyes radiating exhaustion, he wrapped her in his arms.

Morgan sagged into his embrace, then pulled back.

He looked away as his mouth pressed into a thin line.

Her stomach clenched. He was furious with her. He had to be. "Wes?"

He kissed her. "I'm fine, babe."

"Ma'am, here's your personal effects." The deputy handed over her cell phone, watch, and cash. "Please sign on the dotted line."

She did.

"Y'all have a good day now, you hear?"

Oh, it'd be better than good after she soaked in a hot bath and pulled on some clean clothes.

Wes took her hand and led her outside.

She drew in a deep breath. The drizzle from the night before had subsided, leaving behind clean, fresh air smelling like Downy. Dawn lit the eastern horizon in a gauzy pink. She followed Wes to his Honda CR-V. "Where were you last night? I thought you were going to meet us, but then the cops—"

"Shhhh." He put a finger over her lips. "I'm sure you're starved. We can talk over pancakes at the IHOP."

"But—"

"It can wait at least until we get some caffeine, okay?" He settled her in her seat and started the SUV. They wheeled out of the parking lot with a chirp of tires.

Morgan could barely keep her eyes open. For a few moments, only the sound of commercials on the radio played. Why was he so quiet? "Are you... are you mad at me?"

When they paused at a stoplight, he ran his hand down his stubbled jaw. A small groan escaped him. "No. Just... tired. I was up all night trying to find you. I finally figured out you were arrested."

Recalling the cop cars lighting up the house's living room in blazes of sapphire light, she twisted her hands on her lap. More images assaulted her. The shouts, the running. Foolish and futile, it turned out. "All of us were arrested for underage drinking and smoking weed. Where were you? I thought you were going to be there."

He took her hand. "I told you I had a study group."

"Wes—"

"Can you wait until I've got some food in me?" He clenched his jaw.

Morgan got it. He was pissed at her. Not that she could blame him. She settled for staring at the Nashville skyline as it began glowing in the rapidly reddening dawn. Would it ever be home? Hah! Hardly. No,

Arlington, Virginia, was home. Why had someone murdered Dad? If he hadn't died, then—

Stop it, Morgan. It happened. Mom ripped you away from your friends and made you move here. Deal with it. She glanced at Wes. Ever since they'd met at a party in September, he'd treated her well. Made her feel loved. He filled that void left by Dad. She settled for resting her head against the window as the sound of the Rocket Roosters, one of the newest country bands around, blared from the speakers.

Twenty minutes later, in a booth with a short stack ordered and coffee steaming in a ceramic mug in front of her, she gazed at her boyfriend of six months.

Wes stared at the scarred Formica tabletop and tapped his steepled fingers together. "Tell me what happened."

"After you texted and said you were running late, Amanda picked me up." Once more, shouts filled her memory. She winced and glanced at her scraped palms, her only reward for trying to run away from the cops. "I told Mom she and I were studying for the math test I was supposed to take today. It was a great party. Everyone was there. One guy brought out the beer. Someone else started passing around a couple of joints. Then the cops showed up."

"I saw the rip in your jeans."

She ran her finger along the tabletop's pattern. "I fell while trying to run away." The cop's words as he arrested her rang in her ears. Miranda rights or something like that. "They booked me and set my bail at twelve hundred. I called Mom."

She paused as the waitress brought their orders. Oh, she really didn't want to talk about what happened next.

Wes let her be. While he dug into his meal, she barely touched hers. Finally, she could stand it no more and set her fork down. She inhaled a shuddering breath. "She told me she was sick of the lies, the sneaking around, everything. She'd missed enough teaching because of me. I could sit in jail until this afternoon as part of my punishment. She'd come and get me after school."

He set his utensils down with a clink. "And she still doesn't know about us."

"Hah! Hardly. She would have made me break up with you since you're in college and I'm only sixteen."

The corner of his mouth twitched upward. Strange.

"Wes?"

He leaned back. "Nothing. I just find it hard to believe she wouldn't come and get you."

She bit her lip as Mom's rejection stung again. "But you did."

"And I need to get you home."

Maybe when she was clean and rested, she could face Mom. Her eyes filled as she followed him outside.

Before opening the car door for her, he cupped her cheek and kissed her. "Promise it's going to be okay."

She could only hope. They pulled into traffic, and she leaned her head against the seat. The brightening morning sun warmed her. The set of country music on the radio finished, followed by commercials. Another set began. She drifted.

The SUV stopped.

They weren't at the townhouse in southwestern Nashville she'd called home for the past two years. She stared at a warehouse of dingy gray metal siding. Metal stairs led upward to a small landing and a door. A man leaned with his forearms against a railing. His biceps bulged from the sleeves of his black T-shirt. He trotted down the stairs.

Only then did she notice they were inside a chain-link fence laced with concertina wire. "Wes? Where are we? I thought you were taking me home."

His tendons stood out from his hands gripping the wheel. "I had to make a stop on the way."

"Where are we?" Her voice suddenly sounded tinny to her ears.

Wes pressed her seatbelt release. "Get out."

His harshness stung. "I-I don't—"

"Get out. Now." He popped open his door.

"Wes?"

Her own flew open, and the man with the biceps dragged her from her seat.

Her Keds scraped cracked asphalt. She struggled as his fingers bit into the tender flesh of her arms. "Ow! Leave me alone! Wes!"

Wes gripped her chin so hard she squeaked. "I need you to come with me and keep quiet."

Morgan began trembling. Suddenly, home seemed like the best, safest place in the world. "I need to go *home*." Caught between them, she thrashed. "No! Let me go!"

Wes's slap knocked away any remaining words. "I told you to be quiet."

With that, her guard practically lifted her off her feet. Metal echoed against the hard soles of boots.

Beeps sounded in her ears as Wes snapped, "Get her inside. Now!"

Her guard slammed her face first into a wall.

She squirmed.

At least until something stung her neck.

Time slowed. Voices distorted. Light blurred as she staggered backward and collapsed to her knees.

"Room Five is ready and waiting. Get her in there," a woman's voice ordered.

Strong hands lifted Morgan to her feet and carried her along a path of hazy light circles. Her guard lowered her onto a queen-sized bed with silky soft sheets.

Someone wrapped some rubber tubing around her arm. Another needle. Everything began spinning.

Just before she passed out, she heard Wes say, "Only the best for my girl."

Friday, March 18, 2016, 2030 hours CDT, Nashville, TN

In love. Jaidon Ash knew no other way to describe his feelings for the woman who stood onstage at the Nashville Convention Center. His wife spoke with fervor. Passion. And the audience? The dim lighting revealed rapt expressions as they ate up her every word. That included his daughter. He fought a smile. Elsbeth's green eyes, so much like his, gazed wide-eyed at her mama. For good reason.

Cassie's upswept blonde hair, snapping brown eyes, and trim figure in its glittering gold dress captivated him. *Love of my life for twenty years. Here's to twenty more, babe.*

His wife wagged her finger. "Human trafficking is everywhere. Know the signs. And if you see something, say something. Sometimes small pieces add up to a big case, and you could save someone's life. Thank you for your time."

Everyone clapped.

Jaidon rose and led the standing ovation. He glanced at Elsbeth again. Pure admiration. She wanted to be like her mama in every way. And was becoming that, especially in the looks department. Had he not known she was sixteen, she could have passed for her early twenties because of her evening gown, makeup, and hairdo. Suddenly, he yearned for everyday Elsbeth in her jeans and sweatshirt, with her hair askew and face clean. Ah, they grew up too fast, these teenage girls.

Cassie joined them, and he kissed her. "Good job, babe."

Elsbeth swooped in for a hug. "Mom, that was great!"

Cassie's eyes sparkled. "You think I did good?"

Jaidon wrapped his arms around her. "Better than good." He released her as several people approached. "I'll leave you to your entourage. Meet you in the lobby in five?"

"Only if we go out for ice cream. I don't care how chilly it is out there. You promised that as my reward." Cassie nudged her daughter. "Elsbeth, I want you to meet some folks."

"Hah. Will do." Jaidon wandered through the ballroom and onto the mezzanine, where he snagged a last glass of Chardonnay. The noise increased as people in tuxedos and evening gowns passed beneath the banner for Forever Free, or "F-Squared" as it was routinely called, an anti-human trafficking organization and Cassie's pet project.

He wanted at least a little quiet and made for a nearby escalator. Along the way, he pressed the flesh of more than a few people who recognized him. A hockey player here. An NFL football player there. The president of one of the record labels for a client of his. A country singer who was also a client.

Finally, he found a bar table downstairs in a corner of the convention center's lobby and pulled his phone from his tux jacket. He checked e-mail. Nothing that wouldn't keep until Monday. No voice mails either. Not surprising since some of his clients were here and others were on the road or vacationing during spring break.

He pulled up his text messages. The Agent had texted him.

I've got the Exotic. You need to come to the club tonight.

He grimaced. People began drifting into the lobby and heading into the chilly evening. He easily spotted Cassie as she rode the escalator downward and chatted with the national president of F-Squared. Jaidon sipped his wine and tapped out his reply. I'll be there in ten.

Cassie collected Elsbeth. Mother and daughter bent their heads toward one another as if sharing a joke.

Jaidon pushed off from the table. "Look at my girls. Pretty as a picture. Let me get a shot of you."

Cassie struck a pose. So did Elsbeth, probably a result of growing up in front of a camera. He smiled. This one he'd frame. "Very nice."

Cassie took his arm. "Are we ready to go?"

He cleared his throat. "Something came up at the club."

Elsbeth blew out a sigh. "Dad!"

He tossed a careless smile her way. "As only a teenager could. It shouldn't take me more than a half hour, okay? Since I drove, I'll meet you at The Igloo. See you in a few."

A veteran of such interruptions, Cassie kissed him. "We'll see you there. Elsbeth, you wanted to meet Clay Hall. I see him over there. C'mon. I'll introduce you."

Jaidon released a breath.

Cassie took her daughter's hand and led her toward where Clay Hall, last year's CMA Male Vocalist of the Year winner, chatted with his wife and a couple of others.

Jaidon headed outside. A valet retrieved his Beemer M5 convertible, and he drove down 8th Avenue to the Gulch. He swung a left and headed east on Division Street. People swarmed the sidewalks. He crossed some railroad tracks and hung a right. Here, near the interstate, though people headed to restaurants and clubs, it was a little less crowded.

To his right, The Music Man's marquis slid by. A line had formed outside as patrons waited to dine and listen to the music of a young lady who showed great promise. With luck, she had some demo CDs in her purse to hand out to any agents who were there listening. He turned down an alley, then made a right onto a street that ran between some warehouses. Chain-link fencing with concertina wire rose up on his right. He stopped at a gate and pressed a code on the pad. It clattered open before closing behind him.

One of his bouncers greeted him as he came up the stairs. "Good evening, Mr. Ash."

"The same to you. Where's The Agent?"

"Inside waiting on you. We've got clients in all rooms tonight, so watch your step."

And we might get more tonight. Yeah, he'd seen men at the benefit dinner who patronized his club for less-than-legal reasons.

When Jaidon stepped into his office, Wes Sampson, also known as The Agent, gripped him in a brief hug. "Hey, man. She's in Room Five."

Jaidon glanced at his watch. "Let's check her out. I've got exactly ten minutes. No more." With a cautious glance into the hall, he noted a guard moving toward Room Two to escort someone downstairs. Time was up. Other clients were waiting. Once they were clear, he darted down the hall after Wes and stepped into the room.

Denelle Brooks, his manager for all things club, stood nearby. She'd pulled back her light blonde hair to the point where it emphasized her square jaw. She didn't crack a smile or say anything in greeting. Not that he expected it. The woman took her work seriously.

Jaidon focused on the girl who lay beneath a sheet pulled up to her neck. Denelle must have combed her hair out because it flowed along the white sheets in a stream of deep copper. Oh, yeah. Bingo.

Jaidon pulled back the sheet. Flawless skin all the way. Not a mole or freckle on her. And filled out more than he expected for a sixteen-year-old. Once more, Wes had promised and delivered. She'd go for the highest rate at his club—and then some in a couple of weeks, if The Distributor agreed. He let the sheet drop. "Is she out?"

The light gray silk of Denelle's dress whispered as she shifted. "She's drugged until morning, at least. I got her cleaned up. She does have some scrapes on her hands and on a knee."

"Those'll heal." Jaidon sat on the bed and lifted an eyelid. A startling blue iris with navy rims. Nothing like he'd seen in a long, long time.

"What do you think?" Wes asked from where he'd propped himself in a corner.

Jaidon stepped to the door. "You did good. Denelle, how soon will she start training?"

"Sunday I'll have her training as a waitress."

"And on the bed?"

A smile curled the woman's lips as her ice blue eyes glinted. "Tomorrow night."

"Perfect. Wes, come with me." Jaidon led the way to his office, all the while making sure no clients saw him. Once behind a closed door, he leaned against the edge of his desk. "You landed a good one. I'm calling The Distributor. I'll make sure you get a bonus."

Wes's eyes lit up. "Thanks. I've started grooming another potential Exotic as well."

"Good deal. We'll talk later." Jaidon watched him go. Then he lifted his cell phone to his ear. After a couple of years, he'd finally scored again. Big time. When The Distributor answered, he said, "Sir, I've found one. I've found an Exotic."

"Tell me," the man said without preamble.

He did.

When the man replied, the faintest traces of an accent colored his words. "Done. Break her in. My son, who I'm training to inherit this side of my business, will be coming to Nashville in a few weeks. He'll take a look at her."

With that, the man clicked off.

Jaidon pocketed his phone and headed into the chilly evening air. Time to rejoin his wife and daughter for some ice cream.

2

Tuesday, April 5, 2016, 2000 hours MST, Sedona, AZ

Sana Jain peered through her binoculars at the two-story adobe structure below her perch in the hills surrounding Sedona, Arizona. Stars winked in the inky black dome of night above them. A chilly breeze sent a shiver through her. She didn't care. Time to move. She glanced at where her fiancé, Suleiman al-Ibrahim, lay on his mat with an observation scope pressed to his eye. "Any movement?"

Thanks to the black camo paint on his face, the only thing she saw were the whites of his eyes as he shook his head. "Nothing."

She shouldered her pack. "We'll be back in an hour."

"Or sooner."

"Want to bet?"

"Perhaps." He reached up and ran his hand down her cheek. "What would the wager be?"

"If I win?" She'd be sure to collect on snuggling with him under a blanket with a fire crackling in the fireplace of the Women's Building. "I want extra time with you tonight. And if I lose, what do you want?"

"Some lingerie for the honeymoon."

Underneath her own camo paint, her cheeks warmed. "For you or me?"

A sexy smile crossed his face. "I believe you know, *eshgham.*" He pulled her to him and brushed his lips across hers. "Go now. Butch is waiting."

As she always did, Sana smiled at his Farsi term for "my love." She scuttled over the ridge to the road where Butch Addison, the escape-and-evasion specialist and mechanic for their team, sprawled in the driver's seat of a black Chevy Suburban. Its engine growled low. She catapulted her five-foot frame into the passenger's seat. "Let's do it."

"What did you bet Suleiman that we'd get in?"

Huh? The heat in her face intensified. "Uh..."

The big man chuckled as he lowered his night vision goggles. They rumbled down the slope under total blackout. "C'mon. Out with it, girl."

She couldn't believe she was saying this. "Some cute lingerie for the honeymoon."

He burst out laughing. "For you or him?"

She scowled. "Funny how I asked him the same thing."

Butch's mirth simmered. "Hah. Not that he's gonna get it from anyone else."

Sana preferred focusing on their task ahead. It should be easy. Pass through the barbed wire at the property's edge. Approach the wall rimming the house. Break in. And gather a haul again. It'd teach the homeowners a lesson, one that Victor Chavez, owner of Sentry Securities, had bet the Marcos family wouldn't learn after their first break-in eight weeks before.

Butch braked the vehicle. No lights flashed since he'd removed the fuse to the taillights. He pulled a do-rag over his bald head. "C'mon. We got a job to do."

They slipped through the barbed wire. A quick dash took them over rocky desert and scrubby grass to the edge of the house's wall.

Butch created a stirrup with his hands and thrust her upward.

Sana drew in a sharp breath as she checked the top. Glass shards, all embedded in fresh concrete, glinted in the moonlight. "We've got glass. Give me the mat."

With one hand supporting her like a cheerleader, he lifted up a thick leather mat she used for such occasions. With it draped over the wall, she dropped on the other side.

Butch jumped up and scrambled over. He landed with barely a sound.

Sana marveled at how a six-four, two-fifty guy could move so quietly.

She observed the house. Only a dim lamp glowed in the den. A stove light glimmered in the kitchen. "No floodlights on. Shock." She darted to the wall next to a set of French doors on the patio and pressed herself against it.

Butch's phone began vibrating. She winced. Even though it didn't ring, it still made noise. He silenced it without a look and nodded toward the door. "Is it open?"

Oh, so carefully, she turned the knob. Unlocked. She'd be collecting her little payout from Suleiman tonight.

"Sana, Butch, beware," Suleiman said through the wireworm in her ear. "Someone—"

She cracked the door. A burglar alarm began screeching and drowned out the rest of his warning.

Sana yelped.

Butch began laughing, and she glared at him as they dashed onto the patio and into the backyard. "I guess Suleiman's going to collect, huh?"

The noise ceased as she pulled out a rag to wipe the camo paint on her face. "I guess so." Footsteps crunched on the pea gravel of the walkway leading around the house. A couple joined them. She pasted a smile on her face and extended her hand. "Mr. and Mrs. Marcos, hi. It's good to see you again."

The husband shook it. "Under better circumstances, at least. For us, that is."

Butch chuckled. "Yes, sir. You had us going. We found a door open and took the bait."

The wife sighed. "I told Amelia and Stefan to lock up when they left."

"Let's go over what happened." Butch gestured to the chairs and couch that made a conversation group on the covered patio. "When we broke in two months ago, we got over a wall with no glass on top, right?

Then we gained entrance through the back door since no neighbors could see thanks to the wall. And no alarm alerted anyone because none was installed. And we found an open window, plus the unlocked back door. We made off with how much that night?"

Mrs. Marcos glanced at her husband. "Fifty grand or something like that in cash, jewelry, and small electronics."

Sana used her phone to pull up a spreadsheet she'd done of their haul in February. "And if we'd had a truck, we would have made off with even bigger items. I'd say this was a success for you two. Had this been a real break-in, that alarm would have sent me running as fast as I could, and I probably would have wound up in the ER after cutting myself up getting over that wall."

Butch rose. "Congrats. You outsmarted us. Vic'll be calling you to set up a closeout visit." Once they retrieved the mat, they walked with the couple out the front door, then continued down the drive to where he'd parked the Suburban. "Finally. Someone who takes the boss's recommendations seriously."

Sana swung into her seat. "It does happen."

"But not too often, not even at the prospect of getting five percent of Sentry Securities' fee back. Chalk up another security assessment test as a success." After reinstalling the fuse so the taillights would come on, he checked his phone, which began chiming. "Hey, boss. We just got done testing the Marcos house. They did a good job..." He laughed. "Yeah, I'm glad they took you seriously. What's up?"

Sana tuned him out as she laid her head against the seat. Weariness from working the early shift at her business, Pause Café, began hitting her, especially because she'd have to do it all over again in the morning. At least she'd earned a good day's fee as one of Victor Chavez's contractors for Sentry Securities. Part of that would go for the wedding in June. And the rest? Into the café.

Butch nudged her. "Hey, Sana. Don't conk out on me yet."

She straightened. "What's up?"

"The boss has a job for us in Nashville. He wants us to gather the team."

"When?"

He stomped on the accelerator. "Tonight. Bad stuff has gone down. That's all I know."

A smile crossed Sana's face. Maybe now she could put off lingerie shopping.

Tuesday, April 5, 2016, 2115 hours MST, Flagstaff, AZ

Sana pulled on a pair of leggings and added a hoodie lined with soft fleece. She shoved her size-five feet into their clogs and headed to the door. Time to see what Victor had in store for them. She stepped onto the back porch of the Women's Building. Ponderosa pine with a faint smell of horses on Last Chance Ranch tickled her nose.

The tense muscles in her shoulders relaxed. Ahead of her, the walls of the box canyon northeast of Flagstaff loomed black against the starry night. Arizona nights were the best. They beat the bright lights of her native Austin, Texas, by a mile. To her left and ahead of her, lights blazed through the glass walls of Victor Chavez's studio, which had become the *de facto* meeting place for the team when they had a job.

Suleiman arrived at the studio just as she did. He took her in his arms. "You did well tonight."

She heaved a sigh. "Though we got busted."

He chuckled, its sound husky in her ears. "What do you plan on getting?"

She anticipated lingerie shopping for their honeymoon as much as a round of rabies shots. "Hmmm. I haven't had time to think about it."

He leaned forward and kissed her. "Maybe that will help."

"Men!" She swatted him on the chest before snuggling up to him. "It'll be a honeymoon surprise."

Butch stood in the doorway, his husky frame blocking some of the light. "Well, hello, you two lovebirds. C'mon in before you heat up the neighborhood with that kiss."

Suleiman released his bride-to-be but held onto her hand. "You sometimes mystify me, Butch."

"Hey, I try. Someone's got to keep you guessing." He returned to the worktable. "How's the guest list coming?"

Ker-plunk! There went her mood. She'd avoided talking about the impasse she and Suleiman had hit on the guest list—until now. She tried procrastination. "It's mostly done."

Suleiman released her hand and wandered to the fireplace. "Except for her parents."

She shot him a dirty look.

Butch stroked his beard, a new product since the previous No-Shave November. "That's a toughie."

"Tell me about it." Sana poured some water from a gallon jug into an electric teakettle and turned it on. She dropped a teabag into a mug with a picture of a rock climber on it. "I don't want to talk about it."

The printer whirred. Butch collected a set of papers and distributed them to stacks on a drafting table. "Just remember it may be better to give them the option of refusing rather than living with the regret of not inviting them."

"I'll take that under advisement."

He gathered everything into folders. "It's only a suggestion." He glanced up as Shelly Wise, the team's computer expert, and Diana Kasem, the team's doctor, joined them. "Hey, you two. Is Skylar coming?"

Diana joined Sana and picked up a mug with a stethoscope on it. "Nope. He texted and said his manager quit on the spot, so he has to close tonight. And Fi got stuck in a snowstorm in Wichita, so she's not getting back until tomorrow or Thursday. I'll fill them in."

"Yokay. We'll make do with what we've got." He handed everyone a folder before thumping across the granite tile to one of the two sleek, modern chairs that created a conversation group in front of the studio's fireplace. "Everyone, gather 'round. Vic wanted us to call him when we were here."

Diana gestured to her folder. "What do we have?"

The chair groaned under Butch's weight. "Info on our newest gig. Briefing sheet's on top, and Vic will go through that."

Sana settled on a couch covered in the same black leather as the chairs. Suleiman joined her. Shelly sat on the other end, and Diana curled up in the other chair.

Butch dialed a number on the conference phone that sat on the coffee table.

Victor's voice boomed off the glass walls. "Hey, everyone. How's it going?"

Butch's gaze swept across the room. "Well. We've got everyone here but Skylar and Fi. They couldn't make it. Actually, Fi's stuck in Wichita in that snowstorm."

"Which is coming this way, I heard. If that warm air from the Gulf doesn't disturb it." The line crackled as if Victor shifted.

"How's Nashville?" Diana asked.

"Good, but I'm ready to come home."

Butch lifted a large mug with an image of a rat on it to his lips. "Don't sound like that's gonna happen anytime soon."

"Nope. Does everyone have the information I sent?"

Sana opened her folder and pulled out the briefing sheet. "Right here."

Victor's voice had a flat tone. "I met with Mary Walton today."

Sana frowned. "As in Gary Walton's widow?"

"Remember him?" Sarcasm tinged his question.

How could she forget? Almost three years ago, Gary had approached her at the gym where she was working in Austin and offered her a free ticket out of her dead-end life. A net positive—until she thought about the way the man had betrayed the Shadow Box team two years before, which had nearly cost everyone their lives. He'd done worse to Victor. He'd turned on his best friend of fifteen years.

"Anyway, Mary's now a widow. No pension, no life insurance payout either since the FBI knows he was involved in some serious crimes."

Diana raised her gaze from her folder. "So she's struggling."

"Something like that. They've got two kids, Morgan who's sixteen and David who's fourteen. They're my godchildren. The summer after Gary passed, she moved from Arlington to Nashville. They live in a three-bedroom townhouse near her folks in the southwestern part of Nashville."

Sana winced. "Isn't that kind of a rash decision? I mean, I thought a good rule of thumb was to wait a year after a life-changing event before making a big decision like that."

Victor drew in a breath. "I can't say I disagree with you. Regardless, Morgan's had the worst time of it. Seems the move didn't wear well on her. She fell in with the wrong crowd. Her relationship with her mom went south. In March, she went to a party where weed and alcohol came out. The cops showed up, and she got arrested."

Sana scanned the briefing sheet. It laid out a rough timeline of events on St. Patrick's Day and the day after. "Her mom didn't bail her out?"

"Nope."

"Why?" Shelly asked. "I mean, if I'd done something like that, I'd have been in deep doo-doo, but Mom and Dad would have bailed me out."

Sana's mood dipped as she thought about her own stint in prison that began seven years before. Under her breath, she muttered, "Not if you're on the skids with your parents."

"I agree, Shelly." Paper rattled on Victor's end. "She told her daughter she was going to leave her in there so she could think about what she'd done."

Butch's mouth worked, but no sound came out. Finally, he drawled, "What? Is the woman nuts?"

"Not mine to say," Victor replied. "When Mary headed over there after school, Morgan was gone. A friend bailed her out, and now she's missing."

"Does the friend have a name?" Butch asked.

"Will Smith."

Diana wrinkled her nose. "And I'm Angelina Jolie. Vic, this stinks. Please tell me she called the cops."

"Oh, yeah. She did. I got a copy of the report they gave her. She had no idea Morgan had a boyfriend, and when they talked to this Will Smith guy, he said he left her at the townhouse. The cops think she's a runaway. Regardless, Morgan's disappeared, and Mary's worried sick."

Sana flipped to the police report and scanned it. Nothing Victor hadn't already covered. "I can understand why she's so worried."

Victor cleared his throat. "I told her I was hesitant to muck in a police investigation. At first, I was going to say let them work their case."

Butch shifted his bulk on the chair and rested his elbows on his knees. "What changed your mind, boss?"

"Clay Hall called."

Sana's eyes widened. "Clay Hall as in the mega country singer?"

Victor chuckled. "Don't go fan girl on me, Sana. Yes, *the* Clay Hall. Remember he's a client of mine, right?"

Wow. Clay Hall. Sana couldn't believe her ears. "Oh, uh, yeah. I'd forgotten."

"Anyway, he's involved in this anti-trafficking organization called Forever Free or F-Squared for short. He went to a seminar a few weeks ago and learned all about human trafficking. He's suspicious, and he actually offered to pay for us to search for her."

For Sana, the choice was easy. "I'm in even if we weren't getting paid."

"We all are." Diana peered at the others. "Right, guys?"

The rest responded in the affirmative.

"I knew you would be." Victor muffled a yawn. "Sorry. It's getting on toward midnight here. Sana, Suleiman, Butch, and Shelly, I want you four to come to Nashville. Diana, hold back until Fiona arrives. You and Skylar read up on human trafficking and the case. As we get info, we'll feed it back to you."

Sana's to-do list multiplied in seconds. Make sure gear bag was up to date. Pack clothing. Call her manager and shift supervisor for tomorrow. "What do we need to bring?"

"Your normal gear bag. Prepare to be gone a couple of weeks."

Good. She could avoid the guest list—and sending out invitations—until they got back. "Will do."

"And read up on that info. There will be a charter plane at the Flagstaff airport first thing in the morning. It leaves at 0700 hours sharp, so be there or find your own way." Victor rattled off the contact information. "I'll meet you at Nashville's General Aviation at 1300 hours. And I've already taken care of your hotel reservations and gotten an additional rental car for you all. I'll see you tomorrow."

"Later, boss." Butch silenced the conference line. Then he fixed each of them in his dark gaze. "Well, gang. Looks like we've got our work cut out for us."

Sana's own stint in prison threatened to parade through her mind. She shifted her gaze to Morgan's picture at the top of the briefing sheet. A cute redhead with innocence in her eyes. The girl must be terrified out of her mind. Sana raised her gaze. "Do we ever."

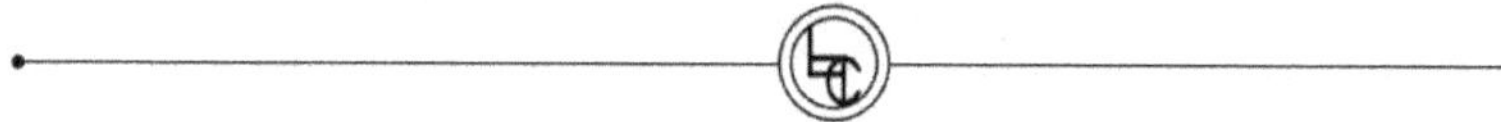

Tuesday, April 5, 2016, 2300 hours MST, Flagstaff, AZ

Sana sat cross-legged on the couch in the common area of the Women's Building and stared at the case file laying open on her lap. Oh, she needed sleep. Not yet. She gazed at Morgan Walton's picture. A pretty girl. More pictures showed her with her brother and mother. And with her father before he passed.

She turned to some full-length shots. Make that a pretty girl who had the figure of a woman and was probably innocent to the world. Undoubtedly, she'd caught the eye of someone who had other intentions for her.

She flipped pages to some bullet points related to human trafficking. Traffickers preyed on those girls and boys who were vulnerable. Isolated. The risk for runaways skyrocketed. But Morgan hadn't been a runaway, right? Maybe not, but for all intents and purposes, she and her mother had ceased talking. Morgan had become isolated from a caring network, which had made her vulnerable.

Suleiman tapped on the door.

Sana waved him inside. "Hey, come on in."

He settled beside her. "Where is Diana?"

"Asleep since she has to be at the hospital at six tomorrow morning."

He kissed her, then nodded toward the file. "I noticed you were troubled."

She wrapped her arms around herself. "That's one way to put it. Sometimes, I wonder about people."

"What do you mean?"

"Like why did Mary Walton rip her children away from all they ever knew? To my knowledge, they'd never lived in Nashville before. At least it's not listed here. I mean, they were in Fayetteville, North Carolina, until Morgan was five, then Arlington."

He fell silent for a few moments to the point where she wanted to tell him to answer. Finally, he looped a strand of her shiny, black, chin-length hair around his finger. "I cannot answer except to say that perhaps she wanted to be close to her parents and in-laws. I am not in her head."

"I know. But..." How could she explain the feelings of sadness she'd felt in her own life when her parents had rejected her? "It doesn't make sense to me."

"Who knows?"

"Yeah." She ran her finger down Morgan's head shot. "I can identify with her."

He rubbed the base of her neck. "How so?"

"After I got arrested, I sat in jail and rotted until I pleaded guilty." Her jaw tightened as memories resurfaced. Over seven years ago, she'd huddled in a cell, desperate for a visit, a phone call—anything—from Mother or Father to show they cared. Nothing. She'd shamed her parents. She'd been cast out of the family and become a stray, unwanted by either of them. Oh, the loneliness that followed that realization. Back then, she yearned for a hug. "To me, it was betrayal at the highest level. If some 'Will Smith' character had professed to care for me and bailed me out, I probably would have believed him."

"Do you think he's a human trafficker?"

She shrugged. "I have my suspicions, but I don't know. It can happen. A trafficker can befriend someone who's vulnerable. They gain their trust. Who knows how? By sleeping with her? Maybe. But it could be just by being her friend. And if things are as rough with her mom as Vic says, I can see why she would readily go with someone she trusted, even if he didn't have her best interests at heart." More memories assaulted her, and her lip trembled. "It was so hard, Suleiman."

He took the folder from her, closed it, and laid it on the coffee table. "We will find her. That, I can promise."

"I'm not so sure."

He kissed her on the temple, then on the lips. "Can you perhaps leave it be for a bit? Perhaps try to be positive about it?"

"I'll try."

He kissed her long and slow before slipping away.

Sana crawled into bed. Once more, it was like someone had pasted her eyes open. Her gaze roamed across the room. First, it landed on a picture of her and Suleiman from the year before when they'd gone to Victor and Deborah Chavez's wedding in North Carolina. They'd not been dating at the time, but a strong friendship had sprung up between them. For that day, she'd worn a sari of beautiful blue. Her black hair shone in the sun and curled just below her chin. And Suleiman? Oh, so handsome in his charcoal gray suit with just a bit of five o'clock shadow on his jaw.

After the team returned from Somalia the year before, where they'd freed a missions ship from Somali pirates, a romance sprang up between Sana and Suleiman that summer and turned into love. She shifted her gaze to a notebook on her dresser. Diana had given it to her as an engagement gift. A wedding planner, complete with lace around the edges and a picture of Suleiman and her under the clear plastic protector.

Her thoughts turned toward Austin, Texas, and the man she'd thought she'd marry way back then. What had happened to Texas Ranger Ryan Flagel? He'd arrested her, then been her only friend when her life had gotten turned upside down after her sudden release from prison where she'd served time for breaking and entering. Then he became what Diana called a near miss, a man she'd thought she'd marry, probably would have, if Gary Walton hadn't made her an offer she couldn't refuse.

Why had she thought of him? Because he'd been that anchor in the storm of a life upended, someone she could trust and who had her best interests at heart when she badly needed a friend. What had happened to him? Sana turned onto her side. And had she stayed, what would have happened with their romance?

But worse, why did she even care?

3

Wednesday, April 6, 2016, 1500 hours CDT, Nashville, TN

"What are we looking for?" Sana asked the next afternoon as she stood in the living room of the Walton townhouse. Rain drummed a soothing cadence on the roof, making her yearn to sleep away the rest of the day with one of those brightly colored throw pillows she'd spotted on the couch tucked under her head. She stopped herself from reaching for a neatly folded fleece of the same color.

Butch rubbed his bearded chin. "We know Morgan and her mama weren't talking to each other. Morgan's probably hidden stuff from her. We need to find it. Okay, gang. Mary's running errands and will be back by five. I want to be gone by then."

"Why didn't she want to be here?" Shelly asked.

"Would you want to be here when someone rummaged through your stuff?"

She shrugged. "Maybe."

"I promised we'd let her know if we removed anything. Let's start with the downstairs. Shelly, you take the garage and deck outside. Sana, you take the living area. I'll do the kitchen."

As Shelly opened the door leading to the townhouse's garage, Sana turned her attention to the fireplace. The family portrait on the mantel almost taunted her. Gary. Mary. Morgan. David. All wearing matching jeans with white shirts and big smiles, the perfect family living the perfect life. She gazed around the rest of the room. No pictures except on the mantel. And all of those with Gary in them. Life seemed to have stopped after his death in the spring of 2014.

She removed each one and examined them. Nothing. The portrait yielded the same result.

An American flag in a case of elegant dark wood sat below the gold-edged frame. She hesitated. This very flag had draped across Gary's casket, which Victor helped carry at the funeral. How had that torn him? He refused to talk much about a fifteen-year friendship that ended so tragically, just enough to reveal that years before the team came together for Operation Shadow Box, a *Quds* agent turned Gary.

Butch put a hand on her shoulder. "You gotta look, Sana. I'll help you fold it."

She took it down and searched the case, then unfurled the stiff cotton. "Did you know Gary?"

"We served together in Special Forces. Seems Makmoud Hidari led an ambush where they captured Gary's whole team. He was the only one who survived."

Sana cringed at the mention of their old foe. "How did Makmoud turn him?"

"Darned if I know. The *Quds* Force knew what they were doing when they tapped him for the job." Butch took two corners. "Let's put this back."

So twisted. Makmoud most likely left Gary with no choices. Suleiman's half brother was good at that. And at the end, he ripped apart a family. From her experience last year as Makmoud's temporary hostage, she'd learned to fear the *Quds* agent.

She needed distraction. Fast. She moved on to the fireplace and the rest of the living room. "I got nothing, Butch. You?"

"Nope." He shut a cabinet as Shelly rejoined them. "What about you, Shel?"

She carefully shook the rain off her raincoat. "Nothing out back or in the garage. Wow. It's so neat in there. Scarcely anything."

Sana winced as they trooped upstairs. Usually, men filled garages with man toys and tools. An empty garage was just another sign of fallout from the tragedy two years ago.

Butch paused on the landing where five doors opened to various rooms. "Shel, you take David's room and his bathroom. Sana, you do Morgan's. I'll take the master suite, linen closet, and attic."

"Roger that." Shelly stepped into a bedroom.

Sana faced a door with a huge biohazard poster taped to the front. She pushed it open. Oh, wow. What a far cry from the way she'd kept her own room as a teenager. Mother and Father had demanded neatness. But Morgan's room? Junk on a desk and dresser with clothes all over the floor and bed. What a disaster. And where to start?

Sana turned her attention to a four-shelf bookcase to the left of the door. Trophies crowded on top, some with medals hanging from them. She peered at the descriptions. Cross country. Track. 5k race winner. 10k race winner. All from Virginia and nothing from Tennessee. Had Morgan tried out? Or had she made and quit the team?

Tons of books lined the shelves. The Harry Potter series, a favorite of hers as well. And the Hunger Games trilogy. Plus the Lord of the Rings trilogy and a host of other fantasy and apocalyptic fiction books. Her schoolbooks lay in a backpack at the foot of the bookcase or in a messy pile beside the backpack. Sana examined each one. Nothing substantial in them or behind them.

What about the dresser? She moved to the wall across from the window. More books sat in stacks with random jewelry like necklaces and earrings scattered everywhere on top. She picked up some beads from what must have been a Mardi Gras party. A pom-pom from a football game caught her attention, as did some memorabilia from another high school, most likely her school in Arlington. Sana sorted through everything and came to some coasters.

She frowned as she picked one up. Purple background with two sets of sixteenth-note triplets shaped like Ms were stamped on it in gold along with the words Nashville, TN, below that in line with the edge of the circular coaster. Interesting. Had Morgan been there for a Mardi Gras celebration? Quite possibly since they were located together with the beads on the dresser. Did they mean anything? It seemed out of place in a teenager's room.

She took them to the desk under the window and set them on top of a laptop.

The rest of the dresser, including Morgan's clothing, turned up nothing other than normal teenager stuff. Sana turned her attention to the desk. Papers lay everywhere, including a note from her math teacher requiring that her mother sign off on homework with a *60* scrawled across the top in green ink. According to the project file, Morgan was failing school. It certainly wouldn't have been possible to study in this room. Pens and pencils filled a cup from her old high school. Paper clips sat in a shot glass. Sana peered closer at it. Hmmm. The same logo as the coasters. She dumped the clips and added the glass to the coasters and laptop.

She found several pictures crowded on the top of both nightstands. Those revealed Morgan with Gary at various stages of her childhood. She was a daddy's girl through and through, and Sana knew Gary had loved his daughter. His death had broken Morgan's heart. *God, why did this have to happen?* A search of the nightstands revealed two joints. Mary must have had no clue her daughter smoked dope. Sana's heart ached for their torn relationship.

Finally, she headed to the bathroom. More mess, this time in the form of makeup strewn across the counter along with a curling iron, barrettes, gel and mousse, and other hair supplies. Birth control lay in a drawer. In the walk-in closet, more empty hangars than not beckoned to her, probably because most of Morgan's clothing was all over the floor and bed.

Sana took a deep breath as she picked her way into the bedroom. She wanted to scream and run downstairs to the living room where nothing dared stray from its assigned place.

"Oh, my..." Butch stared at the mess. "Please tell me you did this."

She grimaced. "This is how I found it. Promise."

"How do people live like this?"

"My thoughts, exactly. I've found some stuff." She gestured to the laptop. "From what I could tell, she's most likely sexually active, smokes the occasional joint, and at some point," she picked up the shot glass, "probably on Mardi Gras, visited a night club with this logo."

He examined it. "Interesting. Isn't she a bit underage to go clubbing?"

"Unless she got a fake ID somewhere."

Shelly crowded inside. "Whoa. And I thought I was messy. What'd you find? I got nothing in David's room, which is completely opposite of this."

Sana handed her the laptop. "For you. I haven't turned it on, but it warrants a look-see."

Shelly set her backpack on the floor. "We'll have to let Mary know we have it."

Sana picked up one of the coasters. "Do you think you could figure out who the owner of this logo is?"

"Sure. It may take some time, but I can."

"That'd be great because I think this is our next clue going forward. What about you, Butch?"

"Nothing in the master bedroom or bath. Methinks Morgan hid everything in her room. It'd be easy to do if her mama never went inside. I did find something interesting in the attic."

"Which is?" Sana asked as they stepped onto the landing.

"Three sets of suitcases. Now if Morgan truly ran away, don't you think she would have packed at least her backpack or a suitcase? Anyway, I think we're done here. I don't know about you, but I'm famished."

Shelly grinned. "Growing boys have to eat."

Butch swatted at her, and she giggled as she ducked. "Says you. Let's go."

Sana led the way downstairs. As Butch shut and locked the door behind them, she hoped Victor had fared well in his visit to the cops.

4

Wednesday, April 6, 2016, 1630 hours CDT, Nashville, TN

Victor Chavez's stomach rumbled. His rear hurt from sitting on a hard plastic chair in the headquarters building of the Metropolitan Nashville Police Department, and he wanted to jump up and run around to loosen his joints. The detective who'd taken Mary Walton's missing persons report hadn't shown his face, even two hours after their scheduled meeting. That as well as the rain dampened his mood. With a sigh, he snapped shut the Lee Child paperback he'd been reading during his trip. Negative thoughts began circling in his mind like buzzards over roadkill.

Time to reframe his thinking by praying for his family and giving thanks for them. Deborah and the kids had settled well into their new lives. The children thrived in their new schools. DJ would turn fourteen soon, and Butch, who owned a mechanic shop in Flagstaff, had found an old car for the three of them to restore. Anna, his oldest stepdaughter, wanted to work at Pause Café when she turned sixteen in three months. In February, he began court proceedings to adopt the children. Hopefully, they'd be Chavez kids soon, unlike the Walton clan since Gary's—

Like the night before when he'd lain awake for an hour and stared at the ceiling while thinking about his former best friend, Gary's betrayal stole the peace he'd worked so hard to achieve over the past couple of years.

"Mr. Chavez?" A woman's Tennessee twang drew him out of his inner turmoil.

Finally. Something else to think about besides Gary. Victor approached the speaker connecting him with the receptionist via the thick glass. "Yes, ma'am?"

"Detective Cruz is on his way. He got detained with a pileup investigation on the highway. Thanks for waiting."

Victor returned to his seat beside Suleiman.

Ever the quiet one, his sniper rested his elbows on his knees as he fiddled with his phone.

Victor wished he had Suleiman al-Ibrahim's zen-like persona. They both wore emotional scars due to the same man. Makmoud Hidari. Years before Suleiman met Victor, Hidari had influenced his half brother to kill Victor's fiancée. Victor's scars came from trusting Gary, who turned him over to Hidari. What made Suleiman so serene while he, Victor, wanted to climb the walls? Suleiman had made peace with his past. It'd taken time and forgiveness to find that.

And Victor? Had he truly forgiven Gary? No. The realization knocked the wind out of him as much as a sucker punch would have. He expelled a hard breath.

Suleiman raised an eyebrow.

The doors leading to the lobby burst open. Two people, a woman and a man, strode through. Droplets sprayed as the man yanked a bush hat from his head and muttered something to his partner.

The receptionist pointed toward Victor and Suleiman.

The man stopped in front of him. "Mr. Chavez?"

Victor rose. "That's me."

"Detective Landon Cruz." The man extended his hand. "This is Lucy Hendricks, my partner. And you're with?"

Victor almost winced at Cruz's crushing grip. "Sentry Securities out of Flagstaff, Arizona. And this is Suleiman al-Ibrahim, one of my staff."

Cruz didn't acknowledge Suleiman, and Hendricks only mumbled something. Cruz led the way toward a glass door. Drops followed him wherever he went. "Yeah, I remember your company. Y'all did the *Peacemaker* thing, right? Boy, a bunch of renegades is what I first thought."

What was with the guy? And was Hendricks a mute or something? Victor's irritation, which had sprouted during his two-hour wait, flourished. "We got the job done. That's all that mattered."

"If you say so." Cruz used his ID badge to let them into the back. A central staircase encased in glass rose up from the middle of the open room. "Sorry about being late. Ten-car pileup on the freeway. We had four detectives trying to sort things out."

"Sounds complicated."

Cruz snorted as he led the way upward one story to an open floor ringed with glass-walled conference rooms and offices. Anemic gray light filtered through floor-to-ceiling windows. He hung his coat from a hook on a cubicle. Almost immediately, water puddled under it. "That's one way to look at it. Luce, how about take them to Conference Room A while I get my folder?"

Detective Hendricks led them toward a row of conference rooms. She stopped at the first one and let them be without a word.

Ever so slightly, Suleiman nodded toward the far end of the room.

Victor noted the camera. Were Cruz and Hendricks watching them?

"What do you want me to do?" his sniper asked.

"Observe. I'll do the talking." They settled in for the wait.

Cruz joined them and tossed a folder onto the table. Hendricks followed with a couple of bottles of water for their guests and settled to his right.

Victor stared at the folder. Not an accordion file like he might have expected. Or even a little thickness. Just a thin file. He glanced at Hendricks's face. She bit her lip and focused on the bland tabletop.

Cruz popped a wad of gum into his mouth. "Sorry. I'm quitting smoking, and gum is my substitute right now."

"Can you brief me as to what's going on with the case?" Victor asked.

Cruz opened the folder.

Morgan's mugshot from a few weeks ago had been clipped inside.

As he scanned a set of handwritten notes, Cruz chomped for a moment. "Morgan Walton was at a party held by some underage friends of hers. Dope and alcohol came out. We found out about it, and we busted it really good. Arrested her and nine of her pals."

"Who called it in?" Victor asked.

"Don't know." Cruz flipped to a typed report. "Vice received an anonymous call. Morgan and her friends wound up getting booked into the holding cells at the Davidson County Sheriff's Department. That's where we send all of our perps. By shortly after midnight, all but her were bailed out."

Victor pulled out his own notebook and checked his notes from talking with Mary and reviewing her copy of the report. Cruz's statements matched those of Mary's. "When was she bailed out?"

"Around 6:15 the next morning."

Victor studied the page. "By a Will Smith."

"Yep. He said he was her friend. Known her for about six months. Her mom said she'd wanted to teach her daughter a lesson by picking her up after school rather than that morning."

What had Mary been thinking? For about the twentieth time, that thought crossed Victor's mind. Some lesson. "I'm having a hard time understanding why someone would do that."

Cruz shrugged. "It happens more than you think. Some parents think the cops should be the disciplinarian."

Don't judge. You told the team not to do that. You shouldn't either. "Did you talk to this Will Smith guy?"

Cruz's jaw worked the gum. "Yeah. He said he took her home and stayed until she let herself in."

Victor cocked an eyebrow. "And you believe him?"

The detective paused from examining his notes. "We didn't have reason not to. He had a legit driver's license. He said he was a friend. The deputy who signed her out said she could tell they knew each other."

"Did you ever suspect he might have forged the license?"

Cruz's glance pierced him like a spear. "I had no reason to suspect it wasn't legit. And believe me when I say the deputies at the jail know how to spot forgeries."

Victor tried another tactic. "How did he know her?"

"Like I said, he's her friend. I guess he met her at some parties even though he was in college."

"Didn't you question why someone who's probably over eighteen was hanging out with a sixteen-year-old?"

Cruz huffed out a breath and grimaced. "Mr. Chavez, I have nothing to prove they were dating."

To Victor, it seemed like Cruz wanted to get them out of there, most likely so he could write his report on that pileup. Time for another route. "What are your thoughts?"

Cruz laced his fingers on top of the file and leaned forward. "What do you know about teenagers, especially teenaged girls?"

Victor's thoughts flew to Anna and DJ. "I've got two teenagers, a daughter and a son. They came with the wife I married a year ago."

"Hopefully you know they're hard to handle."

Oh, yeah. That was one way to put it.

"Especially the girls." Cruz worried his gum some more. "Their hormones... Man, it's drama. My wife and I barely survived our daughters. When they moved out, we went on a vacation. A long one."

"And your point?"

Cruz's lips flattened, and his fingers tightened where they laced together. "My point is, teenaged girls run away a lot. Some last a day, then return home. Some longer."

"And some never return."

"Agreed." The detective began drumming his fingers on the table. "Truth is, we don't look for runaways."

Had Victor heard right? He rubbed his chin as he tried to digest that bit of information. "Meaning there's no ongoing investigation."

Cruz glanced at Hendricks for a long second. "Nope. None. It's not illegal to run away."

"That's not right."

Cruz put his elbow on the table and pointed at him with his pen. "Hey, I don't make the rules, here, got it? Even children can run away. But I have to say everything mobilizes for children under ten."

But not for teenagers. What was wrong with the world today?

"When Mrs. Walton called us, I took her report. As a courtesy, I talked with Will Smith. He told me they were friends. Period. He left her at the house. Period. I did what I normally do. I sent the report down to our Runaway Unit, and they entered it into the database kept by the National Center for Missing and Exploited Children. If she gets arrested somewhere and her name pops up in that database, we'll make sure she's reunited with her mom."

Victor clenched his jaw. "I still can't believe it. There's got to be something you can do."

Again, Cruz's gaze shifted to Hendricks, who continued gnawing her reddening lip. He refocused on his guest. "Mr. Chavez, let me get one thing straight. I understand your concern. Truly. I do. But many times, these kids wind up with friends. They stay with them until they realize how good they had it with mommy and daddy. Then they return. Sometimes, that can take a bit."

Victor glanced at Suleiman, who sent him a warning signal with a slight shake of his head. He couldn't quit. Not now. "And sometimes, they wind up on the streets and vulnerable. What's the risk that a girl will get trafficked? It's huge, like almost doubles if she's a—"

"How many detectives do you think we have on staff in the Investigative Services Bureau, Mr. Chavez?"

"I don't know."

"Around eighty or so when we're fully staffed. Which we're currently not." Cruz slapped his folder shut. "And every one of us is overwhelmed. Nashville's a big town. We're stretched thin. Now you tell me which felony or horrible wreck we should ignore to go after a runaway teen? The ten-car pileup a couple of hours ago? Or the double homicide up in the northern part of town?"

Point taken. Victor's stomach twisted, and his hands tightened until his nails bit into his palms. "Mary's been through hell."

"Oh, she told me. Lost her husband two years ago, right?" Cruz's eyes narrowed. "Why do you care so much?"

Victor kept his gaze steady on him even as his mood further nose-dived. "I care because I'm Morgan's godfather. Her dad was my best friend."

Cruz examined him as if he were the one who'd taken Morgan. He toyed with the gum wrapper, then shook his head. "Okay. I get it. I'm sorry, Mr. Chavez, but our hands are tied."

Again, he glanced at Hendricks as if he dared her to speak up.

Victor shifted. "Then I take it our visit here was fruitless."

"We did what we could."

"Would you be good if we did our own investigating?"

Cruz chewed some more as he stared him down. A contest between two alphas, to be sure. His phone began vibrating. He checked a text and groaned. "Great. Another call. I've got to get going—again."

Victor closed his notebook. "So, you're cool with us doing our own investigation?"

Cruz grabbed the folder. "You'll share?"

Victor rose and shrugged into his leather jacket. "Absolutely." He resisted adding, *But you said we'd not find anything.*

Cruz tossed a business card onto the table as his phone began chiming. "Here's my card. Luce, print them a copy of the file, will ya?"

She nodded and led the way to a cubicle across from Cruz's. Victor had his copy within a minute.

Something about Hendricks bothered him. She didn't meet his gaze and kept her notepad folded in her arms like a protective shields.

"Detective Hendricks, thanks," Victor said.

She offered a tight smile that faded.

"Luce!" Cruz called. "Convenience store robbery. Let's go!"

Once they'd signed out in the main lobby, Victor flipped through the stapled papers. The same exact thing he'd received from Mary. He huffed out a breath. "That so did not go to plan. He had zero to add."

Suleiman followed him through the deluge toward where Victor had parked his Toyota Camry. "Detective Cruz is hiding something."

Victor cringed as rain pelted him. "Why do you say that?"

"His partner's body language. Everything screamed she wanted to talk but was too scared to do so. And something seems off about that driver's license. If not a forgery, someone supplied it to this Will Smith person."

"And Morgan vanished after he took her home."

"Could she have truly run away?"

Victor turned onto the freeway and groaned at the stopped traffic. "We'll see what the others found out. Then we'll know."

5

Wednesday, April 6, 2016 1845 hours CDT, Nashville, TN

As her gaze darted to the hotel's front doors, Sana ripped open a teabag, dropped it into a paper cup, and added hot water. She retreated to a corner of the lobby where the team waited for Victor.

Shelly sat cross-legged on an asymmetrical lime green chair that looked like something out of a Dr. Seuss story. She pecked away on her laptop as she summarized their visit to the Walton townhouse. Butch sprawled on another chair of orange fabric that seemed too small for his large frame. He spread *USA Today* on the table in front of him.

Sana curled up in a third chair done up in bright blue and stared out the window. The intensity of the rain outside increased. She shivered. "What's holding them up?"

Butch leaned back. "Traffic. This is what got Fi stuck in Wichita. Should be outta here tomorrow."

"Let's hope." Thoughts gnawed at her. "Can I ask you a question?'

"Sure."

"Do you think Mary loves her daughter?"

He rubbed a hand across his bald head. The small silver hoops in his ears glinted as he studied her. "I'm sure she does. Vic told me things were different before Gary died. They were a close family."

"Why the sudden change?"

He folded the paper into a neat rectangle. "Grief does things to people. I know she loves Morgan regardless of what's happened."

Could a family not have love? She thought about Mother and Father. Distant. That was one word she'd used to describe her relationship with her parents. Their love for her had depended on performance, be it in school or gymnastics.

Butch gazed at her, his eyes slightly narrowed. "What about you?"

Her stomach knotted. Had he read her thoughts? "What about me?"

His fingers smoothed the velvety texture of the chair's fabric. "Your relationship with your folks."

The tea in her cup began trembling slightly. "I don't know the definition of a close family. Love in our house had to be earned."

"You sure?"

Her heart ached as she remembered the portrait she'd seen at the Walton townhouse and the envy she'd felt. She really didn't want to go into it. Not now. And certainly not in public. "Uh, yeah."

The doors to the hotel swished open, admitting a blast of wet and cold as well as Victor and Suleiman. Victor jerked his head toward the elevators. His orders were clear. Upstairs. Good. End of topic between Butch and her.

Once ensconced in his suite on the fifth floor, Victor folded his arms across his chest and leaned against the bar of the kitchenette. "What a day. Did anyone get food?"

Shelly settled at the worktable. "I ordered pizza for us right before you showed up. They'll text me when it comes."

"Bless you." Victor pulled a bottle of water from the small refrigerator.

Butch flopped onto the couch. "How were the cops?"

"As friendly as ever." Victor glanced at Suleiman, who fought a smile as he seated himself on the other end of the couch.

Sana perched on the couch's arm and took her fiancé's hand.

Victor held up a file. "Seriously, they were of no help. None. This is all they had. It's just the report Mary got. Running away is not illegal. Therefore, the cops didn't pursue the matter."

"What?" Shelly drawled. "That's it?"

"Yep."

Butch glanced at Sana. "Then we have a problem. You see, we searched the townhouse. I found suitcases in the attic. Three sets of them."

"And her backpack was on the floor in front of her bookcase," Sana added. "From what I could tell, all of her clothing was there." She shuddered. "Her room was so messy."

A small smile crept across Victor's face. "Even messier than Shelly's?"

Shelly only raised an eyebrow as she continued working on her laptop. "Hey, I resemble that remark."

Victor swept a hand through his hair, leaving dark spikes in its wake. "We've been cleared to do our own investigation so long as we keep the cops in the loop. While we were sitting in traffic, I called Mary and asked her to list Morgan's friends in Arlington. Suleiman wrote them down."

"You want us to call them?" Butch asked

Victor took a swig of water. "Yep. Did you find anything else?"

Sana handed Victor the shot glass and coasters they'd retrieved from the townhouse. "We found these, plus a couple of joints and her laptop."

Victor frowned as he examined them. "I have to say, it's a very interesting logo. Any idea of what it's for?"

"My guess is a club," Butch said. "A music club, maybe independently owned and not a chain."

Victor rubbed his chin. "Music clubs are a dime a dozen here. Shelly, do you think you can locate it?"

"Oh, yeah. And I'm going to check all of the social media accounts to see what I can find for Morgan."

Victor handed over the papers he held. "Here's the police report Detective Cruz provided. It's got a picture of this Will Smith guy. Mary didn't know him."

Chalk another one up for family relationships. Sana's chest tightened as she folded her arms. "That's not surprising."

"Nope. You're right, Sana, it's not." Victor pushed away from the bar. "Okay. This is what I want you all to do. Shelly, get going on the social media angle and this logo. Butch, let's you and I split out that list. We've got eight names total."

"What about us?" Sana asked as she gestured to Suleiman.

Victor scribbled something on his notepad and ripped off the sheet. "Then why don't you two go and get the pizza?"

Hmmph. They were now relegated to gofer status. Pain shot through her jaw, and she forced herself to take a deep breath. "Why can't we help?"

Victor fixed her in his gaze. "Because the list isn't that long. Seriously. Shelly, text them when the pizza shows up."

Her gaze never leaving the laptop's screen, she replied, "Will do,"

Whatever. Sana shoved through her room's door and beat feet to the fourth floor.

Suleiman followed close behind her. "Sana."

She swiped her card through the reader, then kicked off her clogs as the door clunked shut behind her. "Of all things!"

He touched her on the shoulder. "What?"

"I wanted to help."

"We are helping."

"How? By getting the pizza?"

"Yes." He drew her close and rubbed her shoulders. "You are tense, beloved. What is troubling you?"

She pulled away, grabbed a pillow from the king-sized bed, and curled up on the couch.

How could she explain what twisted in her head? The Waltons had been a close family. Yet none of the three surviving members had known anything about Gary's betrayal. "When we were at the townhouse, Butch tasked me with searching the family room and Morgan's bedroom. When I was doing the family room, I saw all of these pictures of them. There was this family portrait. They all wore white shirts and jeans. And they looked so," the green-eyed monster reared its head, "*happy*. And Morgan had all of these pictures of her and her dad on her nightstand. They were close and loved each other." She stared at the dark television but didn't really see it. "I never got that with my parents."

Suleiman reached up and rubbed the base of her neck. "You sound jealous."

I am! Not that she would admit that. Tears stung her eyes. "It's torn Morgan up." She took a deep breath. "I guess in some ways, I envy her."

He didn't say anything, only cocked his head as if waiting for her to continue.

"I imagine Gary spent a lot of time with her, loved on her, knew her as a person. I never got that from Father. I mean, I don't call Father Dad. He demanded to be called Father."

"Yet he supported you."

She glowered. "Are you defending him?"

His fingers feathered her cheek. "I am trying to understand your relationship with your parents."

"To him and Mother, it was all about honor. Keep the family name clean. Make them proud at gymnastics and school and whatever else I did." Her words tumbled over one another like a swollen waterfall. "I had to earn his love. He loved my grades and wanted me to go to an Ivy League School. When I applied to UT and won a full scholarship behind his back, he got angry with me. I guess as a way to make up for that, I majored in computer science and worked at his company to please him." That infernal lump filled her throat. No, she wouldn't go further, not into the deepest, darkest, nastiest part of her life where it had taken a wrong turn over a cliff. "I denied who I was to please him. I guess... I guess it made me so angry."

Suleiman took the pillow from her arms. He cupped her cheek. "I can see this has upset you."

She took a deep, shuddering breath. "Morgan lost her daddy to Makmoud's schemes. She then lost her support network when Mary moved the family here from Arlington."

Suleiman wrapped her in his arms and rested his chin on her head. He stroked her hair. True to form, he fell silent as if measuring his response. "Sometimes, we must set aside our emotions before they cloud our judgment."

Oh, spoken like a true man. She smarted under his words. Until she realized he was right. The year before, her anger had nearly spelled the end of both her and the team. She had to keep her emotions in check on this one. Morgan, if she were indeed in trouble, counted on that.

Suleiman nuzzled her temple. "Promise me no rash decisions this time?"

"Promise."

He kissed her.

Oh, his lips. They could wipe away all worries.

He gathered her close. Forget that little rule they'd set up. She warmed as he tightened his arms around her.

Their phones pinged.

With a sigh, he picked his up. "The pizza is here."

As he led her into the hall, Sana glanced at her engagement ring. A decent-sized diamond, one purchased by Suleiman with some of his earnings from their *Peacemaker* foray the year before. A symbol of his love for her and a promise of what lay ahead. Why couldn't she trust her future husband with the hardest parts of her past, especially when she knew all about his? The answer eluded her.

After stopping by the lobby, they trooped upstairs with three boxes in hand.

"Bad news," Victor reported when they arrived. "Butch and I called Morgan's friends in Arlington. All of them answered up. No one's seen or heard anything from her since mid-March. It's a safe assumption that something bad's happened."

Sana's throat constricted. "I'd say you were right."

Victor picked up his phone. "I'm calling Skylar. We need the whole team on this."

Sana's gaze swung to Suleiman. Trouble had come for Morgan and stolen her away. Now, they had to find her before she disappeared forever.

6

Wednesday, April 6, 2016, 2115 hours CDT, Nashville, TN

Awareness. Slowly, it returned to Morgan as she waited on an order at the pass-through window of the restaurant's kitchen. Flames danced briefly in a pan a chef handled. She took a deep, cleansing breath full of luscious scents of steak and salmon. Her hearing sharpened, and she noted the clang of pans, the head chef demanding more asparagus. Amazing.

What a far cry from the past several days of living in a fog. All thanks to surreptitiously dumping her meals that day into the trash. The nights the girls worked tables, Miss Denelle laced their food with drugs to keep them compliant. Morgan wouldn't even think about those nights she worked the rooms, as one of the girls had called it at supper a few days ago. If she did, she'd start crying and completely collapse.

As her mind cleared, a memory resurfaced. She'd turned thirteen that summer, and Dad took her to a cabin in the Shenandoah Valley for a daddy-daughter weekend. His words, as they sat around a fire pit one night and roasted marshmallows, came back in a rush. "As you grow up, you may find yourself in situations that your gut says aren't right. Listen to your gut. And try to escape before fighting your way out."

Now, her gut screamed at her to get out of there. That's all that mattered. Going back to the townhouse wasn't an option. But her friends in Arlington? What about Uncle Vic? Her godfather would take her in. First, she had to get out of there.

How?

The chef shoved two steaming plates onto the pass-through window's shelf. "Order's up, Emmaline."

That was her. None of the girls knew anyone's real name. To them, she was Emmaline since she dwelt in Room Five upstairs. If she dared deviate? Hanna had gotten beaten good because she'd introduced herself to the girl in Room One, Amy, with her real name of Tonya. Morgan wouldn't make that same mistake.

She took the food, placed it on a tray, and delivered it to a table of two, a finely dressed couple who'd come to hear a young woman who played the piano like Morgan wished she could. Did either of them know what happened upstairs? Not that she dared to say anything. To do so would mean certain death. At least that was the word on the upstairs hall.

As she returned the tray to its proper place, she scanned the restaurant and committed its layout to her rapidly sharpening brain. Piano on a stage in one corner. Bar across from it. Dining room full of patrons. Miss Denelle, as the girls called their madam, also managed the restaurant. Resplendent in an ice green silk dress with her white-blonde hair in a bun, she conversed near the bar with a handsome man in a suit whose waves of brown hair just touched his collar. One of the girls had said he was the owner, but Morgan didn't know his name.

What about the bouncers? She gazed at the one guarding the way upstairs. Black cargo pants and T-shirt. At least six feet tall. Thick neck. Muscled arms and torso. Five more replicas of him made up the bouncer crew. A shiver wracked her frame. They could toss her around like an empty grocery bag.

Someone rose from a table of six businessmen. He approached the bouncer she studied. The man held up his phone. The beefy bouncer unfurled his arms and checked it.

Morgan winced. She knew what the man wanted. Forty-five minutes with a girl earned the club's owner five hundred dollars. During her nights upstairs, Morgan earned the owner twenty-five hundred. Bile filled her throat. She had to get out somehow. But could she get through those bouncers who guarded all exits, including the kitchen?

A disturbance caught her eye. The bouncer at the front door argued with some potential customers who were obviously drunk. Kayla, the girl in Room Eleven, served as hostess. She didn't do anything, just stood there and swayed very slightly. Drugs must have kept her in their grip.

The bouncer stepped outside to take care of the drunkards.

Now. Escape while she had the opportunity.

At a fast walk so as not to attract attention, Morgan made for the unguarded front door.

Kayla wouldn't stop her. She couldn't.

So close. Twenty-five feet.

Then fifteen.

She'd have to run for her life once she got outside.

Five feet.

Cold fingers grabbed her arm. Miss Denelle yanked her so hard she cried out.

Her pale blue eyes pierced Morgan's soul. Her square jaw and other severe features hovered inches from Morgan's face.

She'd forgotten about the madam.

Miss Denelle dragged her away from the door. "Where do you think you're going?"

Morgan struggled. "Let me go! I don't want to be here!"

The bouncer returned.

Miss Denelle shoved her toward him. "Get her out of here. Now!"

Morgan's legs weakened. Her courage crumbled, and she began crying as the huge man marched her through a sea of patrons toward the door leading upstairs. She was dead.

Behind her, Miss Denelle made excuses for her behavior. "She's not feeling well. We'll take her upstairs for some rest."

Once behind the closed door of the stairwell, the guard wrapped his arms around her chest and lifted her off the floor. His feet pounded up the steps. The door slammed again.

Miss Denelle's harsh words echoed around the narrow stairwell. "You're a fool, Emmaline. Such a fool. And now you're going to pay for it."

Morgan sobbed. "Please, Miss Denelle, I'll be good. Please don't beat me!"

Her guard shoved her into her room. She tumbled onto the bed and flipped over. "I don't want to do this anymore. Just let me go. I won't say anything to anyone."

"Too late." Miss Denelle jerked her chin at the bouncer.

The guard raised his hand to strike her.

Morgan braced herself for the pain.

"Stop it right now," a male voice growled.

She dared open her eyes.

The owner gazed down at her with some of the greenest eyes she'd ever seen. He focused on Miss Denelle. "She can't have a mark on her, do you understand?"

The woman glared at him. "She tried to—"

"The Distributor's son is coming tomorrow night."

Miss Denelle's eyes widened.

Morgan's breath shuddered out. This Distributor guy must have been really powerful if his name cowed Miss Denelle.

The owner stepped forward. He lifted his hand.

Morgan flinched.

His fingers feathered her cheek and sifted some of her hair. "She needs to be pristine. Am I clear?"

Morgan's sucked in another breath. Maybe he'd protect her.

His focus remained on her as he spoke. "No bruising or anything, or else we'll lose our one and only chance this year."

Chance for what?

The owner turned away. "Contain her by some other method. You understand?"

"Yes, sir." Miss Denelle shifted her attention to Morgan, "Cuff her."

Morgan started crying again as the bouncer chained her wrists to the brass headboard of her bed.

Miss Denelle sat down on the edge and tied a piece of rubber tubing around her arm.

"Please don't," Morgan begged through her tears. "I'll be good. I promise."

The madam snorted. "You broke my trust tonight, young lady. I found that food you didn't eat in the garbage. Then you tried to escape. You're lucky you're an Exotic because it kept you from getting the snot beaten out of you." She kneaded the tender skin on the inner part of Morgan's forearm. "Since you cost me tips tonight, you'll be chained and quite compliant."

Miss Denelle uncapped a needle and slid it into her arm. She pressed the plunger.

Almost immediately, Morgan got the sense everything would be fine. She floated high above the bed. The room started spinning. Dad appeared, his blond hair glinting in light from somewhere. He reached out his hand. "Morgan, you're escaping." Then he faded. No, she wasn't. Hardly. *Daddy, I'm sorry I couldn't escape. I'm sorry. I'm sorry. I'm sorry...*

7

Thursday, April 7, 2016, 1730 hours CDT, Nashville, TN

Victor cheered with the rest of the fans in the bleachers as the two baseball teams lined up for a final slap of hands. David Walton's team had been victorious by one hard-fought run. Beside Victor, Mary Walton clapped, though her motions seemed strained, almost like she were an automaton. His heart ached. If only he could do something to assuage her grief. Hopefully finding Morgan would return some light to her eyes.

Then there was his own ghost—Gary's betrayal. Again, it had stolen sleep from him the night before. He struggled to push it aside. Not an easy task when finding Morgan meant reliving why she'd wound up in a hard spot.

David Walton passed through the gate leading to the field. The boy sported Gary's blue eyes and blond hair, and it didn't take much for Victor to imagine he would look more like his father in a few years.

Victor clambered down the bleachers. "Hey, man."

David's eyes lit up, and a smile spread across his face. He gripped him in a brief hug. "Uncle Vic! Mom said you were here."

Victor slapped him on the shoulder. "Yeah, and I'm glad I could see you play. You were great. Say, want to go and grab a Coke? I know it's chilly and windy." He gestured at some nearby trees rocking in the stiff breeze. "But I'm parched and want to catch up. I can take you home."

"Let me tell Mom." David hustled into the stands and kissed his mother on the cheek. They chatted for a few seconds before he rejoined Victor. "She said it's fine."

Victor fished the rental car's keys from his pocket. He led the way to a white Toyota Camry. "Where's the best place to go?"

"The Burger Shack. It's our hangout." He gave Victor directions until they pulled into a parking lot sporting a red and yellow marquis with a giant burger and soda on it. "Too bad it's close to supper. They have great burgers here."

Victor smiled as he remembered Clay Hall taking him to one. "I've had them before, and you're right. They are good. But yeah, I'm not going to be called down for ruining your dinner."

That elicited a flash of a smile. With a Coke in hand, David slumped on a concrete bench at a table in the sun. His brow pinched, and dark circles smudged under his eyes. "I'm scared about Morgan."

Victor raised his gaze. The wind pushed puffy white clouds across a clear blue sky. "I know. Me too."

"Is that why you're here?"

He refocused.

David hunched in his baseball jacket, and one leg jiggled up and down.

"Well, I was here on other business, but your mom called me Tuesday night. She told me what happened."

David rubbed his hands on his pants legs. "Yeah, like my sister disappeared."

He rested his elbows on the table. "How have things been since—"

"Since Dad died?" David cut his eyes toward him. His Adams apple bobbed.

Again, the strong resemblance between father and son startled Victor. "I'm sorry, if it's—"

"It's okay." David ran his fingers across the concrete top of their table. "I don't know what happened to Mom."

"What do you mean?"

He began picking at a pockmark. "It's like she's turned into a different person. You remember, right?"

Victor smiled as he recalled sharing many a cookout with his ex-wife as well as Gary and Mary. "Yeah. I've known her for eighteen or so years."

"You know how she was always bubbly and outgoing? Dad always said she was like a ray of sunshine. She could always tease me out of a bad mood."

"She did the same with your dad. And even me."

David took a long pull of his soda. "She's different now. She barely says a word. She'll get home from work, fix supper, and then go to her room and watch television, grade papers, or read." He rubbed his arms as he rocked back and forth slightly. He aimed his next words at the table. "And downstairs, it's like she built a shrine to Dad. I mean, she's got that portrait we had done when we were here for spring break two years ago. And the flag that was on his coffin. And pictures of us with him."

Victor placed his hand on his shoulder. "Maybe she doesn't want you to forget him."

"Like we would!" David clenched his jaw. "Once, Morgan suggested that she move some of the pictures, that it was hurting her every night to see everything when she was downstairs. Mom went on this screaming tirade and told Morgan she was dishonoring her father."

Coldness gripped Victor. He tried to compare present-day Mary to the woman he'd known in the past. "Wow."

David resumed his picking. "Morgan spent the rest of the night in her room crying."

"How soon after you moved here was that?"

"A month after we moved into the townhouse." David winced as his nail broke. He brought his finger to his mouth. "Seven months after we came here. Morgan had been going out for track, and she quit the next day. Said she hated the coach."

Victor's chest tightened as he gazed at his godson. A boy forced to be a man too soon. His sister had vanished, and he worried about his mom. It was too much, especially for someone who wasn't even fifteen. "How about you?"

The boy's shoulders rose and fell in a shrug. "I dunno. I mean, I guess I make friends pretty easily, a lot more easily than Morgan. When we started school, I asked about the baseball team, and one of the first people I met was the first baseman. His name's Chase, and he's pretty cool. When the season started last year, I felt right at home."

Oh, Victor wished Morgan had stuck with track and cross country. "Does she have any friends?"

A shudder rippled through David's shoulders. "Yeah. Some of them creep me out. I mean, she's really gotten into going out with them. A lot of them drink and smoke and vape. And some of them seem a lot older."

"Is she dating anyone?"

He shrugged.

Victor leaned forward. "This is important. Can you help me out here?"

The boy glanced around. "There's this guy."

"Oh?"

His shoulders rose and fell again. "Yeah. I just remember during her sophomore year, she sulked a lot. Or that's what Mom said. She seemed really down even though she said she had friends. Then sometime right after school started this year, she got all happy, almost like she'd been in Arlington."

Victor digested that one for a moment. "Do you have any idea why?"

"No. I just knew she'd go and hang out with her friends after school and then party during the weekend. Lots of weekends, she didn't get up until noon or later. I don't blame her. She and Mom clashed a lot." David winced as if remembering some of their arguments. "Then later in October, Chase came over, and we were tossing the ball back and forth in the middle of our cul-de-sac one Saturday afternoon. Morgan sat on the steps and watched us." David's brow knitted. "A car pulled into the drive. She jumped up. This guy got out." He winced again. "It was gross. I mean, they were kissing and stuff. I think it embarrassed Chase. It did me. She told me to tell Mom she was spending the night with friends."

"No name?"

"No. She never did introduce him."

Uh-oh. Victor had a bad feeling who the person was. He pulled out a copy of Wes Sampson's picture. Shelly had used Sentry Security's credentials, accessed the Tennessee Department of Motor Vehicles, and found a match for Will Smith—and a guy named Wes Sampson. She'd printed a clear, color copy of Wes on her portable printer.

"He's cute," she'd remarked as she handed it off to Victor. "Morgan must have thought so too."

Now, he unfolded it to reveal a young man with brown hair just long enough to show a little curl. "Is this the guy?"

David's eyes widened. He picked it up and studied it. "Y-yeah. That's him. Definitely him. He's like, twenty-nine?" He stared at Victor. "Are you kidding me?"

"I wish I was." Victor shook his head. "Sometimes, people look really young for their ages. His name is Wes Sampson."

"Do you think he has something to do with her disappearance?"

"I'm sure he does. He's the one who bailed her out."

David drew in a sharp breath. He closed his eyes and gripped his hair with his hands. In a small voice, he asked, "Will I see her again?"

Victor gazed at a nearby table where a father laughed with his teenaged daughter. The image tore at him. Gary's death had ripped his family apart. Somehow, David had managed to survive. But Morgan?

"Uncle Vic?"

"Oh, sorry." He refocused his attention to her brother, whose eyes radiated anxiety. He badly needed his reassurance. With a deep breath, Victor replied, "If it's in my power, it'll happen. That, I can promise."

8

Thursday, April 7, 2016, 1930 hours CDT, Nashville, TN

Sana shut the door to the black Ford Explorer that was their rental vehicle for the duration of their stay in Nashville. "What are we looking for?"

Butch paused from entering his credit card information into a parking meter. "You tell me."

She rolled her eyes as she peered around the parking lot across the street from The Music Man, which was almost full that time of evening. "I mean, Shelly did all of that work to find out the logo belonged to a music restaurant called The Music Man. You and Suleiman were here earlier today. The least you could do is to tell me what you saw."

As they began strolling toward the sidewalk, Butch laid his arm across her shoulders. "First things first. We're playacting as a dating couple, right? You're acting like you want to break up with me."

She nudged him. "Maybe I do."

He drew her closer. "Hah."

The scent of Old Spice hit her nose. "Seriously, this feels weird, like I'm running around on Suleiman."

That earned a hearty laugh. "No worries there. Trust me when I say he's got your heart. So. Back to business." They approached a warehouse with a renovated front façade. A semicircular awning of deep purple fabric had The Music Man's logo emblazoned on it in gold, just like on the shot glass and coaster. Another couple gazed at a menu posted in a glass case by the door. A bouncer stood beside it and answered their questions. Butch slowed as if looking for something. "Seriously. What do you see that's strange?"

"Where?"

He nodded to the right of the building. "Take a quick look down that alley there."

She did. "I see chain-link fencing. With wire on top."

"Score one, baby. That's exactly right. It's a decent-sized lot that can hold about twenty cars." He held up his phone to compare the Music Man's frontage with a photo he'd taken earlier that day. "The fencing takes up two-thirds of the building's back side. There's an upstairs back door, which is accessible by metal stairs behind the wire. The nonfenced portion has a back door on the ground level. Dumpster's out back as well. Let's not forget the cameras. One at the gate, two on the lot, one on the upstairs door. Then there's one on the back door that's ground level."

As they crossed the street, Sana remembered her cat burglar days and the reconnaissance they'd always conducted. "Five seems to be an odd number. Do you think they're on two separate systems?"

"Yep, 'cause I see three on the front." Butch nodded as they approached the entrance. "Let's shelve that discussion." He smiled and entwined his fingers with hers as they stopped at the bouncer, who blocked their way. "We got ourselves a reservation for two. The name's Addison. Seven-thirty."

The man met Butch's gaze as if challenging him, then nodded toward Sana. "Let me check your bag, ma'am."

Sana handed over her small purse. At least she'd remembered to take out the knife she always carried.

He rustled around inside it before returning it to her and acknowledging them with a nod. "Go on in. Lisa will take care of you."

Butch opened the door and stepped aside. "Madam, after you."

Sana approached a podium, which was empty as the hostess seated the other couple before returning. She studied the young woman with ginger hair streaming down her back. She wore a little black dress. A girl, maybe sixteen, if that. The makeup layered on her face made her look older. Not that it mattered. Teens could work the hostess podium at a restaurant.

A ghost of a smile crossed the girl's face. "May I help you?"

Butch's hand tightened around Sana's. "Yeah. We've got a reservation for two at seven-thirty. Last name is Addison."

"Seven-thirty." The girl drew out the words. She picked up two menus bound in black leather with The Music Man's logo embossed in gold on them. "This way, please."

She led them to a table of shiny dark wood along one side of an exposed brick wall. As she set the menus on top, her motions seemed deliberate, careful, as if she had to think about each one. "Enjoy your meal."

Once settled on a booth bench so she faced the restaurant, Sana immediately swept the area with her gaze, just like Suleiman had trained her almost three years before. A moderate crowd for a Thursday night. About a quarter of the tables remained empty. To their left between the corner and a door, a baby grand piano glimmered under stage lighting. A microphone hung above the keyboard. A placard announced Joylene Sanders as both singer and pianist. Sana picked up her menu as her gaze roamed across the tapestries along the exposed brick, something that undoubtedly helped modulate sound.

Butch turned to survey the restaurant. "I like the atmosphere. Great décor. High ceilings with fabric draped nicely. Fabric on the walls so it don't echo in here."

"You're starting to sound like an interior designer."

He slid around so he sat beside her. "Skylar knows a thing or two about that, and he told me there're three things that make or break a restaurant. Hit two of the three, and you'll most likely succeed."

Sana fought a smile. "And what are those?"

He ran his finger along the menu. "Good food. Good décor. Good service. They scored on the décor. And the food if it's as good as I think it will be." He raised his gaze as a waitress approached. "We'll see about the service."

A young woman, dressed in a black frock with a black apron, approached. Her smile didn't reach her eyes. "Good evening. My name is Faye, and I'm to be your server tonight. May I get you anything to drink?"

Butch nudged Sana. "You go first, baby."

She ordered a glass of Merlot and a tea. Butch ordered a draft IPA.

Faye listed the specials. As she spoke, her voice never varied in pitch.

Whew. Sana inwardly shook her head at the forty-five-dollar rib eye she mentioned. Too expensive for her—and too much food. She gazed at Faye's retreating back where her brown hair swung gently from side to side.

Butch inched closer to her.

Automatically, she slid over a little to give him some room. "Why'd you do that?'

He nudged her. "Baby, we're on a date, not a business dinner. Now I know I'm not Suleiman, but can you pretend? Otherwise, anyone with half a brain will realize we're scoping this place out."

She grimaced but snuggled next to him.

"That's better." His lips moved against her ear as he murmured, "Tell me what's wrong with our waitress."

She tried a smile as Faye brought their drinks.

The waitress moved in steady movements that lacked fluidity.

"Seriously."

"She spoke in a monotone as she gave the specials list."

"Yup. Agreed on that."

She watched as Faye tended other tables before heading to the kitchen. "Her movements seem deliberate, almost like she has to consciously think of them."

Butch draped his arm over her shoulders, and his Old Spice once more tickled her nose in a pleasing aroma. "Score one for you. What else you see here?"

She scanned the area. "Four doors, one on each wall. All guarded by bouncers."

"Don't that seem a bit much for an upscale restaurant and music club?"

Sana noted the men, all who were dressed alike in black cargo pants and black T-shirts. And all just as big as Butch. "Maybe. The restaurant's running three quarters full, and the clientele seem to be all well dressed."

He chuckled. "Yeah, we're probably the least well dressed."

She laughed as she pulled back and studied his jeans and black shirt. It looked like he'd even polished the silver hoops in his ears as well as the silver on the toes of his cowboy boots. "I wouldn't say that." She picked out Faye waiting at the pass-through window in the back. "Our waitress seems a little on the young side to be serving alcohol. How old do you think she is?"

"I have no idea. Makeup can do wonders. What else?"

Exasperated, she lightly elbowed him in the ribs. "Butch!"

"C'mon, girl." His fingers teased the ends of her hair where it curled under her chin. "Talk to me. This is important."

Sana sipped her wine as she gazed around the restaurant. An older woman, cloaked in a dress of icy gray silk, floated between the bar, the waitresses, and the kitchen's pass-through window. "There's an older woman who's a manager. And then the bartenders and cooks."

"Who are?"

Would he stop? "I don't know their names."

"Not thinking you would. But who are they?"

"Guys." Suddenly, it clicked. "There are no women bartenders and no male wait staff."

Butch fiddled with his pint glass. "When Suleiman and I were here earlier today, we saw no women arriving except for the manager. Not even any cooks."

She digested that one for a moment. "The girls are only hostesses and waitresses."

"Exactly. You done good, Sana." He lifted his glass and sipped it. "Hmmm. And I have to admit they serve most excellent stuff. I won't argue with that."

Her mind whirled. Once more, she focused on Faye as she worked a couple of other tables.

The manager's gaze roved across the dining room. The uninitiated would say she was being a good manager and keeping an eye on her people. Sana would have agreed if she didn't possess the knowledge she did. She angled her head toward Butch as if they were involved in intimate conversation. Well, they were. "What you were saying is that you and Suleiman saw only men arriving, save for the manager."

"Bingo." Butch rewarded her with a kiss on the temple. Again, his lips tickled her ear. "No girls came or left. That makes me suspicious."

He straightened as Faye approached to take their orders. Salmon all the way for her. A steak, though not the special, for him.

As she finished her glass of wine, Sana continued her sweep of the room. The manager swung by each table to check on customers. She paused at a table of eight men. A business dinner? Most likely if their loud laughter and booming voices meant anything. Three bottles of wine sat in ice buckets next to the table. The manager rested her hand on one man's shoulder as if she knew him well. She leaned over and held a whispered conversation with him, then reached into the front of her dress and pulled out a slip of paper. She flashed it before stowing it once more.

Interesting. Sana filed that away for future reference. She returned her attention to the doorways. Three of them, including the main entrance, had red exit signs above them. But the fourth along the back wall was blank. It didn't lead to the outside.

A man stepped through, dressed in a khaki suit and a collarless white shirt. His wavy, dark hair brushed his jacket, and his square jaw had probably attracted more than one woman.

Sana easily recognized him from pictures Shelly had shown her. She leaned her head against Butch's shoulder. "That's the owner."

"Jaidon Ash?"

"Uh-huh. Also president and CEO of Music Man Productions, one of the top music tour management companies in the country."

Butch set his glass on the table. "Shel's been busy. What else did she pull up?"

"She got that far before she said she absolutely had to get some sleep."

"Yeah, when she told me she'd stayed up until 0330 hours this morning, I told her to pace herself."

"Not when someone's life hangs in the balance." Sana straightened as a young woman, her dark hair in an up-do, joined Ash. Her body shimmered in a silver-sequined evening gown. They talked, and she laughed as if they had the easy way of friendship. Must have been Joylene Sanders, that evening's entertainment.

Jaidon stepped to the microphone and introduced her. Then she took a seat on the bench and began her set. Oh, she was good. Really good. But apparently not good enough to be on the radio. Otherwise, she wouldn't be singing in a club.

Sana leaned forward and rested her elbows on the table. "What about Joylene? You think she's involved?"

"Nope. Probably not. The waitresses?" Butch once more tickled her ear with his lips. "My gut says they're drugged up a little to be controllable."

The lights dimmed. The sconces on the wall glowed even more, sending the edges of the room into shadow. She had to admit Butch was right about his assessment of a restaurant's success. The food was heavenly, the wine some of the finest she'd ever tasted. The music was most excellent, and combined with it all, the lighting produced a romantic atmosphere. She wished Suleiman were by her side instead of Butch. But maybe that had been for good reason. Butch kept her focused.

Motion caught her attention. One of the men from the table of eight rose. He approached the manager, who now stood by the bar. Once more, she produced the paper and pointed to it, then the man's phone.

Sana kept the man on her radar.

Booming laughter distracted her. In the corner to the left of the stage, an African American man in a white suit sat in a round booth meant for a larger party. He had a green handkerchief, green shirt, and green hat band on the white hat he wore despite being inside. And the sunglasses. Strange. He talked with Ash, who took a seat beside him. Colleagues? Maybe. Then the man leaned on his elbow and apparently got down to business.

"Baby, take a look," Butch murmured.

Sana picked up her tea glass and watched over the rim as the businessman who'd approached the bar earlier got up and made his way to the door at the back. He almost vanished into the shadows. A phone's light flared, and the bouncer checked something, then let the man through.

"Butch."

"I see it. Dang it, I wish there was a way to take pictures without being obvious."

She returned her attention to White Suit. The manager approached him. Another man in all black, who probably exceeded Butch in size, blocked her way.

White Suit said something, and Black Suit stepped aside.

The manager listened for a moment, then nodded before retreating toward the bar.

"Butch, if you get a chance, check out that guy in the white suit in the corner."

Ever so slightly, he shifted. "I see him."

"Who is he?"

He shrugged. "Darned if I know. He screams pimp to me."

Her blood chilled. "You think he's running something upstairs? I saw that guy go up."

"Check the time. Eight on the nose. My money says he comes back down by nine."

This could be a long wait. Sana ordered another glass of Merlot from Faye, who cleared off their empty plates. She'd have to sip this one slowly. They both ordered dessert and observed.

Men, some who were sitting at the bar, approached the back door at ten-minute intervals. Sana's appetite vanished as she imagined what was going on behind that door. She refocused on the booth in the corner.

Ash and White Suit continued conversing. Ash shook his head, then motioned to the manager. For a moment, the woman debated something with Ash. A sharp jerk of his chin ended the conversation, and she headed toward where Sana and Butch sat.

Her smile came across as stiff. "I take it you enjoyed everything? Faye was good to you?"

Butch draped his arm across Sana's shoulders. "Yes, ma'am. Everything was. Miss Faye is bringing us dessert and a last round of drinks. Then we'll take the check."

"I'll see to it."

Sana watched her go. The woman talked briefly with Faye, who handed her what must have been their bill. A moment later, she presented it to them in a black vinyl book with The Music Man's logo embossed in gold on it. "I'll be your cashier when you're ready."

"Interesting," Butch murmured as he examined the bill and laid a company credit card on it. He added cash for a generous tip. "Normally, waitresses cash out their own tickets."

"Unless they're super busy, which they're not." Sana's gaze shifted between the door at the back and White Suit. The man leaned on his elbows as he sipped some wine and swayed slightly to the music. He scribbled something on a notepad. Was he a club owner? Or pimp?

The manager took Faye's arm and brought her over to the corner. White Suit appraised her and spoke. Faye nodded.

Sana's lip curled. "Pimp."

Butch nudged her. "Smile, baby. You look like you want to kill the guy."

"I'm wondering if he's the pimp running things or if Ash is. I'm pretty sure our waitress is a prostitute."

Butch tightened his arm around her. "Maybe. Hold tight. Let's just listen to some music for a bit longer."

Sana's mood dipped downward. She traced the manager to the bar, where she ran Butch's credit card. She dumped the cash tip into a jar before returning Butch's card. Would that go to the waitresses or straight into her pocket? Once more, Sana followed the woman with her gaze. No waitress ran bills.

At eight forty-five, the back door opened. The man from the business party slipped through.

Sana's cheeks heated. "Whatever happens behind that door isn't good."

Butch's fingers teased the ends of her hair. "That's one way to put it. And I have a feeling Ash is involved."

"What about that other guy?" Sana asked.

"Maybe."

White Suit rose. He murmured something to Black Suit, who nodded. They headed toward the front.

Butch kissed Sana's temple, then murmured, "Let's go. Maybe Mr. Pimp will have something to say when we see where he goes."

With that, Sana rose, and they followed the pair toward the entrance.

9

Thursday, April 7, 2016, 2000 hours CDT, Nashville, TN

"I hate hookah bars," Victor muttered as the dark blue Honda CR-V he and Suleiman had followed from Sampson's house turned into a parking lot located near the edge of Vanderbilt University's campus. The building's marquee glowed in bright blue with the words Salah Hookah Bar in neon pink and the same thing, he was sure, in yellow Arabic underneath it. "You think we have to go in?"

A smile quirked Suleiman's lips. "You are the one who wanted to interview him in a public place."

Victor scowled. "I rescind that. At least here, I do."

Suleiman rolled down his window. "Would you like pictures instead?"

Victor winced as the smell from those sitting on the concrete patio next to the building wafted into the car. Gross. Like the nastiest cigarettes, except three times worse. "I'd rather talk to Sampson."

A grin crossed Suleiman's face. "Ah, such tough choices."

Victor grimaced. "I don't want to throw away my clothing because it reeks."

Suleiman laughed. "You would not have liked me when I was younger, then."

"Huh?"

The young man ran his finger down the case of the 35-millimeter camera sitting on his lap. "I ran away to Marseilles when I was sixteen and worked at a piercing parlor. I was part of the punk scene. When Makmoud kidnapped me in 2010, I had bright green hair and many piercings. My girl and I would frequent hookah bars. When he kidnapped me, Makmoud threw me into the shower because he said I stank of hookah smoke. He hates it as much as you."

Victor's mind spun. Strange that he had something, probably the only thing, in common with his nemesis. No. They had one other thing in common. Or person. Gary. *I don't want to go there. Again. I can't.* "I didn't know any of that."

Suleiman shrugged with the nonchalance of a man at peace with his past. "It was a long time ago. I am a different man now."

No arguing that. He had matured so much in two years. "How's Sana? I know the wedding plans have worn on her a bit."

Sulieman stroked his stubbled chin. "Only the guest list." He pursed his lips, then shook his head. "She is very torn about including her parents. And then this case happened. I think it is... troubling her."

"Her and everyone." Victor straightened when another car pulled into the parking lot.

Wes Sampson, who'd been waiting in the light by the door, ceased his pacing.

Suleiman raised the camera to his eye. Using the telephoto lens, he snapped several pictures of their quarry, then stilled. "We may have a problem."

"How so?"

"His friend is Narat Jain."

Victor stiffened and drew in a breath.

The camera's shutter whirred. "I would recognize him easily enough."

Victor squinted as the pair headed inside and settled at a hookah near the windows. Time for him and Suleiman to scram. "How do you think they know each other?"

Suleiman flipped a switch on the camera. "Narat went to Vanderbilt for both of his degrees. Perhaps they schooled together."

Their options to have a nice, public discussion with Sampson had faded. Time for Plan B. Victor hated Plan B because it could land them in potential trouble with the cops. "Let's head to Sampson's place."

"It is risky."

He put the car into gear. "Agreed, but now, we have no choice. None at all."

Thursday, April 7, 2016, 2130 hours CDT, Nashville, TN

Plan B meant Suleiman picked the lock on the side door of Sampson's garage. Once inside, Victor flicked on his penlight. Its red glow revealed that Sampson used one half of the two-car garage for what just about every other American used their garage for—storage. The half closest to the side door held man toys, unused lumber, and yard equipment. Plus some antique furniture. The other half remained blank as if Sampson actually parked his CR-V inside. "Going operational. Call signs from here on out."

Suleiman chuckled. "As Five always says, Roger that, One."

Using a stepladder he found, Victor popped the cover on the garage door opener's light and unscrewed the bulb. They crouched behind a shelf holding paint cans and assorted painting accessories and settled in for the wait.

An hour and a half later, the garage door began humming upward.

Time to rock and roll, as Butch would say.

Headlights swept across their hiding place as the CR-V pulled inside. Its engine shut off, and Sampson climbed from the SUV. He fiddled with his key chain, which probably held an alarm fob. "Dang bulb. Why couldn't it burn out during the day?"

With his hand, he guided himself along the hood of the Honda to the stoop leading inside. He pressed the button for the garage door. Its hum filled the air.

Using the noise as cover, Victor darted to their quarry. He jabbed his pistol into Sampson's side with his left hand and snatched his keys from him. "Don't move or say a word, Wes Sampson."

He froze, then struggled until Victor stilled him with another jab. He handed the keys to Suleiman. "Two, take these and get us inside."

Sampson squirmed. "Wh-who are you?"

"Someone who wants to have a chat with you." Victor shoved him into a laundry room. He trussed his hands behind him with a cable tie, then pushed him through a kitchen and onto a couch in the small den. "Don't move. Got it?"

"Look. I-I don't know what you want. It's not l-like I've got a lot of money here. And no guns. Please. Don't hurt me."

Victor took a step back. "No worries if you tell us what we want to know."

Sweat beaded on Sampson's brow, and a vein pulsed at his temple. He struggled to a sitting position. "T-tell you?"

Victor raised the pistol. "Stay where you are. Two, get the recorder ready."

Suleiman reached into his jacket and pulled out a digital recorder. He turned it on and placed it on a side table.

Victor stashed his pistol and pulled out a photo of Morgan. He tossed it onto a glass coffee table and flicked on his penlight so white light glowed, first in Sampson's eyes and then on the photo. "You recognize her?"

Sampson calmed and lifted his chin as if he'd prepared for a discussion about Morgan. "Never seen her in my life."

No great surprise there. Victor put his foot on the coffee table and leaned forward with his arm on his knee. "Oh? Do you mean to tell me you bail out total strangers?"

Sampson cocked his head. "What? I don't know what you're talking about."

Victor pulled out another folded sheet of paper. With exaggerated care, he smoothed it onto the glass and shone the light on it. "I'm not so sure about that, 'Will Smith.'"

Sampson shrugged. "Okay, so I did. So what? She's a friend. I took her home. Why are you harassing me, dude? I could call the cops on you, you know. I mean, you broke into my house and everything."

What a jerk. Victor pulled out another photo, this one a picture Shelly had printed from Morgan's social media accounts. He studied it with exaggerated care. "I spoke with Detective Cruz at the Metro Nashville PD. He said he talked with you after her mother reported her missing. You told him you were friends." He placed the photo on the coffee table beside the other one. "Somehow, I think you're a bit more than friends with her, meaning you—at the age of twenty-nine—are dating a sixteen-year-old. That's dangerous territory for you."

Sampson's eyes flicked between Victor and the pictures as he gnawed his lip. "Why do you care?"

With his foot, Victor shoved away the coffee table. He braced his hands on his knees and got in his face so they were almost nose to nose. The penlight's glare lit Sampson like a spotlight. "Do you have a sister?"

Sampson's expression again slid into neutral. "Yeah. I've got two."

"How old are they?"

"One's twenty-five, and the other's twenty-two."

Victor glanced at Morgan's picture. "Your younger sister. Is she in college?"

"Yeah. So what?"

He returned his gaze to his quarry. "Is she pretty?"

Sampson shifted. "Uh, yeah."

Oh, the sarcasm.

Victor began pacing. "What would happen if she came to you and told you someone had taken advantage of her? Had slept with her and abandoned her?" He stopped toe to toe with him. "What would happen if she disappeared?"

Sampson's lips flattened. "I'd kill him."

Victor got in his face again. "Then let's get one thing straight. When I hear Morgan's been missing for three weeks... When I hear someone bailed her out... When I know someone lied to her about his age, my protective instincts kick in. Understand?"

Sampson's eyes widened. "Who are you, man? Why do you care so much?"

"That's for me to know."

The glow of the penlight caught sweat sheening on Sampson's forehead. "What are you going to do? Kill me?"

"Nope. But when I turn over the evidence I have to the cops, someone else might. Right?"

Sampson didn't budge.

"Somehow, I think you're not working alone here. I think you answer to someone, and that someone would kill you if he found out the cops arrested you."

Sampson jerked back as if Victor had stung him.

Victor glanced at Suleiman and resumed his pacing. He stopped and hooked his thumbs on his belt. "I'm going to make you a deal. You tell me what you know, and we'll leave you alone. I won't run to the police with what I have." *At least not yet.* "You don't tell me, you cop an attitude, and I'll turn over everything to them. You understand where I'm coming from?"

Sampson sagged against the cushions. "How do I know you won't go to the cops anyway?"

Victor smirked. "You'll have to trust me on that one. Where did you meet Morgan?"

He drew in a sharp breath. His gazed flicked between the two intruders. "At a party. You know I look young for my age. I use that driver's license when I head to high school and college parties. She was there one night. Man, she's a looker."

Victor tensed.

Ever so slightly, Suleiman shook his head as if warning him.

Focus. You've got to focus, Chavez. He shifted his attention to Sampson. "When did you start dating her?"

"Last fall. She needed a friend, you know what I mean? Her mom hates her, and well, her brother's still a little young. I listened to her. When I asked her out, she said yeah."

"And her mom?"

Sampson shrugged. "She's clueless. She never knew about us."

That added up to everything David had told him. Inwardly, Victor winced. "Did you sleep with her?"

With wide brown eyes like a deer's, Sampson gazed at him. "What?"

Victor enunciated each word. "Did you sleep with her?"

This time, the smirk belonged to Sampson. "Yeah, and man, she was a vir—"

"Shut up!" Victor charged him.

Suleiman grabbed him before he clocked Sampson across the nose. "One, he is not worth it."

Sampson shrank back. "What's with the call signs? Are you some secret agent—"

"I suggest you respect us." With a *schnick*, Suleiman held a switchblade to his face. "I am very proficient with a knife. Remember that."

Sampson let loose a string of cuss words.

Victor stepped back and let it flow. He raised an eyebrow. "Are you finished?"

He fell silent.

Victor folded his arms. "How did she wind up in jail?"

Sampson sneered. "What? You don't know?"

Victor waved him away. "Oh, I know she was at a party. And someone gave you a legit driver's license under an alternate identity to pick up under-age girls."

"Naw. I—"

"Remember, the cops can get you dead to rights for statutory rape. Then there's the whole forgery thing. Tell me the truth, or that's the way it goes."

"How do I believe you?"

Victor punched Cruz's number into his phone. "You see this number? It's for the detective who interviewed Mary Walton."

Sampson's lips curled like he knew something about Cruz he shouldn't.

"Better yet, I've got connections with the FBI. You talk to me or them."

He blew out a breath. "Okay. Okay. I knew she was going to be at a party with lots of drinking and at least some weed, maybe more. I told her

I'd meet her there, and she got a ride with one of her friends. Except I was the one who phoned in the tip about the party."

"You wanted her to get arrested."

Sampson rolled his eyes. "Well, yeah."

"Why? Somehow, I think you were instructed. You wouldn't do something like that of your own accord. Someone was paying you, right?"

Sampson's Adam's apple bobbed. "This won't get to the cops?"

"You have my word."

In the dim light, his cheeks began reddening. "I was paid to bail her out, okay?"

Victor had struck a chord with him. "What did you do with her? And don't tell me you took her home. I know better than that."

"I took her somewhere."

"Where?"

Sampson drew in a stuttering breath. His feet shifted as if he wanted to flee.

Suleiman brandished the switchblade.

Victor punched in the number to the Nashville FBI office. "The FBI or me, Sampson."

He cleared his throat. "All right, already, okay? I took her to the back of The Music Man."

"Who did you hand her off to?"

More sweat broke out on his brow and trickled downward. He began shaking his head.

Victor was losing him. "I need to know."

Sampson began rocking back and forth. "I-I can't tell you. He'll kill—"

"Wes—"

"Please! Th-that's all I know. Okay? Please!"

Once more, Victor glanced at Suleiman. His friend nodded. "Sampson, you know you've now confessed to sleeping with a minor. You know what that means, right? Statutory rape."

"I-I can't. I'll die if I say anything more."

"Sampson—"

"No!"

Victor tried a few more questions. Nothing. Sampson had shut down. He hated to admit defeat, but he had enough to know at least a next step. He had to know one more thing. "Tell me something, Sampson. How do you know Narat Jain?"

Sampson cocked his head. "Who?"

This time, Suleiman spoke. "Narat Jain. We know you spent some time at a hookah bar with him."

Sampson's brow furrowed. "He and I... well, we're friends, got it? I met him while he was in college when he interned at the insurance company where I work. When he's in town, he calls me up."

Victor rubbed his chin as he considered the young man's answer. Could be truth. Or not. But was it relevant? He had no idea. And they'd get nothing further. He leaned forward and got in his face one more time. "We'll stop this conversation here. But think about it. And if you can get the guts up to give me a name, here's my number." He tossed a business card onto the glass. No name. Just a number. "If you go to the cops about us, let me remind you of two things. First, you're in way over your head. And second, they know we're in town. Understand?"

"I-I do."

"Then have a good night." With that, Victor switched off the penlight he'd kept focused on Sampson and headed toward the laundry room.

Sampson called, "Hey! What about my hands?"

Suleiman turned. "You figure it out, my friend."

With that, they slipped from the garage and darted through the night toward the car. Once safely inside, Victor blew out a breath. He started the engine. "Thanks for keeping me sane back there. What do you think?"

"The Music Man." Suleiman fell silent. "It will be interesting to see what Butch and Sana found."

Something nagged at Victor. "You think we should have covered our faces?"

"We kept our lights focused on him. That would have blinded him."

Victor released a slow breath. "True. Let's just hope that doesn't come back to bite us on the butt."

They headed to the hotel in silence as Victor tried to process everything Sampson had told them. The punk had tricked Morgan by spinning a web of lies the gullible teenager had swallowed whole. He'd gotten her to trust him, then broke that trust by turning her over to someone who most definitively didn't have her best interests at heart. The question remained as to whom.

They arrived at the hotel. No Butch or Sana waited for him in the suite, only Shelly, who watched a television show. She muted the sound when they entered. "Hey."

"They're not back yet?"

She shook her head. "Nope."

Worry pricked at Victor. Without hesitation, he dialed Butch's number.

Voice mail answered. Victor left a message, then did the same thing with Sana.

Suleiman shifted. "This concerns me."

"Me too." Victor stared out the window. "Let's hope they call soon."

10

Thursday, April 7, 2016, 2145 hours CDT, Nashville, TN

Sana's footsteps quickened as she and Butch followed White Suit and his bodyguard westward to the heart of The Gulch. Crowds thronged the street in search of good music and good food. White Suit and his companion continued their march, which forced her to duck between people. She stood on tiptoes to see them. If only to be a few inches taller than five feet even! She stopped. "I lost them."

Behind her, Butch's heavy steps pounded out a steady cadence. "I got them. We're good. Keep going."

She sucked down a breath of chilly air and wished she'd brought her jacket. By a miracle, the crowd thinned as the pair turned into a night club.

While waiting for Butch, she gazed at a sign above the entrance. This one had a similar awning to the Music Man's but in a fabric that looked almost like black velvet with white writing.

La Femme Nue.

Her high school French came rushing back to her, as did the chuckles of some of her guy friends as they'd put different words together in phrases. The Naked Lady? Her lip curled. It figured. A topless bar. "I don't want to go in there."

Butch came up behind her and put his hand on her shoulder. "Baby, we've got to see this to the end."

She refused to budge. "I don't want to go in there."

His grip became firm. "We've got a guy to question. Can you put on an act for just a little longer?"

"Not if I see topless—"

"Then cover your eyes, for cryin' out loud." Butch massaged his temples as if weary from her prudishness. He pulled her through the glass doors and into a small foyer.

A young woman in a sparkling silver cocktail dress smiled at them from behind a podium of dark, polished wood. "Welcome to La Femme Nue. Do you have a reservation?"

Sana couldn't believe her ears. Topless bars took reservations?

Butch didn't release his hold. "No, ma'am. We thought we'd just come on in."

"Ah, I see." The hostess studied a tablet. "Hmmm. We're totally booked through eleven."

"Do you have a bar?"

She nodded. "That, we do, and it's wide open."

"We'll take that." Butch almost yanked Sana into motion. "Come on."

She took a deep breath. Time to take one for the team. Only once. As they pushed through a curtain into the large room, she stopped in shock. Far from being a topless bar, La Femme Nue was a jazz club, a nice one. And a crowded one. All of the tables for four were occupied. Candle centerpieces on small mirrors filled the room with a golden glow. The notes from a quartet of bass, drums, saxophone, and guitar wound around her like one of her cats. A black woman sang a jazz melody in a mesmerizing rich alto.

"Man, she's good." Butch drew Sana toward the bar and pulled out a chair for her. "Madam?"

She hopped onto it and leaned against polished copper. Where was White Suit?

Nowhere to be found. But she did see Black Suit, the bodyguard, standing in a curtained alcove off the far end of the bar. Was that the outline of a door there? Hard to tell. She leaned into Butch so her head rested on his shoulder. "Do you think he's where the bodyguard is?"

"Probably." He straightened as a young woman in a dress of deep blue silk with a Mandarin collar approached the other side. "Good evening, ma'am."

She inclined her head toward them. "What can I get you two to drink? And to eat?"

Butch patted his belly. "Oh, we've already had supper. But I'd love a beer."

"And you, ma'am?"

"A Merlot." Sana kept her gaze on Black Suit. She almost felt him watching them.

The bartender set their drinks on cocktail napkins.

Sana glanced at her watch. Ten o'clock passed. Then ten-thirty. No sign of White Suit. Lovely. "Butch."

"Baby, can we at least keep pretending like we're on a date?"

She scowled at Black Suit, who hadn't budged an inch. "I'm in breakup mode now."

Butch sighed and tilted his head toward heaven. "What do you want me to do?"

She tapped her fingers on the bar. "I want to talk with him."

He muttered something under his breath about impatient women. "Be patient, and we'll get our chance."

If he told her that one more time, she'd scream.

Shortly before eleven o'clock, Black Suit shifted. White Suit stepped through the alcove's curtain. Still wearing his sunglasses and hat, he strolled into the dining area like a big cat winding through the jungle.

Sana flew off her seat toward him.

Before she could get three steps, Black Suit blocked her path. Yeah, he'd pegged them the second they'd walked in.

Sana tried to peer around his bulk. Impossible since he had a good two inches and maybe twenty pounds on Butch. Dang, he was huge! "I need to talk with your boss."

He didn't say a word, didn't move an inch.

White Suit continued to the stage. He thanked the singer and explained there would be a ten-minute break before the last set began. The club would close at midnight.

Sana darted around the bodyguard.

With lightning-fast grace, he snagged her arm.

Youch! She flinched as his fingers dug into her skin. "Ow! Let me go!"

Butch got in the bodyguard's face. "Take your hands off her!"

With his other hand, Black Suit pushed Butch back.

He stumbled into the chairs. One fell over with a clatter.

Those at the tables nearest to them turned their heads.

Butch's face reddened. Lips flattening, he tensed to charge.

Sana struggled against the bodyguard's iron grip. "Butch, no!"

White Suit inserted himself between the two men. "Hold it right there! Loquacious, unhand the lady." He pointed at Butch. "And you, sir, back off. I highly advise that before Nashville's finest crash this party."

Loquacious released Sana.

She sat down hard on her chair.

White Suit nudged Loquacious back a few inches. "Something tells me you two aren't here for the music, though fine jazz it is tonight. Lucinda's the best at what she does."

Sana took a deep breath to soothe her rattled nerves. "No, sir, we're here because we have some questions for you."

"Oh?" The man examined her from top to bottom. "And what would those be? You see, I know you followed us from The Music Man."

More breaths chased away the adrenaline leftovers. "Then why didn't you say something?"

"'Cause I figured you'd show up here at some point." He laughed a deep, rich laugh. "Monique, some of your finest Chardonnay for me, if you would." He gestured to the far end of the bar so they could talk in relative privacy. "Come here." A small sigh indicated his weariness as he eased onto a chair. "Before we begin, might I ask your names."

Sana glanced at Butch, who nodded ever so slightly. "I'm Sana Jain."

"Ah, Sana. A pretty name for a pretty lady. And you, sir."

"Butch Addison."

"From Louisiana, right?"

Butch cocked his head. "How'd you know?"

"Your accent." The man smiled. "This club is not the only La Femme Nue out there. My first one was in New Orleans. Opened that one in 2005. I opened this one five years ago as the Great Recession began easing."

"And you are?" Sana asked.

The man tipped his hat. "Call me Sugar."

Monique set a glass on the bar. "No one knows his real name. Only his mama. You two need a refill?"

"Water," Sana responded.

"Me too. Gotta drive home, ya know," Butch said.

Sugar raised his glass. "To an evening with new friends."

Life seemed to take a bizarre turn, like straight off the end of the road and into an alternate universe. Never had she imagined she'd clink glasses with a suspected pimp.

Sugar leaned forward on his elbows. "Sugar wants to know why the lady followed him all the way here."

Sana gathered her thoughts. "We saw you at The Music Man. You were talking with the restaurant owner and his manager."

He chuckled. "Ah. Jaidon Ash. A fine man on the surface."

Butch set his water glass down with a clunk. "But not really."

"Yes, sir, you are correct." Sugar studied him as if determining how much he should reveal. "And why are you so interested in my dealings with Mr. Ash?"

Sana glanced at Butch, then refocused her attention on their unlikely host. "Because I think you're running girls out of that restaurant. Like a prostitution ring." Her gaze hardened as she thought about Morgan. "We were there long enough to spot a door where johns go through to get somewhere else, presumably upstairs if our intelligence is correct."

"Hah." Sugar started chuckling softly as he shook his head. "Sugar says you're mighty brazen to level such an accusation. Just why do you care so much?"

Butch slid off his chair and put a protective hand on Sana's shoulder. "A friend's daughter who lives here in Nashville has disappeared. We've been hired to try and find her."

"Hired? My, my, my. This is getting interesting. By whom?"

Sana refused to back down. "Clay Hall."

"Now there's a fine singer." A mystical smile flitted across Sugar's lips. "I know where he's involved. Forever Free. I know them well. They're an anti-trafficking organization."

Sana frowned. What on earth? "How would you?"

"'Cause I work with them, you understand?"

Yep, she'd fallen through a black hole and into an alternate universe. "Uh, no."

Sugar sipped his wine and set it aside. "I like you, Sana Jain. Sugar knows how such a situation like what you saw could be misconstrued. Let me set the record straight. You're right about what you saw. Behind that door at The Music Man is a brothel upstairs. Girls alternate nights. Either they work upstairs, or they serve as waitresses and hostesses."

Bingo. At least part of their assumptions had been correct. Sana glanced at Butch as he returned to his chair. "We saw you talking to our waitress."

"That's right." Sugar nodded. "You did. And you know why? I was buying her freedom."

Sana's jaw dropped. A guy who dressed like a pimp buying a girl's freedom? She didn't know what to say.

Sugar laughed again. "Gotcha, didn't I?"

Her cheeks warmed. She'd been so far off the mark on this one. "I have to say, you did."

Butch's eyes narrowed as he stroked his beard. "Who do you think is running them?"

"Why do you care so much?"

"This girl who disappeared—Morgan Walton—may have been at The Music Man at some point."

Sana pulled out her phone and brought up a picture of the shot glass and coaster. "We found these when we searched her bedroom at home."

Sugar examined them. "And those led you to have supper there."

"I also scoped out the place earlier," Butch said. "Things about it didn't look normal. Like the fence with concertina wire on it. And only upstairs access behind the wire. And too many cameras focused on that one area."

Sugar moved the wineglass in small circles, which left wet contrails on the copper. "The man does his homework. You're right, Mr. Addison. Very right. You think the girl's been taken for prostitution?"

Sana swallowed hard. She pulled up another picture, this one of Morgan's sophomore year portrait. "Have you seen her?"

Sugar gazed at it. "Hmmm, hmmm, hmmm. I have." He met her gaze. "You need to understand something, Sana Jain. Tonight's visit wasn't my first. I go there about once a month for two nights in a row. It's my chance to scope out any new girls. I saw her about three weeks ago. Something told me Mr. Ash had landed himself a good one."

Tears filled Sana's eyes. "She's sixteen. Just a girl."

"I figured as much. And she's a very pretty girl." Sugar cleared his throat. "You want to know something? You're right to say Mr. Ash is involved. He's very involved. The first time I visited, I suspected. I started a friendship of sorts with him because, like you, he thought I was a pimp."

Butch's pencil moved as he made notes. "How does it work?"

A slight smile flitted across his lips. "It's simple, really. I see a girl. I make him an offer. If he accepts, then Sugar walks away a happy man, and a girl gets her freedom. He refuses, I move on."

Sana's head spun, and she burst out, "But why don't you just go to the cops?"

His stiffened.

She'd stepped in it. Big time.

The man only gazed at her before taking another sip of Chardonnay. "Sugar says it's much more complicated than that. You see, Sana Jain, Mr. Ash is one of the most upstanding members of this town. He's a high-fallutin' businessman. His clients at his business are some of the biggest in the music industry. And his clients for his other, not-so-legit business? Some of the most powerful men in this region." He lowered his long-lashed gaze to his glass. "And besides, I don't like cops. Or feds. I try to keep them out of my hair. If I had any hair, that is."

"Everything is not as it seems," Butch murmured.

Sugar shifted on his chair. "Exactly, Mr. Addison. What I at first was trying to do was to buy your friend's freedom. Mr. Ash refused, said she wasn't for sale, which was odd. But your waitress?"

"Faye."

"Which isn't her real name." Sugar squinted as if trying to peer at something only he could see. "Mr. Ash had Denelle Brooks bring her to the table."

Butch's pencil paused. "She's the manager?"

"Yes, sir, indeed she is. A cold woman if I ever saw one. She's also the madam. Keeps the girls in line. Heaven forbid any of them overstep. Mr. Ash offered up that pretty little waitress of yours." A slight smile flitted across his face. "I'm going back there later to get her out. You can count on that."

Sana's heart eased, if only a little.

Sugar glanced at his watch. "Speaking of which, I need to be going. Mr. Ash is a hard man. If Sugar is a minute late, a second late, he breaks the deal." He rose and nodded to Loquacious.

They weren't finished! Sana hurried after him. "But we need—"

"Come back tomorrow, Sana Jain." Sugar stopped and slid something from an inner pocket of his blazer. He pressed the small rectangle into her hand. "My card. And leave yours with Monique. I'm not going to lose the freedom of one girl in a futile attempt to save another."

With that he strode toward the entrance.

Sana almost ran to keep up. She burst into the chilly night.

Sugar and his bodyguard had already vanished into the thickening crowd.

She kicked the ground with her size-five boot. "We'll never get her."

"Let it go," Butch murmured when he'd caught up to her. "C'mon. We've got enough to formulate our next move." He gazed around them. "And I promise. We'll get Morgan."

11

Thursday, April 7, 2016, 2350 hours CDT, Nashville, TN

Reality teased the edges of Morgan's consciousness as she lay on her bed. Memories of the past several horrific days rolled over her like tidal waves. After her arrival three weeks before, she awakened with weakened limbs and a blurry memory. Miss Denelle roused her, then told her to dress in a little black frock she provided. She trained as a waitress that first night. She'd liked the dress—until she realized she couldn't keep it. That mystified her.

She found out why the second night. She asked for her dress since she had to waitress. Oh, no. Miss Denelle made it clear that tonight, her only clothing would be the robe she was wearing. What? Why? Then she got her instructions. Men would visit her. She was to do what they wanted.

Morgan panicked. A couple of bouncers wrestled her to the ground. Miss Denelle injected her with something that made her not care so much when johns came on an hourly basis. A professional football player from the area and one of his pals. A businessman in town for work. Someone Important from the local political scene. Another guy who she recognized as an insurance executive. They went home with their dirty little secrets while she remained locked in hell with each new trick she turned sending her deeper and deeper until she wondered if she had a way out.

Each visit, each vile act they made her perform, stole a bit of her soul until she wondered if she had one left. She'd failed the night before at her one attempt to escape. Only the owner's visit saved her from a severe beating. Why remained unclear, even as her fogged brain recovered from the last dose of drugs.

Now, Morgan rolled onto her stomach and gripped the silk sheets. She opened her eyes and stared around the room. Soft light from sconces lit the pale lavender walls. Her robe hung on a hook, where she'd left it after her last shower. A dresser, for show since nothing inhabited its drawers, sat across from the bed. Her shoulders heaved as she thought of the last man, another lonely soul from out of town. She hated herself for giving in, but she had no choice. At least she was finished for the night and had showered off her makeup.

The lights from the sconces brightened as the lock on her door rattled.

She peered over her shoulder.

Miss Denelle entered. "Get up, Emmaline." She snatched the deep blue, thigh-length silk robe from its hook by the door and tossed it onto the blanket. "Get dressed. Indra's coming to do your makeup."

Morgan pushed herself upright. "Why?"

"Shut up. Just do as I said."

Or there will be a beating. That much hung in the air like a putrid mist.

The door shut.

Morgan climbed from bed. She pulled on the robe and tied the sash around her waist. Normally, she would have loved the blue silk with its beautiful, embroidered flowers on it. Not now. Not when it symbolized her bondage. She sat cross-legged on her bed and chewed another nail down to the quick. She closed her eyes. A deep breath calmed her. That eased the tremors that seemed to grow worse with each passing day of working the johns.

Someone tapped on the door. Morgan would have recognized that noise anywhere. Indra, the girl in Room Nine who had to be in her early twenties. And a genius with makeup. She bustled into the room and set her kit on the dresser. "Let's get you made up real pretty."

Morgan shifted. "Who am I going to see?"

Her friend, whose real name she didn't know, shrugged. "I have no idea. I think the boss man himself." She pulled out a brush and a small spray bottle. "Here. Let me brush your hair."

Morgan closed her eyes as Indra sprayed something. The bristles running through those strands calmed her. Her tense shoulders relaxed a little. Her mind wandered to Mondays. That was the only day they got off and could roam the hallway under the watchful eyes of the bouncers.

The girls often congregated in someone's room. Each wore a different-colored robe, their only clothing save for their waitress or hostess outfits, which Miss Denelle kept under lock and key. Morgan had met them all. Indra with skin the color of dark tea and sparkling brown eyes. Amy of the blonde hair and green eyes. Faye, a young girl, maybe younger than Morgan, with dark hair, fair skin, and dark eyes that remained timid and beaten. And others whose real names she'd never know.

Would she ever leave? If she did, what would happen to someone with wounds so deep in her heart? Tears welled in her eyes as Indra began working on her face.

"None of that, girl."

"I... I can't help it."

"I know." Indra ran her hand down her arm before focusing on applying eye makeup. "But don't start crying, or you'll ruin your mascara."

"You're such a genius at making us look beautiful," Morgan murmured. "You should be a makeup artist."

"I wanted to work in that industry." Indra fell silent as if considering what to share. "At least until I met Wes."

Morgan drew back and covered her mouth with her hand.

Indra, eyeliner poised, stared. "Easy! Don't make me leave a mark on you."

Morgan tried to make the connection as her brain continued to clear. "Sorry. How did you meet him?"

Her friend resumed her work. "Sorority party at Vandy. He kept saying I was beautiful, that he had a modeling job for me. I posed topless.

A stupid idea. We went out for drinks a week later. Then I wound up here."

Morgan had thought Wes cared for her. He acted like it, had been her friend and listened to her angst. Now, she knew him for who he really was. A creep. A traitor. Her gut clenched. Anger. Maybe that would keep her going.

Indra finished with the lip liner and lipstick. She helped her friend stand. "There. Take a look."

Morgan gazed into the mirror hanging above her dresser. Oh, wow. What a makeup genius. Her blue eyes almost glowed in the dim light. Her lips were full and glossy. Her hair streamed like copper silk over her shoulders and even had faint sparkles of glitter in it. If only for a moment, she felt beautiful. "You're so talented." She fought the tears. "Sorry. I'm tearing up. Thank you."

Indra smiled and tucked a strand of hair behind her ear. "For what?"

"For making me feel beautiful." *And a little stronger.*

Indra hugged her. "When I was growing up, Mom told me that because we bear God's image, all of us are beautiful. It's hard to remember, isn't it?"

Morgan could only nod since the lump in her throat choked off anything she could have said. God's image-bearer. That stuck with her even though she'd never gone to church.

The knob turned again.

Miss Denelle glared at them with ice blue eyes, and the room's temperature seemed to drop a few degrees. "Indra, back to your room."

"Yes, ma'am." Indra scurried through the door.

Morgan lowered her gaze to hide the small streak of rebellion that had reappeared.

"Emmaline, come with me."

Morgan rose. She kept her eyes down. Somehow, she'd survive. Somehow, she'd fight back. And maybe she'd live to see freedom.

Operation Music Man

Friday, April 8, 2016, 0010 hours CDT, Nashville, TN

As the bouncer shut the door behind Sugar and that hulk of a bodyguard of his, Jaidon scowled from the leather chair in his office at The Music Man. Saralynn, known as Faye to the johns who visited, would go with the jazz club owner.

The man had asked for Morgan. Hah. Over his dead body would he allow Sugar to buy first Exotic he'd had in four years.

Saralynn had gone for a measly one hundred grand, not like the million-plus Morgan would most likely command at the next auction. The thing was, most of the money went straight into Jaidon's pocket with a bonus for Denelle. The Distributor didn't need to know about his little side business with Sugar buying the freedom of a girl here and there. There were always others to replace her. Always. The commodity never ran out.

His phone pinged, and he picked it up.

His head bouncer for that night had texted. Mr. Narat Jain is here to see you.

Jaidon thumbed his screen. Show him upstairs. The girls have finished seeing their last johns of the night.

He greeted The Distributor's son as he stepped through the door. "Narat, so good to meet you. Your father has spoken very highly of you."

The men shook hands. "The pleasure is all mine. How fortuitous that I consider Nashville to be a second home." Narat Jain settled on a chair. "Wes told me he landed a looker."

Jaidon sat down across from him. "I promise you won't be disappointed."

Narat's face slid into neutral. "You're sure she would go at a good price?"

"Absolutely." Jaidon frowned. "What did you say? Redheads are in high demand. Especially if they have blue eyes."

Narat picked at an invisible thread on his khakis. "And only if they have no blemishes like freckles or moles on their skin. As you know, Mr. Ash, blue-eyed redheads without blemishes are hard to come by. Father can attest to that because he hasn't found one in years, even with our network across the country."

Was it suddenly hot in here? Jaidon undid the top button of his collarless shirt. "I promise you, this one won't disappoint."

Someone tapped on his door before it cracked open. "Mr. Ash."

Ah, Denelle. The one woman he trusted to take care of the twelve girls under his care so they could churn out money. "Come in."

She opened the door. Her pale blue eyes peered at him, and the room seemed to cool. "I have her here."

Jaidon leaned forward. "Bring her in."

Denelle tugged on someone's arm.

The redhead, Morgan Walton, if he remembered Wes's pronouncement correctly, stepped inside.

Denelle shut the door behind her, leaving the girl alone with the two men.

Narat rose. He gazed at her face and reached up. He ran some of her coppery hair through his fingers. A smile tipped his lips. "A lovely hair color. And lovely blue eyes. First impressions are good, Mr. Ash."

"I'm glad to see that. Morgan, undress, please."

She met his gaze as if startled he'd used her real name. She hesitated.

Jaidon added a little more force into his voice. "Undress. Now."

She undid the sash of her robe, but it remained hanging on her shoulders.

Not that Narat seemed to mind. With a deft flick of his hand, the material piled on the floor at her feet. He walked around her as if appraising a sculpture of fine ivory. "You were correct. A nice, full figure. And not a blemish on her. Not even a freckle."

"Is she what you were looking for?"

"As an Exotic?" A smile curled Narat's lips. "Absolutely. I know of several invited guests who are looking for the likes of her."

Jaidon's mind raced. "How much could she command?"

"At least four."

Jaidon's eyes widened. "Million?"

"Oh, yes." Narat picked up the robe. "You may dress."

Morgan slid it back on. Her head remained hanging, but she cinched the sash extra tight.

On his desk, Jaidon pressed a button that summoned Denelle to take the girl back to her room. Once she was gone, he leaned forward. "A drink, my friend?"

"Absolutely."

He pulled a couple of crystal tumblers from his credenza, added ice, and poured some of Kentucky's finest over the cubes. He handed one to Narat and raised his glass. "To a good find."

"I'll drink to that." Narat clinked glasses with him before sitting back. He started chuckling. "I knew it. I told you Wes has talent. Where did he find her?"

"Darned if I know. He has a knack with the ladies. He spots them, friends them on social media, then works them until he sees an opportunity. Fortunately, he chooses his timing well."

"I'll say. Sending him your way when you were setting up seven years ago was the best thing Father ever did."

Jaidon frowned. "Just how do you two know each other?"

"Father told me to make contact. I did so when I was in college and interned at the insurance agency where he works." Narat shrugged. "Let's just say we became friends. He's my sister's age, you know."

"No, I didn't know that."

"Too bad Father wouldn't have approved of their dating. They would have hit it off. Both outspoken, independent thinkers, rebels in their own way. When I saw him earlier tonight, I told him I was going to view a result of his work. I'll let him know he scored. Big time."

"When are you headed out?"

"I'll take her with me when I go on Sunday morning. Until then, I'm visiting friends in the area." Narat's eyes gleamed. "Tell me something, Mr. Ash."

"Call me Jaidon. What would that be?"

The skin at the base of Narat's collar reddened, and he lowered his voice as he said, "Could I have some time with her?"

"With our Exotic?"

Narat's lips curled. "She is beautiful. A fantasy of mine."

Jaidon chuckled. "She's finished for the night, so of course. Enjoy her, compliments of the house. But only if you tell me one thing."

Narat raised an eyebrow.

"What will be your opening bid?"

Another lip curl crossed the son of the Distributor's face. "I'll recommend the bidding open at eight million."

12

Friday, April 8, 2016, 0015 hours CDT, Nashville, TN

"We let him go," Victor stated in his suite after Sana and Butch shared the debrief of their visit to The Music Man and their chat with Sugar. The dark circles under his eyes and stubble on his jaw showed exactly how long of a day he'd had, which didn't seem to be ending despite the fact it was past midnight.

Sana stared at her commander. "What do you mean? Why?"

With his arms folded across his chest, Victor leaned in what had become his customary position against the kitchenette bar. "Because I want to link him to whoever took Morgan."

Inside her clogs, Sana's toes curled. Her pulse quickened. "That was Jaidon."

"We don't have definitive proof." Butch rubbed his eyes, then pawed at his black shirt. "Man, sometimes I hate these smoke-free rooms. I need a smoke after tonight."

Sana faced him. "There's a whole lot more girls than Morgan. Don't you remember?"

Butch yawned long and loud. "Yeah, I do,"

"I don't care. We need to get those girls out. All of them. I mean, the girl who waited on us tonight. Her name's Faye. She couldn't have been any older than Morgan. I don't care how old they are. This Jaidon guy is holding them in bondage."

Victor closed his eyes and pinched the bridge of his nose. Whether praying or trying not to say what he really thought, she didn't know. He took a deep breath, then held up a folder. On its tab was the title of their mission. Operation Music Man. "Sana, what's our mission objective?"

Her chest tightened. "To find Morgan and get her back to her family." She ground those words out. "But what about those other girls?"

"What's our objective?"

Of all things! She clenched her jaw. "I told you."

Suleiman, who sat on the couch with her, took her hand as if to warn her about disrespecting—and disobeying—their commander.

Victor stiffened, then drew in a slow breath and released it. Almost too quietly, he stated, "Our primary objective is to find Morgan and get her to safety. Sana, I understand your concern. Truly, I do. We're collecting information, right? You and Butch did that tonight. Suleiman and I did too. We're building a case we can hand over to the cops. Sure, some of the evidence may not be admissible, but it's going to give them enough to really start investigating so they can bring the perpetrators to justice."

"But—"

"Let me finish." He raised a hand. "In the meantime, we still don't have enough to act, do we?"

She set her jaw. "I think we do."

"Do we know where they're being kept?"

Her fists tightened until her nails bit into her palms. "Upstairs! We know the upstairs entrance is behind the wire. Why else would it be except that it leads to the girls?"

Victor tossed the folder onto the bar. "Are they being rotated on and off site? What are the guard numbers? What are other security measures? How well are the guards armed?"

His questions, though wise, infuriated her. He had her there. Some of her energy dissipated, leaving behind a weariness so profound she wanted to crawl into bed.

With a sigh, Victor lowered himself onto a bar chair. He kept his focus on Sana as if he were speaking only to her. "I promise that when we're ready, we'll act. Matter of fact, the rest of the team is meeting us here tomorrow afternoon. Until they get here, I think we can do some more digging." His gaze slid to Shelly, who'd watched the exchange between her boss and her best friend with wide hazel eyes. "Shelly, see what you can find on Jaidon Ash, Wes Sampson, and Denelle Brooks. Everything." He shifted. "Butch, call up Mr. Sugar. We'll go and have a more in-depth chat with him. I'm hoping he can be an ally in this."

Sana couldn't ask for anything more. She had to be patient.

Victor's phone rang. At his "Hi, Skylar," she tuned him out by peering at the photos Suleiman had taken earlier that night. She gathered them in a stack and glanced at the laptop he'd set on the coffee table. His report from their visit to Wes Sampson glowed on the screen. She flipped to the first photo.

Wes Sampson. The very one who'd sent Morgan into bondage without a care in the world. *You didn't care about Morgan at all. Instead, you probably only cared about that finder's fee you likely got.* Boy, he'd better hope she didn't lay hands on him. She committed his face to memory.

She shifted to some more photos, which revealed a glowing marquee. A hookah bar. Wes pacing outside. Then someone else showed up. This guy had darker skin, but his face remained unclear as if Suleiman had hesitated to zoom in for a closer shot. Then he did as Wes's friend held the door. The last photo was a close-up of his face.

Sana's stomach dropped. Suddenly, she felt far away, as if she were at the end of a long pipe listening to Victor's conversation. She couldn't rip her gaze away from the picture. She'd know Wes's friend anywhere.

Narat Jain.

Her brother.

She drew in a noisy breath. "I-I don't understand."

Suleiman took the photo from her and placed it on the table. "Wes and Narat know each other."

Hot, angry tears filled her eyes. "But... how?"

He rubbed the back of her neck. "Wes said they met when Narat interned at his insurance firm while in college."

"Why is he in Nashville?"

"Apparently visiting a bunch of friends."

Her thoughts zig-zagged like a scared rabbit being chased by a coyote. She tried to get them to straighten out. "But..."

"It is probably a coincidence."

It had to be. She knew her next-down brother liked to return to Nashville because he had many friends in the area.

She wanted to be alone. She glanced around.

Victor had stepped into the bedroom as he talked with Skylar.

Butch chuckled during his chat with Sugar.

Shelly completely tuned everyone out as she focused on her work.

Knees shaking, Sana stood. "I'll be downstairs."

Suleiman caught her eye. "I'll go with you."

"Can I be alone?" She realized that sounded rude. "Please?"

His gaze clouded. He nodded.

She slipped into the hallway, then raced downstairs to her room. She kicked off her clogs and threw herself on the bed. Her shoulders heaved a couple of times as she struggled to push down her emotions. *So Narat's in town. Big deal. You know he likes to come here at least once a quarter. He has lots of friends in the area. Why does one of his friends have to be Wes Sampson?* She raised her head from the pillow. Her cell phone sat where she'd tossed it onto the duvet.

Picking it up, she skimmed through her contacts until she found his number. She dialed. It went straight to voice mail. Of course. It was almost one, and even Narat admitted that he started fading around midnight. Old age, they'd joked only a few weeks ago.

"God, why?" she whispered into the darkness. She rested her head on a pillow and stared through the filmy curtains in her window. A light from the parking lot cast a pale glow through the room. She closed her eyes as she hugged another pillow to herself. She drifted.

"I met someone," she told Narat one hot June afternoon shortly after she'd finished her second year of college in 2007.

His warm, dark eyes held her gaze. "Father told me. He also told me he didn't approve."

Her rebellion flared. "I don't care what Father thinks. I stopped bowing to his wishes three years ago."

Her brother, a recent high school graduate who was mature beyond his years, shrugged. "I understand. Which is why I'm going to Vanderbilt. To get from underneath his thumb."

Sana's heart ached. "You're his favorite, you know. A son. A responsible son destined to follow the path he wanted."

"And it's a burden." Narat sipped his water and stared at something over her shoulder. "A true burden."

"I have a way for you to get back at your father," Taz, her boyfriend, whispered into her ear the following week. They lay together beneath the sheets at his warehouse apartment. He wove his fingers through her long, black hair.

"How so?"

He sat up. "Come with me. I'll show you."

Once dressed, she followed him into another warehouse. Her jaw dropped at the goods she saw. Electronics. Paintings. Sparkling jewelry.

Taz faced her. "We're gradually fencing this. You help us, you get a cut."

"I'm in only if I can keep what I steal."

"Done."

Three weeks later, at the age of twenty, she committed the first of several crimes.

Almost a year later in May 2009 after she pled guilty and turned state's witness, the judge's voice echoed across the Texas courtroom. "I hereby sentence you to four years in prison, six months of that time served already."

Tears had poured down Sana's face. She risked a glance at Father.

His face a mask of anger, he glared at her from the gallery. Shame on her for dishonoring the family! The six months she'd rotted in jail attested to that. A week after her plea deal, Sana rode a prison van to Gatesville to serve her sentence. She whipped around as the door to her cell clanged shut. The bolt turned.

She rushed to it. "Father! Please save me! Please! I'm sorry!"

In the hotel room, she shifted her head from side to side. "No, Father. Please!"

She stilled and sank further into slumber.

"Narat is now my oldest." Father's voice boomed as if from heaven. "Not you. You're cast out of the family and are a stray."

Sana's breath shuddered out of her, and her eyes snapped open. Tears wet the pillow as reality slowly returned.

She felt rather than saw Suleiman sitting on the edge of the bed. His long, slender fingers reached out and took her hand. She held on for dear life but didn't face him. "I don't want Narat to be involved."

That came out as a croak.

He released her and stroked the hair out of her face. "Neither do I, *eshgham*."

Her shoulders quaked. Her emotions began running away like a train hurtling down the tracks. Once more, images from her past pushed their way to the forefront. The startling sadness in Ranger Ryan Flagel's eyes as deputies led her from the courtroom. He'd arrested her, then become her only friend on the outside. Her side flared as if it remembered the shanking she'd survived early in 2010. Then came Ryan again as he sat by her hospital bed when she'd clung to life by a thread.

Suleiman's tender words broke into her past. "Tell me what's on your mind."

He'd never understand everything that had happened once she'd rebelled against Father. Taz's seduction, her loose living, the way Taz had played upon her rebellion and enticed her to commit no less than ten break-ins. Sana bit down so hard on her lip she tasted blood. "I... I can't."

A sigh, the only hint of Suleiman's frustration. His lips brushed her ear. "I love you, Sana Jain. And I am here for you. Please remember that."

He slipped from the room, leaving coldness where his warmth had been.

Sana pulled another pillow over her head. Maybe one day, she'd trust him totally with her past. Today wasn't that day.

13

Friday, April 8, 2016, 1030 hours CDT, Nashville, TN

Weariness. It tugged at Sana as she, Butch, Victor, and Suleiman climbed from the Ford Explorer Butch drove. This time, they'd found street parking right outside of La Femme Nue. A delivery truck rumbled by and pulled to the side of the road at a nearby restaurant. At a coffee shop, two people sat at tables and chatted in the chilly morning air. Shoppers already crowded the sidewalks as they strolled to and from places of business.

She faced the awning of La Femme Nue. This time, Sugar had told them to go through the club and out back.

Cradling a Starbucks cup of their strongest in her hands, she followed Butch's broad back inside. What a difference a few hours made. The restaurant was empty. Silence reigned. But even with the lights on and daylight pouring in from the open door at the back, it maintained its elegance.

"Hey, everyone!" a chipper voice called.

Monique. The bartender from last night. Except now, she looked like she was ready for a day of hanging out in a park. Her coppery curls gleamed in the overhead light, and she wore denim cropped pants and a long-sleeved T-shirt. A single gold chain with a heart gleamed against her brown skin. Was she Sugar's girl as well as a bartender? "He's out back waiting on you since it's too nice a day to stay inside."

Suleiman took her hand as they headed through the club. Sana squeezed it. She should have apologized for spurning his support the night before. But she'd wanted—no, needed—to be alone to digest her discovery.

The group stepped into the light.

Almost immediately, Loquacious, clad in all black again, stepped into their path.

Sugar's voice floated to her along with a sweetly delicious floral scent. "Let him search you, Sana Jain. You and your friends."

She knew better than to protest.

Loquacious was professional and thorough. She offered a smile.

His lips twitched upward.

She stepped into paradise. Wow. She would have never expected such an elegant patio in the middle of a city. Gardens framed paths of pea gravel and stepping stones. They arrived at a conversation group of rattan furniture with a pergola sporting Carolina jasmine vines over it, hence the glorious scent she'd smelled. A fire pit with edges wide enough for people to sit dominated the middle. Low flames rose above coals.

Resplendent again in a white suit but now with a deep blue shirt, hat band, and handkerchief, Sugar rose from a chair. "Hello, Sana Jain. And I see you brought some friends today. Sorry for the search, but Sugar wanted to make sure you weren't carrying a pop gun or anything. Have a seat and tell me who the rest of you are."

Victor picked an easy chair across from Sugar. "Victor Chavez. Team commander and owner of Sentry Securities."

"I checked out your firm this morning. Quite impressive. Especially that *Peacemaker* job last year and kicking some Somali pirate butt. Former fed. But not working with the feds now, right?"

"Nope. Not since 2014."

"That's good 'cause I would have tossed you out on your ear if you were still one. I don't like feds." Sugar switched his attention to Suleiman, who joined Sana on a love seat. "And you are?"

"Suleiman al-Ibrahim. Team sniper and observer."

Sugar tipped his hat. "And engaged to the lovely Sana Jain, I see."

Huh? Sana cocked her head.

Sugar laughed. "Your body language conveys it all, Sana Jain. As does that beauty on your finger."

She blushed as she glanced down at the diamond on her left hand.

"And Mr. Addison, good to see you." He nodded toward a tray of juice and glasses on the edge of the fire pit as well as a tray of pastries. "Please have some. Monique's going to join our little conversation."

The young woman settled on the other end of the couch from Butch.

Sana pushed her mind to the business at hand. "Can you tell us what happened to that girl? To Faye?"

"I got her."

"For how much?"

"I won't say. Human lives are not to be priced with a dollar value. But I did have to pay to get her freedom. Understand?"

Point well taken. "I do. And I agree."

"I thought you would. Let's just say she's somewhere safe until one of my girls from New Orleans can take her to a safe house I have set up down south. Just in case anyone gets any ideas to take her back." Sugar leaned forward and poured himself some juice. "Miss Faye will get the proper counseling through Forever Free to help her through this. And if they can reunite her with her parents, they'll do that." He gestured with his glass to Monique. "Sugar wanted her here today so she can tell her story. It speaks better than anything else."

Monique shifted on the cushions. "I was in your Morgan's position five years ago."

Sana stared. What? This lovely young woman with the lively eyes? The one who seemed much more at home in jeans and a T-shirt than a cocktail dress?

The woman pulled a pillow to her. "I'd run away from home in a small town in Louisiana. I found my way to New Orleans. There, I met someone who promised me a job."

Victor pulled out a notepad. "How old were you?"

"Seventeen. I thought things were so miserable at home. Thought I could handle it on my own. Turns out, I knew nothing about the rest of the world. The guy said I was pretty, that he could find me a modeling job and give me the money I needed to make a start. The next thing I knew, I was locked in a room, beaten, and shot up with heroin." Her eyes glimmered with tears. "To make a very long, sordid story short, I got pregnant with a john's baby. My pimp forced me to have an abortion. That... that was awful. I wanted to die."

Victor, who'd begun scribbling, paused. "Sugar, when did you come in?"

Sugar inclined his head in her direction. "I'll let the lady say."

"This went on for five or so years. Then he showed up." She nodded at her boss. "He didn't touch me. Instead, he told me he'd bought my freedom. I was going with him."

Stunned, Sana listened to the rest of her story. Monique's struggle to break free of drugs at an inpatient facility, then in a group home where other girls freed from trafficking lived with a house mother. She'd cleaned Sugar's house for a fair wage, had health insurance for the first time ever.

"One day, the pimp found out what had happened to me," Monique continued. "Sugar was getting ready to open his club here in Nashville, so he sent me to work the bar. I'm living with a couple of other girls." Her eyes cleared, and that sparkle returned. "I got my GED a few years ago and am finishing my business degree at the community college. I've got a safe place to live. People who care about me, including a beau who's a pastor." A small smile crossed her lips. "I'm free to leave La Femme Nue, but Sugar says the manager's job is mine when I get my associate degree."

Sana's stomach knotted, and she wanted to slink away. She'd so underestimated the man she'd first assumed to be a pimp. Questions flew through her mind and threatened to burst onto the scene. Finally, she blurted, "Sugar, why do you care so much?"

He gazed at her, and she worried she'd stepped in it.

Then he smiled, this time a gentle smile. At the edges of his sunglasses, which he'd not taken off, his eyes crinkled. "Because my mama was a prostitute. My daddy was a john I never knew. She raised me as best she could. Oh, yes, I was lucky because I was smart and had a grandma who took care of me. Mama got AIDS in 1985 and barely lived long enough to see me graduate high school. I had a full ride to LSU and took it. But Sugar ain't never forgotten Mama. She's here." He thumped his chest. "I vowed I'd never follow that lifestyle of being a pimp or being in a gang. Most of Sugar's friends? Gone. Murdered or dead because of a drug overdose. I'm the only one of my initial friend set left. About ten years ago, once I built up enough cash, I started rescuing girls. Monique was one of my first. She put up with my shenanigans and missteps."

Victor studied him as he chewed on the top of his pen. With a knit brow, he stared at his notepad. "Butch said you were trying to buy Morgan's freedom."

Sugar reached for a pastry. "Oh, yes. I know The Music Man and Jaidon Ash are dirty. Not that there's enough proof to get an arrest warrant. Not to mention that some of Nashville's best and most powerful are clients."

In other words, Ash was most likely beyond the reach of the law. Sana's jaw tightened.

"I make a habit of going there to find girls. You know they waitress on alternate nights. That's when people spot the merchandise, choose what they want for the next night."

"How do they do that?" Victor asked.

"I've been around enough to see it in action. They approach Denelle Brooks, the manager and madam. She gives them a website where they can download an app. They have to access it with a fingerprint." Sugar bobbed his head. "Clever, I know. Now they have proof of who's been paying their little brothel a visit. So if they go down, they've got a long, long list of johns to take with them. Not that anyone gives it a thought. Except me. With Morgan, I saw her that first night. I instantly recognized she was a mere teenager. And someone who was new and terrified."

"When was this?"

"Within a week of her arrival at the club."

Sana met Butch's gaze.

The big man's lips curled as if he had an idea in mind. He leaned forward. "Mr. Sugar."

Sugar laughed that deep, rich laugh from the night before. "I like that. What is it, Mr. Addison?"

"I have a plan."

"Then do tell."

He spelled it out. Sana straightened as she listened. It was a good one, especially with Skylar arriving shortly. But the question was, would it work?

Friday, April 8, 2016, 1345 hours CDT, Nashville, TN

As he strode to his car in the parking lot of the Metro Nashville Police, Victor wanted to stamp his feet and holler like a toddler. Detective Lucy Hendricks had told him Cruz was out of the office. More than that, the case was closed. In Cruz's mind, Morgan had run away. Period.

"I've got evidence that points to the contrary," Victor had said.

"He'll be back later this afternoon," Hendricks replied. "Good luck on convincing him."

Victor stared at her. "What does he have on you?"

That earned him a cold look before she stepped to her desk to answer the phone.

Now, Victor approached the Camry and clicked the fob.

The lights flashed.

"Mr. Chavez!" a woman called.

He turned and found Hendricks trotting toward him, almost at a run. He leaned a hip against the fender. "What is it? Because apparently, I wasted your time, and now, you're wasting mine."

Hendricks skidded to a stop. Panting slightly, she took a breath. "I'm sorry I didn't help you, but there's something more I didn't want to mention in there." She jerked her head toward the building.

He folded his arms. "Like what?"

"Cruz was ordered off the case. That came down from the chief."

Interesting. It jibed with what Sugar had said that morning. "Why? Do you have any idea?"

Her lips pursed, and she shook her head. "Not really. I think it has to do with Wes Sampson. The thing is, we've had an uptick in girls getting reported as missing with the results being reduced to running away. Like happy, normal girls at college who suddenly vanish. The one thing they seem to have in common is Sampson."

Stunned, he stared at her. "That's all you know?"

"It is. Cruz knows more since he started taking those missing persons reports."

"Where is he?"

A ghost of a smile crossed her lips. "He has his favorite hot dog stand by the Parthenon. But you didn't hear it from me."

"Hendricks, thanks." Victor hopped into the Camry and sped toward the Parthenon in Midtown. It was a ways west, but then again, Cruz probably spent little time at the office. Twenty minutes later, he shut the door and headed onto the Parthenon's grounds. He found the food truck, then the detective sitting on a bench with a hot dog poised for entry into his mouth.

Cruz grimaced when he noted Victor's approach. "How'd you know where I was?"

"I figured it was a little late for donuts. Hot dogs were my next best guess, so I took a chance."

"Hendricks told you."

Victor shrugged. "She says you come here to hide on Friday afternoons."

"No." Cruz squinted at him in the bright afternoon light. "I come here on Friday afternoons to get a hot dog at the hot dog truck and enjoy not being bothered for once."

Victor seated himself on the bench beside him. "So sorry to interrupt you, then. I can leave."

"You're here. Why did you come?" He took a big bite.

"I wanted to catch you up on what I and my team have done. And it's a lot." Victor ran through everything, from searching Morgan's home, to finding The Music Man, to nearly wringing the truth from Wes Sampson. He held up a folder. "Here's what I have."

Cruz set the hot dog aside and thumbed through the information before stuffing it inside his leather jacket. "You and your team did quite a bit in twenty-four hours."

Victor gazed at the replica of the Parthenon in the distance. "We want to get Morgan back."

"I get that. Truly, I do. And I'm not unsympathetic. But the case is closed."

"So said Hendricks." Victor shot him a look. "Was that your choice?"

Cruz glared at him for a moment and picked up his Pepsi can. It shook slightly as he sipped. "Where's the evidence?"

Victor stared. "I just handed it to you. It's right there in that folder."

"It's not admissible."

"What?"

"If anything, I could haul your butt in and charge you and your pal for kidnapping."

I cannot believe I'm hearing this. Victor shook his head. "Look. As I said, Wes is really close to thirty. If anything, judging from what we've found, you could arrest him for statutory rape since Morgan's almost half his age."

"Not on inadmissible evidence, I can't."

"He lied to you. He said he took her home when in reality, he took her straight to The Music Man."

Cruz crumpled his hot dog wrappers. He rose. "Let's take a walk for a bit."

They headed toward the Parthenon. As they walked, Cruz fished a cigarette pack from an interior jacket pocket and shook one out. He cupped his hands and lit it.

"I thought you said you were quitting."

"Hah. I lasted three months this time. That's two more months than last time. Dang job." He took a drag. "I saw no evidence in that folder definitively linking Morgan to The Music Man. Sampson could have dropped her off to someone who used the club as a meeting place."

Oh, Victor hated to admit that. "I know. Except for Sugar's placing her in the club."

Cruz let the cigarette hang by his side as they continued their stroll. "Marvin LaMott, or Sugar to you, is shadier than you could ever imagine. I make it a habit to get to know the club owners around here, and I know he opened La Femme Nue just a few years ago. I had him checked out. The feds say he's clean, though I suspect he's just as neck deep as anyone in running girls."

Victor clamped his jaw shut. He knew better than to argue with someone who'd already come to conclusions, even though they were the wrong ones. "My gut says he's above-board. But I'm not sure about Jaidon Ash, the owner of The Music Man."

Cruz stopped and stared at him. He raised his cigarette to his lips and took an uneven drag. "You know something? You've got some nerve."

"Huh?"

Cruz continued his walk. "How much do you know about Jaidon Ash?"

"He's had the club for a little over ten years. He also owns Music Man Productions."

"Which is one of the biggest tour management companies out there. And I'm not talking rinky-dink tours. I'm talking about big, world tours for artists not just in the country business but rock, rap, you name it." He listed several singers Victor knew. "He started that business twenty years ago, and during the Great Recession when a bunch of his rivals went under, he survived and kept all of his staff. Now I know that here in Music City, most of our rich people are singers, but I can tell you one thing. He's up there with the wealthiest other businessmen."

Victor's heart sank. "So in other words, he's untouchable."

"No one's totally untouchable. But he's pretty close. He's very visible on the social scene and in the community. He's got friends in high places. And MMP's always listed as one of the best places to work in Nashville. His wife's involved in charity work, big time. And—"

"Who asked you to drop the case?" Victor's eyes narrowed as he studied the detective. Like Hendricks, something unsettled Cruz, kept him silent.

Cruz glared at him with such venom that Victor wondered if he'd slap cuffs on him right then and there. "Remember what I said about high society? That's not just rich people. And I'm three years from retirement. Dang job," he muttered as he turned and walked on. "I need this pension, Chavez. And you simply don't have enough evidence for me to act."

They came to a stop next to an unmarked Dodge Charger. Cruz ground out his cigarette before pointing at him. "You bring me something concrete, something I can sink my teeth into, I'll open that investigation." He yanked at the driver's door. "You get something I can run with, you call me. You don't, it was nice knowing you." With that, he slid into the car.

Victor watched in frustration as the detective headed back to work.

So much for getting official assistance. He blew out a sigh and stared at the receding car. That was okay. He could manage. The team would manage. If anything, all of them were capable, Together, they were formidable. And tonight, he'd find out with his own eyes if Ash held Morgan. If he did, Victor would stop at nothing to free her.

Nothing.

14

Friday, April 8, 2016, 2015 hours CDT, Nashville, TN

Victor approached The Music Man with Butch and Skylar James, the team's resident intelligence and procurement officer who'd arrived earlier that day. All had dressed well for this adventure. Skylar, now the proud owner of two restaurants, one in Las Vegas and the other in Flagstaff, sported his trademark navy blue suit, blood red shirt, and navy tie. He swaggered—yes, swaggered—something Victor had never achieved and usually envied.

A bouncer blocked their path and lifted his chin as he eyed Butch. "You were here last night, right? You back again already?"

Butch strutted up to him. "I brought my lady last night. Tonight's a guys' night. Got a reservation for three for Addison."

The bouncer asked to see Skylar's jacket pockets. He obliged, and the man nodded. "Go on in."

They stepped into the large space.

"Nice," Skylar murmured. "This Jaidon Ash may be many things, most of them despicable, but he's done this up right."

A hostess, a blonde who appeared to be in her teens, greeted them with a slight smile. She led them to a table to the right of the entrance. The stage was in the opposite corner from where they sat near the bar.

Victor's earpiece, which he'd inserted so it wasn't visible, crackled.

"Six and Seven approaching," Diana Kasem, the team's doctor, murmured. She and Fiona Mercedes, the team's pilot, had come with Skylar and would now act as decoys when Victor put Plan A into motion.

"Two and Three are also inbound," Sana said. She and Suleiman would provide covering fire if needed. And if they had to go to Plan B, they'd attempt to gather intelligence about the area behind the door.

Victor took in everything. Bar in the corner so it wouldn't block the view of the stage. Tables along the wall and on the floor, all aligned to provide clear views of any performers onstage. The raised dais sat beside a corner booth opposite the bar. Tonight, black velvet covered a piano. The trim of two guitars glittered in the overhead lights. An unplugged show. Should be interesting—if they were there that long. Hopefully, they wouldn't be.

Waitresses, all in black dresses with bar aprons, circulated between the kitchen and tables.

One woman ruled them all. Denelle Brooks, the manager, stood out in an ice green dress with her hair pulled back in a severe bun. She reminded Victor of a teacher he'd once had, a woman who'd never hesitated to rap his knuckles with a ruler even when such thing had become unacceptable. Denelle's eyes roved the floor. She glanced at the bartender, who seemed to be the only man working out front.

A young woman approached them. Her coppery hair was the only thing that keyed him in to who she was. Morgan. Boy, makeup made girls look so much older. He would have pegged her in her early twenties had he not known she was a girl of sixteen going on seventeen that August. Even though a faint smile crossed her lips, no recognition flashed in her eyes. "Welcome to The Music Man. I'm Emmaline. May I get you something to drink?"

Emmaline? Thankfully Sugar had provided an interesting tidbit while they shared lunch earlier that day. Ash had revealed it to him one time over drinks. Each girl worked her johns under an assumed name that matched their room number, and one side of the hall worked the johns while the other waited tables. Morgan must be residing in Room Five.

Plan A looked good since Morgan was their waitress. He'd talk to her enough to gain her trust. When Fiona and Diana created a distraction, they'd slip out a side entrance. Suleiman, who was on overwatch with his sniper rifle, would cover them. A direct and simple solution to their very complex problem.

The redhead approached with their drinks.

Victor took his Cabernet. As the others received their drinks, he observed her. She spoke more slowly, so differently than the effervescent girl he remembered the last time he visited the Walton house when Gary was alive. Chatterbox. That's what he'd told Gary, who'd agreed with a laugh. She had to be drugged, most likely to keep her calm and pliable. Those blue eyes fixated on him longer this time, as if she recognized him but couldn't place him. As she turned away and headed to the bar, a chill raked up his spine.

Denelle Brooks watched her closely, almost as if she were under a microscope. Did the manager know her foes lurked in the herd of customers like wolves in the disguise of sheep? How could she? He filed that thought away for future reference.

Butch, who sat across from him and Skylar, shook his head and mouthed, "No go."

Victor had to agree. No way could they grab Morgan, not when the madam kept an eye on her. If they did, they'd create total chaos, which could backfire in a big way. He didn't want to imagine the scenario. He'd be accused of drugging Morgan and kidnapping her, and Cruz would probably take great pleasure in having a solid excuse to lock him up.

Fiona and Diana stepped through the entrance and greeted the hostess. They were seated on the other side of the restaurant against the wall.

Victor rested his elbows on the table so his watch, including the microphone Shelly had installed, was near his mouth. He attempted to smile at something Butch said as he murmured, "Plan A is a no-go. Time to implement Plan B."

Friday, April 8, 2016, 2020 hours CDT, Nashville, TN

Clad all in black, Sana and Suleiman crept down a little-used backstreet toward The Music Man. One block southeast, I-65 roared as cars traveled in and around Nashville. Auto fumes drifted downward. Had it not been for a stiff breeze that had sprung up, Sana would have felt smothered.

Victor's directive crackled in her ear worm. Plan B it was. Trickier but more interesting in her mind. Up ahead, the concertina wire lacing the top of the chain-link fence behind The Music Man glimmered in the anemic glow of the streetlights. No way could they get inside, not without getting cut to ribbons, and certainly not with the eyes of the cameras glaring down at the parking lot. They'd be busted the second they splatted onto the pavement in a bloody mess.

Their best bet was the ladder on the side of the restaurant that led to the roof. Butch and Suleiman had noted it when reconning the restaurant the day before. The key would be to get there without getting spotted by patrons arriving at the restaurant. The deepening dusk helped conceal them.

They pressed against a neighboring warehouse before darting to the side of The Music Man. A mess of pallets hid them from the front. To her left, the ladder rose up.

Suleiman unholstered his pistol and jerked his chin upward.

With a black shemagh over her face, Sana ascended. With his pistol resecured, Suleiman followed, and they crept along the roof in slow steps to avoid making noise.

Suleiman took up overwatch out back so he covered the parking lot and upstairs door.

Sana inched along the tar paper as she recalled the plans Shelly had found online from the local planning department. The Music Man's AC units were on the roof, meaning the intake vent also resided there. If the plans were accurate, it would lead down into a main shaft for the second floor, most likely to where they kept the girls.

She glanced at her fiancé. As he began assembling his sniper rifle, she unzipped her backpack and removed a spool of cable with a camera in a clear sphere at one end and a monitor at the other. She threaded the camera end into a vent. Using controls like those for a remote control car, she guided it into the upstairs shaft. Vents passed by the lens. She carefully pushed the orb through the slats on one that was in the middle of an upstairs hall.

Perfect.

So long as no guard looked up, she'd be invisible to those in the hall. She could angle the cameras set at ninety degrees to give her an indication of the activity happening not ten feet below her. With a small recorder at her lips, she began dictating her findings in a low voice. It didn't bode well for them. Two guards at either end of the hall, both armed with pistols and radios. A john showed up precisely at 8:50 and went into a room. Ten minutes later, another john followed into a different room on the same side of the hall.

Bile built in her throat. Save for the footsteps of the johns, no sounds came from the microphones attached to the cameras. She murmured into her recorder, "No noise emitting from the rooms. Must be soundproof."

She withdrew the camera and headed down the other direction so she eavesdropped on a small lobby with two closed doors. One of the doors had a combination lock. At 9:20, another john approached. A lobby guard punched in a number. Sana wrote it down and confirmed it ten minutes later.

Suleiman's voice filled her ear. "A car is approaching."

Sana withdrew the camera so it rested just inside the vent. She grabbed her 35 millimeter camera and stole to the edge of the roof.

Suleiman's breath hissed through his lips as a male figure climbed from a CR-V. "Wes Sampson. Three, take a—"

"I'm on it." She snapped several photos as the man bodily removed a feminine figure from the passenger side.

"One, Wes Sampson has arrived with another girl," Suleiman reported. "Be careful."

Friday, April 8, 2016, 2045 hours CDT, Nashville, TN

Victor's mind raced. Plan B would take longer and might be riskier, but it was the only plan they had left without completely regrouping.

Morgan took their order, this time with Denelle closer than ever. Yeah, she wasn't going to let the girl out of her sight.

After Morgan drifted to another table, she approached them and laid a hand with elegant icy pink nails on Butch's shoulder. "And how's everyone doing?" Her voice rasped a little, as if she'd been outside smoking or had strained her voice. She smiled tightly at Butch. "You were here last night, weren't you?"

"Yes, ma'am." He flashed an easygoing smile. "With my girl, then. This is a guys' night. I've got my pals visiting for a weekend of golf."

"And you all are?"

"This is Vic." Butch nodded toward the team leader. "And Skylar."

"A pleasure to meet you, ma'am," Skylar drawled in his finest, honeyed Virginia accent. "This is a very lovely restaurant."

Her face didn't change expression, almost like she'd overdosed on Botox. "I'm glad you like it. Anything you need, let me know. I promise you Emmaline is our best." With that, she moved on down the line of customers until she was a few tables away.

"Guys, something popped up. Wes Sampson is here out back," Sana softly reported. "He's got a girl with him. Maybe the replacement for Faye."

"Roger that. Keep an eye on them." Victor went back to his observations as they shared drinks and laughed like old buddies hanging out.

The door leading to the back, which had fallen into shadow, opened. The person stayed and chatted with the bouncer guarding it before strolling into the dining room. Sampson. Crap. Victor's blood chilled. He hadn't expected the man to put in an appearance in a public place. He came toward them!

Victor's mind darted in all directions. He had to get out of there. Now. Before Sampson spotted him and raised the alarm. "Six, Seven, I need a diversion."

"One diversion, coming up." At the ladies' table, Fiona rose. She laughed and gestured toward the restrooms. Then, as if still calling to her friend, she headed to intercept Sampson. She stumbled, almost fell into him. He caught her, and all of his attention turned in her direction as he righted her. She took his arm and led him toward the bar.

Victor frowned and looked at his cell phone as if a call had come through. "Guys, I'm going to take this outside." With that, he slipped into the night air and faked taking a phone call from his wife. He stood close enough to the bouncers that they could hear his end of the conversation. A few minutes later, Fiona murmured, "One, all's clear. He headed to the back again."

Friday, April 8, 2016, 2050 hours CDT, Nashville, TN

Jaidon yawned as he gazed at the monthly reports from March. A killer one for Music Man Productions. That much he knew from his stint at the office earlier that day. And for The Music Man? Decent. At least on the legitimate side. He'd made enough to pay Denelle, the cooks, and the bartenders as well as those who'd sung for him. But on the illegit side? Stellar. Every girl's calendar filled up quickly, especially Morgan's.

He smiled as he thought about his conversation with Narat. It blew him away that the girl could potentially fetch an opening bid of eight million. Even four million would net him a wonderful mil. What would he do with it? From the last payoff four years before, he'd bought them a house on St. John for cash.

Not that Cassie had ever questioned him. She never did because the briefcase containing cash from an Exotic's auction always arrived at the club. Then, he'd parsed it out over a period of months and told her the club had done well. He'd do the same with this payout. But where would he invest the cash?

Letting himself dream a little, he accessed sites for houses in Aspen and Vail. They'd always gone skiing except for those couple of years during the Great Recession when things had been awful for everyone. He already had Elsbeth's tuition at her private high school and potential private college covered. Maybe he'd set some money aside for first class travel.

Or, maybe, just maybe, he'd donate some to Forever Free. Wouldn't that be so suitable? His lip curled. Sugar had tried to buy Morgan. No way, no how. Not when she'd net him a huge sum in a week.

Jaidon knew what F-Squared did. Sugar did the dirty work of buying girls their freedom. Then F-Squared helped rehabilitate them and reunite them with their family—or ease them back into society if a reunion wasn't possible. Or, at least to hear Cassie talk, that's what they did. He endured her work with them. At first, she said it was to be a volunteer with something other than Elsbeth's school. But now? His wife had gone nuts over F-Squared.

It wasn't like he could demand that she quit.

She'd start asking questions if he did.

Jaidon went back to checking the restaurant's financials. Then he sighed and closed the program. Nothing that wouldn't keep until Monday. Right then, all he wanted to do was introduce the Mickelsons, then head home and let Denelle manage them for the night. It was the least he could do after staying at the club until one the night before to pacify La Femme Nue's owner. At least Wes had already netted Jaidon a pretty decent replacement for the plain Faye. A blonde, one with gray eyes. Not an Exotic, but hey, he already had one of those.

He was about to shut down his computer when the door burst open.

Wes stumbled inside. He leaned against it, his eyes wide as if he'd seen a ghost.

"Wes?"

"Did I tell you about last night?"

Puzzled, Jaidon shook his head.

Wes began babbling so fast that he ordered him to slow down. Someone had paid him a visit, someone who knew Morgan. He'd been interrogated. Inwardly, Jaidon shrugged. So this man knew about the way Wes had lured her, then brought her to The Music Man. Nothing he'd said implicated him, Jaidon. And Wes would keep his mouth shut. He had more to fear than Jaidon since The Distributor knew him well.

Wes's eyes widened some more. His martini shook, and Jaidon feared he'd pass out. "He's here."

"How do you know? I thought you said you were blinded by lights the whole time."

"I caught a flash of his face. Dude, I'd recognize him anywhere."

With his hands on the arms of his desk chair, Jaidon leaned forward. "Tell me where he's sitting."

"To the right of the bar if you're facing it." Wes described his face.

"Get going. Take care of the girl. And I'll take care of him."

Doubt crossed Wes's face.

"Promise he'll not bother you again. And now I've got to get going myself."

Wes left, and Jaidon followed. He headed downstairs and, along with Denelle, greeted the Mickelsons in the green room. He led them onto the stage and introduced them. Thanks to the glare of the stage lights, he determined only shadows, not identity, of the man who had panicked Wes. He'd take care of that. Once they brother-sister duo began playing, he stepped off the stage and wandered the restaurant.

Friday, April 8, 2016, 2100 hours CDT, Nashville, TN

Victor returned to his seat and slid onto the bench beside Skylar. "Thanks for the save, Seven."

Through his earpiece, Fiona chuckled. "Think nothing of it. Though I feel like I need to wash my hands after touching Wes Sampson."

Victor studied the restaurant. "Eight, what are your thoughts?"

Skylar sipped a glass of Cabernet as he studied Morgan serving a nearby table. "Plan A's definitely out. Plan B may take a little longer, but it's our only option."

"I agree. Let's do it."

Morgan brought their supper dishes. As she placed them on the table, Skylar devoured her with his eyes. Had Victor not known the necessity of it, he would have punched his friend on the nose for looking at a sixteen-year-old like that. He glanced at Denelle. The woman stared at her girl. Was that a small smile on her face? Maybe she realized Skylar was interested. If so, all the better for the next step.

Skylar murmured, "Watch the man in action." He rose to get a drink from the bar, then strolled to the woman. Denelle said something. He laughed and touched her on the arm as if they were old friends. From the front of her dress, she produced a slip of paper and held it up. Skylar tapped something into his phone. He showed it to her, and she nodded.

With bourbon in hand, he returned to the table. "Boy, talk about feeling dirty."

"Oh?"

"I've been many things in my life, but a john going after an under-age girl is not one of them." Skylar reached into his jacket and pulled out a small case.

"You're clear," Victor murmured.

He carefully slid the thin latex onto his finger. "Fake fingerprints. Never leave home without them. And now," he manipulated his phone, "I've got an eleven o'clock with Emmaline tomorrow night. Boy, she's popular. I got the last slot." He removed the latex and slid his phone into an inner pocket of his suit jacket.

Ash moved from table to table nearby as he briefly chatted with various customers. He stopped at theirs. "Gentlemen, I take it things are good here?"

"Oh, very," Skylar replied. "Most excellent food. And entertainment. And the help. Exquisite."

Inwardly, Victor cringed. *Skylar, don't overdo it.*

Ash clapped him on the shoulder. "Good to hear."

He winced. Suddenly, the delicious steak he'd downed sat like a rock in his stomach. It would have to happen tomorrow night. They had to get Morgan out. If they failed, Jaidon and his crew might clamp down so tightly she'd be beyond their reach.

Operation Music Man

Friday, April 8, 2016, 2110 hours CDT, Nashville, TN

Uncle Vic. The man had to be him. From her place at the bar as she waited for the drinks for the trio of guys, Morgan couldn't keep her eyes off them. He was, wasn't he? Uncle Vic. The drugs kept her brain fogged just enough that she couldn't quite make the connection. Why was he here? Such a thought wearied her mind. She let it drop.

"Order up for Emmaline," the bartender said as he set the glasses of wine, beer, and gin and tonic on the blotter.

She shifted them to her tray. As she did so, she felt those eyes on her. Miss Denelle watched her oh, so closely. She approached the table again and set the drinks before the guys. Up close, she noted the man with dark eyes and hair. He had to be Uncle Vic. She doubted herself. She hadn't seen him in two years, and then, it'd been at Dad's funeral. Before that, maybe three years. The question rose in her chest. She had to ask. Had to find out.

Until she felt Miss Denelle's sharp gaze on her back.

She couldn't unless she wanted to be locked up.

Morgan moved on to other tables. She filled a couple of drinks of water. Two pretty ladies on the other side of the room tried to engage her in conversation. The drugs didn't allow for that, and she backed away before they noticed something was wrong with her. She cleared away the plates of the guys. All the while, Miss Denelle was near. Did it have to do with what happened last night?

Morgan's eyes teared. She didn't want to remember last night. Not at all. Not being treated like a piece of meat during an inspection. Or afterward when the man's visitor had come to her room. She hadn't had anything in her system then. She assumed that would have made it better. No. It'd been worse. He'd—

She stopped the thought and stuffed it down with all of the other memories. Anger. If she got angry, maybe that would help. Again, she felt Miss Denelle's eyes on her, daring her to show any kind of emotion. She wouldn't. She'd survive. Her anger withered like a vine in harsh sunlight.

Miss Denelle came to her. Over the swell of the music, she said, "Emmaline, I need the checks for those three men."

Morgan leaned against the bar as she sorted through her orders.

"Faster, young lady, you understand?"

"Yes, ma'am," she whispered. She found the three orders, ripped off the slip, and handed it to her.

"And I got you an appointment tomorrow night." Miss Denelle nodded in the direction of the trio. "You see that blond one?"

Oh, she hadn't missed the way the man had ogled her. He was cute. If she'd been older... But now he revolted her. She didn't want to imagine what he'd ask of her. "I-I do."

Miss Denelle ran their bill. "He's got an appointment with you for eleven tomorrow night. Meaning you're full, if I remember your appointment sheet correctly."

Tears clawed at her throat. The drug made it easier to suppress them. She retreated to the pass-through window for another order and delivered those. She allowed her gaze to drift to where the trio had sat. They were gone. Her one possible hope of escape was gone.

She'd just have to hold on—and wait. For what, she didn't know.

Friday, April 8, 2016, 2115 hours CDT, Nashville, TN

After his tour of the floor, Jaidon retreated to his office as he thought about the three men Wes had pointed out. They seemed like normal customers. The blond guy and his dark-haired companion sat on the bench with their backs to the wall and the bald one across from them. They seemed a hundred percent involved with their meal and conversation.

Had Wes imagined the whole thing?

Probably not because The Agent wasn't prone to panic.

Jaidon opened the program for his surveillance cameras and pulled up one for that part of the restaurant. He zoomed in as best he could. Good. A clear shot of the man with dark hair. Wes hadn't been totally accurate with his description, but he'd been close enough for Jaidon to worry. He noted the bald one. He'd been there the night before with a woman.

With a sigh, he scrubbed his hands through his hair. "Why now?" They were so close!

He grabbed his phone and texted his head bouncer. I need you upstairs. Now.

That would bring the bouncer who controlled the kitchen and supervised the other guys.

A moment later, a beefy guy with a buzz cut of dark hair joined him. "What's up?"

"We have an issue." Jaidon printed a screenshot of the dark-haired man and handed it over. "We think this guy has less than honorable intentions, like he's here trying to steal the Exotic."

"This guy?" The bouncer studied the picture. "What did he do?"

"Rough up The Agent. I want him taken care of."

The man raised an eyebrow. "How far?"

"All the way." It had to be done. "Follow him to wherever he's staying. Then take him out and whoever is with him."

"Will do." With that, the bouncer left to carry out his orders.

Now, Jaidon shut down his computer. With a sigh, he stuffed his wallet into his pants pocket and snagged his phone off the desk before shutting off the lights. He slipped down the steps, then outside via the green room. As he slid behind the wheel of his Beemer, he raised his phone to his ear.

Cassie answered.

The tension melted away, and he smiled. "Babe, I'm on my way home. Fire up some popcorn. Let's watch a movie together."

15

Friday, April 8, 2016, 2230 hours CDT, Nashville, TN

"I'm struggling," Victor said as he slumped on the couch of his suite and pressed his phone to his ear.

On the other end, Deborah, his wife, remained silent for a few moments. Most likely, she thought through everything he'd told her, especially earlier in the week. His close friendship with Gary. The betrayal. The way Victor thought he'd dealt with it. Until Mary Walton called him, desperate for him to find Morgan.

"It's not that I didn't want to take the case," he continued.

"But you didn't realize it'd reopen old wounds."

He remembered Gary's announcement so many years before. "Yeah. I mean, Morgan's my goddaughter. When she was born, Gary asked me if Olivia and I would be their guardians if something happened. Not their parents but us."

"Are you still their guardian?"

He rose and paced. "To my knowledge, that never changed except for when Gary removed Liv's name after we divorced. Until I moved to Raleigh in 2009, I was like an extension of the Walton clan. Morgan called me Uncle Vic. I love her like my own daughter." The lump rising in his throat stunned him. "I thought I'd come to grips with what Gary did to me. Truly, I had. But I'm struggling to move past it."

"Gary and Mary trusted you enough to make you guardian if something ever happened." Again, a little more silence as if Deborah pondered her next words. "To me, that means Gary admired and respected you, even if at the end it didn't seem that way. More than that, he trusted you to take care of his children if he and Mary passed at the same time. Despite everything that happened almost two years ago, that trust never wavered."

Victor collapsed onto the couch. He pinched the bridge of his nose to keep the emotion from choking off his voice. His breath came out ragged. "Maybe that's why I'm struggling."

"And it gave me another thought."

"Which is?"

"When Morgan gets out of this, why don't we ask for guardianship of her?"

Stunned, Victor remained silent.

"I'm sorry. Maybe this isn't the—"

"No, no." A smile broke through his somberness. "I actually... like the idea. But you know the courts would want reunification if at all possible."

"I was just thinking that if things are as bad as you say they are between her and her mother, it might be counterproductive, especially after what she's experienced, for her to return home. She'd be ripe for running away again and winding up right where she is again or worse."

Victor shuddered at the "worse" scenario. Hope blossomed anew. "It might work. I just don't know the legal side of it."

"Let me figure that out. You said Clay Hall works with Forever Free?"

"He does."

"Maybe he could give me the name of one of their attorneys." Deborah took a breath. This time when she spoke, he could hear the smile in her voice. "Speaking of legal things, I got a letter today from the courts. Your date to adopt the kids is June 10, right before Sana and Suleiman's wedding."

Joy exploded across Victor's spirit. "Praise God!"

"Absolutely. And Vic," her voice softened, "let's pray about asking for guardianship of Morgan. I... I don't want to run out ahead of God."

"Agreed." A sudden lump of emotion choked him. "And we need to do our homework at the same time."

"Give me Clay's number, and I'll start researching on Monday."

"Will do." Victor muffled his yawn. "Sorry. It's late here. I'll call you tomorrow. I love you."

"Love you too."

After texting her Clay Hall's number, Victor sat there for a moment and tapped his phone on his hand. What Deborah had proposed was a wild shot. But one that just might work. And her wise words about his struggles with Gary's betrayal? He realized how true they were. Gary had always trusted Victor, even though they'd literally come to blows two years before. Morgan was like Victor's daughter. And fathers protected their daughters. Gary couldn't do that from the grave. But Victor could. He would. He'd find Morgan, protect her at all costs. In the meantime, he knew what he needed to do. Rising, he muttered, "Leave this where it belongs, Chavez, which is in the past. And get some sleep. Now."

He picked up his Bible from the couch's side table. It was always the last thing he read before closing his eyes, a habit he'd developed nearly two years before when he'd started walking with the Lord.

No reading glasses. Since the year before, the print had gotten too blurry without them in some lighting situations, and he'd found himself coming down with headaches. Curse that male pride of his. He'd finally caved and visited his optometrist a month ago.

With a little smirk on her face, the doctor told him the news he hadn't wanted to hear. "You need reading glasses."

Then came the hard part. Keeping up with them. Deborah simply laughed and told him to go to the drugstore and get several pairs to keep around the house. Maybe he would after he got back. Now, he realized where his lone pair resided. In the cup holder of the rental Camry he'd been driving. He'd placed them there when checking his phone at a traffic light on the way home after supper.

Grumbling, he shoved his feet into a pair of moccasins, then slid his key card into the pocket of his sweats and snagged his fob off the worktable. He headed down five floors and into the evening air. Thanks to the crowded conditions at the hotel, he'd parked on the end in a dark section of the lot between a Ford F-250 and a minivan.

The locks clicked. He leaned in to retrieve the glasses.

Footsteps approached.

He withdrew as two shadows blocked either end of the narrow space where he stood. One brandished a baseball bat.

Victor leaped onto the hood of the Camry and slid across. His feet hit pavement.

His assailant tackled him, feeling like a boulder had landed on him.

Victor jabbed him hard with his elbow.

The man groaned and fell away.

Victor rolled to his knees and staggered upright into the grill of the pickup. The bat flashed toward him.

He jerked to the side.

The blow, meant to break ribs, knocked the wind from him. He ducked again, and metal crumpled as the bat slammed into the pickup's hood.

He turned to dart toward the safety of the hotel.

Someone swept his feet from under him.

Victor wheezed as he collapsed to the pavement. His head bounced on the hard surface. Stars exploded before him.

He rolled over just in time to see his attacker raise the bat like a club.

This was it.

He braced himself for the killing blow.

A man shrieked.

Unable to move, Victor groaned as his side began throbbing.

Something pinged off another car.

Running feet told him his assailants fled.

"I missed. Vic!"

"S-Sana?" His brain had a hard time connecting the name to his mouth. He rolled onto all fours and tried to rise.

The world tilted. He collapsed to the pavement.

"You are safe." Suleiman. When had they shown up?

Victor drifted in and out of consciousness.

More running footsteps, this time toward him. Someone turned him onto his back. "Vic, don't you pass out on me." Diana. She lightly slapped his cheeks and shook him.

Victor tried to push himself onto his elbows. "I-I'm..."

He sank into blackness.

"Vic." Pain on his cheek roused him. Her blurry face above. It sharpened. Behind her, both Suleiman and Skylar stood guard, their pistols out and raised.

On his other side, Butch leaned over him. "You got ambushed, boss. They got you pretty good. You think you can stand?"

"I... I need to stand."

"In a moment."

"Seriously, I'm fine." Yeah, right. About as fine as someone who'd gotten hit by a train.

"Bull." A light flared in his eyes as Diana checked his pupils. "You were in and out of consciousness. You need to go to the hos—"

"I'm fine. Let me stand."

Diana and Butch grasped him by the elbows.

Somehow, he made it to his feet and wavered.

Diana put her hands on her hips. "So like it or not, you're going to the ER. And Butch."

"Yes, ma'am."

"I think our location's been compromised." Her gaze swept the parking lot. "Sana, Suleiman, what'd you see?"

"Four men in ambush. I don't think this was a random hit." Sana patted a pouch around her waist. "Those goons had better be glad I didn't have my knives on me."

Butch fixed his gazed on Victor. "I agree with Diana, I think we need a new base of operations. You got Clay Hall's number on you?"

Suddenly, Victor's legs began shaking. "You're... you're right. I'll..."

He faded into blackness.

Friday, April 8, 2016, 2330 hours CDT, Nashville, TN

The movie's final credits rolled across the screen. From where he sat at home on the couch with his feet propped on the coffee table and arm around his wife, Jaidon observed Elsbeth. His daughter curled up on the chair perpendicular to them. She remained still, but those green eyes, so like his, sparkled. Most likely, another idea for a story percolated in her mind.

Cassie reached out with her socked foot and nudged her. "What's going on in that little head of yours?"

Elsbeth blinked. She straightened. "Do y'all mind if I head upstairs? I want to write for a little bit before I go to bed."

Jaidon glanced at the clock on the mantel above the fireplace. Eleven thirty. "Of course not. It's not like it's early."

His daughter rose and kissed both of them goodnight. Her footsteps pounded on the stairs as she scurried upward to her wing of the house.

"I have no idea where that girl gets her imagination," Cassie murmured with a shake of her head. "We're going to have to make sure she cuts her light out tonight."

"Nah. Let her write. Sometimes people work best at night." Jaidon inhaled the perfume Cassie must have put on earlier that evening before he'd arrived home. He wound some of her blonde hair around his fingers, which exposed the tender flesh of her neck just below her ear. He kissed her earlobe. "Want to adjourn upstairs?"

She stilled. "Absolutely."

He swung by the kitchen and grabbed a bottle of wine, two glasses, and a corkscrew. He followed her up the steps and through the double doors of their suite.

Low light filled the room. Cassie had already turned back the satin sheets. The evening breeze whispered through the screens of the open windows, bringing with it heady scents of flowers already blooming. Outside, the faint azure light of the pool cast a glow into their room. Low music played, a sexy number he remembered from their dating days. She began dancing.

Oh, my...

Jaidon opened the bottle and poured them both glasses.

She sipped hers as her eyes beguiled him.

He faced her and ran his hands down her arms.

Her eyes glossed. She squeezed his forearm, then ran her fingers down her neck to the collar of her button-down shirt.

He pulled her close as he began kissing her in earnest.

His phone, which he'd tossed on his dresser, vibrated. A familiar number flashed up.

Dang it! He stiffened. *No, I don't want to answer it.* He shoved it out of his mind.

Until it did the same thing.

"Jaidon," Cassie whispered in a breathy voice.

He released her. "I've got to take this."

She put her hands on her hips. "Really? Is it work?"

"Something urgent. But stay right there." His smile felt brittle, fake. "I'll be back."

Once downstairs behind the closed doors of his study, he dialed the number. "Is it done?"

"Someone rescued him," his chief bouncer said. His breath hissed inward. "They... dang. One of them had a shuriken. Got me good in the shoulder."

"A shuriken?"

"As in a throwing star. It went deep, man. I'm still bleeding."

"So he's still alive."

"Yeah. I'm sorry. Truly. I am. But that girl..." He could almost see his bouncer shaking his head. "She may be tiny, but boy, she kicked our butts. Would have taken all of us down with those dang stars except we knew when to call it quits. We got out of there."

It figured. Wes's unnamed assailant remained alive. Jaidon ran a hand down his face as he considered the implications. Just when he'd thought he had things in hand, they spun out of control. Was this person a threat? Oh, yeah. Whoever this man was, he was now on alert. Maybe the bouncers' attack would send him running home with his tail between his legs.

No. He'd keep coming after Morgan.

Jaidon squared his shoulders. He inhaled through his nose, then exhaled through his mouth. His pulse settled. If this man did, he'd find himself in the Cumberland River. No qualms. No doubts.

"Jaidon?" his bouncer asked.

"Oh, sorry. I zoned out. Don't worry about it."

"You're sure? I can send someone back there to keep an eye on things. We can get them in the a.m."

"Yeah, do that. Go home and get cleaned up, okay?"

"If you say so."

"I do." With that, Jaidon tossed his phone onto his desk and rubbed his chin as he paced the large room. He paused and gazed out the window at the backyard pool, remodeled with funds from starting the brothel. Elsbeth would play there this summer with her friends, just like she had the previous few summers. Except her swimwear had graduated from a one-piece to a bikini. He thought about the private school she attended. Great student-teacher ratio. She did well, had been on the honor roll for the past several years. Most likely, she'd head to college at a school like Duke or Harvard. He liked to brag on her, the apple of his eye, his pride and joy, and whatever other cliché would describe a father's love for his daughter.

Could tonight's incident bring the whole thing crashing down? No. Morgan had finished waiting tables. Denelle made sure she was secure in her room and lightly drugged, per his direction. She'd stay that way all the next day. Tomorrow night, she'd see her last round of johns and net the club another twenty-five hundred. Then Narat would take her to Texas to get her prepared for the auction. Jaidon would be fine. Then more than fine after next weekend.

This time, as he headed upstairs, he left his phone in the study, but the ambush remained in his mind. This man, whoever he was, remained a threat, and he doubted he, that lady friend of his, and any of his other pals would remain where they'd been staying. Jaidon would need to be on high alert.

He paused outside the door. Low music continued playing in the suite. His mouth went dry when he noted Cassie once more dancing, this time in a negligee. He forced the incident from his mind.

Instead, he had eyes only for his wife. He drew her close. As he crushed her to him, he pushed that niggling worry to the back of his mind. He'd be okay. And then in a week, he'd be at least a million dollars richer than he'd ever anticipated in his life.

16

Saturday, April 9, 2016, 1400 hours CDT, Nashville, TN

Sana lay on the roof of the warehouse that neighbored the eastern side of The Music Man. Across the alley and one story below her at the restaurant were a row of windows that looked like slits. Was that the only way the girls saw daylight? Was anyone there at the moment? She couldn't be sure since the bright sun masked any movement from within.

The night before, they'd checked out of their hotel and found shelter at a guest house on Clay Hall's sprawling estate outside Franklin, which lay southwest of Nashville. Victor had sustained a mild concussion and one nasty bruise on his side that made him wince when he moved. The doctor's orders had been clear. Minimal stimulation. Meaning, he was down for the count for tonight's operation. At least they were almost ready. Sana needed one more data point, which she now gathered.

She returned her attention to the task at hand, photos of the large window the architectural drawings showed overlooked a stairwell. It led to the lobby on the second floor and a room on the first where entertainers waited before singing. She raised the 35-millimeter camera she'd brought and took aim.

The shutter whirred. She checked the photos. All showed what she needed. Time to return to the estate and grab a nap before she and Suleiman headed out to set up.

Sana slid away from the edge of the roof. Once safely out of sight of anyone on the second floor of The Music Man, she stashed her camera in her backpack and crept to the ladder on the far side. Back on terra firma, she strolled to the mouth of the alley. She turned left, which would lead her past The Music Man and toward her car.

Maybe she'd swing by a coffee shop on the way home. She'd seen an independent one near where she parked the Camry she'd borrowed from Victor. As she walked those blocks, she dialed his number. At his answer, she smiled. "Vic, hey. How are you doing?"

"Oh, hurting like nobody's business." He grunted as if he shifted position. "I feel like I got hit by a bus."

"I'm sorry."

"Did you get what you needed?"

"I think so. It looks like the latch in the window is hand-operated and doesn't require a key. I'll study the pics when I get back. Is there anything else anyone needs?"

"I don't think so... Yeah, I just talked to Butch. He says we're good."

"And we're sure the mark will be working the rooms tonight?" Sana asked. Her gaze flicked upward. One coffee shop, coming up.

"Yep. Shelly reviewed the video several times. The girls who are in the odd-numbered rooms are working the johns tonight. And since Emmaline equates to Room Five, that means her."

A smile curled Sana's lips. Oh, she couldn't wait to get Morgan out. "Then we're on go for tonight. They're not going to know what hit them."

"They won't. When will you be back?"

Sana slowed. Did she hear scuffling behind her? She whipped around. Nothing. She took a deep breath. "Hopefully in forty-five minutes. I'm going to get some tea first."

"See you then."

Sana slid her phone into the back pocket of her jeans. As she did so, she gazed around her as uneasiness quivered up her spine. No one near. She'd imagined she'd heard someone following her.

Operation Music Man

Saturday, April 9, 2016, 1430 hours CDT, Nashville, TN

"Dude, you done good," Narat Jain drawled in his native Texan accent as he and Wes strolled The Music Man from the back to the front. At that moment, none of the girls roamed the interior of the restaurant. In the back, the head chef hollered at someone. Pans clanged. In the corner, a bartender placed wineglasses in their racks. The Music Man geared up for another night. Most likely, Denelle Brooks had begun drugging the girls who would work as tonight's waitresses.

Man, what a cold woman. Narat shivered just thinking about her. Yeah, she got the job done, but boy, she creeped him out. Why, he didn't know.

"Hey, you want to hit some clubs tonight?" Wes asked as they reached the front door.

Narat pushed through it. "Yeah, that could work. Maybe..."

The words died on his lips as a petite Indian woman with chin-length black hair strolled past him.

Was that... No. Sana was in Arizona.

Wasn't she?

"You okay?" Wes asked.

"Yeah." Narat's pulse skittered upward. "Let me call you later, okay?"

"Uh, sure. See ya then." Wes turned right and headed toward his car.

Narat hurried to catch up to the woman. He'd call to her. And if he was wrong? He'd say she reminded him of one of the women he admired most.

His quarry raised a phone to her ear.

He drew closer and caught her end of the conversation.

"Vic, hey. How are you doing?"

Narat paused. He knew of only one Vic in Sana's life, the man who'd originally been her boss in Arizona. Now moving quietly like a jaguar, he kept pace with her.

"I'm sorry... I think so. It looks like the latch in the window is hand-operated and doesn't require a key. I'll study the pics when I get back. Is there anything else anyone needs?"

Confusion washed over Narat. Why was Sana in Nashville, more specifically, near The Music Man?

She slowed at a coffee shop. "And we're sure the mark will be working the rooms tonight?"

Narat's blood chilled. Something was definitely up. He knew she sometimes did contract work for Victor Chavez. Was that why she was there? Her terminology indicated that she knew darned well what went on in the upstairs hallway of The Music Man. Her knowledge wasn't what he wanted to learn at that point.

"Then we're on go for tonight. They're not going to know what hit them."

Narat ducked around the corner of a Ford Transit van. His heart hammered in his ears as he listened to his sister's sharp intake of breath. Then she said, "Hopefully in forty-five minutes. I'm going to get some tea first."

He remained stock still. His mind whirled with all he'd overheard. Sana was in Nashville at the very place where Ash held Morgan Walton. She'd been gathering information about a window with a latch that was hand-operated. Huh? That didn't make any sense. What did she knew about girls working the rooms at The Music Man? More than that, something was going to happen. Tonight. From her smug tone, he imagined it would be more than just her.

His mind roamed back to when he'd visited Arizona the summer before, shortly after she'd had surgery on her shoulder. Good times. He'd met her friends, a strange community.

Victor Chavez had radiated intelligence and leadership. Suleiman, of course, was Sana's new love, and he and Narat hit it off well. Butch Addison was a nice guy, but something told Narat not to mess with him. Shelly Wise, Sana's best friend, was all geek. The rest of the crew were friendly. They were a close team, a unit of sorts. Had they worked together during that year or so in 2013 and 2014 when Sana had practically vanished from her brother's life? Could it be that this same unit meant to thwart Ash's plans?

Narat couldn't let that happen.

"Hey, you wanna move or something?"

He jumped and whirled.

A deliveryman with a dolly full of boxes stood there.

"Oh, uh, sorry." Narat scurried further down the street toward his car. Only when he slid behind the wheel did he dial his friend's number. "Wes, hey."

"What's up? You know where you want to go tonight?"

He ignored his question. "We've got problems."

"Huh? What?"

"We need to go and see Ash."

"But I'm on my way to—"

"Now, Wes."

His friend blew out a sigh. "Okay. Fine. Meet me at my house, and we'll go from there."

Narat dropped his phone onto the passenger seat and cranked the engine. With any luck, they'd get this sorted out and be prepared for any kind of ambush Victor Chavez would throw their way.

17

Saturday, April 9, 2016, 1600 hours CDT, Nashville, TN

"You got it! Watch out! Here it comes!" Jaidon called as Elsbeth in her position as goalie braced for the charge of the opposing team's strikers. One of them lined up for a shot. The ball flew toward her. Elsbeth caught it and rolled on the ground. She hurled it toward a team member, who passed it downfield.

"Good job!" Cassie called. She clapped and cheered as Elsbeth kept an eye on the action.

As play continued, Jaidon shaded his eyes from the bright sunlight. His phone vibrated on his hip. He glanced at it. A text from Narat. Huh? He wasn't supposed to show up until tomorrow morning. That much Jaidon had made clear when he left the restaurant earlier that day. He pulled it up.

We need to meet. Now. We're at the soccer field. Meet at the bridge on the river.

Who was we?

Jaidon's eyes narrowed. He kissed Cassie on the cheek. "It's hot out. You want me to get you a drink?"

"Sure." She smiled, then turned to talk to some of their friends.

Heading along the walking path that spread throughout the park, he came to a bridge leading over the Harpeth River. Narat leaned against the railing and gazed at the water. Wes paced with his hands shoved into the pockets of his khakis.

Jaidon didn't slow. "Let's walk."

As the trio meandered along one of the paths, Jaidon glanced around. No one paid them any attention. "What's going on?"

Wes hunched. "Bad stuff."

Narat shot him a look. "I noticed someone lurking near The Music Man earlier this afternoon."

Jaidon scrubbed his hands through his hair. "Who?"

"My sister."

His thoughts froze. "I'm not sure I follow."

Narat's gaze darted around. "I want to talk about this somewhere else."

Jaidon stopped. "I'm here with my wife and daughter."

Narat shrugged. "So tell them you had something come up and that a couple of coworkers will take you to the office, then home."

"She'll ask—"

"Then lie," Narat replied. "It's not like you haven't already done so for years."

The nerve of him! He glared at The Distributor's son. But yeah, Narat was right. If he told the truth, told Cassie where the money for the reno of the pool and the house on St. John had come from, she'd leave him, maybe even kill him herself since she came from a rough background. "All right, then. Meet me at the main entrance in five."

With that, he got two drinks and took one to his wife. "Cassie," he murmured just above the noise of the game.

She raised an eyebrow. "What's up?"

"Something came up at work." He didn't specify the club or the company.

She ran her hands down her blonde ponytail. "Oh?"

"Yeah. Two buds came to get me. That's how urgent it is. You mind if I head out to take care of it? I'll have them drop me off at the house." That way, she wouldn't come to the restaurant.

"Will you be home in time for supper?"

"Should be." As he learned forward and kissed her, he earnestly hoped so.

A half hour later, Jaidon realized that might not be the case. He rested his elbows on the arms of his leather chair at his office in The Music Man. His stomach clenched as he listened to Narat summarize what he'd overheard from his sister. He sipped his drink. "If they succeed, we're toast. Understand?"

Narat, who sat in one of his visitor chairs, nodded. "We're not going to lose the Exotic."

Jaidon twirled a pen in his fingers. "Agreed, we're not. Who does your sister work for?"

"A company called Sentry Securities."

Jaidon leaned forward and typed the name into Google. The company website flashed up. Victor Chavez was the owner, and his picture on the website confirmed he was the man who'd visited the restaurant the night before. "Is he a one-man show?"

"Oh, no. He has others who work as contractors for him when needed. Sana's engaged to one of them, a guy named Suleiman al-Ibrahim. Her wedding's in June. Did you google Victor?"

"Of course. He's listed as the sole owner of Sentry Securities. He's former Secret Service, former bodyguard to the stars." He sneered at that.

"Google him and *SAS Peacemaker* together."

As he sipped his soda, Jaidon did. A cuss word flew from his mouth as he read a couple of articles related to the *Peacemaker* incident the year before. His breath stuttered, and his gut tightened when he realized the skill of his foe. The man was formidable, had thrown together a plan that had rescued a billionaire's daughter from certain slavery. "Was Sana involved?"

"Most certainly." The younger man shifted. "I've been out there. I've seen people she called her friends who were most likely on the team. It's the real deal, Jaidon, not someone playacting. These guys function like a true special operations team."

A shiver worked his way up his spine. "Oh, I don't doubt it. But let me tell you something. They're not going to stop us from getting the

Exotic out of here. And they're not going to bring me down." He pointed his straw at The Distributor's son. "You understand?"

Narat nodded, as did Wes.

"Good. Tell me about your sister."

Narat shifted. "She's skilled in ninjitsu. A black belt. She also spent time in prison."

"For what?"

"She was known as the Ninja Cat Burglar in Texas way back, about seven or eight years ago. She got arrested, pled down, and spent almost two years in Gatesville."

Jaidon started chuckling. "I can't imagine what your dad did."

"Disowned her." He twisted his fingers on his lap. "I'm the only contact she's had with our family since she got out of prison. We're close."

Jaidon shoved that remark aside. "How did she wind up in Arizona?"

Narat shrugged. "She told me she'd gone to work for the government. At least until summer of 2014."

Jaidon steepled his fingers as he thought about what he'd learned. He opened the video from last night and zoomed in on the trio of men who'd come into his restaurant. There. He spotted Victor Chavez. And the big, bald guy who'd come in with a petite Indian chick the night before. He opened another file, this one from Thursday night, and scrolled through it until he found what he was looking for. He turned the monitor. "This your sister?"

Narat nodded.

"You recognize the guy beside her?"

"I saw him when I visited her. He's a nice guy."

"I don't care if he kisses babies and hugs puppies. He's a danger if he's associated with her and Chavez. What's his name?"

"I don't remember."

"I can find out." Jaidon pulled up the reservations system. He found Thursday night. "Ah. Butch Addison." He focused on the blond guy who'd visited with Denelle last night. One look at the brothel's app told him what he needed to know. "Skylar James has an eleven o'clock with Emmaline. Interesting."

Wes shifted. "What do we do? I mean we don't know where—"

"Let me think about this some." He picked up his pen and twirled it in his fingers again as he considered his options. Chavez was shrewd. No biggie. So was he. A smile played about his lips. "I have an idea. Here's what I propose."

With growing confidence, he laid out his plan.

Narat nodded. "It'll work. It's got to work."

Jaidon's stopped twirling his pen. "Exactly. It doesn't? More than The Music Man will be coming down."

Oh, yeah, his marriage would collapse. As would the entire network of The Distributor. And he, Jaidon Ash, was not going to be responsible for that. He turned to Wes. "When Narat leaves tonight with his sister and Morgan, you go with him. It's probably time you took a vacation, right? And Narat, you be here at eight. Got it? Mr. James will get the surprise of his life. And so will Sana and her pals."

Narat gave him a ride home. While they'd been inside, high clouds had overtaken the sun. A chilly wind sprang up, signaling the growing chance for storms that night.

Throughout supper, a grill-out affair with Cassie, Elsbeth, and her best friend, his mind churned through his plan. He tried to hide it from his wife and daughter, but when he accidentally called Elsbeth's friend Morgan instead of Moira, Cassie pulled him aside and asked, "Morgan. Who's she?"

"A singer we're trying to land for a tour," Jaidon lied. "She's wanting a lower fee than what we charge and said she'd rip up the contract if we didn't work it out today."

Just then, Elsbeth asked her mom a question.

The incident dropped, and Jaidon let it be. His mind swung back to the plan. It would work. And when it did, Morgan would be well on her way to Texas and the auction that would follow. Meaning, he'd be all the more rich by the next weekend.

18

Saturday, April 9, 2016, 1930 hours CDT, Nashville, TN

Numbness. The nights she worked the johns, Morgan shoved her emotions deep down into a dark corner of her soul. It was the only way to survive. Now, she huddled in the room with its warm glow and soft-colored walls that normally would have relaxed her. If she got out of there, she'd never, ever paint her walls a pale lavender. Ever.

She sat on the bench at the foot of her bed as Indra applied her makeup. Something teased at the edge of her mind, something the young woman had told her Thursday night. "I'm an image-bearer of God."

Indra paused.

Had she said that out loud?

"What's that?" Her friend brushed some rouge onto Morgan's cheeks.

"You said your mom told you we're God's image-bearers."

Indra sighed and lowered the brush. She stared at her hands. Her words held tears. "I've lost hope."

"We can't, Indra."

When her friend raised her gaze, her eyes were wet. "I wish." Then she seemed to shake herself. "Let me get you finished so you can do me."

She finished her work in silence, and Morgan returned the favor. The two girls hugged, and Morgan whispered, "We have each other. And we're God's image-bearers."

Maybe if she repeated it enough times, she'd believe it.

She curled up on her bed with her arms around her knees. She yearned for Monday when no johns would bother her. How would these men be tonight? Demanding? Gentle? Some had been embarrassed to be there, as if they knew they were doing wrong. She'd wanted to shout at them that they were, that they were breaking their vows to their wives. The drugs kept her thoughts from reaching her mouth. Others didn't care and were sometimes cruel. They were fulfilling their lusts and maybe even their fantasies as they took bits of her soul when they left.

As eight approached, she eased onto the bench in front of her bed. She knew the routine. Greet them. Tell them she was Emmaline, here to serve them however they wanted, rather than Morgan, scared sixteen-year-old who'd been brought here against her will. Things would then progress—as her thoughts digressed—from there until they left forty-five minutes later. Then she'd run into the shower as if the water would remove everything they'd done to her.

Hateful.

The knob turned on her door.

She glanced at the clock on her dresser. Eight o'clock. Time for her first client. Her lights dimmed as they always did.

Slowly, she turned her head as it opened.

The owner stood there, his shoulders back, his chin held high with a satisfied smile on his face. Was he going to take a bit of her as well? "Morgan, come with me."

She tried to process his request through the haze of the drugs. "I-I don't... understand."

He leaned his hip against the doorway and tucked his hands in his armpits so only his thumbs were visible. "You're not going to work tonight. Instead, you're going to stay with me in my office."

Why? His request was strange. She stilled. "I..."

He grabbed her arm and jerked her to her feet. "Now."

Morgan stumbled along beside him as he pushed through a door and into the small lobby she remembered from a few nights before. The bouncer standing guard only raised an eyebrow. The owner shoved her into his office.

When the door shut behind her, she froze, unable to move at all, as she stared at Jaidon's visitor who'd inspected her like a piece of meat two nights before.

A slight smile flitted across his face and vanished.

The owner shoved her to the man, who pushed her to the floor so she sat with her knees to her chest behind the door.

The owner rummaged around in his desk as he said, "I want you to be quiet now."

She remained where she was. "I... will be."

"I can't bank on that." He loomed over her with a needle and syringe. "So I'm going to ensure you will."

She stared at him as he uncapped the needle. A tear trickled down her cheek. "Please... I'll... be... good. Promise. No more—"

"Sorry." He shoved up the sleeve of her robe and tied some rubber tubing above her elbow. "I need to make sure. And when you wake up, I promise we'll take good care of you."

She doubted that. She winced as he injected the sedative. She began repeating in her head what she'd said earlier to Indra. *I'm an image-bearer of God. I'm an image-bearer of God.* Her world began tipping. Whatever he'd given her was far stronger than anything she'd experienced before. *I'm an image-bearer...* She relaxed into darkness.

Saturday, April 9, 2016, 2200 hours CDT, Nashville, TN

Sana and Suleiman crept past the warehouse on the eastern side of The Music Man. They stopped, and she peered around the corner. Uh-oh. A bouncer leaned against the back door leading to the kitchen, He brought a cigarette to his lips. A smoke break or a guard? She didn't know, but it meant one thing. They'd have to find another way in. No worries. They'd planned for this. They withdrew and scurried to the far side of the warehouse. "Guard at the back door. Taking alternate entrance."

"Be careful, Three," Victor cautioned over her earpiece from where he and Shelly manned the computers at Chad Hall's guest house in Franklin.

He didn't have to remind her. If she messed up in the crossing between the two buildings, she'd wind up as a wet spot on the pavement below. She wiped her hands on the legs of her jumpsuit, then scaled the warehouse ladder. Suleiman followed, and they headed to the opposite side.

Soft light emanated from the slit windows on the second floor of the Music Man. Shadows moved, but she discerned nothing else. The chasm looming before her was twelve feet wide, enough for a delivery truck. She lifted her chin, straightened her shoulders, and thrust out her chest. She ran hard toward the parapet.

She sailed across, hit the opposite parapet, and rolled to dissipate her energy. She came to her feet with her tranquilizer gun out ready to fire if anyone got suspicious. Five minutes passed. Nothing.

Suleiman tossed her pack to her, then his own pack holding his two rifles. He joined her a moment later. He murmured, "Get set up while I do the same."

No worries there. Sana pulled out the spool holding her camera. As she began threading it through the intake vent and into the hall, something niggled at her, like a faint itch she wasn't sure was there. No one had come to check when they'd landed. And nothing from Butch and Skylar, who'd headed to The Music Man an hour earlier for Skylar's appointment with Emmaline.

A raindrop hit her on the cheek, followed by a cold gust of wind. Over the western horizon, lightning flickered low and threatening. Storms were rolling in. She shivered.

Suleiman crept to her side. He took her arm and pressed his lips to her ear. "Sana? What is wrong?"

She bit the inside of her cheek and tried a smile that quickly faded. "Let me get this threaded. Four, tell me when to stop."

Shelly replied, "You're good. Keep going. Okay. Stop. I've got the girls' hall—all of it—on my screen. No one seems the wiser."

"Three, looks good," Victor said. "Five, sitrep. Is Ash here?"

"Negative, at least down on the main floor," Butch replied. "Denelle introduced the latest set."

"Roger that. Be careful because he could be upstairs."

Sana secured a length of rope around a pipe sticking out of the roof. She slid into a climbing harness and attached herself to the rope. Oh, so carefully, she walked down the side of the wall and paused. Below, nothing moved.

On the sidewalk to her right, people strolled by without any clue of what transpired in the alley. Sana pulled out a set of glass cutters. She secured the suction cup to the window just above the lock and ran the cutters in a circle. Carefully, she removed the glass circle and undid the lock. Within seconds, she had the sash up.

She glanced upward.

A flash of lightning silhouetted Suleiman's head.

She gave him a thumbs up, then slipped inside.

Her fiancé's words sealed her fate. "Removing rope."

Sana crept up a flight of stairs and paused at the fire door. Just on the other side of the slit of glass, a bouncer stood next to the door leading to the girls' hallway. He had a pistol at his waist and a watchful gaze.

Sana's hands tightened into fists. She forced them to relax, then once more rubbed them on her quads. She glanced at her watch. 2245 hours. The next john, who'd be seeing another girl, would arrive in five minutes. Then she'd act.

2250 hours. A man came up the stairs from the restaurant. This one looked like some sort of businessman or politician in his khakis, blazer, and shirt undone at the collar.

The bouncer keyed in the combination and opened the door for the john, who stepped through.

She shifted and drew her tranquilizer gun.

She pressed the crash bar and pushed open the fire door.

The bouncer turned.

The gun clicked, and a dart embedded itself in the man's arm. He slapped at it, then began slumping toward the ground.

Sana rushed forward as the wall of human flesh plummeted toward her. She caught him, then staggered and sank to her knees before lowering him to the floor. Her gaze flew to the door to Ash's office. No light emanated from underneath. Good. He must have been out like Butch had surmised.

"Eight, guard neutralized. No one's in the office," Sana whispered into the boom mic hanging in front of her lips.

Down below, a door closed.

"Eight in," Skylar murmured.

Sana reloaded and raised her tranq gun until she got a visual on him. She reached into her pack and pulled out a silenced Beretta. And a knife. Best to have him armed to the hilt when facing a goon at the end of the hallway.

He winked at her as if to say, "Got this one."

She nodded and punched the combination. The lock clicked. She let the door shut behind him. *Lord, let this work. Let him get Morgan out.* She'd stay put until he gave the all clear, then head out the back door with him.

"Eight here. We've got a problem," Skylar murmured.

"What happened?" Victor asked.

"Morgan's not here."

Sana stilled. This couldn't be.

Victor drew in a sharp breath. "Come again?"

"She's not here. And man, talk about soundproof rooms."

Victor clipped his words. "Eight, get out. We've been blown. E&E. Now."

No! Sana's mouth went dry as her heart raced. They had to find Morgan.

She turned and faced the door through which he'd gone. She'd back up Skylar, then—

Pain exploded in her head. She crumpled to the ground. *Move! Attack! Go!* Her arms and legs refused to budge.

Someone ripped away her shemagh and headset.

They dragged her into another room.

She blacked out.

Operation Music Man

Saturday, April 9, 2016, 2310 hours CDT, Nashville, TN

Trouble. Skylar James knew it when he saw it, and a neatly made bed with no Morgan Walton defined it tonight. He heard nothing from the hall, which didn't bode well either. "Morgan's not here. And man, talk about soundproof rooms."

Victor's reply chilled him. "Eight, get out. We've been blown. E&E. Now."

"Eight, a bouncer's headed your way," Shelly warned. "They're on to you."

Adrenaline exploded inside him. He drew his silenced Beretta as he took a deep breath and released it. His heart rate slowed. He popped into the hall.

The bouncer at the end toward Ash's office raised his gun.

Skylar fired.

The man collapsed.

He dropped the bouncer at the far end with another shot, then raced toward the door leading to the fire escape.

Where was Sana? "Three, you heard One. Get out of there."

No sound.

"Three?"

Someone else burst into the hallway. Skylar took him down. He backed toward the door.

"Five here." Butch's breath huffed into his ear. "Compromised. Getting out through the back. Now."

A bullet whistled past Skylar's ear and punctured the glass on the upper half of the door. He ducked through. "Two, cover me."

"On it," Suleiman replied. "Six, Seven, cut the fence."

Just beyond the wire, the black Ford Explorer, its lights off, skidded to a stop. Fiona jumped out and began cutting the chain-link fence. Diana covered her from the other side.

The fire escape shook as Suleiman landed beside his teammate. "Go, Eight."

Skylar bolted downward.

Butch burst through the ground-floor door. He stepped to the side as someone blasted after him.

Suleiman's tranq rifle clicked.

The man fell.

"Go, Five. Now!" he shouted.

As Butch raced toward the Explorer, Skylar hit asphalt. He shot another man coming through the ground-floor door.

"Two, watch the door!"

Suleiman took a couple of steps down, then ambushed another attacker as he came onto the fire escape's landing.

Skylar raised his pistol. "Eight covering. Two, get out of there."

Suleiman raced down the stairs, and both men dove through the gap in the fence. They piled into the back of the Explorer.

Skylar found himself squeezed against the door.

"Six on egress," Diana reported as she stomped on the accelerator.

"Three..." Suleiman panted.

Skylar wiped the sweat on his brow. "Missing. I think she got compromised."

Suleiman swore under his breath.

"Shutting down frequency," Shelly reported. "We're on cell from now on."

Skylar faced forward. Sure, he and Sana had had their differences over the years. But she was family now. And family didn't leave anyone behind. They'd find her. Hopefully before it was too late.

Saturday, April 9, 2016, 2320 hours CDT, Nashville, TN

Pain brought Sana out of her blackness. Her hands were numb. So were her ankles. Then came the sound again. Skin on skin. And more pain from a slap. Someone jerked her arm.

Sana winced as she was dragged to a sitting position against a desk.

Ash knelt in front of her. In the dim light, his eyes had widened to the point where she saw the whites of them around those emerald irises. His nostrils flared. "You thought you were so smart, didn't you?" He popped her across the face again. "You thought you could come and rescue Morgan. Well, I have news for you, Sana Jain."

How did he know her name? She closed her eyes.

Pain in her jaw jerked her to reality.

Ash gripped her chin and forced her to look behind his door.

Her heart sank.

Morgan slumped unconscious in a corner.

He released her. "You were wrong. I still have Morgan. And guess what? She's going to net me a lot of money. *A lot.*"

The cry stuck in Sana's throat.

Ash struck her once more.

She moaned.

Ash turned his gaze. "It was your brother who alerted us."

Stunned, Sana stared at Narat towering over her. How had he known their plans? How?

"Narat, you know what to do, right?"

Her brother's image blurred.

"She knows too much now," Ash said. "On your way out of town, kill her. Dump her body in the river before picking up Wes."

Narat's Adam's apple bobbed. "That wasn't part of the plan."

"We're out of choices and time, got it? Get rid of her unless you want to wind up in jail. You got a problem with that?"

"Narat, no," Sana whispered. Her head throbbed all the more.

Ash kicked her. "Shut up. Go on, Narat. Get your car and meet us out back. I'll get two guys to help you load up." He picked up a cell phone and dialed.

Dizziness assailed her. With a groan, she slid along the front of the desk until she lay on her side.

Above her, the conversation raged. "What do you mean, they got away? Really?" Ash cussed. "Get rid of the evidence, and get Denelle to close early. Say there's been a fire in the kitchen or something." He kicked the desk. Hard. "I don't care what she says. And send two guys up here. Now." He hung up sneered at her as he brandished a strip of cloth. He pushed it into her mouth and cackled as he tied the knot. "Have a nice life, Sana Jain. What's left of it."

As the door opened to reveal two bouncers, he turned away.

One man tossed her over his shoulder. Her head banged against the door jamb as they passed into the hallway where Ash kept the girls.

Footsteps clanged on metal stairs. A car chirped. A trunk shut. The man shoved her into the foot well of the front passenger seat.

Narat accelerated down the street, then sped up even more. Streetlights flashed by overhead. Darkened windows kept her separated from the safety of the world outside.

He gripped the steering wheel so tightly that his knuckles were white, even in the dim light. With one hand, he released her gag. "Why did you have to be here?" He slapped the steering wheel. "Now I have to kill you."

Sana struggled against her bonds. No give. She couldn't feel her hands. Or her feet. Of course, soon she wouldn't feel anything. "How... how did you know?"

He spat a curse word in her direction. "I saw you outside The Music Man. Imagine my surprise when I saw my sister—my sister!—strolling past, chatting with her boss as if she didn't have a care in the world."

Her stomach dropped as rain began pounding down on the car's roof. Her aching mind whirled to her conversation with Victor earlier that day. *Then we're on go for tonight. They're not going to know what hit them.* No... She scrunched in the foot well. Dizziness assailed her.

Sweat trickled down his temple. He muttered over and over again, "I can't. I just can't."

"I love you."

He cussed at her. "You've put me in a terrible position."

Tears filled her eyes. "I do. You're the only one in my family who cared enough to stick around after—"

"Shut up!"

She flinched as he decelerated.

They swung around a corner and skidded to a stop.

The dome light flashed on.

He slid from the car. A second later, the passenger door opened. He yanked her legs around so her ankles were exposed.

Sana's head hit the central console. More stars sparked.

Her feet and hands came free.

Narat heaved her from the car.

She collapsed in a heap on the wet sidewalk.

He loomed over her. "I'm going to tell Jaidon I killed you, okay? But instead, I'm leaving you here, in one of the worst parts of town. Maybe I'll be right. Or wrong. That's up to you. You see, I do love you, Sana. But you got in the middle of things beyond your control."

Tires chirped as he sped away into the chilly darkness.

Numbness remained in Sana's hands and feet. Somehow, she crawled to a streetlight. Chest heaving, she leaned against it. Where was she? The street sign didn't help at all. Further down, more streetlights were out. The rain stopped as the tingles increased to the point where she wanted to scream.

I have to get out of here. She tried rising but only succeeded in toppling face first onto the gross pavement. As she lay there, she stared at a nearby bench. Somehow, she reached it and collapsed onto its slick surface. Her fingers gripped nasty wads of leftover gum. Bass music played as a car came down the road.

"Oooh, baby, you look like the Black Widow," the passenger in the front seat hollered through the open window of a car. Bass shook the windows, and LEDs lit the wheel rims and undercarriage. It slowed and backed up. The driver called, "What's your price tonight?"

She stared at them.

The car sped around a corner.

She had to get out of there.

Sana pushed to her feet. This time she swayed as she tried to orient herself. In the distance, the tall buildings of downtown glowed in the mist. She'd head in that direction. If she could find someplace open like a fire station or all-night McDonalds, she could phone the emergency number they always had for missions. Vic would find her. She began limping in that general direction.

Somewhere in the distance, gunshots popped. She cringed as the realization that she was alone and completely unarmed sank in. She hurt so much even her wits had deserted her.

More bass rattled her bones.

Crap. Maybe she'd better duck into the shadows.

"A hundred for an hour with you," that first guy called.

"Not interested," she replied.

"Two hundred. I'm good for it, baby."

"Leave me alone!" With that, Sana hobbled into the shadows of a nearby pocket park.

Car doors slammed.

"I'm gonna get me some Black Widow." The driver's taunts followed her as she ducked into some bushes. She could hide.

Footsteps pounded on the sidewalk.

Or not. She was on their turf and totally out of her element.

Sana dodged to the right.

She blasted into a low chain-link fence. It rattled, revealing her location as surely as a flashlight's beam.

The passenger chortled. "C'mon, babe. We good at what we do."

Sana heaved herself over the fence and landed face first in a mud puddle. The man's vile description of what he'd do to her floated over her.

No. She staggered upright and darted through a yard to a residential street.

Behind her, the fence jingled. Another car, bass booming, came down the street, this one at a slow pace.

Her pursuers had called buddies.

Chest heaving, Sana assessed her options. Poor at best, deadly at worst. Keeping to the shadows, she stumbled across front yards. As if they were toying with her, the second car kept pace.

God, please. Conceal me. Please! Where was a fire station when she needed it? Heck, even a cop car would do. Anyplace where she could seek shelter.

She made it to a small commercial area.

The second car screeched to a stop. Two doors slammed. "We got you now, Black Widow!"

Someone hooted.

Oh, no you don't. Sana noted the tall buildings in the distance, then fled into an alleyway. She'd go through there, then lose them on the other—Oh, no! Ahead of her, someone had built a fence. A dumpster sat against it. No problem. She'd done leaps like that before.

Sana's legs began shaking.

She tensed to jump.

And smacked into the fence.

She tumbled to the pavement. The fall knocked the breath from her, and she wheezed.

Someone laughed. "See, Black Widow? You can't run from us."

Sana drew in a noisy breath. She climbed to her feet and made another leap.

Her fingers came into contact with the fence's top crossbeam.

Fingers like talons grabbed her waist.

No. She'd not let them take her. She struck out with her elbow.

The glancing blow only enraged her attacker.

He slammed her into the dumpster.

Sana's head cracked against the metal. She moaned and sagged into the trash at its base.

The guy grabbed her throat. "You do that again, I kill—"

"Unhand the lady," a booming voice commanded.

The pressure released.

Sana raised her head. She began trembling as she pulled herself to a sitting position.

Four more forms, three massive and one tall and slender, blocked what little light was left.

"I ain't letting you have her," her assailant growled.

"Sugar says you have no choice."

Sana's vision began tunneling. Her chest heaved. She barely heard grunts, followed by cries and running feet.

Hands touched her face. She yelped as they feathered the knot on her head.

"Hold on, Sana Jain. We've got you."

"Sh-Sugar?" she mumbled.

Strong arms lifted her.

Briefly, she gazed at the concerned face of Loquacious.

She passed out.

19

Sunday, April 10, 2016, 0030 hours CDT, Franklin, TN

"I can't believe this. I truly can't believe this!" The words tumbled from Victor's mouth as he paced in front of his team.

Skylar slumped together with Fiona on the guest house's love seat. Shelly focused on the closed lid of her laptop and ran her finger along the outline of the University of Maryland sticker she'd stuck on it. Diana stared at the ground. Butch fiddled with his cigarette pack as if he were dying for a smoke. From where he sat beside Sana on the couch, Suleiman didn't dare meet his commander's gaze. He rubbed his fiancée's back. And Sana? Her head drooped as she pressed an ice pack to it.

"What happened back there?" Victor asked. "How did they know we were coming? By all intents and purposes, we were secure."

Sana's shoulders quaked. A small sob escaped her.

Victor turned his attention to her. "Sana, what is it?"

"Narat knew."

He stared. "Your brother? But... how?"

She raised her face and gazed at him. Tears tracked down her cheeks. "He... overheard me talking with you."

Right. Sana had called him earlier that day. They discussed any additional data needs. He'd been so confident, so assured they'd get out of there with Morgan and without a problem. Hah. Foolishness on his part. Total foolishness. "I'm not sure I understand."

She closed her eyes, and her face contorted as if she fought another sob. "He-he must have seen me when he came out of The Music Man. He followed me, overheard our conversation."

Oh, no... "And you talked about operational details."

Hurt washed across her face. "*You and I* did. All I did was mention Morgan and that we were going to get her out."

"And it was enough." Victor slammed his fist onto the granite bar. "And now she's gone. We don't know where they took her. And we nearly lost you, Butch, Skylar, and Suleiman. All because you—"

"How was I supposed to know he was behind me? Geez, Vic, cut me some—"

"It was enough." Victor threw his hands up as he muttered under his breath. "Your carelessness nearly cost everyone their lives."

Sana's head jerked as if he'd slapped her. "You know something? I'm done with this. You can finish the debrief without me." With that, she blasted into the damp, chilly air.

Victor heaved a sigh and ran his hands through his hair. What a miserable end to a horrible evening. They should have done this in the morning, not tonight when everyone's emotions were raw. "We'll reconvene at 0900 hours tomorrow. Get some sleep."

Murmuring followed. One by one, the team dispersed: Shelly and Diana to their rooms, Skylar and Fiona outside along with Suleiman.

Butch was the last to leave. He muttered something under his breath and shook his head. "You blew it, boss."

Oh, too right. Victor had realized it the moment he dressed Sana down in front of everyone. Was he right? Hardly. His frustration had gotten the best of him, and he didn't stop, such was the state of his wounded pride.

Victor rubbed a neck tense from a day of stress. His side began aching again. So did his head. How could he fix his torn relationship with Sana? He couldn't think about that right then. Morgan was gone. Sana had nearly died. Butch, Suleiman, and Skylar might not have come back. All due to Sana's missteps. No, that was a lie. Maybe she'd talked out of turn, but he hadn't stopped her either. He winced.

Hard-soled shoes slapped on the stone walkway outside.

Victor drew in a breath. He really didn't want to talk to anyone right then.

Sugar stepped through the open French doors, this time without Loquacious.

Victor refused to look at him. "Sorry. You caught me at a very bad time."

"I heard that little tiff you had with the team. With Sana Jain."

Victor's cheeks heated, and his chest tightened.

His unexpected ally eased onto the love seat. "Sugar says you've got some fences to mend."

Victor slumped onto a bar chair and stared at the microwave in the kitchen. "I know. I screwed up. Big time. Sana. Well..."

"She's a special lady."

"I know. I know." Victor winced as his side throbbed. He retreated to a recliner and gently massaged his temples. "She may be small in stature, but she has a huge heart. She cares deeply for Morgan."

"You know why?"

"I can hazard a guess."

Sugar cocked his head.

Victor stared out the open French doors. Butch and Suleiman chatted in low voices with Fiona and Diana. He shifted his gaze to his new friend. "I think she knows what it is to desire a parent's love and acceptance, but not receive it, just like Morgan struggled."

Sugar leaned back on the love seat and stretched his arm out along the back. He crossed his leg with one ankle on his knee. "My, my. She sounds like quite a lady. Loquacious has taken a shine to her."

Victor cocked an eyebrow.

Sugar chuckled. "Oh, not in that sense, Victor Chavez. He sees her as his little sister. So when Ash got his claws into her, we were going to move heaven and earth to find her."

Victor faced him. "How'd you do it?"

He picked at a loose thread on the love seat's arm and studied Victor through his dark glasses. "I knew things weren't right. Let's just say Sugar has contacts in this city. I put guys on Narat Jain, had him followed when he screeched out of the parking lot. And Sana, that little lioness, is distinctive enough, especially in that Black Widow outfit she had on. My guys kept me informed. The second Narat Jain dumped her in a bad part of town, I started working additional contacts. We found her. That's enough, right?"

Victor didn't press. He knew how valuable a role Sana played. If only she'd exercised a bit more caution. No, that wasn't right. He bore equal responsibility here. And earlier? He'd broken one of his biggest rules for himself: reprimanding someone in private, without an audience. He winced at the thought. Though he knew he needed to, he didn't want to apologize to Sana just yet. Not until his emotions settled. "Why doesn't Loquacious speak?"

"When he was ten, I was a senior in high school, literally a month away from graduating. His mama and my mama were good friends, and we were neighbors. I still remember that night. We'd gotten back from some honors thing at the high school and were sitting on the stoop of her house talking. Man, it was hot." He stared at something in the distance. "We heard the car first, a big one, a big engine, big bass. I think that scared him. Mama must have sensed bad juju because she said it was time to leave. We headed down a couple of houses to where we lived. That's when we heard the gunfire."

"They died?"

"His mama and his sister, yeah. He'd run behind the brick wall of the porch, which was the only thing that saved him. Mama and Grandma took him in. Then when Mama passed a few months later, Grandma took care of him. Then when she passed while I was in college, I took him up to Shreveport with me and made sure he finished high school." Sugar shook his head. "He hasn't said a word since. No sir, not at all."

"No doctor could help?"

"Oh, we tried, Grandma and then me. We sure did. But nothing. He's got nothing wrong with his ears or vocal cords. He just won't speak. Once

I started down the road I've taken, I offered him work as my bodyguard." He inclined his head toward the door. "But he recognizes bravery and guts when he sees it. And a tender heart. And Sana Jain's got it all."

Victor grimaced and rubbed his chest. "I know."

"Then I have two requests for you, Victor Chavez."

"Name them."

"Be a man and apologize."

Ouch. That hurt. A feeling of heaviness settled over him.

"And let me work with you. I could be your ninth member." Sugar leaned forward and took off his sunglasses. Earnestness radiated from his eyes. "Because believe me when I say I want to get Jaidon Ash and get him real good."

Victor considered his words. "We'll discuss that in the morning when we're all fresh. Right now? I need rest—after my apology."

"Fair enough." Sugar slid his sunglasses on his face. As he passed Victor on his way out, he clapped him on the shoulder. "You're a good man, Victor Chavez. Don't you forget that."

If only Sana would think the same thing.

Sunday, April 10, 2016, 0045 hours CDT, Franklin, TN

Sana hunched on a bench overlooking a pond on Clay Hall's estate. She wrapped her arms around her knees and rested her chin on them. Who cared if it was chilly or the bench wet? She didn't. Morgan was gone, most likely never to return, all thanks to her.

A lit path ringed the pond and cast glimmers on the surface. Water dappled as a fish seized a meal. From the guest house, not a sound emitted. She glanced toward it. Cigarettes flared, probably Butch and Fiona, maybe even Suleiman since he hadn't quite kicked the habit.

Footsteps came closer.

She uncurled from her tuck as she recognized Suleiman's lean silhouette and the broad one of Loquacious. So he hadn't been smoking with his friends.

Suleiman took a seat beside her and wrapped his arm around her shoulders.

She stiffened. "You're not going to ostracize me?"

"No, *eshgham.* Why would I do that?"

She pouted. "Because I screwed up. And according to Vic, I'm solely responsible for Morgan's disappearance."

"I do not think he said that. He only voiced concern that—"

"Whatever." *Thanks for the lack of support.*

He drew in a sharp breath. "For what it is worth, it could have happened to any of us."

What was he trying to say? Pain creased her throat as she stared hard at the pond. For the thousandth time, she replayed in her head her conversation that afternoon with Vic. "I had no idea I was being followed."

"I know. But avoiding conversations about—"

"I get it, okay?" Her chest tightened. "I realize it was an error, but I had no idea I was being followed."

He closed his eyes and shook his head. "Sana..."

"You were the one who said not to worry about it. You and Vic. That it was probably nothing, that they were just good friends."

Suleiman pulled back and stared at her. He rose, putting more distance between them. "What are you trying to do? Blame me?" He shook his head. "No, Sana, I am not—"

"I thought you were here to support me."

"I am—"

"No, forget it." She sprang to her feet. "I don't need your support."

"Fine, then." He muttered something and kicked the ground. "Until you can get over your one-woman pity party, I have nothing else to say. Get some rest, and I will see you in the morning."

He left her by herself.

Maybe not since Loquacious stayed nearby. The big man kept several feet away but remained close. Like she needed protection now. Hah. Maybe from her own tongue.

She sagged onto the bench as the heaviness in her heart intensified. Now she had to make amends with her fiancé. What else could go wrong?

Another set of footsteps came up the path.

Loquacious stirred and blocked the way.

"It's okay, Loquacious," Victor said. "Thanks for looking out for her."

The big man patted Victor on the shoulder and headed toward the house.

Sana resumed her contemplation of the pond. If she listened closely enough, would she hear church bells in the distance marking the first hour of the new day?

Victor drew in a breath, then slowly released it as if groping for the words to say. "I owe you an apology."

She clamped her jaw shut lest she mouth off at him to stop holding her solely to blame for what happened. Especially since he hadn't stopped her.

Victor seated himself beside her and clasped his hands between his knees. He glanced at her, then at the pond. "Ever since I've had command of people, be it when I first started in the Army, in Special Forces while deployed in Iraq, as a whip agent with the Secret Service, or as commander of Shadow Box, I've made a practice to issue reprimands in private. I violated that tonight, big time. I'm sorry."

His words did little to soothe her tattered pride. "That hurt me."

He paused for a moment as if considering his words. "I know. And those are words I wish I could take back, but I can't. Please know I do value you."

The words shot out of her mouth before she could stop them. "Why did you blame me, then? As if I were solely responsible for everything that happened? I mean, we were both talking, and you never said anything about mission silence."

"Sana—"

"And to hear Suleiman talk, it seems like everyone blames me for what happened to Morgan. And I'm—"

"If you hadn't said anything—"

"So now it's all my fault." Tears began trickling down her cheeks. "Completely mine. Gee, Vic, you could have told me to shut up."

"It's not good practice to discuss tactics in public."

She turned her back on him and swallowed her sob.

He put his hand on her shoulder. "Sana—"

"Leave me alone."

Its warmth withdrew. He drew in a ragged breath. "I did what I came to do. I apologized. I can't help you if you don't get that chip off—"

"I don't *need* your help," she hissed. "Leave me alone. Just... leave me alone."

He obliged her.

She risked a glance over her shoulder. Victor, head down, hands stuffed into the back pockets of his jeans, wandered toward the guest house where Butch stood with Skylar. He was probably going to talk about what a miserable failure she'd been. Butch slapped his friend on the shoulder, and they sat down on the patio's wrought iron furniture.

Sana sagged onto the bench as she stared at them. She should be there planning their next move. No. She shouldn't have violated the unspoken rule of maintaining silence about the mission in public. She'd had an innocent conversation, one she'd never expected to be overheard. But Vic was right. It'd been pure carelessness on her part. She'd erred, and Narat had discovered their plans. Why couldn't they see it was an honest mistake?

I truly didn't know he was there. Really. I didn't. I screwed up. Hot tears pushed to the surface. *I'm not worth being in the pack anymore. I'm a stray again, just like when I got released so suddenly from prison and didn't know where to turn.*

She yearned for people who totally got her. Victor didn't. Not even Suleiman. A name flitted across her mind.

Once upon a time, in a state far, far away, Ryan Flagel had understood her. He'd understood all of those emotions that had flown through her when her release from prison upended her life. He'd been that safety net she'd so badly needed, had even taken her under his wing and given her a place to stay. Until—

Her cheeks heated. Even thinking about the way they'd begun dating a few months after her release seemed disloyal to Suleiman. But hey, she was once more a stray who yearned for belonging and knowing she was worthy. Too bad Ryan wasn't close enough to provide that.

20

Sunday, April 10,2016 0800 hours CDT, Franklin, TN

Victor tried to figure out what his team looked like. College friends who'd partied it up a bit too hard the night before? No. None of the other seven looked green. No one lay passed out on the floor. However, Shelly still wore her nightshirt and pajama pants as if she'd pulled an all-nighter. Her curly sandy blonde hair was back in a loose ponytail, and she had smudged her glasses. Like they'd seen a sad movie? Well, Sana had red eyes with dark circles under them, meaning she'd most likely cried herself to sleep thanks to his mouthing off again. Oh, why couldn't he control his tongue?

Then it hit him. A sports team. More specifically, a basketball team that had just gotten a butt-kicking from the opposing team and now faced the coach. He didn't want to be the kind of coach who berated his players. He needed to encourage them, to mend some fences—fast. Otherwise, everyone would crash and burn, and their unity would disintegrate.

Then Morgan would be lost to them for good.

He glanced at Clay Hall and Sugar, both who looked like they'd actually had a decent night's rest. His attention returned to his team. *Lord, let me get this right this time. Please!* He took a deep breath. "Bad stuff went down last night, didn't it? We got snookered. And it hit us hard in different ways."

Sana gazed at him before hanging her head.

His heart ached all the more. He felt as if he were speaking directly to her when he added, "Do I think all is lost? No. We need to regroup, put that collective brainpower we have to use and figure out our next step. Then we take the next one and the next one after that until we find her. If we keep the pressure on our enemies, we can do this."

Hesitantly, as if afraid he'd lash out at her, Shelly raised her hand.

He nodded in her direction.

From where she sat on the couch on one side of Sana, she said, "I have an idea."

"The floor is yours."

"While you all were rushing to save Morgan yesterday, I got this crazy idea in my head. You see, ever since we found out who owned The Music Man, I've been researching Jaidon Ash."

Victor leaned against the kitchen bar. "What are your thoughts?"

"Why not hit him where it hurts?"

With a cup of coffee in hand, Skylar reclaimed his spot on the love seat with Fiona. "I'm not following."

Shelly ran her finger in a circle on her steno pad. "I know because I haven't had a chance to share this with anyone. Jaidon's been married almost twenty years. He and his wife, Cassie, have a kid, a daughter who's sixteen. Yet he's selling girls to johns, right? Why not take the battle to him? Put him in the position where *his* daughter is the one who's missing?"

A slow smile played about Skylar's lips. "Dang, girl. I didn't think you had a nefarious bone in your body."

As if thrust into her own world, Shelly jumped up and began pacing. "We make him witness it, and then the only way we give it up is if he confesses as to what happened to Morgan."

Curiosity stirred in Victor's soul. But he had lines he wouldn't cross. "We're not going to kidnap anyone."

Shelly faced him, and her eyes gleamed behind her smudged glasses. "Who said anything about kidnapping? We literally take the battle to him.

We set up the bonus room of their house to look like she's been kidnapped. And we get it on video."

Skylar's lips curled as his brow wrinkled. "Again, I'm impressed." He snatched up a pen. "At least with the bones of it. Tell me more."

Victor began jotting down notes too, as did Butch. As Shelly explained, that twinge of hope blossomed. It could work. It was complicated, but her steno pad full of scribbled pencil marks clearly indicated she'd pondered it all night, including everything that could go wrong. It was risky, but the payoff would be huge. And it was their only chance of quickly cracking this case wide open.

Finally, Shelly wound down. "That's all I've got."

Butch grinned. Positively grinned. "Oooh, this is gonna be good, real good."

Victor had to agree. "Okay. This is what we need to do. Shelly, what do we know about Jaidon's Sunday routines?"

"A lot." She rifled through her pages. "I tracked his cell phone movements for the past six months. When they're in town, he sticks close to home on Sundays. Oh, and I've found something interesting." Her eyes glittered. "He's an early adapter of automating his home. I mean, everything. His fridge, his air and heating system, his lighting, his alarm, even his window blinds."

Victor raised an eyebrow. "So you're saying..."

"I got into his home computer system via the IoT—"

"Which is?" Skylar asked.

"Oh, Internet of Things or IoT. Anyway, I got into his network through the IoT for his window blinds. That enabled me to access and control the rest of his house. Anything you want, I probably have. Like here's one thing. They keep a pretty tight ship during the school year. Sunday nights, his daughter's on the computer and then her phone until nine or so. Then she goes upstairs, gets ready for bed, and her lights cut off automatically at ten. The blinds close at eleven. The rest of the lights go out at eleven. And the best thing?" She flipped to another page. "Elsbeth is all over social media. I've got tons of pictures we can use."

Everyone jumped with ideas, and a solid plan formed, one they could use in a short span of time.

Victor stared at his notepad. Tons of things to think about. "Good. Anything else?"

Shelly turned to the team's intelligence officer. "Skylar, I want to download that app you got last night. If I can break into it, then maybe I can find a whole list of johns who have partaken of the forbidden fruit."

Gratitude for the unity and talent of his team filled Victor and for their willingness to forgive his missteps from the night before. "It's going to be tight, but I think we can pull it off. While everyone's getting ready for tonight, I'll take all we have and start summarizing it. Depending on what we find out from Ash, we might have enough to bring the FBI into this. Butch, I want you to take the lead in getting set up. Suleiman."

His sniper and observer raised his gaze, one that was somber. Clearly he and Sana had yet to make up.

"You and Sana head out to Ash's house. Put it under observation and see what you can find. Speaking of which..." Victor frowned. "Where's Sana?"

Suleiman rose. "I'll find her. Then we will go."

That was all Victor could ask for. "Gang, let's get to it. We've got much to do."

Sunday, April 10, 2016, 0840 hours CDT, Franklin, TN

Sana found comfort in the barn. She always had. When the team had fallen apart in the summer of 2014 and Suleiman hid in his work and schoolbooks, she fled to Last Chance Ranch's barn. There, the organic scents and soft nickering of the horses reminded her that God's creation was so much more loving than humans who did cruel things to each other.

As she rubbed the velvety nose of a horse in Clay's barn, her thoughts ran to what was going on at the guest house. Everyone was all excited about planning the mission to wring information from Ash about Morgan.

She would have been as well if she hadn't gotten the teenager into that situation.

"Sana?"

She cried out and whipped around.

Suleiman stood in the open door. A shaft of clear spring sunlight framed him and gleamed off skin rapidly browning in the sun. His biceps filled the sleeves of his T-shirt, which on the front had an outline of the Mushroom, Flagstaff's hardest rock climb, and the words, *Don't get 'shroomed'* on it. Since he was one of the few people who'd successfully climbed it with her, she'd given it to him the Christmas before as a joke. He stuffed his hands into his back pockets. As he joined her, his hiking boots whispered across the fresh hay in the aisle.

Her nose quivered at the aftershave his freshly-shaven cheeks.

He drew her close, and she laid her head on his shoulder. "When you slipped away like that, I worried."

She couldn't meet his eyes. "You all had it under control. Why did you need me?"

"Because we like your ideas. Truly, we do."

She risked a glance at him before returning her gaze to the mare in front of her. The horse snuffled her hand.

"If this is about last night, it could have happened to any of us. No one blames you."

She shrugged.

"Sana..."

"I think people do. I mean, Shelly practically ignored me all night."

"Because Shelly got her idea then. And you and I both know when she gets focused, the whole world vanishes."

She exhaled but refused to look at him.

Suleiman lifted her chin with his finger and cupped her cheek. Sorrow filled those gray-brown eyes of his. "I am sorry you are hurting. You have much to offer. To this team. To me. To God. Remember that, my dear Sana."

Impossible. How could strays have anything to offer anyone? She averted her gaze to the other end of the barn, where a door stood open. It led to a corral where two very pregnant mares stood with their heads over the fence.

He cleared his throat. "Regardless of your current feelings, we have been tasked to observe the Ash house. To see what Ash does today. It should not tax you too much since you are still recovering. When his family heads to bed, we will commence final operations."

What choice did she have? Victor didn't tolerate team members bowing out simply because they didn't feel like doing a menial task.

He took her hand and kissed her fingers. Before they headed to the guest house, he whispered, "I love you, Sana Jain. I always will."

Within an hour, in the western 'burbs of Nashville, they'd located Ash's residence. Estate was more like it. The man resided on four acres, half of it wooded with no neighbors in sight, and in a house of stone with a nice patio and pool out back. A portico shaded an outdoor sofa and two chairs. What a far cry from the car trunk where Morgan had probably resided the night before.

At about eleven, the floor-to-ceiling windows on the lower level were pushed back to allow the crisp morning air to flow into the house, letting the outdoors came inside for them. Jaidon, clad in long pants and an untucked button-down shirt, strolled into the warm sun in bare feet.

A shiver worked its way down Sana's spine as she remembered his malevolent gaze from the night before. To his family, he portrayed himself as a kind husband and father. She knew better. Once he'd seated himself at a conversation grouping in the sun, he unfolded a newspaper.

A woman, a book and notepad in her hand, joined him. Must be Cassie. Her dark blonde hair spilled past her shoulders, and she sported pajama pants and a sweatshirt.

Then came a girl with the same blonde hair as her mother. Sana focused her camera on her and snapped a few pictures. Her face free of makeup, she reminded her of Anna, Victor's oldest stepdaughter, or Morgan—or what Morgan had been before the events in March. Innocent to the world. Where was she now? Probably tied up somewhere in the dark. This teenager, Elsbeth, slouched in a chair on a patio of expensive stone beside an expensive pool.

From their position under a camouflage net at the edge of the woods, Suleiman adjusted the directional listening device. Almost immediately, the earpiece Sana wore hummed to life with the crinkling of a newspaper and faint sound of a radio playing somewhere in the background. Then Elsbeth began chattering about school stuff, things that should have been on Morgan's mind had Elsbeth's father not intervened. Homework. Friends. The prom, which was coming up in a couple of weeks. "You're going to be back for that, right, Dad?"

Ash smiled at his only child. "I wouldn't miss it for the world. Of course, just a few weeks ago, you were even more dressed up."

She blew out a sigh. "That wasn't the same."

He laughed. "Because you were with your parents."

She folded her arms and lifted her chin. "Exactly. But, that gave me an idea for my term paper." Elsbeth glanced at her mother. "I'm going to write about human trafficking and its impact on girls' lives."

Ash stilled.

Sana's lip curled as she remembered the man's arrogance from the night before. *Yeah, why don't you talk to your dad about the damage he's done to lots of lives?*

Then Ash smiled. "That's a great idea. Your mom can give you some ideas on sources to research."

Stretched out on a chaise lounge to soak up some sun, Cassie lifted her head. "When's the paper due?"

"Mid-May."

"Then you've got time for lots of research."

"But not today." Elsbeth focused on a notepad in her hands. "Today, I want to continue working on that story I started after our movie Friday."

So it went the rest of the day. The family headed inside but kept the windows open as they shared lunch. Then Ash came back outside and lay on the couch under the portico. Laughter came from the den, then the sound of a piano and the alto of a woman singing, most likely Cassie. A typical Sunday afternoon for a wealthy American family.

Toward dusk, the Ashes headed out for some supper. When they returned, they opened only the French doors onto the patio. Conversation was much harder to follow, but it seemed as if they spent the majority of time in the family room and kitchen.

Thanks to the windows, Sana had a great view of Elsbeth as she perched at the kitchen island and did her homework. Precisely at nine, she kissed her parents good night and headed upstairs. Cassie followed a few minutes later. Only Ash remained sitting on the couch, his elbows on his knees, his chin resting on steepled fingers, his brow furrowed. He straightened and sipped what was his fourth glass of wine and stared at the fireplace.

Did he think about the night before?

Sana hoped his soul thrashed within him.

He had no idea of what was coming at him later.

Then something uncurled within her. She was a liability. She shouldn't go, lest she do something foolish to tip off Ash once more. Sana glanced at Suleiman.

Lying prone on his mat with a scope to his eye, her fiancé was in his element. He'd be fine without her. The whole team would be. So tonight, she'd stay with Shelly back at base.

21

Monday, April 11, 2016, 0100 hours CDT, Franklin, TN

Victor's mind churned as he and Butch rode in the panel truck with their gear and two team members in back. Hours earlier, as they'd begun final preparations, Sana announced, "I'm staying back."

Victor, who'd been carrying one of the props they'd built to their rented truck, stopped. Skylar took over before he dropped it. "Come again?"

Keeping her eyes on the concrete floor of the second, unused barn on the Hall estate, she repeated, "I'm staying back. I'd be a liability to everyone, and I don't—"

"Sana, are you feeling okay?" Fiona hoisted a case holding the needed video cameras. "I know you have a concussion—"

"Just a little headache." Sana raised her hand as if to ward off any additional reassurances. "Besides, if I don't trust my own judgment, how can I expect you to?"

Victor had let it go and left her behind. But it bothered him. "Hey, Butch."

His deputy glanced at him. "Yeah, boss?"

"Do you think Sana's concussion kept her from coming?"

Butch pursed his lips, then shook his head. "Don't know. Probably. I also think she's started second-guessing herself too much."

"I know." Victor sighed. It was clear the mission had shaken her confidence, and he couldn't figure out a way to help her get it back.

"She's kind of taken a beating, ya know?" Butch slowed and turned into a parking lot. "How 'bout let's sort this out later, 'cause we're at our destination."

Victor couldn't argue. He had to stay focused, lest another op go belly up. That'd be a record for him. Two in twenty-four hours.

"Four, you there?" he asked into his boom mic.

Shelly's reply came through loud and clear. "Roger that. Four's ready to go. Three's with me."

He released a small breath. At least Sana had finally come out of the room she shared with Shelly, which was where she'd been when they'd headed out.

Victor peered around the deserted shopping center a couple of miles from Ash's neighborhood. "We're at Checkpoint Bravo. Six, Eight, where are you guys?"

Sitting with Diana in the Explorer, Skylar replied, "Ready and waiting."

"Two, Seven, you guys comfortable back there?"

Fiona replied from the cargo area, "Yeah, but this is getting old. Fast."

"Just a bit more. Four, we're in position. Take the alarms down."

"Roger." A moment later, Shelly added, "Alarms are now down, and cameras are feeding on a loop I recorded last night."

"Turn on the heat."

"Done," Shelly replied. Using her command and control of the home's thermostat, she switched the home's central heat on. "Heat on. Let me know when you want to cut it off."

Victor straightened. "Eight and Six, let's do it."

Diana's breathy reply filled his ears. "We're on it."

Victor closed his eyes and envisioned Skylar and Diana creeping to the air intake of the heating system. They would deposit a combination of nitrous oxide and sevoflurane gas that would plunge Jaidon and his family into a deeper sleep with no other effects than having a good night's rest. They should wake in the morning fine.

"Done," Diana reported. "Now we get to wait an hour while it dissipates."

He checked his watch. Two in the morning. When they'd be in a deep sleep. A perfect time to strike. This time, the only noises in the truck's cab were muted sounds of heavy metal emanating from Butch's earbuds as he psyched himself up for the mission. Victor fiddled with his phone and accessed the local news for Nashville. Nothing about the events the night before at The Music Man. Fine with him. He watched the numbers slide by on his digital watch. 0130 hours. Then 0140 hours. Then 0150 hours. Finally, an hour passed. Victor tapped Butch on the arm. "Let's do it."

The earbuds came out, and the earpiece went in. Butch put the truck into gear, and they rumbled toward the Ash estate. It had both a circular driveway out front and a driveway that went to the three-car garage that loaded on the side. And thanks to the pines at the edge of the road, no one could see them once they arrived. Shelly now had control of the lights and had plunged everything into darkness save for the pool.

Victor opened his door.

Butch released the lock on the cargo area, and he raised the roll-up door as quietly as he could.

Fiona hopped down, followed by Suleiman. Both took up sentry positions around the truck.

Victor peered at the second floor. The master suite was there, and he didn't notice any motion indicating anyone was up. "Let's do it. Six and Eight, meet us around back."

"We're on our way," Skylar replied.

They regrouped at the French doors under the portico. It took Skylar only a moment to pick through the locks. Diana went in first with a sensor device to detect gas concentrations. She returned a few minutes later. "We're clear."

Butch smirked. "'Cause we didn't have to drag you out?"

She shook her head. "Sensor says we're good. I even checked upstairs. No one moved at all."

Victor stirred. "Let's do it."

The team set to work. Once again, he marveled at the way they moved exactly as they'd rehearsed. Butch and Skylar brought in the wood frames they'd covered with dull gray fabric. Diana and Fiona joined them with the tripods and cameras while Suleiman assisted with the metal bed frame and mattress. This is where Victor missed Sana because it took a little longer to get ready.

Fiona nodded to him. "Cams are ready. Check with Four."

"Four, did you hear that?"

"Running checks." Clicking followed as Shelly typed something. "Good. Camera's up and running. Check that tablet."

Victor pulled an iPad Shelly had given him from its case. A video app showed the bonus room, now outfitted to look like a holding cell, all the way down to fabric walls in a drab gray. Skylar placed Elsbeth on the bed and pulled a sheet and light blanket over her. They'd laid a chain on the bed so it snaked out from under the blanket. The better to project a prisoner image. "Perfect. Five, you're set up?"

From downstairs in Jaidon's study, Butch replied, "Ready. Coming your way."

"Let's do this, then." Victor strode down the exposed walkway to the master suite. He pushed open the doors.

Neither Ash nor his wife stirred at his entry. They lay side by side. Cassie faced the front windows. Ash sprawled on his back, a faint snore emanating from him.

Victor stepped to his side. His lip curled. For a moment, he wanted to shake him awake and scream at him for Morgan's location. He couldn't. Not when her life was at stake.

Diana pulled out a container that looked like a perfume bottle from her pocket, the antidote to what she'd sprayed into the HVAC system. The fine mist settled over Ash's face.

Now all they had to do was wait.

Monday, April 11, 2016, 0300 hours CDT, Nashville, TN

Jaidon's eyes snapped open. Absolute stillness. Nothing moved. No sound either. Not surprising seeing it was in the wee hours of the morning. Speaking of wee, he had to go. Now. He shouldn't have had four glasses of wine. But Elsbeth's determination to write her term paper on human trafficking bothered him. Maybe he needed to persuade her to research another topic. Except she was like him. When she got something on her mind, she wouldn't give up on it.

He pushed himself upright. His world swayed a little. Yeah, he should have avoided that fourth glass. His mind remained foggy as he did his business. He wiped the sweat from his forehead. Why was it so warm in here? He hoped he wasn't coming down with something. Especially since he was leaving on Friday for Texas. He splashed some cool water on his face, then dried it with a towel and turned toward the bedroom.

Someone grabbed him, and a huge hand muffled his yelp.

He struggled as his much larger attacker wrestled him to the floor and slapped tape over his mouth.

His breath wheezed out through his nose as the man put a knee between his shoulder blades.

The man grabbed his wrists and tied them. The same with his ankles.

Jaidon couldn't move. Cassie. Elsbeth. Where were they? He began sweating as his hands clenched and unclenched behind his back. A blindfold sent him into complete darkness.

The intruder lifted him off the floor and tossed him over his shoulder. They descended the stairs.

He couldn't let them take him from the house. He squirmed.

Instead of the sounds of the outdoors, he heard the hum of the refrigerator as it turned on.

His assailant slammed him onto a chair and lashed him to it. Pain burned across his mouth the tape was ripped away, then the blindfold.

Bright light blinded him. His eyes teared as they tried to adjust to it.

He couldn't see a thing beyond the glare. Cassie and Elsbeth. Where were they? He couldn't seem to catch his breath. He began hyperventilating, and spots appeared in his vision. *Calm down, Jaidon. Now. You can't help your wife and daughter if you're a blithering mess on the floor.* Somehow, he rasped, "Where am I?"

"At home," his attacker replied. "Men, cut the lights."

Abruptly, the bright light ceased. A low glow from a lamp in a corner silhouetted three unwelcome visitors. One's massive form loomed over him, probably the one who'd manhandled him. The other two were tall and slender.

And where was here? Gradually, his eyes adjusted to the gloom. He picked out the albums, the autographed posters, the awards that hung on the walls of his study. A tiny bit of relief unfurled within him. Until he thought about Cassie and Elsbeth. He strained against his bonds. No give. A flash of nausea crossed him. Voice shaking, he said, "Look, if it's money you want, you can have all of it. Just... leave my family and me alone."

One of the slender men stepped closer. "It's not that simple, Jaidon Ash,"

"Cassie..."

"Your wife? She's fine." With his hands behind his back, the slender man, who Jaidon surmised to be the leader, did a circuit of the room. "Looks like you're into music. Really into it."

Calm down. You can't reason with the man if you're irrational. He took a deep breath and steadied a little. "You seem to know me."

Leader, who was masked like his pals, shifted his gaze toward his prisoner. "From what I remember, you're a big name in this town. Tour management, right? You own Music Man Productions? More than that, started it twenty-one years ago with not a dime in your pocket. Matter of fact, you didn't draw a paycheck for the first six months."

Coldness spread in him. This man had invaded his home, knew way too much about him. "Why. Are. You. Here?"

Again, the man ignored him. "I also read somewhere that you started a night club with a similar name as a way for your wife to have a place to sing."

A heavy feeling settled in his stomach. "How did you find that out?"

Leader curled his lips. "I can read, Jaidon Ash. And I can research with the best of them. That's quite a portfolio you have—including a brothel. And when did you set that up? During the Great Recession, if I remember correctly. Your club was going under and would have taken everything else—Music Man Productions, your cars, your house—with it. The brothel got you out of debt."

His chest tightened, and dizziness assailed him. Was he having a heart attack? His chest heaved as he took a deep breath. How had Leader found out? Or had he? Was he just trying to make him react? "Now why would I do that? I'm one of Nashville's most upstanding citizens."

Leader whipped around. His dark eyes glared at him. "Can it, Ash. I know the truth. And I know you're not operating alone. Someone else paid off that debt you owed on The Music Man."

Again, Jaidon jerked at his bonds. No give. "I don't know what you're talking about."

Leader bent and got in his face. "Word gets around, my friend. I know you're in the business."

Maybe deflection would work. "Who sent you? Sugar?"

Leader withdrew. "Who? I have no idea who you're talking about." He began pacing in front of him. "But I do know you hold Morgan Walton."

Jaidon allowed himself a smirk. "Yeah, you think you're all cool. But I know you work for Sugar. And no, I don't have a Morgan because I don't have a brothel."

Leader paused. "She goes by the name Emmaline at your restaurant. Lots of people remember her. She's a pretty redhead. No, a beautiful one."

"Seriously, I don't know what you're—"

"You're a fool!" Leader grabbed his chin. His eyes had widened so Jaidon could see the whites. "Let me tell you one thing. I'm going to ask you a series of questions. And I want answers. Got it?"

"No," Jaidon growled.

He backed away and stared at an award Jaidon had received from the Country Music Association. He glanced at his prisoner. "You see, I don't know a Sugar. To me, sugar's what you put in tea or in a birthday cake.

But I do know you're in a dangerous business. I know about your brothel because I'm in the business myself, and I want a certain girl out of yours because she could fetch a large sum of money."

Maybe he could still talk his way out of it. "I don't—"

"I hate to have to do this. But, if I don't get her, I have a great substitute." Leader extended his hand to the other slender man, who gave him a tablet.

The big man moved a small side table so it sat in front of Jaidon. Leader fiddled with the tablet, then set it on the table so it faced him. Jaidon gasped. Its screen showed a girl in a bed somewhere in a room with gray walls and muted light. Two masked women stood in the room with some sort of rifles across their chests. Jaidon opened his mouth, then closed it. He'd recognize Elsbeth in repose anywhere since he'd watched her sleep from the time she was a baby. She seemed unconscious. Was that a chain protruding from the bed?

Sweat once more built on his brow

"Recognize your daughter?" Leader asked in a quiet voice.

"I... I... What have you..." Jaidon's voice trembled.

Leader leaned against the door frame of his study. "Yes, that's your daughter. The apple of your eye, right? Your pride and joy? She's got her mama's beauty and heart, doesn't she? And your passion. Matter of fact, I heard she wants to write a paper about human trafficking." Leader barked sarcastic laughter. "How ironic."

Somehow, this man knew everything about them, even events from hours earlier. But how? They must have been watched. "Where is she? When did—"

"She's in a safe location. I can promise you that. But she won't stay that way, or in that location, for long. Now tell me where Morgan is."

Jaidon slumped against his bonds. His head spun. Elsbeth was living his worst nightmare. Big time. "I... I don't have her anymore."

Leader straightened. "What do you mean?"

How did he phrase this? If The Distributor found out... He didn't want to know the consequences.

"Let me show you something else, Ash." Leader picked up the tablet and fiddled with it. He set it back down on the table.

Jaidon gaped at the pictures. Since he followed Elsbeth's social media accounts, he'd seen them before. Elsbeth at the winter dance a few months ago. At Christmas when she'd gotten a pair of diamond earrings from him. With her brand new Honda Accord at her sixteenth birthday last fall. "I..."

"Those are only some of the... less revealing pictures we found of her. And they're going to go to hole-in-the-ground-dot-com if you don't tell us what we want to know. You know that site, right?"

Oh, did he ever. He used it frequently to sell girls who'd ceased to be of value to the brothel.

Leader flipped the images back to Elsbeth's still form. "I put the word out, these pics go out, and suddenly, we'll be pulling down lots of cash for the sale of your daughter. How does that sound?"

He couldn't let that happen. These goons had Elsbeth. And who knew about Cassie? He grimaced. He knew all too well what happened to girls who vanished into the depths of human trafficking. "Okay. Okay. What do you want to know?"

Leader nodded to the other slender man, who pressed a button on a digital camera sitting on a tripod. "You've got someone above you. I know you do. Who is he?"

"The Distributor."

"I need a real name, Ash, not some cutesy nickname. Who is he?"

Jaidon swallowed hard. He'd be betraying Prasata. Big time.

Leader tapped the tablet. "You refuse our questions, and she disappears, remember?"

"All right, all right. Prasata Jain."

"Oh?" The leader folded his arms across his chest. "And who is he?"

Once Jaidon started talking, it was like he'd tapped a relief valve and couldn't stop. "He's some big president of a computer corporation in Austin, Texas. But that's his legit job. He came from India while in college and brought the family trafficking business with him. He said the States was the perfect place to expand it."

"And you shipped Morgan to him."

Jaidon winced at the amount of betrayal he'd just committed. "Yeah. His son came and got her. He's in neck deep with it, like he's an heir of some sort."

"Where did he take her?"

Sweat trickled down Jaidon's chest. Why wasn't the heat cutting off? "It's hot in here."

Leader didn't budge. "The temperature's fine, Ash. Keep talking."

"He... he has this event every year on his ranch outside of Austin in the Hill Country." He closed his eyes when he realized what would happen if Prasata found out. "It's an invitation-only event where buyers from all over the world come to buy pretty girls. We who work for him get to go as well. We call those girls Exotics because they have unusual looks."

"Like who comes?"

Jaidon shrugged. Last year's party washed over him. Though he hadn't sent an Exotic, he'd enjoyed the weekend all too much. "Sheiks. Tycoons who are a whole heck of a lot wealthier than I am. Movie stars. Trust fund babies. Even a couple of reps for world leaders."

"When does this happen?"

"Next weekend."

The leader shifted. "I assume he has a guest list, then. Where does he keep it?"

"What? You want to go or something?'

The leader shrugged. "Maybe. Where does he keep it?"

Jaidon smirked. "Where you'll never find it."

Leader tapped the tablet again. "Remember what I said? Be nice and tell me where he maintains that guest list."

He shuddered as he remembered one time when he'd visited Prasata. "Where he keeps everything else related to the business. He has this tablet with him at all times. Kinda like yours, only fancier." Suddenly, he felt cooler, as if the temperature had begun dropping some with his confession. "He's... he's got this crazy sticker on it, a tarantula. Man, he's into those things. It creeps me out because he keeps them all over his offices at work and home."

Leader glanced at his crony. "Where does he normally work with it?"

"Work and home. But work's a fortress. If you wanna steal it, it's gonna be hard."

"Oh, I think we can handle that."

Silence fell. Then Leader spoke slowly and deliberately. "So, you're telling me that Morgan is now in his clutches?"

Jaidon nodded. "Exactly. Jain's son and Wes Sampson took her down there last night. Trust me, she's knee deep in heavy security right now."

"Oh, I'm sure." The leader glanced at his pals.

Did Jaidon detect a faint nod? Elsbeth. Desperation struck him. "Please! Elsbeth is all we have. We can't... She's my life. You're right on that one. Please, please don't take her away. Please!"

"Oh, no worries on that end. Six, join us," Leader said. He returned his attention to Jaidon. "Here's what's going to happen. Because I'm a man of my word, we'll return Elsbeth to you. And you're not to go to anyone with this, understand? Not to the cops because if you do, they get the whole video from us. Not to Prasata Jain, because if you do, those pics I showed you go up on the Hole-in-the-Ground website. You're to go about your business. Then Thursday, I'll contact you with further directions, got it?"

"I-I..."

Leader bored into him with his dark, dark gaze. "Got it, Ash?"

Nausea swelled in him. "Yeah."

Another person, this one with the shapelier curves of a woman, joined them.

The leader got in his face. "You see, we have enough to act. 'Night, 'Night, Jaidon Ash."

Spray hit him across the face.

Then it was lights out.

22

Monday, April 11, 2016, 0330 hours CDT, Franklin, TN

Sana blasted into the night. Nausea surged through her. *Lord, don't let it be true. No! It can't be true!*

But it was.

Prasata Jain, her father, one of the most admired and respected people in Austin, headed up a human trafficking ring of national proportions.

Her feet flew faster. The lights around the pond's path flashed by. She hit a bark trail. "God, no!"

She couldn't deny it. She'd sat right next to Shelly as her friend recorded Ash's confession.

Meaning one thing.

All of her memories she'd had while growing up—her gymnastics, her schoolwork, her family—shattered. No. Exploded into oblivion.

She gulped down chilly night air filled with the fresh, clean scents of trees in bloom.

Her cries became audible. Her vision clouded.

"Who am I? Who am I?"

She ran harder—until she collided with an electric fence at the edge of the Hall property.

Its shock knocked her onto her rear. She curled into a ball and sobbed.

Everything she'd known gone. Like when she'd been released so suddenly from prison. *Stray. You're a stray, Sana.* That little voice got louder and louder.

"I..." She gave up fighting it.

Then, she sensed a presence, a big one. Loquacious. He gathered her to him, held her, and rocked her like a child. She clung to him. Oh, did she feel like he was a big brother! In the short time of knowing him, he'd learned to read her moods. He must have sensed her distress and followed her.

Finally, her sobs wore her out as she huddled in his arms. Despite his presence, loneliness surged over her. She should have been with the team, with Suleiman. Suleiman should have been holding her. Except he wasn't here—and she'd spurned his kindness that morning. No. She'd taken herself out of play this time, maybe for the better.

"I competed in gymnastics for ten years," she murmured to her protector. "I never questioned where our money came from. I just thought..."

Agony choked her off.

"I just... I just thought Father's company was doing so well." She shuddered. "Other kids I knew? Their dads worked second and sometimes third jobs so they could compete. Father never had to do that. I just thought..."

She began crying again. Sana Jain, the great gymnast who'd never shown emotion after her first meet, now wept as if there were no tomorrow.

Loquacious just held onto her. Finally, with her still in his arms, he rose. Sana tucked her head under his chin, much the same way she'd done the year before when Butch had carried her off the plane after the mission in Somalia. She closed her eyes.

Fatigue weighed her down to the point where she had no strength left. A memory surged over her, one from shortly after she'd been released from prison and lived in the mother-in-law suite at Ryan's house. It was the day after her release. Ryan left her at his house with a promise to return that evening.

Sana did something foolish. She walked over six miles in the wrong kind of shoes and got caught in a horrible storm. Bedraggled and in total pain, she returned home to find Ryan pacing the length of his porch. Later that night, as they sat on his porch swing with glasses of wine in hand, he said, "I know this has been hard. Your life has been dumped on its head. Big time. It's hard to go through."

She stared at the dark liquid. "Am I the first stray you've brought home?"

She risked a glance at him.

His hazel eyes remained on her as he lifted his goblet to his lips. He drew a deep breath, and she braced herself for the fallout of her remark. "Most 'strays' I arrest and throw into jail aren't repentant. First, you're not a stray. You're God's child. Second, you're repentant."

Now, as she sagged against Loquacious, she missed his acceptance.

No. I truly am a stray. And I'll never be anything else.

Monday, April 11, 2016, 0530 hours CDT, Franklin, TN

A touch drew Sana out of an exhausted sleep. She didn't want to wake up, didn't want to return to the reality where her father sold girls to the highest bidder. But her eyes snapped open. She lay precisely where Loquacious had placed her just a couple of hours before—on the couch of the guest house. Somewhere outside, a rooster cackled to greet the day.

The under-the-cabinet lights in the kitchen cast a gentle glow across the open room.

Suleiman knelt beside her. His long fingers feathered her forehead. She gazed around the rest of the room. Skylar and Fiona sat beside each other on the love seat. Diana perched on one of the arms. Butch had taken the recliner. Shelly curled up on another easy chair, which was where she'd been since Loquacious had stepped into the house with Sana in his arms. Victor sat on a straight-back chair from the kitchen's table.

Lovely.

Her lip trembled as she sat up and pulled on her shirt hem.

Suleiman handed her a mug of peppermint tea. “Sana, I love you.” He gestured to their teammates. “*We* love you.”

Weariness surged over her. All she wanted was to crawl under the covers and not come out—ever. As her eyes filled, she kept her gaze pinned to the floor. “I’m sorry.”

“For what?” Victor asked. “Sana, please. Look at me.”

Somehow, she garnered the courage to comply.

He took a deep breath, most likely trying to figure out how to tell her she was no longer part of the team. “What Jaidon Ash says about your father doesn’t change our thoughts about you.”

“I don’t see how that’s possible.” Her voice rasped after too many hours of crying.

“We know you, girl,” Butch said. “Heck, if there’s anyone more opposite of you, it’s your daddy.”

Keeping his gaze on her, Victor leaned forward. “Nothing we discovered tonight impacts your standing with the team.”

“Sana, we’re here for you,” Diana said.

What stunned Sana was that every single member of the team, even Fiona with whom she’d almost come to blows several months before, agreed without hesitation. Their support stunned her.

Victor rested a notepad across his knees. “We need your help. You heard Ash’s confession, right?”

She winced. “Every bit of it.”

“Then you know that most likely, Morgan’s at your dad’s ranch.” Victor set a laptop on the coffee table and pulled up a map of Texas. “Can you show me where it is?”

Sana rose. Her legs shook, from exhaustion or weakness or something else, she didn’t know. She sank to her knees and studied the map. It took a moment, but she located the sprawling ranch in the Hill Country west of Austin. “It’s here. It’s called West of India or WOI Ranch.”

“When was the last time you were there?”

She tried to remember. “Years ago. I was in high school, so at least ten, more like twelve, years ago. Father bought it when I was a little girl, maybe when I was five. That's it because I'd just started competing in gymnastics when he took us out there for the first time."

"Can you describe it to me?"

"Boy, it's nothing like it was when he bought it." She shook her head. "Back then, it was a three-bedroom ranch house with two outbuildings for ranch hands and an old barn where they kept the horses."

"And now?" Victor manipulated the mouse. "Google Earth is showing something different."

"The main building's like a hacienda. U-shaped with a pool in the middle. A portico closes the end of the U. I think the only building he left standing from the original was the horse barn."

"What of the staff?"

She shrugged. "My intel is years old."

"It's better than nothing."

"Maybe four guys? I'm not sure."

Victor scribbled something down. "Does anything stick out to you about the ranch?"

"Yeah." A memory bubbled to the surface. "After I hurt my ankle for the second time, I needed to get away, to take some time to think about retiring from gymnastics. I knew Father was headed to the ranch for a guys' weekend." She straightened. "It was around this time of year. I asked if I could tag along. He said no, which surprised me." She remembered the push of anger behind those words. "It wasn't just that he said no. He got angry about it. Said it was his time with his friends, period. Even though I promised I'd totally keep in the background."

"Maybe it was one of those auction weekends," Skylar suggested.

Victor nodded. "Could be. Sana, we need access to his guest list. Where would be the best place to lay our hands on it?"

"Not his work." She shook her head. "It's like a fortress there. It's got so much security—at least it did years ago— that it'd take way too much planning. The house is a much better place. He'll keep his docking station in his study, and most likely, he doesn't do anything related to this... side venture away from there or the office."

"I think we can work with that." Victor finished writing, then tore off the pages from his notepad. "Butch, you and the rest of the crew draw up some plans to get ahold of the guest list. And see if we can't get some imagery of the ranch. We'll need to act fast."

Butch took the list and nodded to Skylar. "On it, boss. Skylar, Fi, Diana, let's go outside."

"What are you going to do?" Shelly asked.

Victor rose. "I'm done dealing with Detective Cruz. Morgan's most likely crossed state lines, which puts this squarely into the territory of the FBI. I'm putting together a package for them while you get with the rest of the crew for their comms and AV needs."

That feeling of unworthiness surged over Sana. "Uh, Vic, I... What do you want me to do?"

He rubbed his chin as he studied her. "Take a rest. You've had quite a shock tonight. We'll regroup later today."

Monday, April 11, 2016 0600 hours CDT, Franklin, TN

He'd definitely lost confidence in her. Double the feeling worthless part. She rose and swayed.

Instantly, Suleiman steadied her. "I will come with you."

She shuffled toward the bedroom. "I really want—"

"And I want to be with you." He looked away and huffed out a sigh. "Please, Sana. I can tell you are hurting."

So let me hurt alone, why don't you? she wanted to shout.

Head hanging, she eased onto her bed and wrapped her arms around herself. She focused on the wrinkles in the sheets.

Suleiman ran his hand down her hair. "Sana, please. I feel as if... as if you are shutting me out. What did we say in there? We care about you. *I* care about you. I *love* you."

"Strays aren't part of the group," she muttered.

"Who said you were a stray?"

"You don't know what I've been through." That came out through the lump in her throat.

"I am trying."

A tear ran down her cheek. "You'll never understand."

"With your help, I can."

No. He wouldn't. Sure, he'd had a hard life. But he'd always found belonging. He'd never been cast out. Leaving had always been his choice, whereas her loose life and poor choices had rendered her a stray. "I-I want to go to bed."

The mattress shifted as he rose. Without another word, he left, the door thumping shut being the only indication he'd done so.

He hadn't even kissed her.

He doesn't love you, even if he said he did, that little voice said once more. *Strays can't be loved.*

She pulled the covers over herself. She dreamed again, this time of New Year's Eve 2011 when she'd rung in the New Year with Ryan. They each had a flute of champagne. As the fireworks began going off, he leaned over and whispered, "I love you, Sana Jain."

That had beat all of the fireworks she could imagine. She knew where she belonged. In his arms. She came awake. Somewhere outside, Skylar said something in his honeyed drawl. Butch replied, and everyone chuckled.

She turned on her side and stuffed her pillow over her head. As she dreamed, it wasn't of Suleiman but of Ryan.

23

Monday, April 11, 2016, 0700 hours CDT, Nashville, TN

Jaidon's eyes snapped open. He lay on his back and stared at the ceiling fan as it lazily rotated above him from its mount on the tray ceiling. A fresh, cool breeze sifted through the screens of the open windows. Birds twittered. In the distance, a horse whinnied. Had Cassie opened the windows without his knowledge? Or had those goons who'd busted into his house? Cassie. He turned his head. His wife didn't lie beside him. The sheets were pushed back, the silky pillows she slept on askew.

They'd taken her.

"Cassie!" He bolted upright and swayed a little as he staggered into the door frame.

Downstairs, something clanked. His wife hummed like she always did when in the kitchen. He noted the tinny sound of the television. She chuckled.

Maybe it had been a dream, one induced by that fourth glass of wine. Dang it. He should have stopped at three, maybe even two. He stumbled across the open walkway toward the wing where Elsbeth had her room.

The door to his daughter's bedroom stood open. No Elsbeth, only sheets pushed back. The stuffed horse she still slept with lay on the mattress. Sweat popped up all over his body. The liars, they'd taken her. She'd disappeared right from under his nose. Unless...

He bolted across the hall to her closed bathroom door and slammed it open.

Elsbeth, her hair in a towel with another one wrapped around her slender form, shrieked. "Dad! Get out of here!"

He backed away.

"What are you doing in here? Get out!"

He leaned against the wall and ran his hands through his hair. His fingers came away wet. Surely Cassie had heard something last night. He joined her in the kitchen.

A smile played about her lips as she dumped a bowl of eggs into a skillet. They hissed. "What on earth? Sounds like you spooked our daughter."

Heat began rising in his cheeks. "I... I was worried when she wasn't in bed."

She stirred the eggs. "Well, it's after seven on a school day."

Huh? When had that happened? With a small groan, he sank onto a bar chair at the island and put his elbows on the quartz as he rubbed his temples.

Cassie eyed him as she stirred the eggs. "I didn't get you up because earlier, I heard you tossing and turning. I figured you needed your rest."

"Something like that," he hedged. So which had that horrid experience been? A nightmare or reality? He rose and wandered to his study. Last night, he'd been tied to a chair. It felt like the wooden chair he'd bought from the UCLA Alumni Association years ago. The goons used a side table. He surveyed the study. The table sat under the window, exactly where it'd been with a family photo and plant on top for the past five years. The chair was in its corner.

Still...

Jaidon knelt and checked the carpet for indentations. Nothing. Using his desk for support, he hauled himself upright. It'd been a dream. A spectacularly weird dream. Or nightmare. Except for the sweating. His face felt damp. Yeah, he remembered sweating. A lot.

Maybe Cassie would know something. He took his seat at his normal place at the island. "What do you remember about last night?"

She flipped the bacon, then pulled the eggs off the burner. "We had some wine. Elsbeth talked about her report, then went to bed at nine like she knows she's supposed to do. I went to bed at ten and read for a bit."

"You don't remember anyone being in the house?"

A frown marred her pretty features. "What? Jaidon, what are you talking about? We both went to bed. I read for a bit while you conked out immediately."

Boy, this kept getting weirder and weirder. "But you don't remember anyone being in the house? And when did you open those windows?"

"When I got up. You were so out of it you didn't stir. And maybe you shouldn't have four glasses of wine in a night." She peered closer at him. "You're obviously a little on the hungover side. Why don't you go and get some rest?"

What could he say? She'd slept well. He hadn't. Because he'd dreamed the whole thing up. Sleep. Maybe that's what he needed. But still...

"Look." She tossed more bacon into a frying pan. "Elsbeth is leaving for school in forty-five minutes. I'm headed to the gym after cleaning up here, then to meet with the interior designer about redoing my study, then to a Forever Free board meeting and lunch. It'll be quiet here this morning. You don't have any meetings, do you?"

"Just a staff meeting."

"I'll even call Tamara for you and ask that she handle that." She approached him and studied his face. "What else is on tap?"

Then he remembered. A rapper was flying in from LA for a lunch meeting with him. Then he had a kickoff meeting for planning another star's national tour. He could cancel the afternoon meeting. But not the lunch one since they guy was flying out from Hollywood for the day. "I've got a lunch meeting."

"Then promise me you'll come home after work. Denelle can handle things at the restaurant."

He winced.

Cassie stepped behind him and felt his forehead. "Wow. You're sweaty, and your forehead's warm. I think it's more than just a glass too much of wine." She kissed him on the hair. "Go and get some sleep, sweetie."

"I will." He took her hand. "I love you, Cass."

She kissed his cheek. "And I love you too. I promise we'll be quiet here."

He retreated up the stairs and shut the French doors behind him, then stared at the bed. Now, only the newly leafing trees rustled in the fresh spring breeze. For a moment, Leader's eyes glared at him from his mask. Morgan for Elsbeth. No. Elsbeth was safe. It had all been a dream. He lay down on his stomach and pulled his pillow to him. He nuzzled it. Yes, it had been a dream. Nothing more. At least he hoped so.

Monday, April 11, 2016, 1000 hours CDT, Nashville, TN

"It's a pleasure to meet the both of you," Victor said as soon as he stepped into the lobby of the Marriott in downtown Nashville.

A tall woman, with her curly dark hair pulled into a ponytail, extended her hand. "Special Agent Wilma Metlock. This is my partner, Special Agent Ray Hannaford."

Victor shook their hands.

Metlock continued, "We got a hotel room upstairs where we can talk in private."

Not that he was surprised. He knew his call to the local FBI office the day before had pulled them from a relaxing Sunday afternoon. He expected they'd already done their homework on him. And maybe on the case. He followed them onto the elevator, then down the sixteenth floor hall to a room.

They'd gotten a suite with a sitting room. Indentations in the carpet marked where they'd moved the couch and tables to positions that would favor them during the interview. Victor took the couch. For a few minutes, they chatted about nothing in particular. He knew the drill well. Get a feel for the person you were interviewing, learn their body language. Then start the interview in earnest.

Sure enough, Metlock dispensed with the formalities. "Tell us why you called again. The desk agent wasn't too clear."

Victor began laying out his case. He silently thanked his experience with the Secret Service when he'd investigated fraud cases and prepared countless briefings for his superiors. He'd deemed it boring work back then. Now, he'd structured everything he knew into a concise but thorough briefing package complete with photos.

As he wound down, Metlock gazed at him from where she sat on a straight back chair with a notepad on her knee. Had she believed a word he'd said?

Victor's chest tightened.

Finally, she drew in a breath. "I have to say, I'm impressed. What you did was risky. Big time."

"We had no choice."

She glanced at Hannaford, then continued, "It strikes me as strange that even though you took evidence to Detective Cruz, he didn't investigate. Even if it was inadmissible, it would have been enough to ask questions."

"I think someone powerful is pulling strings. Cruz is afraid he'll get fired." Victor sat back. "May I ask a question?"

Metlock mirrored him. "Of course. And I'll answer it if I can."

"Has anything related to human trafficking in this area come to your attention before?"

She tapped her pen on her pad as if thinking about how much to reveal. "It has. You know it's an issue all over the country."

Victor nodded.

"And runaways, both girls and boys, are significantly at risk."

"Because of overloaded systems."

"Right. Typically, we refer them to local law enforcement because we don't have the manpower to run these cases down. And unfortunately, running away isn't illegal, so most take no action. But this one," she leaned forward and tapped some of the photos, "what you've shown us, even if the evidence isn't admissible, is enough for us to step in because it's now crossed state lines." Again, she glanced at Hannaford. "We'll open up an investigation today. And don't worry about Cruz. We'll address this with him."

"What about Morgan's being shipped to Texas?"

Hannaford cleared his throat. "Many states have task forces related to human trafficking, and we have reps on them. Texas has one led by the Texas Rangers. They may know something about Prasata Jain's involvement, or at least a person's involvement who goes by the moniker The Distributor."

Victor scribbled that note down. "Who should I contact down there?"

Hannaford scrolled through his phone. "Ah. Here it is. The Texas task force leader is Ranger Ryan Flagel." He read off the contact information. "He should be able to read you in as much as he can. And I highly suggest you take a copy of what you presented to us along with you."

"Done."

Metlock lifted the folder he'd given them. "This is ours to keep?"

"Absolutely." Victor placed his Sentry Securities business card on the coffee table. "And I'm available if you have any questions."

"Thank you." They rose and shook hands. Metlock gestured for him to precede them into the hallway.

Something niggled at the back of Victor's mind. A question with an answer they might have. "Agent Metlock, I have a request and a question."

She paused. "What is it?"

"The request is that you wait until Sunday to move on ash, after we've hopefully gotten Morgan out. You understand, right?"

She nodded.

"The question is, did you know Gary Walton?"

She lifted her chin and closed her eyes. The door thumped closed behind her. "We'd better sit down for this."

They returned to the conversation group.

Metlock eased onto her chair again and gazed at the coffee table as if considering her words. "I knew him, worked with him in Counterterrorism until I transferred here in 2013. I thought he was a good guy."

She didn't voice the rest. Gary had betrayed both agency and country by becoming a double agent for the Iranian *Quds* force.

"Morgan's his daughter."

She frowned and pulled the girl's picture from the folder. "You know, I thought she looked familiar. I just couldn't place why."

"Did you ever meet her?"

She slid the picture back inside. "Years ago at an agency picnic. She was a little girl then."

Victor chose his next words with care. "Gary was my best friend for fifteen years. I know he betrayed the FBI. He betrayed me as well." His side flared from both the beating he'd taken Friday night from Ash's goons and the one two years ago from Gary. "I'm Morgan's godfather. She... she and her family became collateral damage from Gary's betrayal. Everything that happened afterward tore the family apart."

The rush of emotion choked off his words.

Her hand on his arm startled him. "I promise that, at least here, we'll bring justice to what happened to her. Work with Flagel's task force. If anyone can find her, it's them."

He could only hope so. With that, he followed the two agents to the lobby. They parted ways with Metlock promising to call if they needed additional information. Victor settled behind the wheel of his Camry. He took a deep breath as images of his beating at Gary's hands receded. Did he feel peace? Not yet. But he now had allies in this lonely battle.

He dialed Butch's number. "Hey. Where are you?"

"Headed to the airport, boss," Butch replied. "How did it go?"

"Better than I expected." He provided a bare-bones outline about his conversation with the two agents. "Tell the pilot to file a flight plan to Austin. We're going to see the Texas Rangers. I should be there in half an hour or so."

"Wilco." Butch clicked off.

Victor sat there for a moment, then pulled out a slip of paper with a message he'd written that morning. He'd text it to Ash to ensure the man didn't decide to run to the cops or to Jain. Then, he and the rest of the team would rain down fire on Prasata Jain's little empire.

Monday, April 11, 2016, 1305 hours CDT, Nashville, TN

Almost there. Jaidon knew it deep in his bones as he gazed at his newest potential client. Lamar Jenks, all decked out in a T-shirt, jeans that probably cost a fortune, and more gold necklaces than Cassie owned, gazed at him through dark, gold-rimmed dark glasses. His manager sat beside him at the outdoor restaurant.

Jenks smiled, revealing a gold tooth. "I like you, Mr. A. I've heard all about you through my pals, and they like what you did with their tours."

Jaidon allowed himself a small smile. This guy's pals consisted of other A-list rappers. And for one who was just breaking into the business, he was wise to listen to his friends. "I think a national tour would work well. I know it seems strange to be working two years out and before your album's even cut, but it can take some time to get tour dates established, especially when you're planning two hundred dates in a year."

The rapper's shoulders rose and fell in a careless shrug. "I don't care. I want to get my music out there, you know? Sell some albums, you know?"

Oh, Jaidon did. Very well. But the album had to be made first, and sophomore albums sometimes didn't happen. "Here's the deal. We'll go ahead and start work on it. Kenya here," he nodded her on his right, "she's going to be your tour manager. Trust me when I say she's good at her job. We'll go ahead and start looking at tour dates once you pay our upfront, nonrefundable deposit. After you do that and get your album cut, we'll set to work on the other items that need to be taken care of, like set design, dancers, etcetera."

Jenks's manager nodded. "That works. You'll send a contract to us?"

Kenya straightened. "This afternoon." She put her elbows on the table and leaned forward. "We've already been working on it. Once I add the finishing touches, we'll send it right on over. Please sign and return it by the end of the week along with the deposit. Then next week, we'll get started in earnest."

A waiter brought a vinyl book. Jaidon slid a credit card for Music Man Productions into it and handed it back.

"We can do that." The manager rose. "My apologies, but we need to get back to the airport. Evening Hollywood engagement, you see."

Jaidon and Kenya mirrored him. He wanted to shake his head at someone who could fly from LA to Nashville and back in one day. "Good seeing you. Thanks again. We'll be in touch."

Jaidon resumed his seat.

Kenya settled beside him. "Like, wow. You're putting me in charge of Lamar Jenks?"

"You're up for it," he told her. "Truly, I think this is a great opportunity for you. Just remember he can get tiring after a while. And he fancies himself a ladies man."

She laughed. "I think I'm a bit old for him."

"That's never stopped him before."

"Then hearing my fiancé's a cop might help. Listen, do you want to get together this afternoon? I could use your wisdom."

Oh, how he loved employees who realized they needed guidance. "Definitely. I've got only one meeting, so set up something on my calendar."

"Will do." She stood. "Let me run to the ladies room. I'll be back."

Jaidon settled in to wait for his card. He pulled out his phone. Ah. A few texts. One from Cassie asking how he was. He tapped out his reply. Much better. More sleep had helped convince him he'd just had a nightmare. Then came one from a nervous client needing reassurance that another project manager had gotten his request half an hour ago. He saved that one for later. Then came a third.

Remember what we discussed last night, Ash. Your daughter. We have her pictures. You breathe a word to anyone, especially to your friend The Distributor, and they'll go up online at www.holeintheground.com. And then Elsbeth disappears because we know where to find her. Got it? We'll be in touch Thursday with further directions.

Jaidon's stomach suddenly turned. He grimaced as it cramped on the meal of swordfish and crab he'd eaten. No. What he'd tried to rationalize as a dream was truly a nightmare, a living nightmare. Sure, they might not have taken Elsbeth, but they could, and he knew it. For a brief, wild moment, he considered calling Cassie and telling her to take their daughter, their only child, down to the house on St. John, stat. But he couldn't do that. Most likely, they were being watched. And she'd ask questions he didn't want to answer.

"Jaidon?" Kenya's voice distracted him. She stood next to the table.

"Uh, hey."

The furrows between her eyes deepened. "Are you okay? You look like you don't feel good."

"I... don't." He grimaced. "Something's not sitting well with me. Listen. Do you mind if we meet tomorrow?"

"We can do that."

"Good, 'cause right now, I think I need to go home and lie down."

"Okay."

He accepted his credit card from the waiter. Without even calculating a tip, he scribbled it on the line. He shoved the pen and book away. "Thanks. And... I can't wait to get started on this. I'll... see you tomorrow."

With that, he bolted to his Beemer, leaving her staring at him and probably wondering just what the heck had happened to her boss.

24

Monday, April 11, 2016, 1730 hours CDT, Austin, TX

In Sana's dreams, a gate clanged shut. She stood on the hard concrete outside the prison that had been her home from May 2009 to March 2011. The warm Texas sun beat down on her head. Her heart pounded. She had a hundred dollars in her pocket, no plan, and no ride to anywhere. *God...* Her mouth went dry.

"You'll figure it out."

She turned. Taz stood there, his arms folded over a gray shirt with the tails out. A lock of brown hair hung across his forehead. Once so sexy. Now menacing. Wasn't he serving a life sentence for ordering her shanking from prison?

"And if not, there's always Ryan." Another voice, this one belonging to Suleiman.

The two men faced each other with her in the middle.

"You're not a stray. You're God's child." Ryan spoke to her that horrible day after her release when she'd walked so much. They sat together on his back porch swing.

"No, you're a stray," Taz taunted in his Aussie accent. He leaned against one of the posts, his hands shoved into his jeans pockets, one leg crossed carelessly over the other at the ankle. He smirked. "You always will be, Sana. It's why I liked you. Sorry about your man, though." He glanced toward the yard. "I had to take care of him. He was coming between us."

Sana followed his gaze.

Suleiman lay sprawled on his back on the green grass. His chest was a mass of red, his eyes open. Sightless.

Sana woke with a cry. Her breath shuddered out, and her pulse thudded in her ears. She lay on the king-sized bed in her Austin hotel room and gazed at the windows. Late afternoon sunlight tinged the sheer curtain with faint traces of gold. Her mind swam as her heart rate settled toward normal.

More than ever, she needed to talk with Miss Merlita, who resided as a permanent resident in one of the prison units at Gatesville. She'd led her to Christ and still mentored her. During her short call to the warden that morning, Sana had scheduled an appointment with the woman. Never mind that she hadn't shared her plans with Victor or figured out a way to get there.

She needed out from the hotel. Maybe from this awful situation she called her life. Walking would help shake the last vestiges of her dream. She pulled on her boots. Her legs carried her quickly along Congress Avenue and across the Colorado River. The tall buildings of Austin's downtown core receded behind her. She kept walking, her feet seeming to have a mind of their own as she passed through neighborhoods of small, over-priced homes. Even as the sun dipped lower, she walked some more.

The area turned industrial, but she noted newly renovated buildings turned into housing, as if during her absence the area had begun gentrifying. She slowed at a set of warehouses. When she'd trained there fifteen years before, one building had housed a gym for aspiring gymnasts, a second a dojo for martial artists. Now, the sports complex contained four buildings, the other two being for rock climbing and ninja warrior training. They bordered a brick courtyard with a splashing fountain. Several parents waited at picnic tables or underneath the shade of a portico. A couple of them cast curious glances her way

Sana resumed her walk despite recognizing Coach's blue Toyota Highlander in one of the side parking lots. She crossed eastward over I-35 with its noise and pollution. The area quickly became even more industrial and rundown. Overhead, planes lined up for their final descent into the airport. Warehouses surrounded her.

Her steps slowed, then ceased as she stopped in front of one. For a year and a half, she'd lived with Taz in its upstairs apartment. She gazed at the fence's gate. Open. Pallets of what looked like industrial pumps were stacked outside. A couple of employees stood nearby as they discussed something on a clipboard. Then she remembered. Taz's holdings had been auctioned off.

One of the men looked her way.

Sana headed toward the warehouse behind it. This one was totally deserted, its gate locked with a heavy chain and padlock, nothing in the parking area. Overhead, a plane roared. Taz's words from nine years before haunted her as he showed her stashes of electronics, jewelry, and paintings he and his crew had stolen over the years. "Babe, you can do whatever you want to with your cut. Keep it. Sell it. I don't care."

She'd kept it. For her, the thrill had come in the thieving, not the selling. What had begun as a way to get back at her parents had turned into an addiction. She'd been too far gone to stop until—

"I forgot how you liked to walk," a male voice said.

Sana stifled her scream and whipped around.

Dressed in a denim shirt, black jeans, and black cowboy boots, Ryan Flagel hooked his thumbs in his belt, where his silver star-in-a-wheel Texas Rangers badge gleamed. "You must be troubled because you always walk when you are. I guess some things never change."

Her mood dipped as she thought about the briefing he'd provided the team when they'd arrived shortly after lunch at the Rangers' headquarters on the third floor of the Texas Department of Public Safety. "Wouldn't you be after what we discovered?"

"Oh, yeah." He glanced around in the sky's fading light. "Hey, you mind if we take this conversation somewhere else? This isn't the best place to be after dark." He called a comrade, who must have been shadowing them from a distance. On the ride into downtown, no one said a word.

Sana felt Ryan's gaze on her, as if he assessed the impact of the team's discovery on her. A lump rose in her throat.

They wound up at the Starbucks where she used to work on Third Avenue near City Hall. Thankfully, the manager who'd hired her wasn't in that day. The baristas had all turned over since she'd left three years before, so no one recognized her or tried to make painful small talk.

She ordered a hot tea. Ryan insisted on paying for it, so once she had her drink in hand, she wandered onto the patio. Her phone chirped. A text from Suleiman. Where are you? I went by your room, and you were not there.

She thumbed her reply. I'm out walking. Where are we meeting?

He named a popular barbecue restaurant near their hotel. Be there at 8:00.

She replied with a thumbs-up emoticon, then slid her phone into her purse as Ryan joined her. "How did you find me?"

"I followed you."

She gaped at him. "You *followed* me?"

A smile played about his lips. "I was delivering a copy of the wiretap warrant we generated to your boss. I saw you leave, got curious, and followed you." He winced. "I just didn't realize how far you'd go. My feet are killing me."

That got a chuckle from her. Her mirth vanished as she considered the reason the team was in Austin. She stared at her drink. "I feel like everything I've lived is a lie."

Ryan sat back in his chair and sipped his brew, a Coffee of the Day if her nose was correct. His hazel eyes, which danced with flecks of gold and green when he laughed, remained serious. He set his cup on the table. "I can see why you feel that way. When I saw you earlier today, I could tell you were upset."

"Is that why you didn't talk to me then?"

A rueful smile crossed his face as he shook his head. "No, I didn't talk to you then because it wasn't appropriate, and I noticed you're engaged," he nodded at the ring on her finger, "most likely to someone on the team.

I don't think he'd appreciate the hashing up of old memories, even if they're fond ones."

He had her there.

"I don't know what to think or feel about everything." She toyed with the teabag string. "When I was growing up, I had no idea where Father made his money. Quite frankly, I never thought about it. As I got older, we butted heads over and over again." She'd outright rebelled when Father had demanded she attend an Ivy League school. "That's one of the reasons why I went to college here in Austin on that scholarship. To rebel, to show him he had no power over me."

She'd expanded her rebellion to include living with a man and stealing for him. "But, in everything that happened, I never, ever..."

Ryan remained silent as if collecting his thoughts. "Do you think everything you did as a child, the life you lived back then, was a lie?"

"Exactly!" She huffed out a hard breath. "I mean, I don't know what to think anymore. And after misstepping in Nashville..." Her words recorded forever in the black and white of Victor's after-action report flashed before her. "It's my fault we didn't succeed. And everything I remember from my past is in shambles. It's brought back so many awful memories of when I was with Taz. I... I feel like a stray."

Again, Ryan didn't say a word, something she'd learned to appreciate when they'd dated.

She hunched and focused on her teabags resting in the cup's lid.

His hand on her arm startled her. He leaned forward. "Sana, look at me."

A blush warmed her cheeks as she stared at his hand, which had already tanned in the warm Texan spring. So masculine, especially when emphasized by the dive watch he wore. Years before, that very hand had cradled her cheek when he kissed her.

He withdrew his comforting warmth. "I don't think any member of your crew blames you for what happens. Or sees you as a stray."

"But after—"

"No. In the very short time I've known all of you, I can see the care you have for each other. And I know it's hard when reality alters."

She lifted her gaze. "How about crumbles?"

"Fair enough."

"But what do I do?"

"About?"

She threw up her hands. "Everything!"

"Whoa. Easy there."

She blew out a sigh.

Ryan leaned forward again, this time on his elbows. "Listen. You've dealt with the part where you were an adult, right? With rebelling, stealing, and living with Taz. You paid the civil penalty. You repented before God. Don't you remember our conversation a few years ago when you first got out of the pen?"

She nodded.

"Then remember you're God's kid and not a stray."

Oh, he got her so well.

"And the part about your father..." He shook his head. "You were a child back then. None of that was under your control. You depended on him to feed and clothe and love you."

"Even with money earned off the backs of girls forced into slavery." Bitterness laced her words.

"Not your fault, Sana. His. He made the decision. Not you. Remember that." He once more touched her arm. "And remember you're not a stray."

She doubted that.

Her phone buzzed. She pulled it from her purse. Suleiman again. Where are you? It's 8:00. I am worried.

She'd so totally forgotten about meeting the team. "Oh, no!"

Ryan smiled. "Meeting your crew?"

"Uh, yeah. At Bailey's Barbecue." She thumbed out that she was on her way, then rose. She winced as her tired feet protested. "Ryan, thanks." She turned to go, then faced him. "Um, where's the nearest Enterprise facility?"

He chuckled. "You too tired to walk three blocks?"

That earned a weary laugh. "No. I need to go see Miss Merlita tomorrow. I have a nine o'clock with her."

He stood and tossed his drink cup into the trash. "I can take you."

She stared. "What? I—"

"I'm headed up that way anyway to interview a suspect for the task force. Let me take you."

Maybe then they could catch up. "That sounds good."

"Have fun. Tell Victor I'll be in touch with him tomorrow."

She waved over her shoulder and hobbled the few blocks to the restaurant.

Monday, April 11, 2016, 2015 hours CDT, Austin, TX

Once she had a tray of brisket, two sides of corn and peach cobbler, and a drink, she found the team camped out at a picnic table on the restaurant patio. Surprisingly, no one else was out there, which made having their conversations about the task force easier.

"Glad you could join us," Butch called from where he sat in the middle with Shelly to his left. He patted the bench to his right. "We got room for you here."

"Sorry I'm late." Her cheeks warmed a little, and she pretended it was from her near run to the restaurant. "I lost track of time."

Butch squeezed Shelly against Diana. "I forgot how much you enjoy walking."

Shelly playfully shoved him. "Hey, you mind moving over a little?"

He laughed. "What? You need to breathe?"

"Er, something like that." She pushed into him again, and he slid over an inch. She groaned but didn't seem to mind.

"Sounds like we've got some swell backup," Skylar said as he picked up a piece of white bread and squeezed a dollop of mustard onto it.

Victor took a sip from his beer bottle. "Yep. And we've got our jobs for tomorrow. You guys get to have all of the fun. Me? I'm stuck at headquarters."

"What's the plan?" Skylar asked.

"Butch, you and Skylar go to the Jain house and plant that docking station. Shelly, you'll be back at HQ with me making sure it works."

"When am I going to get to go to the field?" she asked.

"Your time will come. Promise."

She sighed. "You all get to have all of the fun."

Victor focused on the other team members. "Suleiman, Sana, Fi, and Diana, you're going to the ranch with some of the task force and—"

"I-I can't make it," Sana muttered before she lost her courage. "At least in the morning." When Suleiman's eyes narrowed, she focused on Victor.

Her commander paused. "What?"

"I-I have an appointment to see Miss Merlita. My mentor. Tomorrow's the only time she can meet." As if a prisoner of the great State of Texas had a full calendar.

He gazed at her as if trying to figure out if she fibbed. Then he shrugged. "You'll be back when?"

"By noon. I-I can join the surveillance team then."

"All right. We'll be running in shifts anyway. Fi and Diana, you've got first dibs." They discussed the task force and their duties. Girls had begun disappearing at alarming rates, not just from the Dallas area but from Austin, Houston, San Antonio, and even small towns. All held two things in common. They were pretty. And their bodies had never been found. The governor had appointed the task force, headed by Ryan, of agencies and local law enforcement from across the state. They felt certain a serial killer wasn't at work but a human trafficking ring was. And they'd begun narrowing down the hub of activity to the Dallas area with suspicions that the activity in Dallas was part of a larger network.

Victor and his crew supplied the missing link. And a name. A huge victory. The task force had begun focusing all of their firepower on Prasata Jain. Now, breaking the case wide open became a *when* and not an *if*. Whether they acted in time to save Morgan became the question.

Sana's supper turned to lead in her stomach. They had to. If they lost Morgan again, she'd have no way to redeem herself. And that was something she couldn't tolerate. Not then. Not ever.

25

Tuesday, April 12, 2016, 0900 hours CDT, Austin, TX

"Man, would you look at this place." Butch pulled to the curb in a utility van the task force had provided, complete with side-panel magnets for the local telecom company the Jains used for their television and Internet. The mansion loomed before them. Italian style. Complete with those skinny evergreen trees he couldn't name. Around the sides, Lake Austin peeked at him with flecks of silvery sunlight skimming the surface. The place where he'd grown up could have easily fit into one wing of the house.

Skylar snorted. "Looks like where I lived with my old man. Except ours was colonial and in Richmond."

Butch stared at his friend. "What?"

He shrugged. "What can I say? The old man knew his business, and I grew up with a silver spoon in my mouth."

"You went to boarding school, didn't you?"

"Day school. I lived at home." Skylar didn't volunteer anything else.

Butch knew better than to probe. Time to get to the mission anyway. He keyed his mic. "Four, you said Tarantula left for the office an hour ago?"

"Yep. Surveillance just reported that he pulled into the parking garage," Shelly replied.

"Okey dokey. We're getting ready to head in." Butch smiled and shut off the engine, then caught Skylar grinning at him. Or was that a gloat? "What?"

"You've got a thing for her."

"Who? Shel?"

Skylar's grin shifted to a smirk. "And you have a pet name for her."

Butch groaned on the inside. He needed to focus on work right now, not on a woman who was both zany and endearing. "Can we get going? Last thing we want to do is draw suspicion."

"On your lead."

"Yeah, yeah, yeah." Grumbling, Butch shoved open the door, and they headed up a wide flagstone walk. "You do the talking, Mr. Silver Lips."

Skylar winked as he rang the doorbell. "With pleasure."

It took a moment, but a young woman, maybe a girl, opened the door. She wore a maid's uniform, even down to the white apron. "May I help you?'

"Mr. James and Mr. Addison here," Skylar said in his finest Texas accent. "We're here on behalf of IntCom. They're doing a survey of the cable and gateway boxes they have in their inventory." He ran his finger down a clipboard. "It says here this house has four units in it. We need to verify the serial numbers on those units."

"Um..." The girl cast a glance into the living room as if someone waited out of sight. She returned her attention to the pair. "I need to see a letter. And some ID."

"Gladly." Skylar handed over a card, as did Butch. Thank goodness for the task force. They'd whipped those out in no time flat. The same with the letter.

The maid opened the door wider and stepped aside. "Please, come in."

Skylar peered around him as if lost. "Can you tell me where the units are?"

"I can." An Indian woman stood in the archway leading to the back of the house. She had her black hair pulled back in a bun. Only a few wrinkles showed around her eyes, which hardened as she focused on the pair.

Skylar offered her his hand. "Ma'am, I'm Skylar James with IntCom. We need to—"

"I heard you." She lifted her chin but not her hand. "Your timing couldn't be worse."

Oh, gotta love the honesty. Did she suspect? Butch spread his arms. "Ma'am, we do apologize. This came up very suddenly. Our offices got hacked, and it wiped out our local equipment registry."

She surveyed him with eyes that reminded him of Sana's. Except Ushma Jain's held a coldness that gave an indication of the loveless household Sana had experienced while growing up. Or maybe that came after she rebelled. "Do what you must. I have people coming over for tea in thirty minutes, so be quick about it."

No problem there. Butch nodded. "Just tell us where they are, and we'll be on our way."

"The study, the den, the bonus room, and our bedroom." With a swish of her filmy skirt, she took Skylar's arm. "Come. I'll show you the bonus room and bedroom."

That left Butch holding the bag containing the docking station. Thank goodness. He glanced at the maid, who'd kept her gaze glued to the marble floor. "Ma'am? Can you show me the study?"

She turned and led the way on toothpick legs that reminded him of a teenager. She had to be no older than twenty or so. They crossed through an arch into a great room that had round tables set up with white tablecloths. Each table had six place settings of fine china and silver. To his left, they passed a wet bar where a bartender could actually work. The counter curved and contained unique carvings that reflected the Jains' Indian heritage. The kitchen island was to the right, and she stopped at a set of closed French doors with smoked glass. She opened one. "It is in here, sir."

He tipped an imaginary hat. "Thank you, ma'am. So sorry to pull you away."

That garnered a little smile and a teen-aged giggle. Something heavy settled over his heart as he slipped inside and left the door cracked. He took a look around. The same twelve-foot ceilings as in the kitchen. A heavy mahogany desk cut in modern lines. Banks of windows made up the other walls, and a pool of azure water glistened out back with the lake beyond. On the interior wall across from the desk was a large television monitor.

Below the TV were three shelves holding glass boxes full of tarantulas. Butch sucked in a breath. A squeak escaped him. He listened.

The maid's knife beat a rhythm against the marble cutting board as she sliced up the fruit he'd seen on the island.

He returned his attention to the spiders. One crawled toward the glass as if it'd seen him. Even though he had grown up in the bayou and lived for months outside while deployed in the desert, spiders gave him the willies. Not that he'd admit it to anyone on the team. He shuddered, and his breath shortened. *Breathe, boy. Breathe. No sense in getting wound up over them.*

Sure. Whatever.

He had to focus. Now. The desk held hardly anything, only a blotter, computer monitor, mouse, keyboard, and holder for pens and pencils. And the docking station. It was right where Sana had said, to the right of the monitor. Score one for her. He pulled out the counterfeit docking station. With one eye on the door, he swapped it for the real one and murmured in a low voice, "Four, you read me?"

"Yep." Shelly's reply came through loud and clear.

"I've got it installed."

"Try your iPad."

"Roger that." Butch pulled a tablet, a duplicate of Jain's, minus the tarantula sticker, from his bag and hit a few buttons. A picture popped up, one of the team. He slid it into the port. "What do you see?"

"A picture of our team." She squealed, which elicited a smile from him. "It's working. I'm mirroring exactly everything that's on your iPad. Looks like we're going to be busy here tonight."

"Hopefully." Butch listened as the maid hummed to herself. "May I disconnect?"

"Go on."

He pulled it loose. He cringed as he approached the terrariums to check the cable box on a small shelf above them—just in case the maid poked her head in. The rat-a-tat-tat of the knife continued.

You can do this, Addison. Since when is a big, bad man like you scared of a spider? Since his big brother Leroy had thrown one on him while he'd slept as a kid.

Butch returned to the great room. Upstairs, Ushma's rich alto rose and fell in time with Skylar's honeyed drawl. He swore that boy could sweet-talk anyone, even a woman as sour as Sana Jain's mama. As he wandered to the foyer, he made a show of checking the cable box in the den and writing something on his clipboard.

As if they were royalty, Skylar descended the curved staircase with Ushma on his arm. "Thanks, Ms. Jain. You made my job easier."

She smiled at him, something that transformed her and revealed bits of Sana. "You're very welcome. Have a good day."

Skylar released her. "Ma'am."

Then the two men were out the door and inside the van. As Butch started the engine, Skylar peered at him. "Success?"

"In spades." Butch put the van into gear. "Though I swear the maid's probably not getting paid."

"I'd say you're right. The sooner we get Prasata's little racket off the street, the better. I think Sana's mom is starved for affection. Makes me wonder if all is not well in the land of Jain."

Butch cut his eyes toward him. "She come on to you or something?"

"Yep. Creeped me out knowing she's Sana's mom."

"I hear ya." Butch rolled down his window. They rumbled down the street. Hopefully, Ushma Jain didn't realize the Jains had been their only customer that day. "Speaking of Sana, what's up with her?'

"Huh?"

"She's been acting weird."

Skylar shrugged. "Given our rocky past, I'd say she always acts weird around me. So what can I say?"

Butch chuckled. "True. Seems this has impacted her way more than she's letting on. It's like she's lost all confidence in herself."

"Not her fault. But let's hope she can regain it because we're going to need her skills before this is all said and done."

Butch couldn't help but agree.

26

Tuesday, April 12, 2016, 0900 hours CDT, Gatesville, TX

Sana's nerves jangled just like they did every time she arrived to see Miss Merlita at the Alexander Unit of the Texas prison system. A stiff wind buffeted Ryan's Ford Explorer. Toward the west, clouds gathered on the horizon, a harbinger of the storms predicted for that night.

She closed her eyes. Again came the flash of the bulb for her mugshot, the handing out of her white prison uniform. That day in May 2009, she'd ceased to exist as Sana Jain and became Prisoner 80249. She wiped her sweaty palms on her leggings. *I'm just a visitor today. Not a resident.* Her hand snaked to the cross necklace hanging around her neck.

"You okay?" Ryan quietly asked as he put his Ford Explorer in Park.

Suddenly, it felt too hot inside. She glanced at the clock in the SUV's dash. "Yeah."

Ryan kept his gaze on her and touched her arm. "You're a free woman now, remember? Totally free."

Did she detect a bit of bitterness there? Because three years before when Gary Walton convinced her to sign on to Shadow Box, a totally clean record came with the contract, meaning she could leave the state if she wanted. She had. She gazed at him.

His hazel eyes remained soft, compassionate.

She cast another glance at the clock. "Let me get inside since I know you have an appointment of your own."

He leaned back. "I'll meet you back here in an hour."

"Good luck with your suspect. Maybe he can be that link we need."

He made a small shooing motion with his hands. "Go on. Tell Miss Merlita I said hi."

She climbed from the vehicle and pulled open the door leading to the administrative building of the unit. She checked in with the guard by showing her driver's license and relinquishing her purse.

The receptionist handed her a claim check. "The warden will be with you in a minute."

An old fear rose. "I'm sorry?"

The woman cast her a glance before tapping something on her keyboard. "He wanted to have a word with you before you saw Miss Merlita."

They'd rescinded her freedom. Sana's breath hitched, and her blood chilled. *That can't be. Gary promised my record was clean. Ryan verified it.* Gary had betrayed his country. Maybe that was it. Maybe because of that, she was once more a stray, destined to get locked up in the pound. Maybe—

"Ms. Jain?" She'd recognize that Texan drawl anywhere. Warden Davis stood above her, a man so tall and broad that he seemed to block out the light.

"Uh, hi."

He smiled, but it did nothing to dispel her fear. "It's good to see you again. Come on back. I wanted to talk with you for just a few minutes before you saw Miss Merlita."

"H-how is she?" Sana tried not to notice the quaver in her voice.

"Doing well. When I told her you'd called, she was very excited." He pushed open a door with a frosted window, then gestured to a wooden chair. "Have a seat."

Sana perched on the edge with her knees together. Her gaze darted to the window. Sure, she could escape, but she wouldn't get far at all before they caught her and threw her into solitary.

Warden Davis peered closer at her. "Is something worrying you?"

She shook her head.

"I can promise you, today your role is that of visitor. I wanted to see you because I received your written request a month ago for Miss Merlita to come to your wedding." Another, gentler smile crossed his mahogany features. "I've decided to grant that request. Miss Merlita has been a model prisoner these years we've had her here. Were it not for the nature of her sentence, she would have been released long ago." He shoved a white envelope across the desk to her. "This letter is the official reply I was going to send yesterday until I got your call."

She placed a hand over her heart as she met his gaze. "Warden Davis, thank you. Thank you so much. When you called me in here, I feared the worst."

He chuckled. "That you were going to become a prisoner?"

She nodded.

"Far from it, Ms. Jain. I wish every prisoner who left here had the same success story." As he stood, his chair rolled back and banged into the credenza. "Well, your call was last minute, so I put you in a conference room. Same rules apply though. No touching. One hour max. A guard will be inside the entire time."

Oh, did she know those rules well. She'd lived by them a few years ago. "Thank you so much."

"You're very welcome." He showed her to the conference room.

An older black woman with gray dreadlocks sat in one of the wooden chairs at a table that could fit eight. A smile broke across her face. She rose. "Well, well, well, look at you, Sana Jain, all pretty in your leggings and top."

Sana ached to hug her. She couldn't. Instead, she pulled out a chair and sat down. "It's so good to see you, Miss Merlita."

"Likewise, sweetheart. You're looking well, like engagement agrees with you."

Her smile trembled as she thought about all that had happened in the past week.

Miss Merlita leaned in as her eyebrows drew together. "Where's your young man?"

Her foolishness from Saturday still rang in her ears. "He's in Austin on business. We're here along with the rest of our team."

A brief smile flickered across her spiritual mentor's face. "Team. Fill me in."

Sana explained the way she contracted with Victor at times, then described the bare bones of Morgan's situation. She couldn't bring herself to mention her discovery about Father.

Not that Miss Merlita bought into her smokescreen. She scratched her chin. "I see. What brings you here when time is of the essence? And don't you tell me it's just to chat. You look as if you might burst into tears at any minute."

That infernal lump choked off Sana's words. Her chest heaved. As she bit back a sob, she whispered, "It's worse than that. Father... he's... he's the one running the whole thing."

"Your *father*?" Miss Merlita opened her mouth, then closed it. "Your father, Sana Jain?"

Shame uncurled inside of her. "Yeah."

Her mentor pursed her lips. "I can see why this is complicated."

Since she had no Kleenex, Sana dabbed at her eyes with the sleeve of her tunic top. It left a mess of mascara on the fabric. "It's like everything I knew crumbled. Who am I? I'm someone who grew up on money earned by selling girls into slavery."

Miss Merlita held her silence.

Sana continued, "Finding that out brought back a whole bunch of bad memories. Like when I got involved with Taz, started sleeping with him, and stealing stuff to get back at Father—who'd all but disowned me. Hah! He, the one who's sold girls into slavery, disowned his only daughter as if he were so high and mighty." She sniffled. "If that wasn't bad enough, Narat's neck deep in this. He overheard me talking to Vic and... If it weren't for me, we would have already rescued Morgan."

"I—"

"And if that's bad enough, Victor blamed me and rightfully so."

"Now do you—"

"Who was I kidding?" Sana tried to tamp down her emotion. "I'm still a stray. I always was."

"Now wait a minute, young lady." Miss Merlita leaned forward and rested her shackled wrists on the table. "What did we talk about all those years ago?"

"What I did." Oh, did she remember those long nights when she'd first arrived in prison and had discovered the good fortune of being Miss Merlita's cellmate. "How much I'd stolen, and—"

"No, Sana." Miss Merlita's voice softened. "What else? What Jesus did for you, right?"

Too choked up to reply, she nodded.

Miss Merlita didn't move her gaze at all. "God loves all of His image-bearers."

Sana couldn't answer that.

"He sent His Son to die for all of us."

As she stared at the dark wood of the table, she doubted that. "I know."

Miss Merlita sat back. The chains clinked in an all-too-familiar reminder of Sana's days in prison. "Huh. You seem to have forgotten. Problem is, a lot of people would rather be their own god, chart their own path."

"I did."

"Until you landed here. You knew you needed a Savior. I remember those conversations well." Miss Merlita rested her chin on her hands. "You felt the weight of your crimes, of your torn relationship with your parents."

"Who've never admitted to their mistakes."

"Yet you forgave. God doesn't make junk. Remember that." Her mentor focused on something on the table. "Have you talked to your young man about this?"

Suleiman. Her heart caught as she thought about him, about last night. She'd been quiet, apparently too quiet for him. As they parted, he snapped at her and demanded to know where she'd walked. His kiss had been perfunctory. As had been his soft, "I love you." "It's like there's a wall between us now. I... I can't talk to him about my distant past. He'd hate me."

"Do you really think that?" Miss Merlita asked.

Sana's stomach tightened. "He wouldn't understand."

"I think you underestimate him. You talk to him. Share this burden on your heart. Take him into your confidence. He's there to be a support for you. And to pray over you."

"Will you do the same?"

"Of course! Let's do that right now."

Sana bowed her head and listened as her mentor prayed for her. Did it offer any reassurance? Not really. How could God love a stray?

When she opened her eyes, she knew a change of subject was in order. "Speaking of the wedding, I found out some good news."

"Oh?"

Some of the heaviness in her heart lifted. "The warden said you could come."

Miss Merlita's face lit up. She clapped her hands together. "I'd be delighted."

"You'll come on Friday and leave on Sunday."

"My, I'd better figure out what to wear. Somehow I don't think the bride would want me to wear white."

That did it. Sana laughed. They caught up. Finally, someone knocked on the door.

The guard, who'd stood in the corner of the conference room as silent as a sentinel, stirred and opened it. "Miss Merlita, time to go."

Sana preceded her into the hall.

In the middle of the small lobby, Ryan chatted with Warden Davis.

With her heart feeling lighter than it had in a bit, she turned to her friend, whose eyes clouded when she saw Ryan.

She returned her gaze to Sana and pasted a smile on her face. "Something tells me there's more to meet the eye than you've let on. Well. I'll see you in June, I hope."

That settled on Sana like a mist. What had she meant? She and Suleiman were going to wed. *We are. Right? Of course. Why wouldn't we?* She stuffed thoughts into a deep, dark part of her soul. Maybe then, she'd forget they'd ever flitted through her mind.

Tuesday, April 12, 2016, 1010 hours CDT, between Gatesville and Austin, TX

"How did your meeting go?" Sana asked as she and Ryan rocketed down the highway. The Explorer swayed in the strong wind. She squinted in the bright morning light.

He remained relaxed, one elbow resting on the sill, his grip steady on the steering wheel. "'Bout the way I thought it would. The guy we busted is what we call an agent. He gets the girls and ships them to a brothel in Dallas. We think there may be a link between him and your father. He knows stuff, but he wants a deal. Less time and a new identity before he spills his guts. So while you go out to the ranch for surveillance, I'm headed to the US Attorney's office with my FBI counterpart to see if we can do just that since this is most likely going to become a Federal case."

"Because of its interstate nature since Morgan crossed state lines?"

"Exactly."

They rode for several more minutes in companionable silence. It was one of the things she'd appreciated about him when they dated. They could read or simply be without feeling the need to fill the void.

Ryan straightened. "Hey, do you mind if we stop off at the house? I haven't been home in a couple of days, and I need to do some cat maintenance."

That got her. She chuckled at his term for taking care of his cat. "Sure, but I promised Vic I'd be there at twelve-thirty to go out with the next surveillance team."

"This won't take long." Ryan put on his blinker and took the exit leading to his house in Temple. The better to split his territory, he'd told her when he'd brought her there after her release.

It remained the same, a cute two-story farmhouse on the eastern edge of town. The memories shook her. That long, long walk the day after her release. The garden where she'd worked during her second day of freedom. The rose bushes. She'd loved their scent. And the detached garage with an enclosed hallway on the second floor leading to the main house. She'd stayed above the garage in the mother-in-law suite. Something was different, though. "You screened in the front porch."

Ryan slid from the SUV and crossed the pea gravel walk to the low steps. The door to the back porch squeaked the same way it always had when she returned from work. "Yep. The cats like it outside, but I didn't want a coyote to get them, or for them to run away." He turned off the alarm and unlocked the French doors. "Want some tea? You looked like you didn't sleep too well last night."

"I didn't." A floorboard creaked under her booted foot. Warm, dark hardwoods, so cool beneath her bare feet during the summer. He still had that black and white teakettle she adored. His boots clunked on the wood as he headed toward his study at the front of the house. Sana remained where she was as a calico cat meowed and strolled into the kitchen. She wound her way around Sana's legs.

She stooped and picked her up. "Oh, Suzy. I've missed you. Ryan said you have a buddy."

Sure enough, a black cat with emerald eyes strutted into the room. She stroked his sable fur. "You, my boy, are handsome."

Ryan joined her and opened a cabinet door. He reached inside and pulled down a couple of travel mugs. "I see you've met Felix."

"That's a good name for a cat."

The teakettle began hissing. "I got him a couple of years ago. After you left, I figured Suzy needed a companion."

She picked up the slightest hint of Dove soap and aftershave. Her cheeks flushed, and she slid a little closer to where he leaned against the counter. He seemed to stare at something much farther off than the refrigerator across the kitchen. "Ryan?"

"Sorry. Just thinking." He rubbed a hand through his hair and dropped a couple of bags into the mugs, then poured the water. He handed one to her. "Why don't you head on out to the porch? Let me feed these guys. I already did their litter boxes."

Sana migrated to the swing out back. She shoved it back and forth with her foot. "I came by here, you know."

He poked his head out the door. "What was that?"

"I..." She'd been visiting friends in Austin and had driven up to his house in February 2015—only to see him come out the door with another woman. Her cheeks warmed. "A little over a year ago, I was in Austin. Dumb me decided to drive up here. I... I saw you with another woman one Saturday morning."

Kibble clinked into a bowl, then he joined her and shook his head. "That was Becca. I don't know. It's like I started seeing her to forget you. It was... too much too fast. So wrong in many ways. We broke up after three months of dating."

Sana's cheeks heated. It felt strange to be the gold standard by which someone else was compared.

Ryan settled on a rocker with his mug. A few more minutes passed, the familiar squeak of wood on wood the only noise. "Fact of the matter is, I haven't been able to forget you. We were quite a pair, weren't we?"

A lump swelled in her throat. "You're probably the person who knows me the best."

He shifted her way. "Your man doesn't?"

Her heart jumped when she met his gaze. "No, not the bad stuff. He knows I did a couple of years in the pen. All of the team knows that. He doesn't know about Taz and my total rebellion against my family." Oh, that gaze of his. So compassionate. "I... You're the one who knows me best. That's what I love about you, Ryan. You knew everything, yet you didn't write me off."

He continued rocking as he sipped his tea. "Did I tell you I'm engaged?"

Stunned, she stared at him. "What? When? To whom?"

A faint blush tinged his cheeks. "Her name's Dakota, and she's a nurse at the hospital here in Temple. We ran into each other at church. I proposed a month ago, and the wedding's in October."

The news hit Sana hard. Ryan, engaged? But...

"Anyway, I didn't shoot straight with Becca, didn't tell her about my wife and the way she died. I didn't want to do that with Dakota, and before we'd known each other three months, I shot straight with her about the way losing a wife and unborn child to a drunk driver had impacted me. She knew the good, the bad, and the ugly pretty much up front."

Sana knew what he insinuated. She couldn't tell Suleiman of her past. He was already angry with her, and that might send him over the edge.

Ryan suddenly rose. He paced and rubbed the back of his neck. "We need to get going."

He locked up the house, and they walked to the Explorer. As she reached to open the door, he turned her. She gazed into those hazel eyes she'd so adored years before. He took a deep breath, then remained silent as if considering how he should voice his thoughts. "Sana, look."

She cocked her head.

"I know what happened with your father rocked your world. I get that. Truly. I do. It'd shake any sane person and make them question a lot of things. And I know you're engaged. And I am as well. I respect the need to work closely with your team, which includes your fiancé, until this is finished. I'm not going to do anything to damage either of our engagements or my relationship with your team. I suggest you do the same."

With that, he headed to his side of the SUV. Case closed. In his mind, it seemed. And her?

He didn't say he wasn't interested, a little voice in her head whispered.

No, he's right. I shouldn't even be entertaining that notion. Period. Especially since he's engaged.

Just think about it. What happens when this is over?

She preferred not to contemplate that right then.

27

Tuesday, April 12, 2016, 2120 hours CDT, Austin, TX

Victor paced in the task force's chamber at Texas Ranger headquarters in Austin. He stared out the window, then shifted his gaze to the folding tables where analysts combed through reams of data, both online and on paper. He found Shelly exactly where he'd left her shortly after their supper of Chinese takeout. Any more takeouts, and he'd have to go on a diet since home-cooked meals weren't a current part of his meal plan. He peered over her shoulder. "Anything?"

She tucked a knee to her chest. "Nothing as of yet. He's at a dinner meeting like he was an hour ago, remember?"

Flagel, who'd spent the entire day with the task force save for a run to Gatesville to interview a suspect, pushed away from the wall. Something hot steamed from a travel mug in his hands. He ambled over to join them. "Our guys reported he left work at six, then went straight to the dinner meeting. It's just now starting to break up."

Victor tapped a pen in his hand. "Do you think he'll go home and go to bed or something?"

"I'm all for the 'or something.' The man's a workaholic, Victor. He'll work before going to bed. And judging from his computer activity, I think he works better at night."

Victor wondered about Jain's marriage. Sana hadn't spoken much about her growing-up years, but when she did, she spoke not of love but of expectations of perfection. How she'd borne up under that kind of stress, he didn't know. He did know she rebelled by becoming a thief and doing a stint in prison that finally set her on the right path.

"Ranger Flagel," one of the analysts called, and the Ranger headed over to talk with him.

Victor stared out the window again. Something seemed off with Sana. She seemed re-energized. Almost too much so. At the moment, she was on the way back with part of the team after a shift of surveilling WOI Ranch. At Last Chance Ranch, shortly after the team had formed, she'd had a boyfriend in Austin but broke up with him not long before the team ran its first mission. She never talked about him.

"Victor," Flagel called.

He snapped his gaze from the window and brought his mind back into the game. "What's up?"

"Jain just got home."

Shelly began clicking her mouse. The large displays at the front of the room came alive as she mirrored her screens to them. She straightened as a password screen popped up. "Bingo! The docking station's working like a charm. I just got his fingerprint."

The computer chimed, and a home page appeared. A program activated, and another password screen materialized. So totally cool. Victor cocked his head. "You're seeing what Jain's seeing?"

"Exactly." A document opened, one that contained a list of names and addresses. "A list. Want to bet it's the guest list for this weekend?"

The task force paused in their work. Victor barely heard Skylar's "Dang!" Instead, he focused on the names. Many foreign. Some he even knew, thanks to his work. An oil magnate who lived in southern California. And a movie star who was a client of a security firm he occasionally contracted with. "This is—"

"Unbelievable." Flagel rubbed his chin. "Shelly, can you get that list?"

"I've downloaded it. We have their e-mails. Hopefully Agent Carpenter and his crew at the FBI can unwind their location."

Agent Carpenter, who'd joined Victor, nodded. "We can definitely do that. Shelly, thanks. We'll get started pronto."

Noise levels at the room's entrance increased. The rest of the team arrived. Butch yawned like a lion after a good meal. Leftovers of camouflage makeup covered Suleiman's face. Diana's cheeks remained flushed. Sana's gaze flicked upward, not at Victor but at Flagel, as if they'd known each other previously. He glanced at Suleiman. His sniper studied his fiancée. Why? He'd have to ask later.

"Vic," Shelly softly called.

He crouched beside her. "What's up?"

"I've tried and tried and tried to get into the app Skylar downloaded Saturday night." She ran a hand through her curls, mussing them. "It's a no-go. He's got too many tripwires around his network and the app for me to access them from the outside."

"Can you break in?"

"It'd take time we don't have. But," her eyes sparkled, "I could probably gain access if I were inside his network somehow."

"Like how?"

"Being so close geographically that I can get into his Wi-Fi. I could go into the field when the rescue goes down."

He was tempted, sorely tempted. Until he remembered the mission objective. Get Morgan out. Then let the task force do the rest. "We need you here on comms."

Her face fell.

He straightened and winced as he did so. "Promise you'll make it into the field."

"Yeah, when I'm old and gray."

Victor motioned for the team to gather around. "What do we have?"

Butch, who'd drifted by a drink cooler, cracked open some bottled water. "It's gonna be tough, boss. The perimeter is huge, and he's got the alarm sensors strung in the fence to look like barbed wire. Suleiman walked the entire perimeter today." He nudged his comrade, whose slumped shoulders and lines around his eyes indicated what a twelve-mile walk in the Texas heat could do to someone. "But I think once we get in, there's not much security until up close. Suleiman's come up with an idea of how to get inside the wire. We get someone on the inside, then get the girls secure and bust a move into the compound from the back way. Shelly, can you pull up that satellite mapping we found?"

Shelly hit a switch. An aerial shot of the ranch's buildings appeared.

Butch pointed to the U-shape of the hacienda. "The building's about a mile inside the wire. There's also a small building that looks like it's built into the wall. And then four outbuildings outside the wall."

Flagel joined the team. "We did a flyby with a couple of drones. It's a dangerous gamble because we don't want people to be suspicious. They seem to have a larger-than-expected retinue of guards."

"Because the girls are there," Sana muttered as she gazed at him.

He didn't look her way. "Probably. But no sign of the girls. We're going to do another flyby first thing in the morning and then probably won't be able to do any more unless we want them to get really suspicious. But we've got concealed surveillance just in case anything breaks loose."

Victor nodded. They had building locations. And a good idea about guards. It was progress, the slow, steady kind that produced results if he remained patient. "So, we've got to find a way to infiltrate their setup."

An FBI analyst approached Flagel and handed him a sheaf of papers. Flagel studied them. "Hey, pull this up, will you?"

The analyst nodded and drew a laptop to himself. "Ladies and gentlemen, our list of folks who are coming."

Each person flashed up on the screen. Sure enough, the oil tycoon living in SoCal. And one of the hottest young male stars in Hollywood. What was the young man thinking? Didn't he know what he was doing? Then the other names. A sheik. International businessmen. One from Germany, another from Bulgaria. And another from Russia. Two who were representatives for international leaders. And the remaining four? Men from uber-rich families across the world.

Victor focused on the Russian businessman. Blond hair. Cold blue eyes. A bit stockier than Skylar, but close enough. "Yuri Sazonov." His gaze shot to Skylar. "Getting you on the inside as Sazonov could work."

His procurement officer, the tails of his light blue shirt out over his khakis, studied the screen. He rubbed his chin, but the corners of his mouth turned up in a grin. "My Russian's pretty good, you know."

Victor's mind began clicking. "Yup. Ash said everyone seems to come with a date, right?"

Skylar's gaze slid to Fiona.

She folded her arms across her chest. "Wait You want me go to into this... this..." words seemed to fail her, "as your date? No sane woman would do that."

"She would if she's the madam who's going to be in charge of the girl. Or if he's buying for someone else," Victor replied. "Seriously, you two have that chemistry and would make a great team."

Butch chuckled. "Possessive girlfriend beats the tar out of boyfriend. I can see the headlines now."

She rolled her eyes. "All right. All right."

"So that's two on the inside. Then we'll add two more." Victor picked up his phone. "It's time to call the ninth member of our team. Sugar."

"And I think we have the way in," Flagel announced. "Make your call, and I'll explain."

28

Thursday, April 14, 2016, 0930 hours CDT, Nashville, TN

Stress. It did weird things to people. Jaidon knew that all too well. Twenty years ago when he'd left a steady, well-paying job to start Music Man Productions, it stalked him, made him worry about surviving. Then eight years ago during the Great Recession, the specter paid a visit again, that time in the form of pacing the floor during the night as he contemplated the notion of losing the club, his business, and his family. Cassie talked him back from the edge.

But this? It was different. He felt physically ill. He didn't sleep. He barely ate. When at the office, he was so distracted his office manager bluntly asked him if everything was okay at home. He also avoided The Music Man. He really did need to check on things. But that would bring him face to face with girls who were part of his brothel.

As he sat at his desk at Music Man Productions that bright, April morning, nausea oozed through his gut. Maybe he should set the girls free, fess up to what he'd done. Hah. Fat chance of that. Eight years before, there'd been the possibility of losing everything during the Great Recession. Confessing would make that a certainty. And the fallout. Prasata Jain would take his family and make them die. Slowly. In front of him. Heck, he'd probably sell Elsbeth into a brothel. Maybe Cassie too.

And then there were those gangsters who'd busted into his house. He still had no clue of who they were. Since he'd betrayed Prasata, he couldn't ask him for help.

Lousy. Lousy. Lousy.

As he sat at his desk at work, his breakfast burbled upward. He stared at the door leading to his private bathroom. His stomach settled, and he popped a Tums. Maybe that would help.

He focused on the signed contract sitting on his desk, the product of his work lunch with the young pop star on Monday. Kenya would handle it well. He tapped out his request for her to set up a meeting to discuss potential venues for concerts and how large they should be. They'd also talk about dates. The rest would wait until the singer actually finished his rap album.

He turned to another matter, that of preparing to meet with his project managers to get status updates on tours in the works and others underway.

His phone chirped. A text message. He swiped down. A five-digit sender.

The same number as Monday's text. Dizziness ambushed him. He groaned. Sweat broke out on his forehead. Fingers shaking, he pulled it up.

Time to act, Jaidon Ash. Call Prasata Jain. Tell him you're ill with norovirus and can't travel, that you'll send your proxy to take your place.

Another message flashed up.

Your proxy will be Sugar.

Oh, no. The man had been behind it the whole time.

You have ten minutes. If I don't have a reply from you by then, Elsbeth's pictures go to holeintheground.com. And I'll be verifying you made the call.

Jaidon's stomach heaved, and he barely made it to the bathroom. He groaned again as his gut twisted again. Finally, he rose and stumbled to his desk.

"Jaidon?" His administrative assistant stood in the doorway, her lips pursed, her brow furrowed. "Are you sick? You're really pale."

"Something didn't agree with me," he muttered. "Shut the door, will you? I don't want the whole office to hear me retching."

"Okay," she drawled. She turned to go, then faced him again. "Maybe you should go home and rest."

The door shut with a little more force than necessary.

He dialed a number.

Prasata's finely clipped English sent another wave of dread through him. "Yes, Jaidon Ash. Why are you calling me? We will be seeing each other tomorrow."

Jaidon began sweating. "I... I'm really, really sick." His stomach heaved again, and he clamped a hand over his mouth. "Norovirus. Hit this morning. I've been puking my guts out." Not too far from the truth. "You know how contagious that is."

"Of course."

"I— There's no way I can travel right now." The lie began rolling off his tongue. "I'd infect everyone on the plane and at the ranch."

"We will miss you, then."

Jaidon scrambled for the right words. "I've got an Exotic down there, so I'm going to send someone as my proxy."

"And who would that be?"

"A guy named Sugar. His real name's Marvin LaMott. Check him out if you want. He's got clubs here in Nashville and also New Orleans. Jazz clubs."

"I will. You can be sure of that, Jaidon Ash. Feel better."

With that, the line clicked.

Suddenly, the room felt too hot while Jaidon went cold all over. Maybe he really was coming down with something. He sat there, elbows on his desk, forehead resting in his hands as he willed himself to calm down. His gaze slid to the clock. He had a minute left to reply.

With trembling fingers, he tapped out a message to his unknown tormentor.

All done. Prasata will expect Sugar.

Let them realize the man would be checked out. Right then, he really did need to go home. Shaking, he loaded his laptop into his bag, slid his phone and wallet into his pockets, and headed to the door.

His admin assistant glanced up. She nodded. "Good to see you actually took my advice for a change."

"I'll see you in the morning. Maybe then, I'll feel better." With that, he fled to his car.

29

Thursday, April 14 2016, 1700 hours CDT, Austin, TX

All Sana wanted was a hot shower and a warm bed. Everything would kick off the next day, and she needed what bit of rest she could grab while she could get it. Hah. The revelation of Father's side business had stolen any hope of sleep. That much she'd come to realize the night before as she stared at the ceiling and watched the numbers of the clock turn over.

Now, she focused on a set of tables and chairs that served as the meeting area for the task force. Victor huddled there along with Ryan, Agent Carpenter of the FBI, Diana, Skylar, and Fiona as they planned to insert Skylar and Fiona masquerading as Yuri Sazonov and his girl. Diana would go along with Sugar to serve as his date during the festivities. No problem there. It was gutsy, but knowing Skylar, he'd pull it off, no questions asked. So would Fiona because she was a good actress. Diana too. Most likely, Sugar'd have no problem blending in.

Ryan's phone jingled, and he lifted it to his ear. He straightened as if someone important was on the other end. His expression darkened, and he strode toward the double doors leading to the third floor lobby of the Texas Department of Public Safety.

"Hey, Sana. Pizza's here," Butch called from where he and Suleiman slouched at a table and chugged bottles of water. "Want to go down with us to get them?"

She glanced at them, then headed to the doors as if needing to go to the restroom. "I need to go to the bathroom."

Suleiman joined her. "Are you—"

"I'm fine, Suleiman."

His lips flattened at her interruption, and he rubbed the back of his neck. "Are you sure? We can talk while we wait."

"Seriously. I'm okay." She feigned squirming. "I gotta go. And I'm tired."

"You and me both, girl." Butch pushed the elevator's Down button. "Let's go, Suleiman. Don't want to keep the pizza guy waiting."

The elevator pinged. The doors shut, but not before Suleiman shot her one last, long look.

Sana peered around her. Quiet ruled. Offices related to special operations unit personnel lined one of the halls. Some were empty, some were occupied since crime in Texas never stopped. Where had Ryan gone?

Her mind whirled as she returned to the lobby and headed down the remaining hall. She really should be focusing on the plan to rescue Morgan, not on old wounds from her past. *Why am I being so selfish? I don't understand.* Except that each time she thought about the plan, her thoughts went straight to the man who held Morgan. Her father.

She peered through the clear glass of a door leading to what looked like the break room.

Phone still to his ear, Ryan paced. He nodded and waved her inside. "Sir, we're really close. We're finalizing details on a plan that will wrap everything up this weekend... No, sir. I don't want to disclose operational details right now. First, they're still in the works. Second, I don't want the possibility of a tipoff. I know Mr. Jain has links to the governor. He contributed to his campaign..."

Sana let the door shut behind her.

Ryan ran a hand through his hair. "Sir, I understand this task force has been ongoing for six months. Please pass along that by Monday, it'll be all over save for the paperwork... Yes, sir. No problem." He lowered his phone and shook his head.

Sana approached him. "What is it?"

"Oh, the governor's been on the director's back, demanding that he disband the task force. For some reason, he thinks we should have gotten the kingpin in six months."

"And crimes get neatly solved in forty-seven minutes."

A rueful laugh escaped him. "Only on television. Or in my dreams." He set his phone down, folded his arms, and leaned his back against the counter. "What's up?"

"I have a question."

"I'm all ears."

She ran her fingers along the counter's smooth edge. "I'm... worried."

"About what? If you're worried the FBI's going to come after you, don't, okay? It's not like you had knowledge about what was going on."

That infernal lump swelled again in her throat. "It's more than that." She met his gaze. "I'm worried I'm never going to recover from this."

His forehead wrinkled. "Why would you say that?"

"My missteps Saturday. I mean, if I hadn't talked out of turn, Morgan would be free. It just..." Her time with Taz resurfaced. She threw up her hands. "I don't know. I just feel like an outsider now with the team, like a stray."

Ryan unfurled his arms and braced his hands on the counter. His hazel gaze bored into her. "Because of what happened Saturday or when you rebelled and shacked up with Taz?"

What could she say? Her eyes filled, and she looked away. "Both."

"I remember you used that term when you first got out of prison. Have you talked with your fiancé about this? Suleiman's his name, right?"

"Yeah." That came out as a croak. "I haven't."

"Why not?"

A tear escaped and trickled down her cheek. "What could I say, Ryan? I lived with a guy? He encouraged me to commit crimes, and I bought it hook, line, and sinker?"

He took a step closer. "Do you remember what we talked about a couple of days ago? When we stopped off at my house on the way back from Gatesville?"

Her mind scattered. "N-no."

"One of the things that broke you and me up the first time was that I wasn't honest with you about losing Molly and the baby. When I met Dakota, I knew she was something special. I didn't want to make the same mistake again. Shortly after she and I began dating, I laid it all out on the table. What happened with the drunk driver who killed my wife and unborn child. The way it impacted me. The way it induced so many fears within me that had kept me from totally committing to you. I came clean with her, and it drew us closer."

Sana put her face in her hands. "Suleiman would never understand."

"What makes you say that? Has he bared all with you?"

Suleiman had, his very deepest, darkest secrets. But that had been different. A little less than a year before, they'd been mere friends, and—

Ryan put his hand on her arm. "I think you're underestimating him."

Sana raised her face. She stepped so close he almost held her. "But you... you know me. You know all of the bad parts of me and still care about me."

"And I'm engaged." With his finger, he lifted her chin. "You need to talk to him. To give—"

"Take your hands off her!" Suleiman's shout rocketed through the room. Something crashed on the ground.

Ryan pushed her away.

Suleiman cocked his fist.

"Suleiman, no!" she cried.

His punch caught Ryan on the cheek.

Ryan yelped, then charged.

Butch yanked him back. "Whoa! Down, boy!"

Victor snagged Suleiman.

Face flushed and nostrils flaring, Suleiman shook loose. He jabbed a finger at her. "And you! I never dreamed you would..."

Her cheeks flamed. Her knees trembled. "Suleiman, please, it's not—"

"You betrayed me! And do not think I don't know who you are, Ranger Flagel. You and Sana dated when..." He made toward Ryan again.

Victor grabbed him in a half nelson. "Stop it. Matter of fact, both of you, get out. Now. Butch, put them in a room somewhere. I'll be there in a moment."

Making sure he kept his body between Ryan and Sana, Butch backed toward the door. "Let's go, Sana."

"But—"

"You heard the boss. Let's go before things get worse. You too, Suleiman."

Her fiancé jerked loose from Victor. With one final glare at Ryan as he rotated his shoulder, he flung open the door. It knocked a hole in the drywall.

Butch found another door and an empty conference room behind it. "The both of you, in there. And try not to kill each other."

Suleiman blasted inside and didn't stop until he reached the window on the opposite wall. He rubbed his wrists and lifted his chin.

Sana's heart almost hammered its way out of her chest. His name rasped out as a whisper across her lips. "Suleiman."

He pierced her with a pained stare. "Why, Sana?"

Desperation stole her voice.

"You know something? I do not want to know." He kicked a chair over. "You betrayed me. That is enough."

"I didn't! I—"

"I know what I saw! It is over."

Heaviness crept into her soul. Trembling, she collapsed onto a chair. "What?"

He faced the window. This time, so softly she almost missed it, he repeated, "It is over. The wedding is off."

Thursday, April 14, 2016, 1730 hours CDT, Austin, TX

Victor's face, neck, and ears felt as if they were going to burst into flame. "I don't know what to say, except I'm sorry. I don't know what got into him."

Flagel flexed his jaw. "Oh, I do. When have men come to blows? Over a woman."

What I saw just couldn't have happened. Victor wanted to bellow and beat his chest at that. Sana had gone from a fast-rising star into someone who was falling apart before his eyes. He shook his head. "She seems to have become a bit..."

Flagel rubbed his forehead. "For the record, I never enticed her, never led her on. I even told her she should be discussing her past life with Suleiman."

Victor's throat tightened. Sana might as well have taken one of Suleiman's sniper rifles and shot him.

Flagel headed toward the closed door. "No offense, but y'all will need to pay for the repairs to the wall." He opened it, then turned. "Sana should be sharing that stuff with him, not me. Her home's in Arizona now. Not here. Especially since I'm engaged as well. And FYI for him, I'm not going to charge him for assaulting a law officer. He should consider himself fortunate."

Victor watched him go before heading in the other direction.

Butch stood at parade rest a few doors down.

Victor smiled. "Some habits never die." He clapped Butch on the shoulder. "At ease, soldier. Sit rep?"

Butch grimaced. "Our love birds ain't love birds anymore, boss."

Victor peered into the room. Across from him, Suleiman faced the window with his arms folded across his chest. Sana slumped at a table, her head in her hands, her slender shoulders shaking.

Where was Deb when he needed her? She'd be able to tease apart what had happened a whole lot quicker than he. Not to mention, he had a lousy track record with Sana as of late.

Butch stirred. "At least Suleiman only kicked over one chair."

Victor faced him. "Go ahead and get supper set up. Chances are I'm sending both of them back to the hotel tonight."

"A good idea. And in separate Ubers or something."

"Hah. Probably." *Lord, bind my tongue so I don't shoot off my mouth this time.* Victor headed inside, shut the door, and leaned against it. "Both of you, look at me."

Sana lifted her face. Paths of mascara and tears streaked her cheeks.

Suleiman's eyes remained cold, almost like hard granite. His arms remained folded across his chest, and he stood with feet planted wide.

Victor pushed away from the door. "Sit down. We need to talk."

Suleiman opened his mouth to argue.

Victor yanked out a chair at the head of the table. "Sit. Down. Now."

With a small harumph, Suleiman did the same at the other end.

Lord, show me what to say here. Please. Otherwise, everything falls apart in the next ten minutes. He took a deep breath. "I don't know what happened there, only that I just witnessed some of the most unprofessional behavior I've ever seen. Suleiman, what were you thinking? You never, ever hit a law enforcement—"

"He was flirting with Sana!" Suleiman spat the words.

Sana shot back, "He was not! He was comforting—"

"Ranger Flagel had no intentions of coming between you two." Victor focused on his breaking-and-entering specialist. He leaned forward. "Sana, look at me."

She didn't.

He jabbed his finger into the table's smooth surface. "Now, Sana."

Finally, she did. More tears trickled down her cheeks.

At that point, he didn't care. "What's happened to you? Yes, I know you were dealt a tough blow last weekend, but your behavior as of late has mystified me. If we didn't need every person to get Morgan out, I'd suspend you until you addressed your issues. But I need you, unfortunately."

Realizing she'd heard enough for the moment, he switched his attention to Suleiman. "And you. You're normally the calm one, the one who controls your impulses. Your actions nearly created a rift with the task force. Not to mention, you could have landed in jail on some very serious charges."

Suleiman lowered his gaze to the table. His cheeks reddened. "But Ryan—"

"*Both* of you in here bear responsibility for this mess." Victor leaned forward with his elbows on the table and his fingers clasped together. "This is what we're going to do. You will set your personal differences aside and act like adults. You will act like the professionals I know you can be and will accomplish your duties." He lowered his voice. "And if you don't, if Morgan disappears or someone on our team dies because of you?" He paused. "I'll never forgive you. Understand?"

Sana's tawny skin turned a sickly yellow. Another tear slid down her cheek, and she nodded.

Victor focused on his sniper. "Suleiman?"

"Yes." He ground out that word.

"Go wait in the hall. I want to speak with Sana alone for a moment."

Suleiman jumped up. He almost ran to the door, yanked it open, and slammed it so hard the glass shook. At least it didn't crack.

Victor focused on Sana.

Tears dripped down her cheeks again. Her chin trembled, and it reached her voice. "I'm sorry."

He couldn't soften. Not yet. "When we get back to Arizona, you'll be on suspension, understand? No contracts until you make an appointment with Deb, sit down with her, and work out your issues. Am I clear?"

A nod answered him.

"And I pray you and Suleiman can work out things between each other. Let's go." He rose and escorted his charges to the elevators. As they waited for one, they kept their gazes pinned to the marble floor. Awkward silence hung in the air like a noxious odor. Down the hall in the task force room, someone laughed. Nope. Not having any of that here. The bell dinged, and they rode the elevator to the first floor. Once outside, he fished his keys from his pocket. "I want you both to go back to the hotel for the night."

A black Cadillac Escalade with Louisiana plates pulled to the curb and distracted him.

Loquacious climbed from the front passenger side. He opened the door to the back.

Ever resplendent in his white suit with a navy shirt, handkerchief, and hat band, Sugar slid onto the sidewalk. His eyes crinkled at the edge of his sunglasses as he smiled. "My, my. It's mighty nice of—uh-oh."

He'd seen Sana's tears, Suleiman's glare. "Sugar says he walked into something bad."

Victor fidgeted with the keys. "That's one way of putting it. Oh, I got you a room where we're staying. I hope that's not too low on your totem pole. We're at the Hampton Inn a few blocks away."

He chuckled. "Not at all. Your boy and girl need a ride back?"

Victor nodded to Sana and Suleiman. "Go with the driver to the hotel."

They didn't argue. Suleiman made a point in climbing into the front seat Loquacious had vacated, leaving Sana to help herself into the backseat. The doors closed with a firm whump. The Escalade eased into traffic.

Victor ran a hand down his face. Yep, he'd forgotten to shave that day. "This is bad." He released a sigh. "C'mon. Let's head upstairs."

They wound up in the same conference room where he'd talked with Sana and Suleiman. Loquacious righted the chair Victor's protégé had kicked over. "Sana's coming apart at the seams."

Sugar shut the door and settled on the chair to his right.

Victor focused on the glass top. "If I didn't need them so badly, I'd have sent them back to the ranch in Flagstaff."

"You want to tell me what happened?" Sugar asked.

"Suleiman happened to walk in on Flagel being a little too close to Sana."

"Your Ranger boy?"

"Yup. I think he jumped to some pretty wrong conclusions." Then it clicked. "I think years ago, when Sana got out of prison, Flagel was there to help her pick up the pieces. I gather they used to be romantically involved, though now he's engaged as well."

"It's more than that, Victor Chavez." The ninth member of the team smiled, revealing a gold tooth. "You see, when dealing with the law, Sugar always does his homework. Your Ranger boy was the one who arrested Sana."

Stunned, Victor stared at him.

Sugar bobbed his head. "Oh, yes indeed. Pulled her out of bed, her and her lover, probably after they'd gotten some time in the sack. He got her to plead guilty in exchange for a lesser sentence."

"Then what..." Why hadn't that been in the file Gary had given him three years before at the start of Operation Shadow Box?

Sugar fussed with his handkerchief. "Gut says he saw her true character, the way her man had lured her into crime. He was there when she was sentenced, but he didn't see her again until she got shanked."

Victor's mouth fell open. "She got—"

"Shanked. She testified against her former lover, a dude nicknamed Taz. He got twenty. She got shanked as a thank you and barely survived."

"I had no idea."

"Like I said, Sugar does his homework when dealing with people."

"Yeah, I can see that." Victor's mind strained at something. "Just how do you have those kinds of resources?"

Another smile crossed the man's face. "I'm a man of many facets, Victor Chavez. Some pleasant, some not so pleasant. Many a woman has thanked me for buying their freedom. And many a man..."

Victor shuddered at what Sugar left unsaid. Something told him not to ask. He cleared his throat. "We found a way in. Come join us in the task force room."

Voices fell silent as Sugar made his entrance. Well, they probably saw Loquacious and thought better about questioning Victor or Flagel. Victor made the introductions.

Flagel's eyes remained guarded, and a red mark formed on his jaw where Suleiman had tagged him. "Pleasure to meet you. Victor says you're going to be on the inside."

Sugar put a hand over his heart. "So long as I have a lady on my arm. Who's available?"

"Skylar's going as one of the buyers, a guy named Yuri Sazonov. And his girl, Irina," Victor added with a nod in Fiona's direction.

"So that leaves you two, then," Sugar said as he studied Shelly and Diana. He focused on Shelly. "You got the computers and comms, right?'

She blushed. "That's me."

He fixed his gaze on Diana. "That leaves you and me, pretty lady."

Diana pushed away from the edge of the table. "I'm your woman, then."

Eager to get through the rest of the evening, Victor rushed on with his briefing. "Then it's settled. From what Ash said, all the sellers will be arriving tomorrow by five. You'll arrive at four. No bodyguards are allowed, as Jain handles all security. And no guns either. Communication will be tricky. Wi-Fi connections are monitored, and cell calls are monitored as well."

Shelly smirked.

He faced her. "What?"

"I've got a way around that." She waved her hand as if swatting a fly. "Do go on."

Victor did. Over the next several hours, they bandied the plan back and forth. Task force members offered their opinions and poked holes in it. So did the remaining members of the team. Of course. He expected just that. Another round of pizza came and went as well. By the time that he finally called it a night, he'd reached one conclusion. Come sunrise Sunday morning, either Morgan would be free, or they'd all be dead.

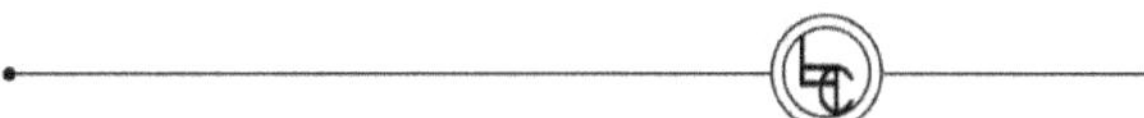

Thursday, April 14, 2016, 2030 hours CDT, Austin, TX

Sana's tears finally exhausted her until she felt like she couldn't move from the middle of the bed. Her stomach cramped from too many sobs and too little food. Muffled noises penetrated the wall separating her room from Suleiman's. It sounded like the television. She raised her head from the pillow. Should she go in there and try to explain?

No. Not when he'd opted to take the stairs six stories to their floor rather than ride on an elevator with her. She'd heard the door to his room slam with a force that shook the walls.

She pushed herself upright. Her head swam, and she put her face in her hands.

Where had she gone wrong?

Too many places. Time for a shower. Maybe that would loosen her mind. With the water as hot as she could stand it, she stepped under its penetrating stream. If only it could cleanse her thoughts as well as it did her body.

It all started when she'd spoken out of turn five days before. Her words, even innocent, had spelled disaster for Morgan and nearly gotten half the team killed. She held herself responsible, and Victor's dressing down in front of everyone widened the crack in her self-confidence. Rightly or wrongly, she blamed herself and assumed the team blamed her. She began calling herself a stray.

Then came Ash's confession and the revelation of who her father really was. It rocked her world and brought back all sorts of bad memories. It only reinforced the notion that she was a stray. When Ryan came back into her life in a sudden, unexpected way, she found it easier to run to him, who knew all of her past, rather than to Suleiman.

"Forgive me, Suleiman," she whispered beneath the noise of the water. "Forgive me for not confiding in you sooner. When we were friends and then started dating, it was so easy to focus on your past instead of mine."

Finally, she shut off the taps and dried on a soft towel. After pulling on a pair of leggings and a sweatshirt, she combed through her wet hair and stared at herself in the mirror. Redness from her tears tinged her wide, dark eyes. She slicked back her chin-length, black hair, which Suleiman loved running his fingers through.

Despite the lump in her throat, she said aloud, "Yes, my past has shaped me into who I am today. But I cannot and refuse to let my past define my future anymore."

How could she battle that temptation?

She returned to the room and stared at the nightstand where she'd placed her travel Bible. She opened it to the Gospels and read about so many of the women who followed Jesus. Like Mary Magdalene, who'd been possessed. Or the woman at the well who'd slept around. Or the woman who'd been bleeding for twelve years with no hope of healing. Strays, all of them, at least to the society of their day. But to Jesus? He healed them. Welcomed them as His followers.

Sana raised her face and stared at the window. The outside light bleached the sheer curtain white. *Jesus, what are You trying to tell me?*

Slowly, like a sunrise, a memory returned from when she'd gotten shanked. While she'd struggled for life in the hospital, she dreamed of being close to fires, of crying out for freedom. Then came Jesus, who pulled her from the inferno and held her close as He took the flaming darts meant for her. She awakened to find Ryan sitting next to her bed. Emotion clouded his face when she told him of her dream. When she returned to prison, she shared her dream with Miss Merlita. Her mentor knew she'd seen Jesus. Within two weeks, Sana was baptized by the prison chaplain and welcomed into a body of believers. She was no longer a stray.

Now, she realized how much she'd isolated herself by choice with thinking she was once more alone and on her own. She'd turned her back on those who could have helped her, including Suleiman. *I can't do that anymore. Jesus, You put me in community for a reason. And I am loved by them.*

Her eyes filled, but she swallowed down her tears. A new peace gradually seeped into her soul. *Jesus, You know me, my struggles, my hurts, the way I can isolate myself. Thank You for reminding me that You loved me enough to die for me. And thank You for putting others in my life who care about me. Now I realize that I'm not a stray. You put me in community with others for a reason, that is to support me and encourage me. Forgive me for my independent nature and my thinking I could go it alone.*

Sana uncurled from her tuck. She needed to talk to Suleiman, to share all that was on her heart. She listened.

Ten o'clock. The television had fallen silent. Was he asleep?

She had no way of knowing. If he was, she'd awaken him so they could talk. Surely they could work things out.

With new energy, she hopped off the bed and pushed open the door connecting their rooms. Sure enough, the television was a black rectangle. But he wasn't in bed, and he wasn't sitting at the worktable or on the couch. "Suleiman?"

She peered into the bathroom.

He wasn't there.

Her heart sank. He'd gone out, maybe to drown his sorrows or something. He probably didn't want to have anything to do with her. Her newly found confidence crashed and burned. She didn't deserve him. Certainly not after today.

New tears pricked her eyes as she stared at the diamond ring on her left hand. Fingers trembling, she slid it free and set it on the nightstand. Her words came out as a ragged whisper. "I'm sorry, Suleiman. You deserve someone so much better than me."

When she returned to her bedroom, she locked her part of the door between their rooms. Without even changing into her nightshirt, she crawled into bed and cried some more. She really needed to get herself together by Saturday at the latest.

She thought about the words she'd spoken to herself in the mirror. As she lay on her back and stared at the ceiling, she tried to coach herself. "Victor's right. I need to be on my A game starting tomorrow but definitely on Saturday. Morgan's counting on that. Jesus, the day You saved me, I was a new creation in You. I know who You made me to be, a lioness who's fearless in times of trouble. I need to focus on that. And after all is said and done, then I'll worry about Suleiman and me."

With that, she turned onto her side and pulled the covers up to her chin. As she closed her eyes, something draped over her, something like peace. Could God be working in her heart? She could only hope so.

30

Friday, April 15, 2016, 1400 hours CDT, outside Austin, TX

In a far corner of Morgan Walton's mind, a deadbolt in a door slid back. She cracked her eyes open. The dim blue light that helped define her prison remained. So did the white noise. Both made her as groggy and drowsy as a drug did. The clamminess of the room where she stayed penetrated her soul. She surveyed her cell. Still six by six with bars stretching from floor to ceiling. The same as the twenty-three other cells she'd counted.

Clear light filled the air and brightened with each passing second. The white noise ceased.

Now she recognized what occupied the shelves lining the wall separating the cells from the bathroom area. Rows upon rows of glass boxes filled with tarantulas. She shivered.

Footfalls echoed through the room, whose ceilings soared to twelve feet high. Not just one pair of steps. Several. Four men and two women paraded down the central aisle separating the cells.

Morgan started. Her blood chilled when she noted a younger man dressed in charcoal gray pants and a white dress shirt with the collar open. He'd been with the owner of the club in Nashville and was the one whose fantasy had been her last nightmare. Now free of the drugs that had held her prisoner while in Nashville, hot anger burbled deep in her gut. She pushed herself upright and huddled with the blanket her captors had provided pulled all the way to her chin. Beneath it, her hands clenched into fists.

The group stopped at the far end. One of them, an older man with salt-and-pepper hair and beard, clasped his hands behind his back and lifted his chin as he strolled up and down the line of cells. His all-black attire save for a sensible silver belt buckle reminded her of a villain from a James Bond movie.

"Welcome, ladies, to the ranch." His English held the faintest traces of accents, as if he'd grown up somewhere else and come to the country years before. "Today is the start of your big weekend."

As if sensing rebellion, he focused on her.

The hair on her arms and nape of her neck tingled. Dad's voice echoed somewhere deep in her soul. *Don't cross him.* She was free of the drugs. She needed to stay that way to think. With lowered eyes, she studied the weave of her blanket.

He moved on down the line. "The festivities begin in a few hours. You see, you're going to be in a beauty pageant of sorts."

But the winner doesn't get a crown. Morgan bit the inside of her cheek.

"Tonight, those who nominated you to attend will be here. You will show them the goods. And then tomorrow night, you will present yourselves to our distinguished guests. Sunday morning, we'll be sending you to a new place."

We're being sold! Morgan dug her fingers into the fabric of the scrubs she'd worn since her arrival. She rested her forehead against her arms and tried to control the trembling that started deep in her core.

His steps resumed, and he returned to his group. "Our guests begin arriving in two hours. Shortly after that, I will see to it that you are fed. And once you eat, you will prepare by showering and dressing. Xenia, show them what they will be wearing tonight."

The man inclined his head toward one of the women, a tall blonde with her hair piled on her head. Tendrils of gold dripped in ringlets to her shoulders. She slid an elegant cape of black satin from her body to reveal a deep blue bikini, plus a sash that said, "Product of Russia."

Morgan's mouth dropped open. She went cold all over as beauty pageant music cued in her mind.

The man handed Xenia her robe. "Chantal, show them what they'll be wearing tomorrow night."

The second woman, a brunette, dropped her own robe to reveal an elegant evening gown of deep red satin that showed off all of her curves. Her sash read Product of France. Her makeup was as impeccable as Xenia's.

Morgan's skin tingled. Her stomach twisted on the meager breakfast Xenia and Chantal, who she now recognized as their caretakers, had served.

"I won't! I won't do this. It's sick!" That came from the cell across the main aisle from Morgan. A curvy blonde with her hair spilling past her shoulders stood and gripped the bars so tightly the tendons on her hands stood out. Taylor. That was the name she'd whispered to Morgan when she'd been coherent enough to think. Taylor from California.

A small smile crossed the man's face.

The girl glared at him. "You're a horrible person to do this to us. And I won't. Not anymore."

For a moment, the man didn't stir. Not an inch. Coiled anger. Ready to strike.

Morgan made it to her knees. Then to her feet. She gripped the bars and started shaking her head. *No, Taylor. Don't. It's not worth it.*

The man's smile melted away. "I'm afraid you have no choice." He shot a glance at the younger man. "Narat."

Narat punched four numbers into a keypad on the cage.

Morgan tried to memorize the combination. Four-six-eight-two.

Taylor backed against the other side of the cell.

The other two men reached inside. They grabbed her and threw her across the aisle.

Morgan jumped back as she slammed into the bars in front of her.

Taylor sagged to the ground. One of the men, who had to be well above six feet and three hundred pounds, snagged her hair. She moaned as he tossed her onto her back and straddled her hips. She thrashed and pounded her fists on his legs. "Let me go! You're hurting me!"

The other guard grabbed her arms and stretched them above her head.

The older man held out his hand, and Narat handed him a needle and syringe.

He knelt beside the girl and ran his finger up and down her arm. Her screams turned to keening as he injected the drug into her arm.

Her guards released her.

She began convulsing. With a moan, she stilled.

Her eyes remained open.

Morgan's legs gave way. She slid down the bars into a sitting position. Her chest heaved as her pulse thundered in her ears. She clamped a hand over her mouth. *I'm going to be sick.*

The older man straightened as the guards carried Taylor's inert form from the room.

As he pivoted on his heel, the older man held up the needle and syringe. "Ladies, your friend, Taylor, received some of the purest heroin available. A death sentence. Does anyone else refuse to cooperate?"

Silence like that found in a recording studio when no one was around.

He focused briefly on Morgan.

She snapped her eyes shut as it clicked. Narat, the young man who'd spirited her from Nashville, was this man's son.

The soles of his shoes once more slapped on the concrete. "The same shall happen to you if you refuse to cooperate. And before you think of suicide by heroin, let me tell you what will happen. She cost me money. And I will collect from her family. They will pay the ultimate price. And so will yours if you choose to die."

Morgan risked a peek

He took in one more strut up and down the line.

She clenched her jaw. She wouldn't look at him, lest he single her out for the same treatment. But Narat?

She felt his stare on her.

She returned it.

Once more, Dad's voice whispered in her ear. *If you're ever abducted, be respectful. It could serve you well later.*

Point taken, Dad. She lowered her gaze to her knees.

The footsteps receded.

Once more, the lights dimmed to that infernal blue. The white noise came on, this time punctuated by sobs from some of the girls. Others sat in stunned silence.

More of Dad's advice flitted through her now-active mind. *If you can find a way to escape, take it.*

She would. Problem was, she didn't see any way out.

Friday, April 15, 2016, 1600 hours CDT, outside Austin, TX

Phase One began as Diana Kasem stood in the middle of what Prasata Jain had just called her and Sugar's guest room. Suite was more like it with rich, dark hardwoods coating the entire area. She passed between two columns of dark wood and railings separating sleeping and sitting areas. In the bathroom were walls of a peaceful golden yellow punctuated by a terracotta tile floor and touches of dark wood and deep blue tile. Big enough for them to hold a party if that was what they desired. Similar colors to that in the bath flowed throughout the suite. Elegant Mexican met rustic western but in a way that didn't clash.

Time to get down to business. She opened her suitcase and dug underneath the more casual clothing she'd brought. From a hidden compartment in her suitcase, she pulled out a small box and turned it on as she began a circuit of the room. Its light remained green throughout her entire tour. Finally, she snapped it off and returned it to its hiding spot. "No bugs, cameras, or anything."

Coming inside from the balcony, her partner-in-crime took off his hat and tossed it onto a desk in the sitting area. "Sugar figures they monitor all cell phone calls and Internet browsing through their central hub."

She kicked off her sandals and crossed a tightly woven Navajo rug that must have cost a fortune. "Most likely since he told us cell coverage was blocked. I'm surprised he didn't get suspicious when I showed up on your arm."

Sugar opened louvered closet doors and unzipped a hanging bag. "Sometimes feigning ignorance is the best course of action. The fact that you were completely agreeable about supper alone here in the suite put him at ease. Maybe this tour gives us some more information. We ask the right questions, pretty lady, and it will."

An hour later, Diana found out exactly what he meant. They met Jain downstairs in the foyer along with three other men, those from Dallas, Seattle, and New York. The rest were due to arrive while they were away.

Had it been under any other circumstances, Jain would have made an excellent tour guide. Diana kept her eyes open as he led them through a massive dining room big enough to seat twenty, a huge great room, and a formal living room. He prattled on about the equipment in the decent-sized gym in the other wing that also held a home theater that could seat fifty.

They headed downstairs to a basement containing an extensive wine and liquor cellar and even a bar for tasting parties with its own seating area next to it. A stout metal door with an electronic keypad seemed too modern, too out of place, to fit with the rustic nature of the house. And what was the room on the other side under? She'd kept her direction fairly well until they'd come down to the basement on a staircase that wrapped along two walls. Maybe the kitchen?

She ran her hand along the rough wood of the bar. "This wood is beautiful. Is it reclaimed?"

Jain paused from his monologue. Obviously, he hadn't expected a question. "All of it is. Old railroad ties is what I believe the interior decorator requested." His chest puffed out slightly. "I like old things as well as new. And that includes my wine and liquor."

She gestured to the door and tilted her head. With an impish smile she asked, "Is that what's behind that door? Your top secret wine stash?"

Uneasy laughter rippled through the small group.

"Ah, you found me out. I may not drink alcohol in my native country of India, but I do enjoy a fine wine or Scotch. Or champagne, as you will see tomorrow night. And yes, you caught me. The finest of the finest, I keep under lock and key, to be shared only on special occasions." With a sweep of his hand inviting them to precede him, he said, "Come. We have much to see outside."

Diana noted the door's location on her left as they headed toward the stairs. Two turns upward brought it to be on her right and indeed below the kitchen. *Thank you, Suleiman and Skylar, for drilling observation skills into my head.*

Once more, they stood in the hallway separating the dining room from the kitchen. The basement door stood across from the dining room between the two openings leading to the kitchen.

Jain led them into the great room and outside. They were on one side of the U-shaped hacienda. A pool filled the space between the two wings. Oh, the lush landscaping of bougainvillea, palms, and hibiscus, plus a myriad of other tropical plants Diana couldn't begin to name. If she dropped her guard, she could imagine she resided at a resort instead of a hacienda where the sale of girls took place on a regular basis.

"Tomorrow night, we will dine beneath the portico," Jain said as he led them alongside the sparkling azure water. He faced Diana and Sugar, who kept an arm around her waist. "I bought this ranch in the early nineties." A rueful laugh escaped him as they passed beneath the portico and arrived at a wide road of smooth stones. "Over time, I tore down the old house and everything else except for that old horse barn you see."

Diana noted where it lay in relation to the rest of the hacienda. "Do you have horses in there?"

Jain chuckled. "Ah, no. It's historic, and my children wanted me to keep it. Our horses are kept outside the walls. Which is also where our ranch hands live."

Who now toted rifles slung over their shoulders. Some ranch hands.

At the barn, two guards tugged the doors open. A black Chevy Silverado pickup with darkened windows eased from the inside. A shell covered the back. They closed the doors behind it and locked them with a chain and padlock.

She glanced at Jain.

His stared at it with an intensity that sent chills down her spine. His nostrils flared. He smoothed over his expression with an ingratiating smile as he gestured for them to continue toward the back of the property.

Why would a truck be in there? And why would two armed guards close the door? Diana slid closer to Sugar. He took her hand as if to comfort her. She needed to get to their room to sort things through—after she finished the blasted tour.

"This way, everyone," Jain said as he led the way through an auto gate at the back.

A half hour later, they returned to their room. Grabbing a notepad, she sketched what she remembered of the layout and stared at it. Something seemed weird as she gazed at the barn versus its location with the kitchen and the basement. She could draw a straight line to it at right angles across the road. Maybe a tunnel? She needed to see what was behind that door.

But how?

Then it came to her. She'd have to sneak downstairs after everyone went to supper.

"Sugar says he needs to get a move on it."

He stood before a full-length mirror and primped by adjusting the lapels of his blazer and his tie. He fastened a tie pin glinting with rhinestones, a Shelly Special that contained a listening device.

In her musings, Diana had nearly forgotten about him. "So sorry. I was thinking."

Sugar smiled at her. "I could tell. Prasata Jain spooked you."

She glanced at her notepad. "That door in the basement hides something big."

"You might be right."

"I'm going to go down there in a bit, see what's behind it."

"That's a plan, pretty lady. Need I say be careful?"

She tapped the earpiece hidden in her ear. "I'll be listening and IMing Four tonight after I get back. I'm not going to be gone long."

He nodded to the diagram she'd drawn. "Sugar suggests memorizing that and destroying it."

She kissed him on the cheek. "I will. Get going, you."

Soon, her earpiece came to life with the rumble of male voices. She easily picked out Sugar's timbre and speech patterns as the men were served appetizers in the formal living room next to the foyer. Jain welcomed them and asked everyone to head to the dining room.

Time to go. Diana cut on the shower in the bathroom. That way, whenever someone delivered her meal, they wouldn't question her absence.

Since she was the only one on the hall, she darted to the staircase and peered over the railing to the foyer.

No guards. At least on the inside. She tiptoed down the stairs and paused. Down the hallway to the right was the other wing of the house with more guest suites on the second floor. She stood in the formal living room, now deserted since the festivities continued in the dining room. Before her stretched the great room, her last hurdle before she reached the kitchen. She had to play it cool, like she belonged there, so none of the maids who rushed back and forth across the hallway to the dining room would question her. She also had to avoid attracting Jain's attention.

With a deep breath, she strolled across the great room. A maid glanced up but said nothing as she placed goblets full of wine on a tray. She hefted it onto her shoulder, then headed across the hall.

Diana caught a glimpse of the dining room. Jain sat with his back to her so he faced the windows with Narat to his left and a blonde woman to his right. Sugar had taken the foot of the table. Smart man. His gaze crossed her, but he didn't react. The rest of the guests were preoccupied with accepting their drinks.

She arrived at the basement door. With one last check, she opened it and slipped inside.

She paused on the small landing and listened. No sound. On sconces to the right, candles flickered. Real candles. More lit the stairs in a soft glow. She tiptoed downward. Additional candles on ironwork flickered on the wall above the couch. She tried to imagine what happened down here. Perhaps some of the intimate goings-on of Jain's trafficking business. Or maybe training girls to be at the beck and call of their masters as they served wine and liquor from the numerous bottles in racks along the wall next to the bar.

She approached the door with its keypad. Digital like she'd suspected. In other words, high tech. Why? Even for an extremely expensive wine collection, a lock and key should have sufficed.

Upstairs, the door leading to the landing opened.

A female voice, so different from the male voices of that night's festivities, called something to someone upstairs.

Diana froze. She had to hide. Now.

She scurried behind the bar and crouched. Hopefully, no one would be interested in a tasting tonight. She risked a peek around.

Heels clicked on the wooden steps. The voluptuous blonde from the dining room came down the stairs. She wore an evening dress and, with her hair piled in golden ringlets on her head, came into the basement. She approached the door. Diana tried to note her fingers as they moved across the keypad. She got the first two numbers, but there were four beeps.

A moment later, the woman came out. She stopped.

Diana pulled back. Had she been spotted?

Then, with muttered words in a foreign language, the woman turned back. Once more, she punched in the code. This time, Diana caught it all. Four-six-eight-two. Bingo. She had to get out of there before she pressed her luck too far.

When she was sure the woman headed to the first floor, Diana retraced her steps to the kitchen.

"What are you doing in here? I thought Father instructed you to dine alone."

Diana stilled. She swiveled on her heel and found Narat staring at her, his head cocked. His dark eyes glinted. Did he suspect? Her mind spun. "What's a good meal without a glass of fine wine?"

A smile flitted across his lips. "Point well taken." He reached for a goblet and a bottle of Merlot. His gaze never leaving hers, he poured it, then toasted her before handing it over. "Enjoy your evening, Dr. Kasem."

"And do not disturb us," he might as well have added.

No worries there. With wine in hand, Diana retreated to the suite. Her heart pounded as she leaned against the shut door. That was too close.

A meal with a cover over it and a glass of wine sat on the small table in the sitting area. A smile crossed her face. She took her meal and laptop out on the balcony. She might not be able to reach a cell tower with her phone, but that didn't mean she couldn't communicate with Shelly. But people would be monitoring her computer. She had to be careful. She logged into the Wi-Fi and selected a movie, then opened the IM program Shelly had installed on her computer. Encryption turned her surveillance information into a conversation with her parents.

Four, Six here.

Got you, Six. What did you find? Shelly's words eased the tension in her chest.

With the movie making it look like she was relaxing, Diana summarized her findings, everything from the pickup leaving the barn to the door in the basement with its four-six-eight-two combination. Hopefully, Vic and Butch would make sense of her observations.

But I don't know if the girls are being held there, she typed.

Another message flashed up.

One says it's a good theory.

Diana kept listening to Sugar's chatter. She had to give the man credit. He'd fit right into the team and knew how to pass along information without seeming to do so.

"Nice round of girls, eh?" he said to the guy who must have been sitting next to him. "Looks like Atlantic City all over again. Miss America. Swimsuit style. Boy, do I ever love a bikini on a girl."

Diana stilled.

"Twenty-three of them. Man." Sugar breathed in as if they were the most fascinating beings in the world. "Product of Nashville, huh? Hmmm, hmmm, hmmm. That Mr. Ash sure does know his stuff. Sugar says she'll go for a pretty penny. Redheads always do."

That elicited laughter.

Diana began typing on her IM program again.

Twenty-three girls. Morgan's here. My gut says they're being kept in the basement behind that door. She recalled Jain's expression when he'd noted the pickup. Not happy at all. More toward anger. *And my gut says the old horse barn houses something. Maybe a tunnel entrance?*

Shelly's words flashed up. *Thanks for the info, Six. One says good work and keep it coming.*

Unfortunately, nothing else of note, just catcalls and bawdy comments from all of the men. Her cheeks reddened. The sooner she got out of this mess, the better. Then came a suggestion from the seller who resided in Dallas. "Hey, that redhead is yours for the night if you want it. Mr. Jain always allows us one last shot at the merchandise."

Diana's jaw clenched.

Sugar's rich, easy laugh flowed across her earpiece. "Naw. I got my woman. My pretty lady's enough for me. Matter of fact, I'm going to go and get me some right now. Enjoy your evening, Mr. Dallas."

A few minutes later, the door to their suite opened.

Diana minimized the window until she laid eyes on her accomplice.

He joined her on the balcony's couch with his elbows on his knees. He took off his sunglasses, which he'd never done in her presence. Something haunted his eyes. Worry. "You make sense of all of that, pretty lady?"

"Yeah. You were great." She closed the program and set her laptop on the table. "And I figured out where they're being kept. Behind that door."

"And you sent all of that to the boss man?"

"Yep."

"Good." His gaze slid to the door leading to the hallway. "'Cause if we don't get her out tomorrow night, she's going to disappear forever. That, I can guarantee."

31

Saturday, April 16, 2016, 0800 hours CDT, Austin, TX

Early Saturday morning, Phase Two of the last-ditch effort to save Morgan began on the twenty-fourth floor of one of the luxury hotels in downtown Austin, the very floor where Yuri Sazonov had checked in the night before along with his girl, Irina Petrova. The task force had surrounded them in rooms of their own before wiring Sazonov's room for sound. Eavesdropping garnered a treasure trove of information.

A driver would pick Sazonov and Petrova up at ten that morning.

Guns were not allowed. Neither were bodyguards, so Sazonov had come on this trip unprotected.

Petrova rose before him and ordered a sumptuous breakfast from room service.

Now, Victor studied the room service cart, which the team had commandeered from the kitchen. Butch would do the driving since Victor had ordered Suleiman and Sana to remain at the hotel for this part of the operation.

Victor peered at Flagel. "You're good with us doing the initial takedown?"

The Ranger delicately rubbed his cheek, where the red mark had turned to a bruise going yellow and blue. "You do the initial entry. We'll follow. It's not like he'll get far, not when we have him surrounded."

Victor faced his escape-and-evasion specialist. "Five, someone needs breakfast."

"Shouldn't Suleiman be doing this?" Fiona asked. "I mean, he's the waiter in real life."

Butch grinned. "Nah. This bull in a china shop can handle it."

Victor undid the deadbolt and security bar and peered into the hall. "There's no one around. Sazonov's girl ordered room service forty-five minutes ago. Get going. We'll be right there with you. Just get him to open up long enough for us to get inside."

"Hokay. Here goes." Butch pushed the cart into the hall.

With guns drawn, task force members crept after him. Victor took up residence on one side of the door, Flagel on the other. Victor nodded to his deputy.

Butch knocked and called in his Cajun accent, "Room service."

Locks slid back, and the door opened the length of the security bar. Sazonov's gravelly bass filtered into the hall. "I did not order room service."

The door shut.

Victor lifted his chin and jerked his head toward the door. He mouthed, "Try harder."

Butch rolled his eyes and knocked again. "Room service."

Sazonov again peered at him. "I did not order any!"

Butch stuck his foot in the door before he could slam it in his face. "Sir, I'm sorry, but I got me here an order here for an Irina Peetroovi."

Victor winced as he mangled the name.

Turning his face to the room, Sazonov asked a question in Russian.

A feminine voice answered.

Grumbling, he slid off the security bar.

Butch pushed the cart inside, which maneuvered Sazonov further into the room.

Victor caught Flagel's gaze.

They burst inside.

Flagel raised his gun. "Texas Rangers! Get your hands on your head. Now!"

Sazonov's shouts filled the room, as did Irina's shrieks. "What are you doing? I am a visitor to this country! You are harassing me!"

The door slammed behind the task force, which now surrounded Sazonov. Flagel holstered his gun. "Let's just say we're trying to save you from yourself." He yanked out a chair from the worktable and pointed. "Sit down." He focused on Petrova. "And you. Sit on the couch and don't move. Understand? Both of you keep your hands on your head." He nodded at one of the members of the task force. "Search the place."

Petrova settled on the couch. Her eyes followed the team as they spread through the suite.

Flagel paced in front of the man. "We know why you're here. In just a couple of hours, you're going to travel to West of India Ranch here in the Hill Country of Texas. While there, you'll see women, most of them teenagers, being auctioned off for top dollar and will most likely buy one. Does any of this sound familiar to you?"

A vein pulsed in Sazonov's temple. "I know none of what you are talking about."

Flagel folded his arms across his chest. "No, I believe you do. The party is this weekend by invitation only."

Victor fished a paper copy of a PDF file they'd pulled from Jain's tablet. He smoothed it on the worktable's surface. "You have an invitation, right? A hard copy, I might add." Victor took a sheet of paper Flagel handed to him. "Looks something like this."

"Found it," a task force member called as she extricated something from Sazonov's briefcase.

Flagel held it up. "And here's your invite."

Sazonov's eye twitched. He lowered his gaze to the invitation.

Flagel widened his stance and hooked his thumbs in his belt. "Thank your lucky stars we got to you before you left. You see, you'll get nice accommodations at one of our safe houses while we go and take care of some business." His gaze flicked to Victor. "I cede the floor to you."

Victor knocked a code on the door to the adjoining room.

"Almost my doppelganger." Skylar said as he and Fiona strutted through the door.

Sazonov seemed to catch on to their plans. "You look nothing like me. I'm... too big for you."

"Nah. Keto diets can work wonders." Skylar strolled to the closet. As he opened the door, he appraised Sazonov with a practiced eye. He chuckled as he fingered the suits. "So perfect. I'm glad you love to be in pictures, Sazonov. It helped me with my shopping."

"You are a fool," Sazonov growled. He focused on Fiona. "And you look nothing like Irina."

Victor couldn't deny that. Irina was a brown-eyed blonde with dark roots while Fiona's hair was dark.

She shrugged. "No big deal, Sazonov. Everyone knows women change hair color like clothes. Even Prasata Jain knows that."

From where she perched on the couch, Petrova spat Russian curse words at everyone in the room.

Fiona chewed her out in the same language, and a shouting match followed. It was like two cats fighting. Finally, Flagel stepped between them and threw his hands up. "Both of you. Just. Be. Quiet. Could you? Please? You're giving me a headache."

Fiona sniffed and smirked as she lifted her chin.

"Who won that round?" Victor whispered to Skylar, who'd watched the exchange with a smile flitting about his lips.

Skylar chuckled. "Seven did, hands down."

Oh, boy. This could be a long day.

Flagel gestured to a team member. "Mendez, take Mr. Sazonov and Ms. Petrova to our safe house. Check in when you get there. And Sazonov, I suggest you cooperate. If you refuse to do so, then you will indeed find yourself under arrest." Flagel turned to Victor. "One, time to get going."

Victor found Skylar in the adjoining room, where he adjusted the khaki tie that matched his suit. Oh, did he ever mirror Sazonov, right down to the gestures. His procurement and intelligence officer had a way about him Victor could only envy.

Ever resplendent in a dress that fit her perfectly, Fiona joined them. She didn't even wobble on the high, high heels Russian women seemed to enjoy so much.

Victor pushed away from where he leaned against the dresser. "Six will have your comms equipment when you get on-site."

Skylar slid Sazonov's invitation into an inner pocket of his jacket. "She told me where she'd leave it. Wish I could say the same thing about a gun."

"Kitchen knives can work too."

"True." Skylar clapped him on the shoulder. "See you on the inside."

As Victor stepped into the hall, his mind turned toward a warehouse on the western edge of Austin. His next destination.

32

Saturday, April 16, 2016, 1100 hours CDT, Austin, TX

Phase Three began two hours after Victor and his team left the hotel. A smallish quad-cab box truck with the emblems of a local event planning company festooning its sides sat in the bowels of the warehouse. Several people wearing the uniforms of the company carried tables and chairs toward the roll-up door at the rear.

Flagel paced nearby with his phone to his ear. Victor couldn't hear any of the conversation, but from the way the man gestured, something agitated him.

Butch rose from his couch in the cargo area of the truck and winked at Sana and Suleiman. "You guys ready to get cozy for a while? It's gonna be a tight fit."

Victor glanced at Sana and Suleiman. Both wore neutral expressions. Game faces. As if maybe Victor's words two days ago had finally gotten through to them.

Victor joined Butch and examined the box he'd helped install beneath the floor of the truck. "I guess I can handle the tight fit."

They both hopped down, and Butch heaved a mock sigh. "Let's just try not to generate too much man stink."

Sana swatted him on the arm. "Or girl stink."

"Yup. Though man stink is worse."

Flagel slid his phone into the back pocket of his jeans and rubbed his hands on the denim.

Victor joined him. "You okay?"

As he chewed on his lip, Flagel raised his gaze to some point only he could see. He didn't answer.

"Flagel?"

That seemed to rouse him. "Sorry. I was thinking."

"About?"

"That was the director again. The governor called him and wants an update. Talk about insistent." Flagel shook his head. "I asked him to wait until later this afternoon because by that point this train is down the track and can't be stopped."

Victor's scalp prickled, and he shot him a sideways glance. "Did he agree?"

"He saw my point and promised to stall him." Flagel rubbed the back of his neck. "Now I've got to figure out what to say without revealing too much." He seemed to shake himself. "Let's get going. We get you guys in and loaded, then we can move." Flagel shifted as they joined the other members of the task force who'd go with the truck. "Remember, gang, if you can, park next to that old barn with the rear facing the wall. Should be easy enough since it's dead across from the portico where these tables will go. Offload everything and be sure to pop those locks so Victor's crew can get out. Then create a scene so they can get into the barn. Got it?"

Carpenter, the FBI agent and lead for the insertion team, nodded. "Roger."

"Get going."

Butch eased into the large box. Victor went next, then Suleiman, then Sana. They all lay so they spooned each other. Finally came the bags containing their gear. Darkness fell as the latches clicked.

"It's getting cozy real quick-like," Butch muttered.

"Think of pleasant things," Victor said.

"Like?" Sana asked.

Victor fought a smile. She sounded like the old Sana again. "Oh, I don't know. Lying in a meadow in the spring."

Butch chuckled. "Gag. You're too funny, man. You want to hear some jokes?"

"No!" everyone chorused.

"Dang. Tough crowd. I think I'll go and eat some worms."

That drew a tense laugh from everyone.

Scraping sounds above the indicated the tables and chairs were being loaded.

The earpiece Victor wore crackled. Then came Carpenter's voice. "Everything's loaded. We're on our way out. Give us forty-five minutes, and we're there. I hope no one needs to use the restroom."

"Very funny," Butch replied.

The truck lurched forward. Soon, it picked up speed and thundered down the highway into the Texas Hill Country. Victor began sweating in the midday heat. He took a sip of water from his Camelbak and tried not to count the minutes until he could breathe fresh air. Finally, the truck pulled to a stop.

"We're from Ace Events to deliver tables and chairs," Carpenter said. "Let me see here. Fifteen tables for four and sixty chairs."

"We've been expecting you," someone replied. "You're late."

"Traffic getting out of town. What can we say?"

"Go on. You'll come to a wall. Go through the gate and park beside that old barn you'll see. Got it?"

"Yup."

"Get going. A Narat Jain will meet you."

The truck continued on its way. They must have been on a dirt road because it didn't slow down and jostled everyone hiding beneath the floor. Dust sifted through cracks in the box. Butch sneezed, a loud guffaw that left Victor wondering if he'd find snot on the back of his neck. So long as Butch didn't sneeze again when they arrived. Finally, they stopped. The truck beeped as it backed up.

"Hang tight," Carpenter murmured.

Victor tapped twice on his mic, indicating he'd gotten the message.

The door to the cab slammed. "Yeah, we're here to deliver tables and chairs. Sorry we're late."

"Get them set up." Narat's voice held a trace of tension to it. "You were supposed to be here at ten."

"Not what my work order said. Here." A pause. Carpenter added, "The longer you stay here and argue, the longer it'll take us, right?"

"Get everything offloaded and be gone in half an hour. My girls need to do their work."

"Guys, let's go," Carpenter said.

Three other doors slammed, and the door to the cargo area rattled upward.

"Four here," Shelly murmured. "Tango Foxtrot asking for an update."

"Trojan horse has arrived," Carpenter muttered.

"Roger that."

Tables scraped across the floor. Then came the sound of locks clicking. "Trojans freed."

Victor again tapped twice in acknowledgment. He listened. A moment later, an argument broke out among two of the task force members.

Their cue to action.

Victor pushed open the hatch and sat up. His back protested. So did his knees, but he didn't have time for stiffness. He stood. Butch and the other two shouldered their packs and followed.

Victor stepped to the edge of the cargo area. He peered around the corner of the truck. Sure enough, a fistfight had broken out. Carpenter, the other guy, and some of the guards were breaking it up. Time to move. He hopped down and landed in a crouch with his pistol up. The rest of the team bolted to the barn. Sana went first through an open stall window, then Suleiman. He followed, as did Butch.

"Trojans inside," Victor reported.

"Roger that, One," Shelly replied.

Victor surveyed the barn's interior. Once dusk settled over the area, Suleiman would take over watch in the hayloft. But until then, they needed to find what Victor surmised to be a trap door. As his sniper and Sana pulled sentry duty, he and Butch began searching the floor.

Just what he'd thought. Concrete with sawdust covering it with tire tracks clearly evident. Sure, the shell of the barn may have been original to the property, but he doubted the original barn had concrete floors. He shoved aside more sawdust. Bingo. His hands brushed a straight line too perfect to be old. He pushed some more aside until he revealed a trapdoor in the floor. It had a handle flush with the door. A digital lock. He'd feared that.

Victor caught Sana's eye and nodded at the lock. Then he cupped his hand over her ear. "Think you can still get inside?"

She crouched and examined it. With a slow smile, she nodded.

Just then, the door to the cargo area of the truck rattled downward and slammed. The locking bar clanked into place, followed by the thump of the quad cab's four doors. The engine grumbled to life. Then came Carpenter's voice. "See you on the other side, One."

Victor gave two taps. They settled in to wait.

Saturday, April 16, 2016, 1830 hours CDT, outside Austin, TX

As she sat on a stool outside her cell in the hacienda's basement, Morgan wanted to die. She rubbed her eyes as she replayed last night's "beauty pageant" in her mind. Awful, awful, awful. She now knew what it felt like to be viewed as a chunk of meat. And if she ever got out of there, she'd never, ever wear a bikini again. Ever. She nearly laughed. Her chances of escape had dwindled exactly to zero.

She watched the guard through dull eyes as he went down the line of glass boxes with a bucket in hand. He dropped something into each.

As she fixed Morgan's hair, Xenia hissed something in Russian.

"What's he doing?" Morgan asked.

"Feeding those beasts." Another few words of Russian escaped her. "I never understood why Prasata keeps those. They scare me."

Morgan shuddered.

Xenia secured one last pin. "There. You are beautiful. Now for your face."

No words passed between caretaker and prisoner as Xenia applied makeup. Finally, she stepped back, then helped Morgan stand. "Come with me."

She wobbled in three-inch heels but steadied as the woman led her to a full-length mirror. Tendrils curled around her face while the rest of her hair was in an elegant twist. Where a girl had been now stood a woman cloaked in deep purple silk with diamonds dripping from her ears and draped around her neck. The makeup accentuated her eyes and lips. It would have been a thrill were it not for the circumstances. Her eyes filled. "Did this happen to you?'

That earned a sharp gaze. Xenia didn't say a word, instead turned her and took her back to her cell. A guard had moved the stool inside.

Morgan stepped to it.

He shut the door, and Xenia gazed at her for a long moment. "My friend, you do what you must to survive. You will learn that."

Tears began filling her eyes.

Xenia reached out and took her hand. "Do not cry. He hates to see ruined makeup, and all it will do is earn you a beating. Can you not cry?"

The lump twisted in her throat and choked off her voice. She nodded.

"Good then. Hold your chin up. Submit to them, and you will be okay."

No, she wouldn't be. Not ever again.

Xenia nodded to the guard and Chantal, who'd been getting the other girls ready. To Morgan's right, they opened a door. Then the white noise came on, and the lights dimmed to that awful blue. All the better to drug them without injecting anything.

Morgan sank onto the stool and rested her head against the bars. She tried to rouse up that anger she knew would help her survive. Despair snuffed it out as surely as a candle in a bell jar.

What would happen to her?

Escape wasn't possible, not with the security around her. Right then, she preferred to die rather than suffer even more abuse. But what then? *You're an image-bearer. You are worthy.* This time, she didn't believe it. *God, are You there?* She nearly laughed. Church had been for Christmas and Easter, Sunday mornings for hanging out as a family. Mom and Dad hadn't thought much about God, and neither had she or her brother. Until now. *God, I'm scared. Save me. Please. Before it's too late.*

33

Saturday, April 16, 2016, 1900 hours CDT, outside Austin, TX

Time to move. All afternoon, Victor had listened to vehicles pulling up and disgorging their wealthy passengers. People chattered as they splashed around in the pool. Glasses clinked. A radio played. Sheer enjoyment while he and the rest of the team sweated in the semi-dark heat of the barn. He even heard Skylar's laugh and Fiona's bell-like giggle. Why did Skylar seem to get all of the plum assignments? When afternoon turned to evening, the noise diminished as people headed inside to prepare for that night's festivities.

Moisture trickled down Victor's back. He took a nip of water from his Camelbak. What he wouldn't give to lounge at the pool at Last Chance Ranch with a beer in hand.

Outside, Narat directed his staff. Music began blasting from loudspeakers.

Over his wireworm, Flagel murmured, "Tango Foxtrot to One. Come in."

Victor stuffed his finger in his other ear to dampen the sound of the noise. "Go ahead, Tango Foxtrot."

"Trojans, we've been shut down."

Victor's breath hissed between his teeth. "Come again?"

"We've been shut down. Per orders of the governor."

The plan they'd so carefully concocted flashed across Victor's mind. Insert his team. Secure where the girls were held. Then call in the cavalry.

He glanced at Sana, who stared at him with wide eyes reflecting exactly what he felt. Shock. He lowered his head. "What happened?"

"We went in to brief the governor about the operation since we were then in motion. And you know what he did?" Flagel muttered something under his breath. "He shut us down. We're to cease immediately."

"Um, we're kind of stuck here."

"Don't I know it." Bitterness laced Flagel's words. Then came footsteps. "We tried to tell him that. And it got worse. He wants our files. All of them."

"In other words, there goes the case."

"We're fighting it. The FBI's in our court on this one." A door closed. Flagel continued in a low voice, "Listen. Shelly's doubled down on her efforts to get into that app. No luck yet, but hey, at least she can keep working on things since she's not a Ranger. And we're not abandoning you. We're regrouping, but it's going to be a bit. Hang tight. I'll be in touch when I can be, hopefully within an hour."

"Roger that." Victor dropped his hand. He hung his head, then studied his crew.

From where he rested with his back against an empty stall, Butch growled something low and threatening. "We're screwed."

Victor rubbed his chin. "Let's think."

Suleiman, who'd taken a knee for sentry duty, shifted. "The best choice would be to abort."

Victor stared at the double doors, which Diana had reported to be padlocked from the outside. At least they'd have some warning if someone approached. "We can't."

Sana, who also pulled sentry duty, nodded.

Victor had three team members as well as Sugar in the red zone. Surely they'd heard that bit of news. "Sana, see if you can get out there and tell me how many vehicles we have that we could use to escape."

Sana slipped outside through the window they'd entered. She returned a few tense minutes later. "We have four Suburbans. Their fobs are in the central console cup holders, and I turned out the dome lights."

Four Suburbans for thirty people. Victor's heart hammered as his mind scrambled. Get in. Get out. Fast. Real fast. "Four, where are you?"

"We're regrouping at Carpenter's house. He's on the western edge of town," Shelly replied. "We should be there in fifteen minutes or so."

"Roger that." Victor thought through the evening's agenda Diana had laid out. At seven-thirty, a reception would begin. Supper would commence at eight. Then the night's entertainment at nine o'clock where the girls would parade before their buyers, before wrapping up at nine-thirty with a silent auction that would last until ten-thirty. Most likely, Jain would send for the girls at half past eight. Originally, the task force was supposed to strike at eight. He wouldn't bank on that happening now. According to the itinerary Diana had shared last night, they had one chance this evening, and that was it.

"Trojans, listen up." He could only hope the others were listening. "Here's what we're going to do. Six and Nine, head down in five minutes."

"Will do," Diana whispered.

Victor continued, "Take out any guards outside the door and get inside. We'll meet you in there. Seven and Eight, follow within five minutes after that."

"Roger," Skylar replied.

"We'll go back through the tunnel and out through the barn to the four Suburbans we found. We'll have to leave everything behind. Then it's out the front door, like it or not."

"Will do," Fiona murmured.

Victor nodded to Sana. "Let's get to it."

Suleiman headed upward to the hayloft to stand overwatch. Dust filtered downward as he established his position.

While Victor and Butch pulled sentry duty, Sana reached into her pack and removed a screwdriver, plus an electronic device. She popped the front off the digital lock and attached two wires, then activated the device.

A moment later, she grunted in satisfaction. "Four-six-eight-two. Father got lazy, apparently."

Lazy or not, they had a way in. Victor nodded. "Let's go,"

She punched in the number. The lock clicked.

"Bingo," Butch peered down a set of stairs draped in total darkness. "We're in."

Victor straightened. "Two, we're going down. Stand by."

He made sure his MP5 was secure on its line against his tactical vest. With a deep breath, he raised his tranq gun, lowered his night vision goggles, and crept down the steps.

Saturday, April 16, 2016, 1930 hours CDT, outside Austin, TX

Narat studied one of their guests, the one who wore a khaki suit and black shirt with a khaki tie of fine silk. He knew the man from somewhere. What was his name? That's right. Yuri Sazonov, Russian businessman. His blond hair glinted in the lights strung around the portico as he chatted with a sheik from Dubai and sipped a flute of some of the most expensive champagne out there. He matched the picture he'd sent. Irina Petrova, not so much. Sazonov had joked that women changed hair color like they did shoes. She kept her arm around his waist and laughed at something the sheik said.

Narat surveyed the rest of the group. The sellers would sit at their own segregated tables so as not to influence anyone's thoughts about the price of the girls. He noted the black man with the tall woman on his arm. Sugar. A gregarious man who'd fit right in with the other sellers. Tonight, he came decked out in his white suit with a black shirt, handkerchief, and hat band that actually had rhinestones on it. His girl's tight curls hung past her shoulders. So totally alluring, especially the night before when he'd noticed hazel eyes flecked with copper. Too bad she wasn't available.

Something bothered him about Sugar. Ash said he was a last minute replacement since he'd succumbed to norovirus. Sugar had professed ignorance about the no-women rule for the sellers. Understandable. Ash must have felt so bad that he hadn't completely briefed his proxy.

Narat set his discomfort aside and returned his attention to Sazonov. He could have sworn he'd seen him somewhere before. Maybe he'd come last year. No. Narat had attended then as Father's understudy. Was he really a buyer? Or an imposter? He thought about other places he'd been the past several months. At work? No. Father had hired no blond like him as of late. Maybe at the country club where he played tennis? He knew everyone there, and no blond man resembled Sazonov.

At a night club?

Ah, yes. The Music Man in Nashville, just not in person. On a surveillance video Ash had played for him. And he'd been with someone, Victor Chavez. That meant one thing. Trouble.

He glanced at Father, who laughed at something a man living off a trust fund said. Xenia, Father's mistress and hostess for the evening, sipped her champagne and tucked her arm through his.

Narat turned away. Father was too busy. He, Narat, would take care of this matter. And keep it quiet.

He'd follow Sazonov.

The group's volume increased along with the amount of alcohol consumed. Sugar draped himself all over the delectable Diana Kasem. Clearly, they might not make it all the way through the night. Sure enough, they kissed and slipped away hand in hand. Narat switched his attention to Sazonov.

The man whispered into Petrova's ear. They shifted to the edge of the crowd, then broke free and headed toward the house.

Narat followed. Something in his instinct pricked. These two were up to no good, and he'd stop it. Now. Without Father's help but with Wes Sampson's. His friend had joined the guard detail after his arrival. He leaned against the wall next to the doors leading to the great room. His hand rested on the butt of the pistol holstered at his side.

As Narat approached, Wes raised an eyebrow. "What's up?"

"We've got a problem. I believe we have a potential situation brewing. Get two more men and meet me near the kitchen."

Wes texted his summons.

Keeping his distance, Narat followed Sazonov and Petrova.

They stepped inside.

He increased his steps into the great room. Laughing, his quarries made a right, toward the kitchen. He hesitated, then bolted into the hall. To his right, the door to the basement clicked shut.

Wes joined him with two others in tow.

Narat nodded toward the door. "They went this way." He reached inside his tux jacket and withdrew his Beretta. "Let's go find out why."

Saturday, April 16, 2016, 1945 hours CDT, outside Austin, TX

Sandwiched between Victor and Butch, Sana paused and listened. Not a sound on the other side of the door. The green of her NVGs showed blank metal with a keypad glowing brightly. Victor punched in the code, and the lock clicked.

Sana shoved her NVGs upward before the dim blue glow could blind her. Tranquilizer gun up at the ready position, she covered the left while Victor took the right. Eyes widening, she stepped back. Before her stood four rows of what she could only call six-by-six jail cells with all but one occupied by girls slumped on stools or standing. All wore evening gowns. White noise filled the room.

She felt rather than saw Butch's shudder. "Ick. Tarantulas. I hate them."

Sana followed his gaze to a nearby wall and cringed. Father had always collected the things. Apparently, he'd become a tarantula hoarder.

At the other end, a bolt clanked back. Along with Butch, she focused her tranq gun on it.

Sugar dragged an unconscious guard through the doorway. "Sugar says it's time to join the party. This guy was cramping our style. Hard to get romantic with my lady if someone else is around."

Victor joined him. "Are Eight and Seven behind you?"

Sugar bobbed his head. "Indeed, they are."

A redhead midway down gasped. "Uncle Vic?"

Victor rushed to her and gripped her hand. "Morgan!"

"Get me out. Please. Get us all out!"

Skylar's honeyed drawl crackled in Sana's earpiece. "On our way. Look for us... right now."

They joined the group.

Sana studied the lock on Morgan's cell. A keypad. Just like the trapdoor lock.

Morgan reached out and touched her on the arm. "I saw someone enter four-six-eight-two."

Sana entered the code, and the lock clicked back. Tension drained from her shoulders. Almost there.

Victor opened the door. "Team, get everyone out. Ladies, we're here to rescue you, but I need your help. Take off your heels and stay as quiet as possible. Gather around me."

One by one, the team released them. Tension eased in Sana's chest. She handed off Berettas to Skylar, Diana, Fiona, and Sugar. They pulled sentry duty and stayed on the perimeter of the group of girls who'd gathered around Victor.

He took a knee. "Listen to me. I only have time to say this once. I want you all to go single file. I'll lead. You'll go through that door over there." He pointed to the door leading to the old barn. "At the top, go to the horse stall on the left at the back. There's an opening to the outside. One of our team will be there to help you through. You'll see four Suburbans. Start filling out the farthest where I tell you. Stay as quiet as you can. Go in through the back and climb into the back seat. Leave the front for us. Got it? I want to see nods."

He focused on each girl. One by one, they obeyed.

"Staying quiet is key, okay?"

Again, more nods.

"Two, did you hear me?" Victor asked.

"Loud and clear." Suleiman's voice reassured Sana. "Getting set now."

Victor straightened. "Nine, you're behind me. Then Eight. Then Seven, Six, Three, and Five. Let's go."

He led them to the door. One by one, the girls filed past him with Sugar counting off. After the first seven, he joined the line.

An alarm blared.

Sana jumped and whipped around.

A gate began lowering across the tunnel's entrance.

She shoved the girls toward the gate. "Go!"

They bolted in that direction.

Skylar pushed four more under and rolled after them. He came to his knees. "Sana, come on!"

She dashed toward it.

It clanged to the floor.

Skylar rattled it. "No!"

Her thoughts began scattering as her senses sharpened. Her breaths came in hard gasps. "Eight, go."

He grabbed her hand. "No, I—"

"Go! Otherwise, you'll get caught."

He stepped back. "We'll get you out. Promise."

She shoved the remaining girls behind her. "Stay in the hall."

Heart pounding, she let go of her tranq gun, which retracted to her combat vest. She raised her MP5 and took a knee with Butch. "Five?"

Butch pressed the scope of his MP5 to his eye. "Get ready."

Sana's training kicked in. Her breath evened. While her pulse thundered in her ears, her hands remained steady. Diana and Fiona adapted the same pose.

The door popped open. Something clanged on the concrete floor.

Flash-bang grenade.

Sana scrunched her eyes closed and plugged her ears with her fingers.

The concussion knocked her off her feet.

Her head swam. She staggered upright. In front of her, Diana and Fiona writhed on the concrete as they recoiled from the effects of the blast.

Guards poured through the door.

Butch, who'd done the same as Sana, rose to his knees.

"Drop your weapons. Now!" Narat called. "Or you and the rest of the girls will die very slowly."

Sana cast a frantic glance at Butch.

He slowly shook his head, then eased to his knees and placed his guns in front of him. He laced his fingers on his bald head.

No! She couldn't. She couldn't let Narat take them. "Five—"

"Do what they say."

She mirrored him.

Narat approached. What she'd do to wipe that smirk off his face! He kicked away her MP5, tranq gun, and pistol. "I see you survived long enough to be a fool again, sister."

With a growl, she jumped him.

Narat tumbled backward and landed with an oomph on the hard concrete. She struck him across the face.

Someone ripped her away.

She staggered but remained standing.

One of the guards faced off with her. He was huge! Probably taller and broader than Butch. In guttural English, he stated, "You did the wrong thing, woman."

"You're not taking me." She circled toward the bathroom area. Maybe she could lose him in the shadows.

The guard struck with surprising quickness. He shoved her—hard. She flew through the air and crashed into the shelves holding the tarantulas. Two collapsed, and glass boxes shattered on the floor.

Sana lay there and tried to collect herself.

She rose to her knees and charged.

It turned to a stumble.

The man only laughed.

He cocked his fist and slammed it into her face.

She skidded on her back across the concrete, then rolled to all fours and tried to rise.

The world swung before her.

As she fell into blackness, one thought crossed her mind.

She'd failed Morgan.

34

Saturday, April 16, 2016, 1950 hours CDT, outside of Austin, TX

Victor charged upward as the alarm blared in his ears. His hamstrings burned. He sucked wind. Hitting the lip of the steps in the horse barn, he stumbled and fell to his knees. He pushed himself upright. Where was Suleiman? "Two... where..."

"Outside. Get everyone out. Quickly."

The first girl burst through the trapdoor.

"This way!" Victor dashed toward the window and plummeted through.

Suleiman had already opened the back doors to two Suburbans.

Victor lightly pushed the first girl toward it. "Over there. Go!"

Suleiman grabbed a smoke grenade from his belt and lobbed it toward the portico, followed just as quickly with a flash-bang.

Shouting and screams answered him.

Victor slammed the rear doors to the first Suburban. "Two, make sure they keep their heads down."

Sugar fell through the stall window. He hit the ground with an oomph, then rose, his front streaked with dirt.

Like lemmings jumping off a cliff, the second round of girls barreled through. Sugar hauled one to her feet and pointed. "There. Go!"

Victor did a count. Too few by far. "Where are the others?"

Skylar vaulted through the stall window. "Caught."

Crap. Victor's palms moistened. "Eight, get in the furthest one. I'll take the next. Nine, with me. Two, with Eight. Now!" He switched the MP5 to full auto and peppered the patio to push people farther into the courtyard. He jumped inside and released his gun. It retracted on its line to his chest. He cranked the engine and shoved the transmission into Drive.

Tires spun until they caught. He wrenched the wheel to the right, and they rocketed through the automobile gate before anyone could close it. Victor stomped on the accelerator as they roared down the road. He checked the rearview. In the deepening dust, he could barely see the shadow of Skylar and Suleiman following.

Up ahead, the gates to the ranch had closed. He tensed. "Gang, hold on!"

They burst through the wrought iron and tore it off its hinges. It glanced off the roof of the second SUV.

Victor's insides quivered. "Eight, you guys okay?"

His radio crackled as they faded in and out of range. Skylar's voice came across through the static. "Thanks for scaring the schnapp out of us."

Victor's breath eased only slightly. "Sorry 'bout that."

"It got us freedom." Skylar coughed. "Dang dust."

Victor tried not to notice he only had four of the twenty-three girls. "Sit rep, Eight. What happened?"

More static crackled. "Someone... made us... alarm... Gates... down..."

Static claimed the rest of the sentence.

"Stay close, Eight. What about the girls and our team?"

"We got seven girls." That came across clearer. "Six, Seven, Three, and Five were caught."

Add that to his four. Crap. Half. Less than half. Victor sucked his breath right back in. "You don't have Morgan, do you?"

"Negative."

Double crap.

"What about the others?" one of the girls asked from in the cargo area. Her voice trembled.

"I'm thinking." Yeah, right. *About how I failed my team and Morgan.*

Another girl in the back seat leaned forward. "Who are you?"

Sugar twisted so he partially faced them. "Friends of Morgan who care about all of you ladies."

Victor's fingers on the steering wheel began hurting. "Eight, are we being followed?"

Skylar muttered something. "Oh, yeah. A couple of SUVs. Two's going to take care of them."

Victor eased the wheel to the left and right, just as Butch had taught them years before in their training. Sparks popped, and the back window shattered. "Girls, get down as far as you can."

The rat-a-tat of bullets penetrated the roar of the engine.

A fireball erupted. An SUV flipped end over end.

Victor's heart nearly seized. Not Skylar and Suleiman and their precious cargo.

"No one else is following," Suleiman reported. "I took down the other two SUVs. It will take more time for them to mobilize."

Victor didn't want to remain vulnerable. And they would, even in Hill Country. He needed backup. Fast. He keyed his mic. "Four, are you there?'

Nothing but static. Not surprising seeing that their long-distance transceiver was on the barn's roof.

Grumbling, Victor fished his phone from a pocket on his tactical vest. Despite his trembling fingers, he pulled up Flagel's number and dialed it.

Flagel's voice boomed into his ear. "Victor! Where are you?"

Thank You, Lord. Victor wanted to sag against the seat. "Flagel, man, am I glad to hear your voice."

"Where are you?"

He maintained his speed. "On the main access road to the ranch. We managed to break out half the girls."

A sharp intake of breath answered him. "What about the others?"

Victor tried not to think about those of his team who'd been trapped. He hung a hard right, heading east on the highway. "They got caught, as did half our team."

That generated a muttered word from Flagel. "I won't ask for details." Then came someone murmuring to him. "Shelly's tracking you via your phone. Listen. You need to get off the main highway. I'm not sure what kind of influence Jain wields around that area, but there's pretty much only one obvious route to and from the ranch."

Victor's gaze roamed around him. "Where do I go?"

Again, more murmuring. "You'll have a farm road coming up in about a half mile. When you get to it, take a right. Farm Road 4820. See it?"

Victor slowed from his rocket pace, lest he pass it.

"You missed it."

Curse this dust. He hacked as it sifted through the air vents. "Do we need to turn around?'

Flagel cleared his throat. "Negative. Take the next one. Ranch Road 2830."

"Crew, brace yourselves." At the sign, he hung a hard right. They skidded around the corner, which earned shrieks from some of the girls. Then came the bumps, which felt like ditches at their speed.

Flagel's voice reassured him. "I see you made the turn. In two miles, you'll see another road, Ranch Road 820. Take a left onto that."

"Roger." Victor kept the Suburban at high speed despite the threat of his teeth rattling right out of his head as they bounced on the rough dirt road. Only Flagel's calmness kept his mind from darting in all directions.

"Good. One more turn. Ranch Road 3281. A right. One mile ahead."

They skidded into one last turn.

"The next turn will be onto a state road. State Road 223. Take that headed east. Two miles ahead. That should get you out of Jain's reach."

Victor could only hope. They needed to regroup. Badly. Finally, they burst onto smooth pavement. He pushed the accelerator down, and the SUV groaned forward.

"Tell me what happened," Flagel said.

Victor summarized their failed escape attempt. His neck tightened. He pinched the bridge of his nose. "Sana, Butch, Diana, and Fiona are back there with a dozen girls, including Morgan. Where are you?"

"Coming to you. We're ten minutes out. Listen. Three or so miles east of you, there's a gas station that's been closed for a long time. Pull over there and wait for us. It's called Loyal Oil and Gas. I sometimes meet informants there. It's got a blue-and-white neon sign that's out. Pull around back, and we'll meet there to regroup."

"Will do. Call us when you're on final approach." A few minutes later, Victor noted the dimmed sign of the gas station. He slowed, cut the lights and rumbled into the parking lot behind the old building. The other Suburban pulled in behind them.

He rested his head against the seat. Two years ago his team had been split and ambushed. Except he, Fiona, and Skylar had been the ones caught. Back then, five had escaped. Now, only four remained free.

He needed air. He yanked open his door and almost plummeted onto the hard ground. Shakes hit him as his adrenaline finally dissipated. He still couldn't think, something that worried him. He needed backup, otherwise, he wasn't sure they could make it in time to save the others. And if that happened, he'd never be able to forgive himself.

Lord, I need Your wisdom. And fast. Show us how to get there and get everyone out before someone disappears forever.

Saturday, April 16, 2016, 2000 hours CDT, outside Austin, TX

"Get up!"

Those two words somehow reached into the black hole where Sana had fallen. Her head pounded. She lay on her back against cold, hard concrete.

Then came a blow to her side. "Get up, I say!"

Her eyes snapped open. She turned onto her side. A large, fuzzy shape crawled in her view. A tarantula. She gasped.

It skittered into the shadows.

Ever resplendent in a tux, Father towered over her. He grasped her around her bicep. "On your knees. Now!"

Sana struggled upright. Her heart sank as she faced the objects of their mission. The girls. All stood in cells. Several mewled. Still in their evening wear, Fiona and Diana occupied two other cells. Her heart sank further when she focused on Butch. He sat on his knees across from her with his hands on his head. A hulking guard stood behind him.

Her worst-case scenario unfolded before her in vivid color.

Father paced between Sana and Butch while Narat and Wes stood off to one side. Father paused and folded his arms. "You never cease to amaze me, Sana. Do you realize that?"

She risked meeting his gaze. "I'm glad I could provide some entertainment."

He huffed out a noisy breath. "You chose to go against me, your very own father."

She lifted her chin. "Who traffics girls."

He slapped her.

Sana's head snapped to the side. That hurt. Big time.

He grabbed her chin so hard she flinched. His nostrils flared, and she nearly swooned at the odor of alcohol and curry on his breath. "You will not disrespect me! You have cost me dearly. Very dearly."

She refused to break eye contact. "At least some of them got their freedom."

It felt so good to say that.

He backhanded her. She tumbled off her knees.

Butch tried to leap to his feet, only to have his guard tackle him and twist his arm against his back. He moaned as the hulk yanked up on his arm and forced him to his knees.

Father grabbed her by the hair. His eyes had widened to the point where the whites practically radiated his anger. His grip tightened, and she gasped in pain. "You are a fool. You always have been. Ever since 2009, you've been worthless to me."

She smirked. "No news there."

He thrust her onto the floor and kicked her on the scar from her shanking.

Pain flared across her midsection. She moaned and curled into a ball.

Father backed off and straightened his tux lapels. A cunning smile spread across his face, and he rubbed his chin. "But perhaps you're not as worthless as I thought. I may have lost eleven pretty girls, but I have gained three women back. Despite your ages, all of you will garner a decent price, enough to begin making up for my losses." He strolled to the cell where Fiona stood. "Yes, I believe that will be the case."

She spat on him.

He flicked away her spittle from his jacket. "Woman, were the time not so tight, I would beat you for your disrespect." He continued to Diana's cell. "Ah, yes. I can see some buyers would be interested in you as well despite the wrinkles at the corners of your eyes."

Father returned to Sana and gloated. "Undress. All the way."

Standing by Narat, Wes stirred.

She gaped at him. "What?"

His lips twitched. "I have to determine your value."

Butch struggled against his guard. "Her value is in the eyes of God."

A yank on his arm earned a yelp.

Sana slowly shook her head. No way. Uh, uh. She couldn't. She wouldn't. Not for him. Not for anyone.

Father extended his hand toward her brother. "Narat, if you would."

Her brother reached into the inner pocket of his tux jacket and withdrew a loaded needle and syringe. He handed it to Father, who held it inches from her face. "You see this? It is the purest of the pure heroin out there. I inject this into your friend, and he dies before your very eyes. You obey me, and he lives."

Butch's guard pushed him face first onto the floor.

He thrashed until they secured his arms behind his back. "Sana, don't do it! You know where I'm going."

His guards laughed at him as one of them shoved up the sleeve on one arm.

No. She'd not let Butch die for the sake of her modesty. Slowly, she rose. The room swayed before her, but she steadied. She unzipped her jumpsuit. Wes reached out and yanked it down. "All the way, babe." He cackled. "Man, Narat, you weren't kidding when you said your sister was hot."

Her cheeks flamed.

Father rubbed his chin as he appraised her. A smile crossed his face. "You will bring in a good price as well, despite that scar on your side."

From her cell, Fiona cussed at him until a guard banged on the bars with the butt of his gun. She drew back.

Nausea swelled inside of Sana. At least her hair swinging in front of her face hid the tears gathering in her eyes. She couldn't bring herself to look at Butch.

Father's footsteps receded a little as he shouted, "Xenia! Get in here." The door leading to the wine cellar opened, and his mistress joined them. "Put a dress on her. Wes, Narat, zip tie her wrists to the bars of her cell before Xenia does her makeup and hair."

"What about him?" Narat asked inclined his head toward Butch.

"I'll deal with him in the morning after our guests leave. In the meantime, we'll proceed now rather than later. If the others who escaped try to tattle to the Rangers or FBI, it will do them no good since the governor shut down the task force. Wes, Narat, bring the girls up in half an hour." With that, Father turned on his heel and headed to the door leading to the wine cellar.

Butch's guards tied his hands behind his back and hauled him to his feet. As they escorted him toward the tunnel, he slowly winked.

That shored up Sana's rapidly waning courage.

She kept her head hung and wrapped her arms around herself. A minute that seemed like forever passed before heels clicked on concrete. Xenia approached with an evening gown of black sequins. She held it up. "Let's put this on." She helped Sana into the dress, then pulled the zipper up. "There. It fits you perfectly despite not having your measurements."

Wes pointed toward an empty cell with a stool in it. "Get in there and sit."

She did so, and he tied her wrists to the bars so she couldn't do anything to take Xenia hostage. She pushed her tears downward as the woman combed her hair and went to work applying makeup. Sana tried to recall happy memories, ones that protected her from what was about to happen.

"All finished. It's okay to look now."

Sana opened her eyes.

Xenia held up a mirror.

Oh, if this had been a happier occasion, like her wedding day, Sana would have admitted she was beautiful with kohl lining her dark eyes and her lips filled out with a dark red lipstick. Now brushed and gleaming, her black hair framed her face and curled just beneath her chin. It shone in the overhead lights. Suleiman. His name ripped at her heart. *I love you, my beloved. I want to see you again, to hold you.* Her chin trembled as she dropped it to her chest.

From where he stood next to her cell, Wes asked, "You think your dad would let me have a go at her?"

Narat, who stood next to him, forced him back a step. "Shut up."

Wes held up his hands. "Hey, I was just kidding."

"Why don't you go wait in the wine cellar?"

Wes cast his friend a long look but retreated without another word.

Narat faced his sister and searched her face.

Despite everything, he'd saved her life in Nashville. "I forgive you."

His eyes widened. Without a word, he followed his friend.

"Until later." Xenia cast one last look over her shoulder before following her master into the wine cellar. The guards left as well. White noise came on, and the lights dimmed to a dull blue.

"You okay?" Fiona quietly asked from the cell next to her.

Sana began sniffling. She stared as a tarantula, one of the many freed that had survived the initial tussle, crawled toward her cell. She yanked at her wrists. The cable ties still held them securely.

"Four of ours got away," Diana murmured.

"Who *are* you?" From the cell on the other side of Sana, Morgan stared at her.

Fiona eased onto her stool. "Uh, we were supposed to rescue you, but that didn't quite go as planned."

"You know Uncle Vic?"

"Very well." The faintest of hope tried to break through Sana's darkness. Suleiman. He'd escaped along with Skylar, Victor, and Sugar. At least, she hoped he had. A lump filled her throat. She winced as the tarantula passed between the bars. Her hands tightened into fists. Too bad she couldn't move them.

"We've got guys on the outside," Diana murmured. "Vic's not going to leave us here on our own."

"If he's alive," Sana muttered.

Fiona flicked at a spider. "Why don't you try to be positive, will you? And what's with all of these tarantulas?"

Sana whimpered as the spider made its way up her skirt and perched on her shoulder. Numbness spread across her. If help didn't come soon, like really soon, it'd be game over. Not just for the three women but for Butch and twelve girls. That was a result she didn't want to accept.

35

Saturday, April 16, 2016, 2130 hours CDT, outside of Austin, TX

Behind the deserted gas station, Victor stared at the guns Flagel laid on the hood of a white Ford Explorer. "That's all you've got among you? Four hunting rifles, two shotguns, and some pistols?"

Flagel nodded in the direction of one of the FBI agents. "That's all Murray had in his house. Plus what you have. And plus plenty of ammo for you guys and for us. Shelly stuffed her pack, and we found some that fit your guns as well. And we've got our own sidearms."

That all came from one house. Wow. Victor joined Shelly. "What do you have?"

She leaned against the hood of one of their SUVs and tapped on her computer. The lights of her jet pack flashed as she accessed aerial photographs of the ranch. Without lifting her gaze from the screen, she replied, "Suleiman reported the alarm sensors were in the perimeter wire of the ranch's fence. It's kind of like an electric fence in that manner. If it's broken or touched, it alerts. The front gate broke it when you all bashed through it."

Flagel shifted closer. "Meaning it's down, right?"

"My gut says they'll at least have strung a wire across the wall until they could get it fixed. So no, it's probably live now."

An idea germinated in Victor's mind. "But they're vulnerable. How many guards do you think they have?"

"Four were in the vehicles we took out," Skylar said.

"And I saw perhaps another dozen or so," Suleiman added.

Twelve remaining. Better odds than previously.

Pulling on a borrowed T-shirt, Sugar emerged from behind one of the Suburbans. "And Mr. Jain decided it wasn't cool for anyone to bring any extra security. It's all on him."

Ah. Jain was more vulnerable than Victor had realized. "They have a dozen left."

Flagel scribbled something on a clipboard. "At least."

Victor surveyed the motley crew surrounding him. Four from his team. Then Sugar. Loquacious had joined the group. That was six. He counted the eight men and women who'd broken rank at the risk of their careers. At least two of them would have to stay behind to guard the girls who'd escaped. Better but not great odds. "Okay. We get into the back gate of the ranch and come through like we'd intended with the task force."

Flagel began shaking his head. "No go."

"What? But—"

"Time's of essence. It's longer between the back and the house. How long, Shelly?"

In the dark, her mouse flashed red as she measured the distances on the satellite image. "Two miles compared to one mile from the front."

Twice as far as to the front gate. Flagel was right. He leaned forward so he rested his arms on the car's hood. "It's going to take time because we've got to use stealth, right? According to the agenda Diana got, the buyers are leaving with their girls starting at eight tomorrow morning. But probably earlier since things went sideways tonight."

"I get it." Victor folded his arms and paced as he tried to come up with a good way to the innermost parts of the ranch without getting everyone killed. His mind must have remained addled because he came up with nothing. "What kind of a plan to you have?"

Flagel's quiet voice penetrated his thoughts. "Sometimes the best entrance is the one at the front. But definitely not by blowing in there. The gate will probably get repaired after the guests leave. That means he has to have at least one guard there, most likely two, and a jury-rigged sensor wire and something else. We take down the guards, and most likely we can get in. The question remains as to the inner wall."

"They are topped with broken glass." Suleiman patted his pack. "We have leather mats. The gates are the same wrought iron as the gate at the ranch entrance."

In other words, more for artistry than practicality.

"We have a couple of short ladders as well," Shelly added. "We carry those in along with the two mats."

"In the basement, they have gates with that alarm system," Skylar said. "Who's to say they won't deploy that again and catch the rest of us?"

Shelly waved her hands. "Oh, you of little faith. If Jain's as techie here as he is at home and work, he's got a smart house. I think if I can get close enough, I can get into his network. It's just been so hard from the outside because he has such tight security from afar."

More pieces of the plan slid into place for Victor. "Okay. Shelly, we get you in close. You'll be close enough that we'll have comms contact. You got those spare comms units?"

"I sure do."

"Hand those out. We all go in. Shelly, you get close to get into that network but stay outside the wall. We'll leave someone with you to protect you. Take down the alarm system and create a new feed for the cameras. Better yet, do you think his lights are wired in?"

She smirked. "Oh, you can bet on it."

"When we start, kill the lights. We're down to six pairs of NVGs, but we'll have to make it work."

"Just be aware they have two of ours," Skylar said.

"Noted. What about the code for the locks?"

"That should be in the security system," Shelly said. "I'll find it, but it'll take some time."

"Then work on that as you tape the feed for the cameras."

She scribbled that onto the small notepad she always kept for her assignments.

Flagel tossed down his clipboard. "It's set, then. Let's get ready to go."

Two agents would guard the girls who'd escaped. They headed to the porch of the gas station to wait it out.

Carpenter and his comrade handed out the guns they'd brought. Victor loaded his and ensured the safety was on before looping it over his shoulder. With one last prayer for guidance, he climbed into the front seat of the Suburban for the ride to his final destination.

36

Sunday, April 17, 2016, 0330 hours CDT, outside Austin, TX

Coyotes wailing woke Narat from his restless sleep. He turned onto his back and stared at the ceiling. A cool breeze wafted through the window. *Go back to sleep.* He couldn't. Too much alcohol? Possibly. He'd used it to self-medicate, to assuage his shame at not standing up for his sister.

Sana. With a groan, he rolled over and stuffed his pillow over his head. He'd always admired her. From the day he'd witnessed her tumbling through the air off the vault when he was a boy to when she'd defied Father to live her own life to when she'd made a new one for herself after getting out of prison. She'd been the rebel, the one to chart her own course even if it led her to prison. Since her release, they'd worked hard to remain close as brother and sister. Her bell-like laughter from better times echoed in his ears.

He was the good child, the son who made his father proud by following in his footsteps. The best schools, a graduate degree in business. Working at Father's company. And where had it led him? To watching a sheik pay out a paltry eight million for his sister.

He grabbed another pillow and punched it. He should have stood up for her when Father made his decision to sell her. He'd stood there, afraid of what Father would say, even when his supposed friend, Wes, made a shameless pass at her. If Narat had spoken up, if he'd objected, Father would have used part of that heroin on him as well as Sana's friend, Butch.

Narat flipped onto his back and laced his hands behind his head. They dug into his scalp. Anger began roiled in his gut as at the humiliation had that washed across Sana's face when Wes yanked her jumpsuit down.

Images from that evening flitted through his mind. The parading of the girls plus Sana and her two friends across a small stage. The silent auction, where clients had come downstairs to bid on them while downing several bottles of fine wine. Seeing the sheik manhandling her stirred more inklings of rebellion inside of him. Then came Wes's unabashed lust for her. Finally, that argument with Father that happened shortly after Sana's friends had helped half of the girls escape.

"Where are the four who went after them?" Father demanded.

Narat, who returned from speaking with the head guard, shook his head. "They got away. We think our men perished."

Father chewed him out in a mix of Hindi and English, ending with, "You're a failure, Narat! I counted on you to make sure things ran smoothly, and what happened? Eleven girls escaped!" He popped Narat across the face. "And who knows what will happen now? I've called the governor. He's promised to shut down any attempts at rescue."

"But I—"

Another slap burned across his cheek. "Fix things and make sure nothing else happens."

Narat wiped a hand across his face. Scarlet coated the top of it.

His father slammed out of the control room to inform his guests of the change in plans.

"What a total..." The head guard, a former Marine who'd seen his own share of foul language and prima donnas during his military career, shook his head. "Mr. Jain's many things, but tonight took the cake."

Narat's cheeks flamed. "Just make sure we're secure."

"I'm on it. Cams are all up with feeds active. We jury-rigged a wire across the gate so the alarm's active. We put stop sticks across the front. Two of my guys are there, and the rest are on zone patrols."

Narat clapped him on the shoulder. "Thank you."

The guard shrugged. "Anything to make your life easier. It ain't easy working for a hard man like Mr. Jain. Matter of fact, I'm done with this gig. I'm turning in my resignation tomorrow."

If only Narat could resign as well.

Now, he sat up and swung his legs over the edge of the bed. Anger nipped at him as he rested his elbows on his knees and rubbed his temples. Sana deserved better. He had to make it right. But getting caught meant signing his own death warrant.

He pulled on a pair of jeans, a black T-shirt, and a pair of moccasins. A pocket knife went into one pocket, and he stuffed his Beretta into his belt at the small of his back.

Silence reigned in the hallway. The double doors to Father's expansive suite were closed tight, sealing off him and his mistress, Xenia. Good. If Father saw what he was doing, he'd be a dead man.

Narat stole down the hallway to the stairs, which were dimly lit by the spotlights in the alcoves highlighting the idols in them.

The guard in the foyer froze.

"So sorry. It's me." Narat joined him at the foot of the stairs. "I couldn't sleep."

The guard gripped his gun and held it across his chest. "Benny's gone, man. I want to kill that big guy as payback."

"Not yet. I'm going to get some fresh air."

"I hear ya."

Narat bid him goodnight and strolled through the great room to the courtyard. All around him, the rooms in the guest wing had finally fallen silent and dark. Perfect for what he intended.

He slipped onto the portico where tables and chairs from that night's festivities remained overturned. The guard patrolling the courtyard jerked his chin in greeting.

Narat paused. Where had Father put Sana's friend?

He had one way to find out.

As if he were out checking on the guards, he first headed to the front gate in the hacienda's wall. Two guards stood there and gripped their rifles. No one chatted. One moved off and began a patrol of the front of the house. Another walked the area around the barn and briefly conferred with one covering the road. Two others worked the back gate and patrolled the length of the rear of the house. A fourth man took the far side.

Then Narat saw him. Since the hacienda had extensive, beautiful grounds, Father had constructed a garden shed against the wall surrounding the hacienda. A guard leaned against the wall next to the door.

After one last glance around, Narat approached. "How is he?"

The man shrugged. "Hasn't made a sound. He asked for water. Mr. Jain said no, but man, everyone needs water. I gave some to him. I hope that's okay."

So like Father. Narat pasted on his best smile. "Of course. I want to check on him myself."

The guard undid the door for him. "Have at it. Holler if you need me."

Narat slipped inside, and the door shut behind him, sealing off any sound thanks to the closed windows and thick adobe walls. Cool and clammy. His nose twitched at the sharp scent of fertilizer and other chemicals. Then he smelled it. Dried sweat. Suddenly, he couldn't seem to catch his breath.

"You come to torture me or something?" That question came as a low growl from the middle of the room.

Gradually, Narat's eyes adjusted so he could at least see shadows. The man called Butch sat on the floor with his hands zip-tied around a central metal post. With a deep breath and a wince, Narat replied, "I've come to get you out."

"And I'm the tooth fairy."

Narat glanced toward the door. "No, seriously. I want to free my sister and all of you." He pulled out his pocket knife.

"If you're going to kill me, it's going to take something bigger than that, pretty boy."

What could he say to convince him?

Forget it. At this point, actions meant a lot more. He cut the zip ties. "See? I told—"

In a flash, Butch grabbed him and slammed him into the pole with his beefy hand closing around his throat and choking off his cry. He yanked Narat's Beretta from his belt and pointed it at the door.

Narat's chest heaved. "Please, I—"

Butch didn't let off on the pressure. "Why should I trust you?"

Narat choked, "I... I love Sana."

That earned a low cuss word and more pressure. "A brother who loves his sister would have defended her."

Light sparked across Narat's vision. "Please..."

Butch pressed harder. "I should break your neck."

"No..."

Butch eased off a little.

Narat drew in a raspy chug of air. "I... want to save her. All of you. But we have to move quickly."

His foe remained in a crouch. "Why should I trust you?"

"Because," Narat gasped, "freeing Sana and all of you is now more important than my freedom—or even my life."

Butch snorted. "How noble."

"If we keep arguing about this, we lose time. Dawn is only a couple of hours away."

Butch lowered his hand. "All right, then. But you turn on me? Betray me or the others? I promise I'll hunt you down and make you pay. Capeesh?"

Narat nodded.

Butch straightened, and his back popped. He offered his hand and helped Narat to his feet. "I hope you have a plan, then."

Oh, no. Something he hadn't really thought through. "Uh, no, I don't."

"Imbecile," Butch muttered almost under his breath.

"No, I'm not." That came from Narat as a harsh whisper. "I have an MBA, and—"

Butch rounded on him. "Boy, let me make one thing clear to you. Book smarts ain't the same as street smarts. And you ain't got a lick of street smarts. Here's the plan." He whispered it to his willing ally. "Now call that guard in here."

Narat opened the door and poked his head out. "Hey, Phil. We have an issue with our prisoner."

The guard straightened from the thick clay wall. "What's that?"

"He's really feeling woozy from all of those chemicals. I'm not sure, but I need you to check to see if I'm right."

The guard muttered something but stepped inside.

Butch had rearranged himself to make it appear like he'd collapsed onto the floor with his arms around the pole.

The guard knelt beside him and put his fingers to the pulse at his neck.

Like a viper, Butch struck and clapped him across the ear.

Phil moaned and collapsed on his side.

Another blow rendered him unconscious. "Hah. Y'all's guards wear black shirts and pants just as we do." He took his rifle and ball cap. "Close enough, but we ain't gonna have much leeway if someone gets up in our faces." He felt in the guard's pockets and came up with some cable ties. He stuffed his pistol in the waistband of his cargo pants, grabbed his rifle, and clipped the radio to his belt. The guard's shirt sufficed for a gag.

Butch towered over Narat. "Let's go. You walk beside me all casual-like, okay? Like we're best buddies."

Which they so were not. Narat got that.

He took a deep breath as they strolled toward the portico of the house. He murmured, "We take the kitchen entrance. Not through the great room."

"Lead the way."

The door came open at his touch. Even after tonight's scare, Father hadn't bothered to order it locked. He had too much faith in his guards and technology. They slipped inside and made their way past a mudroom and half bath on the right and laundry room and the closed doors leading to two maid's quarters on the left.

Narat reached toward the knob to the basement.

"Narat, man. You couldn't sleep?"

Wes. Narat's blood chilled. Had he seen Butch? The man had vanished. He swiveled and found his former best friend standing by one of the dining room entrances. "No. Not after tonight."

"Hey, I'm sorry about earlier."

Where had Butch gone? Narat focused on Wes. "I said years ago you and Sana should go out, not that you should take her to bed."

Wes kicked at something on the floor. "I'm sorry. I know I—"

A beefy arm wrapped around his neck while a hand covered his mouth. He struggled for a moment. His eyes rolled back, then he sagged in Butch's grip.

"Where did you go?" Narat whispered. "It's like you—"

"I saw him before you did, pretty boy." Butch hoisted Wes across his shoulders. "Lead the way."

Narat opened the door to the basement. Candles flickered in the sudden breeze. Obviously, the maids had forgotten to put them out.

At the bottom, Butch patted Wes down for his weapons, then zip-tied him and used his shirt for a gag. He stuffed him behind the wine bar. "Let's go. Now."

Narat punched in the code.

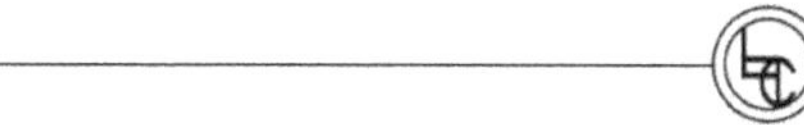

Sunday, April 17, 2016, 0415 hours CDT, outside Austin, TX

Clad in scrubs, Sana lay on the floor of her cell. Like water from a leaking pipe, memories of that horrible night dripped into her soul, filling it with deep sorrow. The abusive handling, the gaping, the bidding among these men. As if they could put a price on a human life. Even now, a just anger burned in her gut, and her hands tightened into fists. That sheik who'd paid eight million for her would get the surprise of his life when he came to retrieve her. *I'm a lioness. God, You made me that way, and I'm not going to go down without a fight. Provide an out for us. I beg You for that.*

In the dim blue light, she focused on Morgan. The girl lay in a heap on the floor. She'd gone to the sheik as well but with a price of twenty-four million. Fiona sat on the floor of her cell with her head resting against the bars and her eyes closed. Six million for her from a Greek businessman who'd seemed to derive pleasure at her foul mouth. Diana, the team's doctor, huddled against the bars with her arms around her knees. She stared at something only she could see. Four million to a rep for a prime minister.

For what had to be the thousandth time, Sana tried her door. Locked. Of course they'd changed the code after the failed escape attempt. Her tarantula friend returned. This time, she let it crawl up her arm and even stroked its thorax. If she stretched her imagination, she could believe it actually snuggled up to her.

At the other end, the door leading to the basement opened. Was it time to go already? When they'd captured her, they took her watch, so she had no way to tell. Instead of a whole entourage, only two forms stepped through.

Narat. Pulse hammering in her ears, Sana pushed herself upright.

Light gleamed off the bald head of the much larger second man. Butch. She'd recognize him anywhere. "What on..."

"At your service, ma'am." He approached. "Your pretty boy brother had a change of heart."

She scrambled to her feet. "Praise God!"

Diana echoed her.

He freed Diana and Fiona. "Code's five-two-nine-one, ladies. Get everyone out."

Butch released Sana and she wrapped her arms around his middle before turning to Narat.

Her brother stared at the floor. "I'm sorry, Sana. I" —his Adam's apple bobbed— "should have stood up for you earlier."

She threw her arms around his neck in a tight hug.

"Sorry to interrupt the reunion, but we gotta get outta here." Butch handed her a Beretta. "Don't say I never gave you anything."

She accepted it. "No worries there. What's the plan?"

He cleared his throat. "Uh, there ain't none yet."

Fiona, who'd been freeing the other girls along with Diana, paused. "What?"

"It's kinda fly-by-the- seat-of-your pants. Narat, what can you tell me about the other guards?"

Her brother stared at the entrance to the tunnel. "We've taken out two. Four perished during your friends' escape."

"What about the others?" Diana asked.

"One in the barn. One outside, but now the doors aren't padlocked."

Butch grimaced. "Too easy for them to access. Sounds like the barn's out. What else?"

Narat folded his arms. "One at each gate. One in the courtyard. And one for each side of the house."

"What about vehicles?"

He released his sister. "I have my personal car."

"Which is?" Butch asked.

"A Lexus sedan."

Fiona snorted. "Uh, we can't put seventeen people in one car."

Butch's brow creased. "I know. What other vehicles?"

"Father's car is within the walls as well. The rest are kept at a parking lot near the guards' barracks, which is outside the wall."

"And he has?" Fiona asked.

"A Mercedes SUV."

Butch slowly nodded as if a plan were forming. "Ah. More manageable. Where are his keys?"

"In the SUV. We're required to keep them in the vehicles in case they need to be moved. They're on the other side of the barn from where we kept the Suburbans."

"Okay, then. Let's think about this for a moment. Barn's out 'cause that guy inside would blow our heads off the moment we raised the trapdoor." Butch muttered under his breath as if he were considering and discarding their options. "We gotta go out through the wine cellar."

Fiona cocked her head. "You sure that's a good idea?"

He shrugged. "Nope, but it's just about our only option, and—"

The radio Butch had taken from one of the guards crackled. "Phil, check in."

Static.

Narat drew in a sharp breath. "That's the guy who was guarding you."

A blip on the radio, then, "Phil? Ray, go check on him. He's not answering."

"Roger," Ray replied.

Butch stiffened. "And we've got about five seconds before everything goes kaput. Diana and Sana, you guys take up the rear. Girls, stay between us, okay? You can't run in flip-flops. Ditch 'em and go barefoot."

Sana kicked off the pair that had come with her scrubs.

Butch crept to the door leading to the cellar. "Girls, as you pass the wine racks, each take a bottle."

Morgan started. "Um, we don't have time to drink—"

"It's a weapon now, honey."

Seeming to understand, she nodded.

Butch cracked the door to the wine cellar. "And follow my—"

"Red Alert! Red Alert! Prisoner—"

Static filled the radio as the lights failed. The alarm blipped.

A couple of the girls screamed.

Butch shushed them.

"Pencil's down, everyone." He pushed through. "Fi, behind me. Then the girls. Narat, in the middle. Diana and Sana, rear guard."

Sana raised her pistol. She sucked in a breath and tried to focus on the golden glow emanating from the wine cellar. It served as a beacon for her.

Diana counted the girls through the door. All twelve passed her.

A dull *whump* echoed through the basement. Someone had thrown open the trapdoor on the other end of the tunnel. Flashlight beams bobbed. Then came footsteps.

Sana's hands grew damp. "Diana, go. I've got this."

Her friend slipped through the door.

Light cut across the basement. Sana winced and tried to duck away.

A man shouted from the tunnel entrance.

She fell to the floor. Bullets tore into the wall above her and sprayed concrete chips. Several bit into her face. She flinched and dove through the door to the cellar. One push slammed it.

Two shots rendered the keypad a mess of wires and plastic.

Behind her, the girls crowded against the bar in the candlelit room. Someone moaned from the other side.

Sana crawled behind the bar and gasped.

Wes struggled against on cable ties on his wrists and ankles.

"Leave him," Narat murmured.

"But—"

"Sister, leave him!"

She withdrew.

Some of the girls whimpered, but for the most part, they maintained stalwart silence. Above, Butch quietly called, "Start coming up. At the top, hang a right, got it?"

"Go," Diana urged them.

Narat nudged the first one onto the landing.

They began creeping upward, too slow for Sana's taste

Something slammed into the door leading to their former dungeon. Something big and heavy.

The line of girls paused. Someone moaned as another *whump* resounded through the small space.

From upstairs came firecracker noises. Gunfire.

Diana gently shoved one of the girls. "Go!"

They began moving.

The door shook again. It began bowing inward.

The last girl started up the steps. Diana followed. "Sana, I'm headed up. Come on."

Upstairs, the door slammed as Diana made her escape.

The door to the cellar blew inward and knocked Sana off her feet.

With a cry, she tumbled to her knees. The Beretta skittered into the flickering shadows.

A man stepped through, the massive man with guttural English who'd bested her earlier that evening.

Sana stretched for her gun but brushed the neck of a wine bottle instead.

He grabbed her ankle and yanked her back before her fingers closed around it.

He flipped her over. His hands curled around her neck.

Sana drove her arms upward and outward.

His hold on her released.

She landed hard on the floor. Pain shot up her spine. She scrambled toward the stairs.

"Not this time." He called her a foul name and gripped her around the waist.

Sana snagged a bottle.

He slammed her into an exposed section of rock wall.

She bashed the bottle against the granite. It shattered and showered both of them with alcohol.

He laughed.

Until she jabbed him in the neck with its jagged edge.

He screamed and dropped her.

Pain roared up the ankle she'd injured twice during her gymnastics career. *God, please...* She pushed with her good leg toward the stairs.

He once more got her around her waist. He tossed her toward the wall above the couch.

Right at the elegant ironwork with candles glowing on it.

She slammed into it, bounced off the couch, and crushed the coffee table. Lit candles tumbled around her. Most went out. A few feebly glowed as the room fell into darkness.

But some of the candles caught the couch's fabric on fire.

Sana sucked in a deep breath, the acrid, smoky smell stinging her nostrils as her attacker approached. Her fingers brushed something hard and smooth. Her gun.

Her training overtook her. Time slowed as she swung around. She fired several shots into his center mass until the trigger clicked. Empty.

He staggered backward and fell against the far wall, then keeled over to one side.

Dropping the pistol, she sagged to the ground.

Until flames began consuming the couch.

Her eyes widened. She tried to rise.

Her ankle gave way. Intense pain momentarily blackened her vision. She sucked in air already hot with smoke and crawled toward the stairs.

"Sana! Help me!"

Wes! She couldn't leave him.

But flames licked at the bar, sealing the fate of Narat's friend. His screams sent shimmies of fear down her spine. No! She couldn't make it to him, no matter how hard she tried.

She started hyperventilating, and her head swam. She made it up the first few treads and coughed. "Lord, get me... out of here." The room spun. "Lord... please..."

She pushed herself up another two. Her injured ankle touched the wood. Pain surged. "God, please."

The flames devoured the wooden wine racks. One bottle fell and shattered, then another. Then another. The flames intensified as they found nearby wooden beer kegs.

She pushed further and made the left turn. Now she had full view of the basement. Sickness filled her as she stared at the bar. A shape writhed. His screams faded. *Wes! No! No!* Nausea surged.

"Sana!" Narat's voice spoke as if from the raging fire.

She coughed out a response. "I'm... coming."

He bolted downward. "Not without my help."

"Wes..."

"You're more important now." He grabbed her under the arms and heaved her upward.

She yelped as a flame briefly licked at her foot. "But Wes..."

"It's too late for him." Narat grunted as he stumbled and fell. A tongue of flame touched his arm and ignited his shirt. He cried out.

"No!" Sana smothered the flame.

"We'll make it." He continued dragging her. They burst into the hallway, and smoke poured after them.

Sana collapsed. "I can't..."

Her vision tunneled.

She felt herself rising as if an angel took her to heaven.

"Sana!" Victor. Had he died as well?

Her world spun, and she slipped into blackness.

Sunday, April 17, 2016, 0445 hours CDT, outside Austin, TX

With his hand firmly on Narat's uninjured arm, Victor bolted through the wrought iron gate in the hacienda's wall. Beside him, Loquacious carried Sana. Soot blackened her blood-streaked face, and she didn't stir in his arms. Victor worried about burns and smoke inhalation, not to mention a myriad of other injuries she might have incurred. Just beyond the wall, they reached the cluster of task force members, who pulled sentry duty on one knee with guns drawn. The now-raging fire at the hacienda bathed everyone in a harsh glare.

With his phone to his ear, Flagel stood behind one of the FBI agents who'd risked her career to stage the rescue.

Along with Fiona and Diana, Butch led a group of girls to safety.

"Fancy meeting you here," Butch said to Victor as he lowered a girl to her feet. "Glad you showed up."

The breath eased from Victor as his shoulders relaxed. "Do I detect a note of sarcasm?"

"Nope. Not at all, boss." They bumped fists. "Just doing a DIY escape."

Victor released Narat, who groaned and cradled his injured arm. "You guys okay?"

"Right now."

"Get into the middle there. Loquacious, we need to check Sana. It's okay to put her down."

Loquacious refused to relinquish her.

Now dressed in a pair of khaki cargo pants and a T-shirt, Sugar approached his bodyguard. "Sugar says it's okay, my man."

Only then did Loquacious take a knee. With utmost care, he placed her on the soil.

Suleiman shoved his rifle to Victor and dropped to his knees beside her still form. He took her limp hand.

Diana knelt beside him and pressed her fingers to Sana's neck. "She's got a weak pulse, but it's steady. Did someone bring my medic supplies?"

"Right here." Skylar handed her a backpack.

As if she'd never been held prisoner or sold at auction, she began assessing Sana's injuries, including a nasty blister on her foot.

Victor crouched on the other side of the former cat burglar and kept silent.

Sana's eyes flickered open. They focused on Suleiman, then fluttered closed.

He brought her hand to his chest. "Sana!"

That earned a sharp glance from the team's doctor. "Easy there, Suleiman."

He kissed Sana's fingers and closed his eyes. His lips moved in silent prayer.

This time, her eyes fluttered open and stayed that way. A trembling smile crossed her face. She mouthed "I love you."

"Praise God!" Suleiman kissed her ever so gently.

She began coughing.

"Help's on the way," Flagel reported as he lowered his cell phone. "I've got BOLOs out for all of the buyers who escaped. Keeping you guys safe is my number one priority right now."

"How many girls do we have?" Victor asked.

"A dozen," Butch replied. "Morgan—"

"Uncle Vic!" Morgan ran into Victor's arms.

He held onto her as tightly as if she were his own daughter. *Lord, thank You. Thank You for sparing everyone and bringing her out.* He pulled back and ran his hand down her hair. "You're okay?"

Tears glistened on her cheeks, but her trembling smile told him everything.

"Bingo!" Shelly cried. She had remained outside and went about her assignments with quiet efficiency. She'd continued as the task force formed a circle to protect the injured. Now, she dug into her backpack and yanked out a flash drive. The LED flickered as she copied something.

Victor joined her. "What did you find?"

"That list." She began jabbering about her methodology and soon lost him.

Victor wanted to scream. "Cut to the chase. Please."

Her eyes sparkled in the glow of the raging fire. "I got into the app. Finally! But it's more than that. I've got lists for Nashville, for New York, for Dallas, for everywhere."

Flagel knelt beside her. "Show me Dallas."

"Right here." A few clicks opened a file of names, all neatly organized in alphabetical order. It even had phone numbers.

He whistled. "No wonder we were shut down. The governor's on there."

Carpenter joined him. "Who else?" He fell silent, and his eyes widened as he took in the names. "Oh, boy. This is huge."

Flagel grinned. "And squarely in the FBI's territory. Finally, I can hand this off."

The FBI agent groaned. "Guess I need to make a call, eh?"

Flagel actually laughed. "You do that, mister."

In the distance, sirens wailed as police, fire, and EMS crews approached.

Victor focused on Sana. She'd rolled onto her side and leaned against Suleiman's legs as she coughed and coughed like there was no tomorrow. Oxygen would soon help her breathe better. She stilled, and their gazes locked. A smile teased her lips, and she gave him a thumbs up.

The tension in Victor's shoulders eased. The failed mission, the agony of losing Morgan, of nearly losing his team, faded. They'd survived, and God had brought them safely through to rescuing not just eleven girls but twenty-three. *Lord, thank You. Thank You for walking with us.*

Mission accomplished. Finally.

37

Wednesday, April 20, 2016, 0730 hours CDT, Franklin, TN

Freedom came in the form of a cami top, pajama pants, and clean sheets smelling of Downy. Morgan savored the softness of the top she wore, the warmth of her pajama pants. A fresh morning breeze tickled her skin and teased her nose with pleasant scents of the azaleas she'd seen upon her arrival the evening before. She lay still and listened. In the distance, horses whinnied. A man said something, and someone laughed. They seemed close, like on the patio she'd crossed yesterday evening when they pulled up to the guest house belonging to Clay Hall.

Climbing from bed, she approached the suitcase on the floor like it was a snake that might strike her. Mom had brought it over the night before. No hugs came with their reunion. No "I'm so happy you're alive!" Just some terse words between her and Uncle Vic. Then she dumped the suitcase at her daughter's feet and practically fled.

"She's in shock," Uncle Vic said. "Give her some time. She'll come around."

Now, Morgan opened it and found clothing in a jumble, as if Mom had found what she could and simply tossed everything inside for her daughter to sort out later. Didn't she care? Morgan tried to focus on the tears in Mom's eyes, that trembling smile. Maybe Uncle Vic was right. Maybe Mom was in shock and didn't know what to think of anything.

Come to think of it, neither did she. Was she, a former sex slave from a brothel, worth anything to anyone? Her eyes filled. *I will not cry. No. I will not cry.* She turned away and stepped to the dresser where Clay Hall's wife had placed some clothing for her.

Ah, leggings and a light-weight hoodie. Perfect for the cool morning air. She pulled those on and ran a brush through her hair as she gazed at herself in the mirror. What did she see in that girl? Sadness, for sure. Emptiness. Was Mom ashamed of what her daughter had done? It wasn't like she'd had a choice. Morgan stopped the thought. *I'm an image-bearer of God.*

With a deep breath, she opened her bedroom door.

Uncle Vic stood behind the guest house's kitchen island and chatted with his wife, Deborah—Aunt Deborah to her. They had an easy way about them, kind of like Mom and Dad had enjoyed. Yearning filled Morgan. So did loneliness. *Dad, I miss you. I miss you so much.* She shifted.

Uncle Vic smiled at her and flipped some eggs on the stove. "Good morning, Morgan. Come on in. Breakfast is almost ready. I hope bacon and eggs are good for you."

She slid onto a chair beside Aunt Deborah. "Anytime."

"Coffee? Hot tea? I've got both since Deb likes her tea in the morning." He opened the door to a stainless steel refrigerator and pulled out a bottle. "Or, I've got juice."

"Earl Gray if you have it."

"I do." He placed a bag in a mug and poured some hot water over it. "Here. The sugar's right there if you need it, as are some lemons and cream."

Morgan gradually woke up as she sipped the hot brew. But instead of the comfort it had been when she was trapped in the brothel, it twisted her stomach. Questions stirred in her mind. Ones she wasn't sure she wanted answered now—or at all. But she had to know. "Uncle Vic, what's going to happen to me? I mean, Mom doesn't want me anymore."

He took a deep breath, and she braced herself for a tongue-lashing about her disrespect and the reassurance of a mother's love for her daughter. He ladled some eggs onto a plate and added two slices of bacon. "I wouldn't say that."

"Then what would you call it?" She hated the anger that pushed against the edge of her question.

His words came slowly, as if he measured their impact on her. "I think she doesn't know what to think. Or feel." He placed the plate before her and fixed another one for Aunt Deborah before settling with his own meal on a bar chair at the end of the island. "I think she hasn't let herself grieve after losing your dad two years ago, hasn't acknowledged that you and David are hurting too, because she's too deep into her own pain."

She stared at her plate.

He tapped it with his fork. "Eat, girl. You can't think if you're stomach's ruling the roost."

That got an unwilling smile from her.

After a few minutes of uncomfortable silence, Aunt Deborah set down her fork. "Vic and I have been talking. I think we both realize how untenable things would be here for you in Nashville."

Suddenly, Morgan's food sat like lead in her stomach. "With Mom?"

"Potentially. Look." A smile crossed her face. "I've heard so much about you from Vic, how he cares about you, how you're his goddaughter. Did you ever stop and think what that meant?"

A lump filled her throat as she thought about Dad. "No."

"It means that if for some reason your parents weren't able to take care of you, he would step in as your dad. He takes that duty very seriously."

Oh, did she know that now. Uncle Vic and his team had risked their lives for her.

He shoved his plate aside and leaned his elbows on the quartz. "We'd like you to come and live with us."

Morgan stared at the veined white rock. She ran her finger along a strip of gray. "I thought Mom would want me to live with her."

He bobbed his head as if to agree. "That is indeed her option. But we also know you two have a rocky history between you."

Morgan couldn't argue with that. The lying. The partying. The drinking. The dabbling in drugs. She and Mom hadn't seen eye to eye since they moved to Nashville. She cringed as she thought about what would happen if she returned to the townhouse.

"Deb and I have prayed about this. We want you to be in a stable place, a place where you can begin recovery and, Lord willing, thrive. We think Last Chance Ranch would suit you well for that. It's in Flagstaff."

Morgan gaped. "Arizona?"

"Yes. All of the team lives there. You'd have four siblings. They're from my first marriage," Aunt Deborah said. "Anna's just about your age. I think you two would hit it off."

Her eyes widened. She opened her mouth, but no sound came out.

Uncle Vic leaned on his elbows. "The big thing is that we want you to heal. Deb's a counselor. She'd be willing to meet with you for however long it would take."

Ever since Sunday night, nightmares had plagued her so much that she awakened screaming, only to have one of the other recently freed girls hold her until she fell back into a restless sleep. The night before, Uncle Vic held her and rocked her like when she'd been a little girl.

His phone rang. He glanced at the Caller ID. "I've got to take this. You two keep talking."

Aunt Deborah sighed as she finished off her bacon. "Hmmm. Anything's better with bacon." She sipped her hot tea. "I know the notion of reliving everything is scary."

She didn't know the half of it. She didn't want to think about the choices that led her to the brothel in Nashville.

"But think about this. Your anger, your grief, your reactions to this experience can be like ingredients that go into a pressure cooker. If left unattended, what happens?"

Morgan rose and shoved her leftover eggs into the trash. "Bang."

"The more you talk about it, the more it's brought to light, and the more it won't feel like shame or a secret," Aunt Deborah continued. "I can be that safe place. We can explore this together if that's what you wish."

"If I went, would I have to obey your rules?"

Aunt Deborah didn't flinch, didn't get angry for her somewhat petulant question. "You'd be part of our household, so yes."

Was that so bad? The more she thought about it, she realized it wasn't. A yearning for a normal family suddenly thrummed deep within her. Then there was that little matter of the long list of johns who'd visited her. If she stayed in Nashville, would they try to take revenge on her? Would they try to hurt David or Mom? She shuddered at the notion. "If I made the move, how would that happen?"

Aunt Deborah sipped her tea for a few moments. "Vic called me to come out here because tomorrow, we're going to court to request guardianship of you. He mentioned it to your mom last night. Though most of the time, the courts like to keep families together, the judge is very aware that you'll be seventeen in August. He wants to speak to you in private about your desires. Then he'll decide."

"How... how long will that take?"

"Up to two weeks or so. In the meantime, Clay's offered to let you stay here. I've got to return home, but Vic said he'd stay since he can work from here as easily as anywhere else."

Morgan swallowed hard. What a choice! A chance at a new life. Maybe her last chance. If she stayed and she and Mom butted heads again... She could wind up right back where she was—or worse. But what about David? Her brother had school, baseball, and a tight network of friends. He already fit in so well. Maybe this—

"Morgan, you want to take a walk?" Uncle Vic stood in the open French doors and shoved his phone into his jeans pocket.

"Uh, sure."

"Grab a mug if you want and put on some shoes. Deb, we'll be back in a bit."

For fifteen minutes, they walked in silence to the far point of the property. Finally, they returned, and he stopped at a paddock near the house where a mare tended her foal. "Foaling season is always a fun time, at least when everything goes well."

Morgan took in the tiny foal as it finished nursing, then wobbled away. "How old is this one?"

"Clay said it was born in the middle of the night last night. A little colt."

"Wow."

Uncle Vic cleared his throat. "Did Deb talk to you about what we're proposing?"

"She did." Something awoke in Morgan and stretched. If she dare let herself dream, she'd say it was hope. "I... I think it could work."

"Good, because I just got a call from Wilma Metlock of the FBI. She gave me a heads up that today and tonight, Metro NPD and the local FBI office are staging takedowns of the brothel at The Music Man. Matter of fact, the FBI is hitting all of the brothels across the country at the same time."

Her mouth dropped open. "What?"

Another satisfied smile crossed his lips. "They're also going after the johns who visited there, which apparently includes the police chief." It faded. "In other words, Nashville is going to be a dangerous place for you."

"Will I... will I have to testify?"

Uncle Vic contemplated the paddock for a moment, then switched his gaze to her. "That's your call. But your statement could put away some very bad people. Long story short, Special Agent Metlock and her partner, Special Agent Hannaford will be here tomorrow to interview you."

Morgan shuddered. It'd be too dangerous for her to stay, which only confirmed that going to Flagstaff was the right choice. "Will you be in the room with me?"

"I'll be nearby. I promise you they're nice people." Uncle Vic leaned his hip against the fence. "Look. I know this will take courage. But you've already shown bravery in the face of danger. You can do this, and it'll ensure that many of those involved will go away for a very long time."

His warm, dark gaze reassured her. "I'll do it. But I do have one more question."

"Sure."

"Is Jaidon Ash going to be part of this arrest tonight?"

This time, his smile turned wolfish. "Absolutely."

Wednesday, April 20, 2016, 1900 hours CDT, Nashville, TN

Finally. Wednesday. Hump Day. Jaidon wanted nothing else but to pop some Tums and stay home. It'd been the same way ever since ten days before when his life had plunged into a living hell. He hadn't visited The Music Man. Instead, the girls from the brothel came to him in his dreams, and he awoke with the tremors and sweats of nightmares.

Cassie worried the stress at Music Man Productions had finally gotten to him and would produce an ulcer any day. He wanted to laugh. No, stress from knowing his illicit occupation might be revealed ate away at his insides.

The news from Texas early Sunday morning hadn't helped. Nope. Not a bit. But nothing else happened. Jain had walked from jail that afternoon and was back at work on Monday. He vowed to get the charges dropped, stating instead the whole thing had been his son's idea. Sure. Like anyone would believe that.

Then, nothing else.

That worried Jaidon. To him, silence meant one thing. Danger.

As Cassie set the supper dishes on the kitchen's island, she clucked her tongue and shook her head. "I still can't believe what happened in Texas. Can you? The news said all but three of the women were minors, and one was as young as thirteen."

"Uh, I haven't been following that." Jaidon forced himself to glance at Elsbeth, who settled on her chair at the island with her phone in her hands. "Elsbeth, no phone at the table, remember? Put it in the basket in the den."

"Dad," she drawled like only a teenager could.

He set a plate of steaks on the granite and pulled out his chair. "Honey, it's talk time right now."

With a heavy sigh, another teen-aged trait, she rose and tossed it into the wicker basket on a console table in the den.

"Elsbeth, if you could get the drinks, sweetie." Cassie took her seat. She took a serving of green beans and passed the bowl to him. "It's horrible. Forever Free's offered what assistance it can in terms of counseling to those girls, especially when it comes to reuniting with their families. It's a huge job."

Elsbeth brought the drinks to the island and took a steak he'd grilled. "I can add that to my report. I mean, my teacher said to make it real. How real could this get?"

Oh, you don't want to know. Jaidon winced as his stomach cramped.

Cassie studied him. "Honey, is your stomach bothering you again?"

He offered a sick smile. "It's slightly tender. I'll be fine. Don't worry."

Elsbeth began cutting up her meat. "Hey, Dad, prom's this weekend. Can I, like, take the afternoon off from school to get ready? All of my friends are." She batted her eyes at him.

What? Oh, yeah. His daughter lived the normal life of a teenager. "Did their parents say it was okay?"

"Yeah. Please? It's not like I get to go to prom every day."

Cassie added her own plea. "Jai, it's a special day."

The best time to ask a dad for something? When he was preoccupied. "Sure."

The doorbell rang. What on earth?

Elsbeth sprang to her feet. "I'll get it. Probably Moira. She said something about coming over to study. And she never can tell time right."

She darted into the hall. A moment later, she returned, a man and woman in suits with badges on their belts and guns at their sides behind her. "Dad, they need to see you."

Jaidon froze. No. Not in front of his family.

The woman, tall with her hair bobbing in a tight, curly ponytail, asked, "Jaidon Ash?"

Slowly, he rose as his stomach once more knotted. "That's me."

"I'm Special Agent Wilma Metlock with the FBI's Nashville office. You're under arrest for human trafficking, exploitation of a minor..."

Jaidon lost track of all of the charges.

Cassie jumped to her feet. "Jaidon, what's this about?"

What could he say? "I'm sure it's a mistake, Cass. Promise."

"No mistake, sir," Metlock replied. "You have the right to remain silent. If you give up the right to remain silent, anything you say can and will be used against you in a court of law. You have the right to an attorney. If you desire an attorney and cannot afford one, an attorney will be obtained for you before police questioning." She turned him and cuffed his hands.

They walked him toward the front door.

"Dad?" Elsbeth's voice pitched upward. "Daddy!"

Cassie blocked their way. "You can't take him! He's done nothing wrong. Why would you?"

The male agent gently nudged her back. "I'm sorry, ma'am. We have a warrant for his—"

"I don't care! Don't you know who we are?"

"I'm sorry, ma'am."

Nausea flipped his stomach even more. "Cass, it's okay. Call our attorney."

Cassie's questions rang shrill as they walked him through the house to the front door. "Why are you doing this? What has he done? Where are you taking him?"

Metlock ignored her and escorted him outside.

Oh, no. Two Metro Nashville PD cars flanked a white Suburban. Their blue strobes sprayed the property with sapphire light. His neighbors next door stood at their fence and gawked.

Heat flooded his body.

"He's done nothing wrong!" Cassie cried from the doorway.

The male half of the FBI couple helped him into the back of the Suburban.

As they pulled away, the last image he had was of Elsbeth clinging to her mother.

For some bizarre reason, Elsbeth's school report flickered through his mind. Make it real? Things had gotten as real as they could get.

38

Monday, April 25, 2016, 1400 hours MST, Flagstaff, AZ

"Butch, thanks for bringing me." Sana opened the passenger door to his Ford F-250. "I think I can get inside by myself."

Butch bolted from the truck and around to the other side. "Easy there. You forget your stature and injuries sometimes, you know? My little lioness."

She scowled but didn't reprimand him. At least he hadn't called her little lady.

He helped her down, and she balanced on one foot as he got her crutches for her. "I'll get your stuff." He shouldered her laptop case and picked up a crate holding her wedding planning materials. "What were you thinking? That you could take everything in on your own?"

"I don't know. I guess I wasn't. Thinking, that is. Or maybe I simply overestimated my abilities." She hobbled to the door. Its sign indicated that the Pause Café crew was pausing for a time of rest and they'd be back tomorrow.

He chuckled and strolled ahead of her to the darkened storefront. "You got your keys?"

She fished them from her purse and turned the lock. The door swung open to reveal a darkened interior with empty glass counters and tables with chairs on top.

"Where do you want to sit?"

Sana nodded at a long reclaimed wood table for eight Butch had made as a shop-warming present for her. "I'll sit here."

"Let's get some chairs down." He placed all eight on the floor. "I'll turn up the heat too. Anything else you need before I head to the shop?"

A lump formed in her throat as she thought about Suleiman. Ever since their return five days ago, he'd avoided her, instead preferring to spend hours upon hours studying. "I miss Suleiman."

Butch lifted her laptop and crate onto the table. "That boy's been studying ever since we got back last week. I guess exams and catching up will do that to a person."

"Yeah, I know." Her heart ached as she stared at her left ring finger. Empty ever since that ill-fated Thursday eleven days ago.

Butch put an arm around her shoulders and hugged her. "Hang in there. You two need to clear the air, and you know how good he is about using his books as an avoidance technique."

Do I ever.

He headed to the door. "Call me whenever you're ready to leave."

"Thanks." After locking up behind him, she crutched her way to the table and shoved a chair from the opposite side around so it sat on the end. With a sigh, she eased onto the chair perpendicular to it and pulled out her laptop.

First things first. She had to get caught up on everything that had happened at Pause Café since she'd last been there, which seemed like an eternity ago in some respects. E-mails took an hour. Lizzie, her manager, had done a great job leaving her with daily updates. She recommended hiring a couple of new employees. Sana agreed, and Anna Fields, Deb's oldest child, would be turning sixteen that summer. She wanted to start working as soon as school ended.

Sana opened her financial program. Ah, invoices. All of which resided in her office upstairs. She took the elevator. Once inside, she fussed around for half an hour by straightening things and gathering materials for next month's schedule before finding the bills she needed to pay.

She began descending the stairs. Halfway down her arms burned. If she wasn't careful, she'd tumble head over heels to the bottom. Just as she hit the last tread, her foot, which sported a blister its entire length and width, brushed the wood. Pain shimmied up her spine, and she wanted to howl to relieve the agony. Boy, she'd be ready for it to finish healing. That and the severe sprain in her ankle.

Maybe she'd brew herself a cup of coffee. Fifteen minutes later, her arms really began aching. Time to sit down. With a deep sigh, she settled on the chair and set her cup in front of her.

Paying the bills took up another hour and a half. Finally, she had nothing else to do. Her gaze shot to the clock at the bottom right of her computer. After five. Butch would be closing for the day soon. Should she call him to come and get her? No. He was doing what she was—getting caught up at the auto repair shop he owned a couple of blocks away. Now, she truly needed to face what she'd avoided all afternoon.

The upcoming wedding.

Or lack thereof.

That obnoxious lump filled her throat. Jain children didn't cry. At least until she'd gone to prison. Somehow, her time in the pen gave her that part of her humanity back.

Out of habit, she checked a website of one of the Austin television stations. The governor of Texas had resigned earlier that day. No surprise there since he'd been one of the johns to visit the Dallas brothel. She clicked on another article. Her breath hissed inward and a chill tingled through her body. Father had held a press conference today. It was meant to announce the launch of one of his company's newest products but turned into a bloodfest related to what happened at West of India Ranch. He reasserted his innocence and stated that Narat, who now resided in a burn center under guard, was the main one behind the recent human trafficking ring. Father twisted it into a vengeance plot fabricated by Narat and her, a way to strike back at the father who'd lovingly raised them since childhood. Especially Sana, who rebelled against him so badly that he'd long ago cast her out of the family.

What?

She closed her eyes and covered her face with her hands. "How could you, Father? You're such a liar!" Her chin trembled. "God, no! This isn't right! Why won't he go away?"

In her initial meeting with Deborah to work out everything in her past, she'd voiced her fear that Father would torment her, even if he sat in prison for the rest of his life. She'd cried, "I don't want him to have that kind of power over me."

"And once you work through things, he won't," Deborah replied. "Sana, look. It's going to take courage, but you've got to realize you're not a stray, but truly, wholly a child of God, who loves you with reckless abandon."

Sana closed her eyes and rocked back and forth slightly. Reporters would surely start hounding her at the ranch and here. It was more than that. Would Father hunt her down? Her and the team? Make them pay? She yearned to talk to Victor, but he remained in Tennessee until the judge rendered his verdict on Morgan's situation.

Then there came that very complicated matter of the wedding.

Actually, it wasn't complicated at all.

Sana reached into the crate and pulled out several boxes. One held envelopes, all lovingly addressed by Deborah and Fiona, the two women at the ranch who had the neatest handwriting. The others held all of the invitations, RSVP cards, and inserts related to the reception. Now meaningless.

She began sniffling. "God, I loved him. I still do! Why couldn't we work things out?"

"We can."

She whipped around.

Suleiman stood in the doorway to the shop.

She ran her hand along the lacquered wood. Why hadn't she heard him come in? And exactly how long had he been observing her?

His footsteps crossed the hardwood planks, in an even, confident stride.

He pulled around a chair so he sat in front of her, as close as her elevated foot would allow.

Heart pounding, she finally regained her voice. "How... how did you get in here?"

A smile flitted across his lips and vanished. "I have my ways. I am a sniper, after all."

Oh, he knew how to make her smile, even when she didn't want to.

He leaned back and crossed one ankle over a knee. That long-lashed gaze wouldn't relinquish her face. "I have missed you."

That lump rendered her speechless.

"We need..." He released a breath. "I realized we need to talk."

"What's there to talk about?" *Way to go, Sana.* She wanted to kick herself.

His slender fingers traced the grain of the wood. "Much."

All of her words, so carefully rehearsed over the days since their return, fled. She closed her laptop and stared at the lid. "I'm sorry I shut you out. And I have no excuse. Truly. I don't."

Suleiman didn't say anything.

She drew in a deep breath. *Don't try to fill the void.*

He didn't break eye contact. "That Monday morning after we rescued you, Victor and I talked. Well, I tried to talk about you Sunday night while you were sleeping, but there were too many things happening."

She nodded. Sunday? She didn't remember much, other than barely being able to breathe from the smoke inhalation. Never mind the blisters on her foot, arm, and legs. And being scared for Narat, who'd suffered a third-degree burn on his arm where the flames had attacked his clothing. By that night, she'd slept with the help of a sedative and breathing treatments.

Finally, Suleiman broke his gaze. "Monday night, we were still in Austin and at the hotel. Victor and I wound up walking the streets of downtown. I was so hurt. I wanted nothing to do with you ever again."

She winced. What could she say? Had he shut her out of his life as thoroughly as she'd shut him out of hers, she would have had the same reaction.

"But then he started talking about last year, about how difficult it was for him to forgive me for my actions, that true forgiveness comes because we, as forgiven by God through Christ, have experienced eternal forgiveness." He sighed and shifted position as lines creased his forehead. "Perhaps I am not making myself clear."

Her lips twitched upward. "You are."

He raised his eyes, and the look in those gray-brown depths shook her. "I forgive you, *eshgham.* I know we have much to sort out."

Her eyes filled, and she grabbed a napkin. "We... do. I do." She bit down hard on her lip as a tear escaped and trickled down her cheek. "I've starting meeting with Deborah. I know I've got stuff from my past to work out." Her heart squeezed when she realized he'd not mentioned the wedding. Maybe that was for the best. Not to wed until they worked things out, that is.

He fingered the box of invitations. "What is this?"

"Our wedding invitations." They suddenly blurred. "I-I guess I should recycle them. I mean, the date's no good anymore."

Suleiman cocked his head. "Why would you say that?"

"Because we're not going to have the wedding."

"Oh?" A smile teased his lips. He leaned forward and took her hands. "We will work through everything together. You and I are a team. I would have it no other way. You have my heart."

Hope threatened to push back the storm clouds.

He slid off his chair. Then, just like the previous November and almost in exactly the same location, he got down on one knee and took her hand. "Sana Jain, will you marry me?"

"Yes!" She tried to throw herself into his arms. It turned into a tumble and pushed him to the floor. Crying, shaking, she stared as he slid the marquis diamond onto her finger.

Then she became aware of clapping.

The whole team sans Victor stood there and cheered.

Heat rocketed up her cheeks as she pushed herself to a sitting position.

With Suleiman holding onto her, she rose.

Butch pumped a fist in the air. "Bravo! Time to celebrate."

Sana gaped as Skylar stepped forward with a cake. "Cheesecake, little lady. Your favorite. Courtesy of my pastry chef. Devin knows how much you like the marbled chocolate variety."

She couldn't reprimand any bearer of cheesecake for using the nickname she hated.

Fiona hustled behind the counter. "I'll get plates."

Diana joined her.

Butch tugged Shelly behind the bar. "And we'll get us some beverages."

Sana felt as if she'd fallen down a rabbit hole—again. Or into an alternate universe. Everyone began talking about nothing in particular, at least until they were settled at the table with beverages in hand and the cheesecake dispensed.

"Hey, what's up with this?" Skylar asked as he tapped the invitation box with his fork. "I thought you mailed these."

"Tomorrow," she promised. "Or, I'll dump them into a mailbox tonight." She narrowed her eyes at Suleiman. "Did you plan this?"

He shrugged, but a smile played across his lips. "Perhaps."

She swung her attention to the best man for their wedding. "Butch! You knew!"

The big man shrugged. "I'm not like Deb's youngest. I can keep a secret if needed."

"Scalawag."

He laughed, then began clinking his fork against his coffee mug. "Hey, y'all, I talked to Vic right before coming over here."

Skylar paused from his conversation with Fiona at the other end. "What did he say?"

"First off, most awesome news and sooner than we expected. The judge ruled that Vic and Deb are now guardians of Morgan."

Everyone cheered.

"They're coming home tomorrow. Morgan will have to go back for any legal things, but she'll be living with us with a monthly allowance until she finishes high school. The judge only asked that she get her degree. That's his desire for her."

Sana's heart lightened. "Good for her!"

"And Vic told me that in June, the day before the wedding, Deb's kids are going to become Chavez kids. They're officially getting adopted on the tenth of June."

She clapped in delight. "We'll have to have some cake and ice cream here at Pause."

Butch's dark eyes took on a mischievous grin. "You know Jaidon got arrested last Wednesday night?"

Diana scraped off the last remnants of cheesecake from her plate. "It was all over the news."

He leaned forward. "It gets even better. He pleaded guilty today to a lot of counts in exchange for a lighter sentence. He's probably going to prison for a good, long time. But, it's what his wife did last night. Seems she's more redneck than I am."

"How so?" Shelly asked.

"She threw all of his stuff out the front door of their mansion and had herself a bonfire."

Sana tried to imagine that picture. She couldn't.

Diana rested her chin on her hand. "I feel for her daughter."

Butch nodded. "Yeah. Especially because everything in her life will be changing. And the police chief resigned. Turns out he was one of the johns on Nashville's list."

"What about Cruz?" Suleiman asked.

"Hah. Here's where it gets really good. Cruz is actually running the investigation related to all of the johns."

Skylar focused on Sana. "What about your dad, Sana?"

She shrugged, but that little ball of fear uncurled inside of her. "He's pinning it on Narat. And me. He had a press conference today and essentially blamed us."

The team's procurement officer snorted at that. "Bull."

Sana gazed at the group around the table. Her friends. Comrades. Ones who'd give their lives for her. She could trust them. "Guys, I'm scared."

Butch frowned. "Why?"

"The press is probably going to show up. I don't want to deal with them. And I'm scared Father will try to come after me. Or all of you. Or Narat."

"He'd be a fool to do that." Butch's reply came quickly. Decisively.

"Why?"

"'Cause he'd have to come through us to get to you. Now your brother? He's probably gonna have to watch his back."

Oh, did she ever know what he meant. She'd gotten shanked in jail as vengeance for testifying against Taz all those years ago. Regret slammed into her. "He's looking at probably twenty years at least. We'll see once he pleads guilty. I wish..."

She wished things had turned out differently for her brother.

Suleiman rubbed her back.

"We love you, Sana." Butch's quiet words reassured her. "We're here for you, okay? And as for the press, we'll take care of them if and when they show up."

Diana rose. "In the meantime, there's a wedding on. And as your wedding director, I say we need to get those envelopes stuffed, stat. Fi, you're at invitations. Sana, the onion skin. Butch, the RSVP cards. Shelly, stamps and return address labels. Suleiman, you stuff."

"What about me?" Skylar asked.

"You lick it."

Butch clapped their intelligence and procurement officer on the back. "Yeah, that way, your big mouth might get glued shut."

Skylar heaved a mock sigh of exasperation. "Very funny, Addison. Very funny. What about you, Diana?"

"I'm supervising."

Everyone laughed.

The conversation turned, and within an hour, only full envelopes remained.

Skylar smacked his lips. "Yum. Envelope glue. Can I have another coffee, Sana?"

She laughed. "Go for it."

Diana surveyed the remains. "We've got a few left over. Anyone else?'

Sana thought about that. Narat would be in jail. Her youngest brother's invitation sat among the ones to mail. But Mother? No. Then her thoughts landed on Ryan. When initially making the list, she'd thought about inviting him. No. She needed to leave the past where it was.

In the past.

With a genuine smile, she shook her head. "We've already invited everyone who matters."

39

Thursday, June 9, 2016, 1750 hours CDT, New Orleans, LA

Sultry jazz floated through the air-conditioned office and bounced off mahogany walls with photos of great singers. A woman's demo tape for La Femme Nue — New Orleans. Yeah, Sugar liked the velvety sound of her voice enough to call her in for an audition to sing at his club sometime during the fall. Uh-huh. She'd bring in the customers, for sure.

On one of his computer monitors, the local news from a station in Austin played, its volume muted. On the other, he pulled up the website for his bank and logged in. He linked to the Bill Pay feature and located the name of a shell corporation for one of his employees in the lesser-known part of his business. He hummed along to the music.

At a tap on the door, he paused the recording.

A woman joined him. Due to today's hot, humid weather, she wore her dark hair up in a bun high on her head. "Boss, you free?"

Sugar gestured for his business manager to enter and leaned back in his chair. "Come on in, Felicia. Come on in. Loquacious out there?"

"Yes, sir. You want him here?"

"Nah. Just making sure he's on duty since we're getting ready to open. What do you have for Sugar?"

She perched on the edge of his desk. "All of the girls from Jaidon's Nashville brothel save for three were successfully reunited with their families."

"Which three?"

"Morgan Walton."

"Victor Chavez took guardianship of her. A win-win for her. That girl's going to go far, mind you."

"And a girl who was codenamed Indra. Her real name is Shondra Penton. She's actually twenty, so not a minor anymore. She has a high school degree with no parents in the picture. Forever Free says she's vulnerable."

Sugar checked the television. Nothing yet. "The other one?"

"Marta Jones is sixteen. Both of her parents are into drugs and booze. They kicked her out for backtalk and general disrespect. She was in a foster home but ran away."

Sugar winced. "Then she has nowhere to go but back into the foster system."

"Right. F-Squared says that's not a good idea at all. I have to agree with them."

Sugar tapped his pen on the desk's blotter. "We got room here in the halfway house?"

Felicia ran her finger down a clipboard. "One reunited with her family, and the other, my admin assistant, Andria, graduated from community college and got another job."

"Bravo." Once more, he noted the television. "Have Patrice set up the rooms for Shondra and Marta. Shondra can be your admin assistant."

"She wants to continue working on her college degree."

"Good. We'll see where she goes from there." He frowned as he pondered Marta's fate. "And see what we can do to get Marta a job. And make sure she knows she's got to get her GED. Can you do that, baby?"

Felicia straightened. "Absolutely. Thanks, Sugar."

With a nod, he dismissed her and returned his attention to the television.

Then a headline flashed up, telling him all he needed to know.

BREAKING NEWS: SOFTWARE CEO AND ACCUSED HUMAN TRAFFICKER ASSASSINATED

Sugar raised the volume and listened to the report. Prasata Jain had arrogantly denied any wrongdoing related to the activities at West of India Ranch in April. No more. As he walked out of his office that evening, an assassin's bullet to his head ended his life. Sugar listened to the report. Good. No arrests. The police had no leads and would continue investigating.

Not that they'd find anything.

Sugar muted the television and focused on his bank account. Without hesitation, he entered a sum total of five hundred thousand for services rendered and hit Send. Below his breath, too low for anyone outside the office to hear, he murmured, "This one's for you, Sana Jain. A wedding gift from Sugar. And may you find peace now."

Saturday, June 11, 2016, 2330 hours MST, Sedona, AZ

Sana gazed at the half moon way up in the black night sky. Peace filled her heart. What a day! It'd passed in a blur, from the moment her bridesmaids and Deborah had sung "This is the Day" to her when she'd awakened to when they'd left the reception in Suleiman's Toyota RAV-4. And now...

She smiled as she thought about her groom.

He'd chosen their place of refuge for the night well, a resort in Sedona. Details were not shared with anyone on the team lest they have a welcoming party upon their arrival.

She leaned on the railing of the balcony.

Suleiman handed her a flute of sparkling grape juice from the bottle he'd brought with him. "Here, *eshgham*."

"Thanks." She took it and leaned into him as weariness from the day suddenly surged over her. "I'm so tired."

"It was quite a day."

She agreed. Laughter from the bridesmaid luncheon echoed in her ears. Then came the cat-and-mouse game of keeping away from Suleiman during wedding pictures before the ceremony.

She'd never forget the way tears filled his eyes during their vows. Ever. Afterward, she savored the feel of her hand in his as they knelt for a song, then kissed for the first time as husband and wife.

Her mind ran back to those days a couple of months before when any hope of wedding Suleiman lay in ashes. But God was good, so good. Healing had begun, and with him by her side, she knew it would continue.

Suleiman brushed a strand of hair from her eyes. "What does Butch say? A penny for your thoughts?"

She chuckled and sipped the sparkling grape juice. "Where to begin?"

He laughed. "Perhaps with the best man? He had eyes only for Shelly."

"That he did." She smiled. On more than one occasion, she'd caught her maid of honor gazing at the best man with unabashed longing. Butch had returned the favor and stuck with her, only to dance with the bride that night. "Do you think that when we get back from Hawaii in a couple of weeks, we'll find that they've gone out?"

He began rubbing her shoulders. "Maybe."

They remained quiet for a few moments. Oh, she loved the feeling of his hands on her shoulders. "Shelly also told me she's looking at a contract in the Bay Area. She'd have to be on-site for a few months."

"Butch will not like that."

"I know. Question is, will they stay together if they become a couple."

"I guess we shall see."

Sana leaned into him. "Want to bet?"

"Hmmmm. Like a few weeks ago when you broke into that house not too far from here?"

She playfully swatted him, and he laughed.

"Perhaps." He turned her so she leaned with her back against the railing.

He nuzzled her hair, then kissed her.

In an instant, Sana saw it all. Her past. Yes, it'd shaped her. But in no way would she let it dictate how she lived now.

Her future. Now wide open. God was good. So good. She'd never forget that. Not then, not ever.

ACKNOWLEDGEMENTS

You've heard that it takes a village to raise a child. It also takes a village to produce a novel, and I have many people I need to thank. First off, many thanks to those who helped in the production of this book. Linda Yezak, your editing is always awesome. Thank you for the way you made a good manuscript great. Thank you goes out as well to Dafeenah Jameel of IndieDesignz who always does a great job with the cover and other images. Also, many thanks go out to my beta readers: Rich Bullock, Jessie Jacobs, Jenny Johnson, Lisa McCool, and Pam Vashaw. Your thoughtful input helped shape the novel into what it is. Thank you to my brother, anesthesiologist Quinn McCutchen, for his input related to anesthetic gases. Your input helped Jaidon's family sleep peacefully.

Thanks also goes out to the rest of the McCutchen clan and Haynie clan. Family support means so much to me, as does the support of my small group, who prayed me through this.

Finally, I want to thank my husband, Steve Haynie. His support, from providing thoughtful feedback during the beta reading phase to serving as my business manager, has meant the world to me. I'm truly blessed. Finally, I'm grateful to God for His blessing of the gift of writing. May I continue to use this talent well.